Renata

THE BEGINNING

Angelina Elias

iUniverse, Inc.
Bloomington

Renata: The Beginning

This is a work of fiction. All of the characters, names, incidents, organizations, and dialogue in this novel are either the products of the author's imagination or are used fictitiously.

iUniverse books may be ordered through booksellers or by contacting:

iUniverse
1663 Liberty Drive
Bloomington, IN 47403
www.iuniverse.com
1-800-Authors (1-800-288-4677)

ISBN: 978-1-4502-7327-5 (pbk)
ISBN: 978-1-4502-7328-2 (ebk)

Printed in the United States of America

iUniverse rev. date: 12/10/2010

Chapter 1

THE GIRL WITH A NEW HOME

"Congratulations to the class of 2000 School of Journalism …Alex Adams, Miranda Castrati, Chase Freeman, Lanai Jackson, Julia Myers, and Kevin Williams." said the Dean as the graduates stepped up to receive their diplomas and hug their teachers. The Dean mentioned more names, but the significance of these graduates was that they were Julia Myer's dear friends from college. Julia was a bright, young girl who was very curious. Julia was curious and impatient; as she had a history of searching for her Christmas presents well before December 25th. This was part of her charm and the beginning of her new adventures.

Julia was exuberantly happy and relieved to be finished with college at the University of Rochester to become a journalist. She smiled and posed as she looked for her parents in the crowd of flashing cameras. As she slowly walked down the steps back to return to her seat, all of her friends clapped and yelled for her as she then tightly hugged them.

In the auditorium, Julia met her father and mother immediately following the graduation ceremony. They took many photographs and celebrated amongst themselves before the formal festivities. Once the roll of film in the camera was full, everyone went to the graduation party hosted by Julia's parents.

The rock music at the party was loud and festive. There was much laughter, fun, food, and drinks to go around. More photographs were taken as well because they had the foresight to bring an extra roll of film.

The party began at 3:00 pm on March 8th, 2000 and lasted until nearly midnight. It was at 10:00 was when Julia's parents and other family members kissed her goodnight. Her father said, "Goodbye Jules" and congratulated her as he left the party. Her parents made reservations at the Hilton Inn in room 3209. Their room was next to a young couple who were heavy smokers.

As Julia's parents were sleeping peacefully in their beautiful room, Julia's father Mark smelled smoke. He told his wife Ida and she mumbled to him that they had probably lit another cigarette next door. But Mark thought otherwise and decided to check.

He sleepily stepped out of bed and walked to the door. At the bottom, orange light and a puffy gray substance began seeping in from under the door.

Mark had made a mistake as to gasp in air. In the hall, people were shouting making their way to the exit in a hurry and one person hit him. There were orange flames crawling up to the ceiling and smoke everywhere and soon in his lungs, making him choke.

Ida got out of the bed in a hurry. She came up to her husband's side and was horrified. They were on the thirty-second floor and she thought even if they tried, they might not have been able to make it. She started to cough and Mark held his Ida close as they rushed down the hall, dodging the flames.

They ran down the hall and felt the floor beneath their feet becoming weaker. Mark saw a fire extinguisher and broke the case with his elbow. He got it out hurriedly and tried to put out the flames.

Ida reached for him, "It's too late Mark! Let's just get out of here!" she pleaded to him.

"Go Ida! Go!" he yelled back, but some of the roof came crashing down and hit his head and her arm as she screamed.

She reached for him as she fell, but he was gone. Tears wouldn't stop pouring down from her eyes. She got up and ran for the emergency exit stairs.

Ida tried with all of her might to try to see, but the smoke clouded her vision and she couldn't breathe. As she was starting to walk down the first flight of stairs, she luckily dodged the part of the roof crashing down behind her. More of her tears blurred more of her vision but then suddenly, further worn-out roof dropped before her and broke the stairs. She was trapped. Ida coughed more, sat on the remaining steps, and cried as she said, "Julia! My dear Julia! Find happiness! I love you!"

The flames spread quickly as the entire hotel burned. There was nothing that could be done. It was over.

Julia Myers was a simple 22-year-old girl who lived in Rochester, New York. She had just graduated from college when she found out that her parents had passed away in a horrible fire. She and her mother's and father's friends attended the funeral. It was on that day when something extraordinary would happen to her to change *another* world…

Many days and nights passed until the sorrowful day of Julia's parent's funeral unreservedly came on March 21st, 2000. Julia was filled with grief the entire time as she spotted their pictures and put a white tulip on their coffin in their honor; the tulip was her mother's favorite flower and white was her father's favorite color. Christina gave Julia a comforting hug before she stepped inside her vehicle when she decided it was time to go.

The drive home was long, almost lingering to her, and she slammed the door shut when she parked in her driveway. She threw everything in her house around- pillows, sheets, decorations, clothes, pens, and papers in the dim lighted house-, broke vases, screamed at the top of her lungs, and shuffled around her bedroom for one item that she could say and write whatever she needed to which was her diary. Julia found a small green journal that she hadn't touched since she was eight while in search for her usual diary, but decided to use the other one instead. She then dashed out of her house, placed herself on a rock in the forest behind her home, and scribbled with an extreme force onto the paper as she tried to hold her tears back, barely noticing a strange light in front of her eyes that seemed to grow larger as more tears swelled around her dark lashes.

Julia's Diary: March 21ˢᵗ, 2000
Dear Diary,
Days have gone by and I had just got back from the funeral and-

Julia was writing in her diary in the small, dense green forest when all of a sudden she was taken to a new world by a bright beam of blinding white light; away from the rest of her family and friends. She had entered a world where *fantasies* became *reality*. She was thinking about starting a new life there in that strange new world, away from the ache of her Earthly life, but wasn't sure. It was all too confusing and terrifying for her to take in all at once...

The white light that blinded and surrounded Julia dispersed into nothing. She fell and was covered to the bone in cold water. Then she realized that she was in a creek- but somehow it was different. Even though she was in the shallow part of it on the banks, she could tell it was deeper and larger than the one behind her house.

Something fluttered in the trees. Quickly, Julia brought herself out of the water and climbed up. The mud on the sides of the bank made her slip, but Julia pulled herself up to find that she was on a forest floor. When she looked up, she saw the green book on the ground near her completely dry. Her mind in a haze, she picked up the book into her hands and felt her stomach drop looking around.

Even though it was still daylight wherever she was, Julia was scared out of her mind. Julia stood up from the ground hastily with her new diary in hand, running her eyes throughout the unfamiliar forest. The rays of sun peaking within from the canopy of leaves made everything seem the colors of dirty orange, mud, washed greens, and charcoaled grays- making it look haunting.

The forest behind Julia's house always seemed to be a pretty lime green and shimmered in the golden brightness of the sun. This place was definitely different. Panicking, she ran.

The soil was slippery beneath her feet, making it easy for her to stumble. She kept running on and on with tears flying behind her and

her feet sore. Her body wanted her to give up, but her mind told her to keep going.

Julia came to a darkened part of the woods, initiating for it to become hard for her to see. Staggering, she fell into a thorny bush, cutting her skin. As she got up, a tree branch tangled her hair when she tried to run again, making her shriek in pain.

Creepy sounds of owls, wolves, and the wild in the area began to squeal and echo through her ears. Almost falling into black, she took off as fast as she could. Up ahead of her she noticed a small triangle shape of light. Sprinting, Julia finally came up to it and rushed through, pushing the trap of leaves and branches.

Bright yellow sun gazed down and surrounded her, making her have to close her eyes burning from her tears. The sudden new warmth calmed Julia. Opening her eyes once more, she gasped.

It was a clearing out of the forest and seemed almost magical. A sea of green and yellow grass flowed like the waves of an ocean. Even the rustling sounds of leaves with the gentle lapping of the waves of the grass in the light, cool breeze seemed to make this new place entirely peaceful.

As though a performance at curtain's rise, flowers displayed masks of bright red, tangerine, and brilliant yellow. Beginning the show, they turned their ears to listen. Rising high into the clouds, blue and purple mountains rang like bells as loud as the thunder. The beams of light shining through the clouds were like spotlights and rang as small bells as soft as a psalm.

Even though Julia was out of the woods now, she could somewhat hear the rhythm of the babbling brook. Imagining it, she virtually saw the fish make the water come to life with their acrobatic jumps. Accompanied by the soaring eagles, greenery, orchestra of birds, and a majestic mountain peak, the masterpiece was surely painted by a talented artistic creator. Yet, a mischievous cool zephyr amidst the tranquility disrupted the beautiful concert.

Dropping to her knees, Julia saw that the sight was nothing short of amazing. However, when she traveled and wandered further than the forest behind her home, it was a highway, not this overture of beauty. Cringing, she thought of the woods she had just come out of and knew this place was not all beautiful and certainly not her home.

Where am I? she thought. *What is this place? How did I even get here?*

Getting up, Julia sat on a boulder while clutching her diary. She opened it and flipped to the first page she wrote in. In an acute glimpse, she saw a small white light disperse into nothing. Frightened, Julia threw her precious diary to the ground and hugged her knees as she thought.

Could that diary be it? How?! Ever since I got it from my grandma, I haven't even touched it. What was it that she said when she gave it to me? I was eight…it was a stormy night. She was babysitting me- it was the same year that she died as well.

Julia stopped. Small, selfish tears she did not want came again. She shook them off as she stood to find some food in this strange, new, and intimidating place.

I'm so hungry. I need to find some food before it gets dark. This is just great! College graduation, I come home to find my parents aren't even here, and then I'm sent to some weird place in a creepy forest!

She stayed by the edge of the woods, picking small things off bushes and other things here and there. After finding some food, berries, nuts, and other fruits she was not familiar with, she settled down next to the boulder again by the beautiful mountain. She watched the sun start to go down as she ate with great comfort.

Finally, feeling somewhat content, she fell asleep. In her dream, she was surrounded by blending colors and an intense sick feeling in her stomach overwhelmed her. Wanting to get rid of the feeling, she forced herself to wake up.

Julia let her sleepy eyes wander towards her diary. She thought it was crazy that a diary could teleport someone, so she picked it up. However, just to be safe, Julia ignored the page that she wrote on earlier to another one.

Julia's Diary: March 21st, 2000 (Continued)

Dear Diary,

I don't know what happened. I'm so scared and cold. I'm in a new place now, not in the forest where I was writing a new diary entry earlier. At first, I was sure it was just my imagination, or that I was just dreaming- hopefully everything- but it turns out that it wasn't.

Julia safely put her diary away, seeing that nothing had happened. Looking around her, it was sunset. The sky was set ablaze with a combination of pink, red, and orange arms speckled with shades of purple. A sudden chill came and she rubbed her arms.

A sharp, abrading, almost explosive sound was made impromptu. Julia jumped and ran her eyes around. The forest seemed to be breathing.

What was that? she thought. *It came from the forest…should I go in there? There might be people.* Julia looked to the setting sun. *I finally found a peaceful place. Should I go back into that eerie forest? I should. The sun's still up and there's a chance that I'll find someone.*

Julia took the first couple of steps slowly. Coming to the edge of the woods, she looked back at the small utopia one last time. Finally, she stepped inside and breathed a heavy breath, not knowing what would soon follow.

To keep herself from becoming scared, Julia crept through the forest at a calm pace. Not knowing where she was going, another boom was made. Shivering, she followed the sound in the dim yellow light.

Julia found that the sound was made near a small cliff and elevated hills in the woods. But it was precisely created behind a bush. She pushed the leaves away to see what had made the noise.

In the small square through the leaves she saw something that let her sigh in relief, yet also confused her. It was a group, of what seemed to be, men gathered round in a circle. They were built like beasts and wore dark clothing from head to toe, jewels, and greedy expressions.

Their clothes were rugged with pieces of armor puzzled on with high boots to protect their feet. The jewels they wore didn't seem to fit them or match- most likely stolen. Finally, their beast-like forms looked to a man in the center of the circle, leaning one foot onto a large stone while peering out into the scenery behind Julia.

He spread his arms to signify the land and said in a husky voice, "Look at it lads! Look at all the land we've finally come to obtain. What do you see in its future?"

"Prosperity!" another man yelled gleefully.

"Ha! Don't make me laugh…I beg you," a man said smugly while holding bandages wrapped around his chest and torso with a large dark coat draped over him, "My broken ribs wouldn't be able to take it. How do you suppose we get the money?" he watched as everyone thought while they looked down to the ground below them, and he shook his head sorrowfully, "We need a miracle."

The first man spoke again after a moment, "It'd be a *real* miracle if a human came. We could sell them and be rich!"

Again the injured man put forth, "But that's never going to happen. We haven't had a human among us for a long time, and even if there was one, who's to say someone couldn't have gotten to them before us and told no one? It's no use."

Julia had heard enough. She let go of the leaves and stood worried. *They're not human!* she thought. *As much as they look human, they're creatures. And they want to sell humans. I better get out of here.*

Turning around in a rush, she accidentally hit something hard. Looking up, she found it was one of the men she had been spying on. He cowered over her as a giant with his head and body blocking any way for Julia to escape. She trembled as he smirked. In one swift move, the man lifted her up by her arm and began to carry, but then dragged Julia to the group as she kicked and screamed.

"Look what I found." he announced in deep voice.

The men gathered round while he held her wrists behind her back as she cried, "Let go of me!"

"What a pretty thing," the first man who talked said as he reached for her.

"Don't touch me." Julia barked as she backed away, almost wanting to bite him like she saw the heroines do in movies.

"Why don't you *try* to escape with your **powers**?" a young boy, probably seventeen, asked.

"Powers? What is this place? Where am I?" she vociferated.

Coughing painfully for a slight moment, the injured man alleged, "Gentlemen, I believe we've encountered a human."

Cheering, the group of men jumped and hollered triumphantly, "What luck has been given to us!" another responded, "We could sell her for a lot more money as well because she's so young and dainty."

The first man spoke once more, "And if we find out where she came from, we can get more mere humans and sell them for more gold," the group of men smirked and lauded amongst themselves for a bit more, but then stopped when he held Julia's chin a bit forcefully, "How did you arrive here beautiful?"

Don't show fear. she thought and then spat down at the man's shoes. At this, he spontaneously reacted by stepping back and then about to hit her. However, the injured man stopped him.

"Maybe this will make her talk," he held his hand towards Julia's neck as fire was ignited on it.

Horrified, Julia backed up and elbowed the man holding her. He gasped for breath as he mistakably liberated her. She ran out of the group as fast as she could back into the forest, kicking up leaves and twigs in the orange light.

The men followed her, she noticed as she turned around to look. Running faster, she looked back ahead of her. Suddenly, she ran into something else and fell backwards with a large thud.

Peering back up, it was a dashing monsieur with blonde hair and practically crystal blue eyes. Julia was petrified. He came almost out of thin air.

She retreated as he reached to help her and said in kind, lovely deep voice, "I'm not going to harm you."

The league of men was closer now. Julia received the man's hand. He looked over to some large trees and boulders before the cliff as he helped her up "Hide," he said guiding her.

Julia hid immediately and watched as the group of men charged at the dashing monsieur. They soon met and started fighting rapidly. She ducked as she watched intensely.

The young man who claimed that he wasn't going to hurt her fought courageously among the men. He used some power, apparently, that seemed to be light as the others used fire, water, and other things. She became terrified.

Powers?! What is going on? What is this place? How can they have powers? They look so human. They couldn't possibly be creatures! What should I do?

Out of nowhere, a man towered over Julia. She fell back in such fright, but he caught her by her hair, laughing diabolically. Julia let out an ear-piercing screech, hanging over a ledge.

"Release her!" the handsome, younger man from before said.

The evil monster laughed once more. He then dropped Julia and fought with the boy. She screamed and caught a strong root sticking out of the side of the ledge. Trying to pull herself up, she slipped.

Thankfully, the young man came to save her just in time. He caught her in his arms and brought her back up onto the ground. Shaking in such terror, Julia looked around as he inspected her, placing her on another large boulder. The group of men was gone. *And it was all because of this young man.* she thought looking back at him.

"Are you all right?" he asked placing some of her hair behind one ear.

"Release her?! Is that all you could think of?"

He was taken back, "A large thank you would suffice."

Julia looked down, "I'm sorry," then back up, sighing and said, "Thank you."

"You're welcome," he looked into her pulchritudinous green eyes seriously, "Now, who are you and from where do you hail?" asked the strange man.

"I'm…my name is Julia Myers. I'm not really sure where this place is, but I'm not from…wherever we are. I don't know how I ended up in this place!" she responded to him nervously with the words rushing from her.

"You shouldn't be here." he said turning away, yet she thought she saw regret in his eyes as if he didn't want to leave her there…

"Wait- what? Who are you?! Please don't leave! I need help."

Before she could say anything else, he dashed away at random. She tried to follow with no luck of spotting him, but instead, she saw a cluster of stars behind every tree and bush in the forest that it led her to. It seemed to be a game of hide and seek, and Julia continued to follow to try to find out where she was and how to get back home. Looking back, she knew she would have trouble finding her home, unless there was another way…

Hopefully I can find that guy again. Maybe he'll be able to help me. she thought determined.

Tearing through the grasses, trees, and thorns, Julia started to become terrified of the unknown territory, but when she looked up at the star-lit sky once again, she found the stars above her getting closer; almost as if they were levitating. Running faster and almost out of breath, she stopped. In front of her, rested a large, majestic palace nestled in rolling hills. Strong, white stone was its fortress to protect it, with a festooned archway made of red brick. The turrets, bridges, windows, and balconies reminded her of *Sleeping Beauty's Castle.* A Bell Tower reached the tips of the clouds, supporting a great, golden bell that resembled some of those at *Notre Dame,* hitting the moonlight, reflecting its shining beauty.

A large, zigzag type road, made of yellow limestone led from the bottom of the forest where she stood, to the entrance of the castle. Then, the cluster of stars transformed into the young man who had saved her earlier, standing at the foot of the roadway. Julia rushed after him before he could get away.

"Wait!" she called.

He turned around perplexed, "You followed me?" he turned back to go up the road, "Go back home."

Exasperated, she flung her arms outward, "I don't know how. And you never answered my questions."

"I don't have time for this. I can't help you." he began walking up the boulevard once more.

Julia pursued him with her stubbornness and feeling of adoration, "You helped me before. Thank you for that, whoever you are...What is your name?"

"I'm...my name is Carson Tabor... And I saved you from bandits. We have many here...I'll say this one last time, you shouldn't be here. Where we are now, there are bandits, creatures, demons, dragons, and many other things that would terrify you. Go back home human. This is no place for you."

"Human? Aren't you as well?"

"As much as I may look like one, the people of this place are far from them. The main reason is our powers."

She paused, "Powers...where exactly are we?"

"On the border of the Pierre and Felpierre Kingdoms."

Julia was confused. Indeed, she was far from her home. She had come to a land where fantasies became reality, and was frightened.

She shook her head, "I have no idea how to get home. Will you please help me?" she asked staring into his eyes.

Carson turned away, but Julia could still distinguish his features in the faded blue light. *His eyes are so clear, beautifully blue. There's something that seems to let them sparkle in the light. All this time...he's been a bit rude, but he seems like he could care.*

Eventually, Carson noticed he was being watched, and he stared straight back into Julia's eyes. He gazed at her emerald, forest eyes once again and was enchanted by them. Carson took a few steps forward, "Fine. You can stay here at my family's castle... As long as you agree to not be a burden."

"I promise," she paused, "So what do you do? That gave you this castle?" she said looking up at the strong, white stone it was made of.

"Yes, well, family is in Parliament. I also work as a trainer in magic. I know you might think that it's a bit awkward."

"Well, if you were me, then you would know if it was weird."

"I guess so." said Carson laughing and nudged his head in the way to the grand entrance, "There are some people I want you to meet. Will you allow me to show you around?" he said in a rich, velvety voice that seemed like he was talking in a beautiful musical fashion, giving a slight smile that gave Julia butterflies in her stomach, so she nodded a little too fast from being so enthralled by his form.

They went inside and looked around. The first thing they saw was the laboratory. In the Kingdoms Julia found herself now in, scientists (or whatever they called them in this new land) dressed in metal suits, swirled chemicals around, and used many different forms of magic. One person even made a bird disappear right before her eyes. She recoiled, still not used to the magic in that world.

The next area she saw was the weaponry room. There were war chariots, armor, swords with matching shields, and much more. All items were neatly arranged and polished to shine like a mirror. Some statues of different knights and warriors were placed randomly about the room- she thought they reminded her of Greek statues.

"You won't need any of these things unless you're in a war." said Carson reassuringly, seeing the slightly frightened look on Julia's face.

"Thank goodness," she murmured, relaxing.

"But the next room you may want to have a good look at."

"And what room would that be?" she asked curiously.

"The library. I figured since you're going to stay, you might have an interest to learn about our world."

"Good idea...thanks!"

Entering the massive library, Julia looked everywhere in stunned silence. Little dwarfs were perched on sliding ladders, books and papers seemed to put themselves away in tall white shelves that covered and wound with the room using stairs, and a white banister as a rail. Tables and chairs were scattered with large stacks of papers and golden pen and ink sets. Julia stepped with caution, making sure not to disturb anything as she wandered around. She carefully pulled up a chair so she could sit in the very center of the room under the glass roof that came to a point at the top.

Wow! A circular library that you can see everything with! There's even gold lining on the walls! This is awesome. I just adore libraries!

As Julia was looking around, Carson went to find a certain book.

"What book do you wish to see?" asked the librarian.

"I'm looking for the book about our world." Carson told her in a hushed tone.

"Don't you already know about our world enough?" asked the librarian with obvious suspicion.

"This is a different case ma'am; I have brought a human." said Carson in an even lower voice.

"Very well," replied the librarian earnestly.

"Thank you." and waited as the old bird-like woman retrieved the book in a tall bookcase next to her.

"Here you are. One book of *Elements*." said the librarian handing the book to Carson.

Then Carson left the librarian with an annoyed glance, stepping up to the gawking Julia, "Are you done looking and ready to read?"

Startled, Julia responded, "Oh, yes, thanks."

Then, without warning, Carson left after giving her the book. This seemed surprising to Julia. Reading his feelings was like penetrating a strong fortress.

Julia eagerly read through the first few pages. The first thing mentioned in the book was the language. It was in all spells and characters. The next subject stated were the ten elements of the world.

After that, she learned the most spectacular and most important thing of all; the life source of the people. The life source was called *Ceylon*. It was designed to help heal, grow, and to use light in special ways she could have never imagined. It also gave them their ability of their powers. A picture of the Ceylon caught her eye; it was a blue crystal broken up into millions of pieces, surrounded by ten single spheres of the ten elements. Then, right when she was reading that it was somewhere in this castle, Carson came, "I got my team ready in the meeting room."

"Oh, ok. Well I wasn't finished reading and-"

"Don't worry," he chuckled, "You can bring the book with you."

She closed the book and hugged it close like it was the most important thing to her, along with her diary, and followed Carson to the meeting room.

"I hope you'll like everyone."

"I hope so, too."

When they got to the door he held it open for Julia and she saw the first person standing in a gray room with a long wooden table and several red and gold chairs. The person was a tall and thin man. He looked about the age of thirty and wore silver pants with a silk blue shirt with silver lining. He also had short brown hair and a thin scar on his right cheek.

"Julia, this is my magic trainer, Christopher."

"Hello Julia. I hope you're ready to learn how to use some magic, but tomorrow just be prepared to get books."

"Oh…well, I'll be ready, nice to meet you." she said confused.

Julia was curious as to why she was going to take magic lessons when she was human. *Humans can't do magic.* she thought.

Then he walked into another room to get the next person.

"Carson, you didn't tell me I was going to do classes."

"Well I thought you might want to, so I got my team and told them to train you. I thought it would be good until you could go back to your world. If you can that is, because I'm not really sure. If you stay, you have to learn to protect yourself." he eyed her, referring to the bandits he had saved her from.

"Ok…but is magic the only thing I'm going to learn?"

"No, I mean if you can't go back than I gave you some extra classes just to help you around here. Is that all right?"

"Well now that you explained it, it is."

"Good. Ah…here comes the social trainer."

Then came in a young girl, who was about the same age as Carson and Julia. She was short, had blonde wavy hair, blue eyes, and she was wearing a short purple dress. To Julia, she looked like a fairy.

"Julia, this is my friend, Veronica. She will help you with social life in the Felpierre and Pierre Kingdoms."

"Nice to meet you Veronica."

"Nice to meet you too Julia." then Veronica gave her a sack of fairy dust as she left, leaving Julia confused as she looked at it, not knowing what it was.

"What is this for?"

"Whenever you need fairy magic. The next person coming in will help you with our government," he motioned his hands to himself, "Such as my family and I in Parliament. His name is Mr. Doddsworth." Carson explained.

Then an old man with pointed ears and glasses came in. He looked like he was in his sixties and wore a red robe with gold on it in shapes of stars and red velvet piping. He also had a velvet red hat and a long silver beard that ran off his chin like a silver river.

The old man smiled as he shook her hand, and then said in a kind, deep voice, and "It was a pleasure to know that I would be teaching a human our government. I've never seen one, especially not as pretty as you."

After a quick greeting, he then left chuckling to himself into the other room.

"The next person specializes in health. Her name is Cassidy."

As such, a small girl came in. She had short curly red hair with green eyes and had a classy look to her pretty face. She wore short, red dress and sauntered over to them. Cassidy also came in startled to see Julia.

"You don't look so well. You should get some rest at least in the next ten minutes."

"Well I think I'm just tired."

"Just giving you some advice. Anyway, I am Cassidy as you heard from Carson, and if you need anything just ring this silver bell."

Then out of nowhere a silver bell was in Julia's hand.

"Thank you."

"You're welcome." then she snapped her fingers and disappeared, leaving Julia in a daze.

"Well, here come the last people you need to meet. They are the best people you can find to teach universal class," he then whispered to her, "Now, the man is very old, and the woman is roughly our age and they're very wise. The man's name is Mr. Clayton and the woman's name is Lori Linda."

Then a very frail old man came out with a book wearing a blue robe with silver moons on it, he had white hair and beard, which looked a white lake with a bunch of rivers swimming off. With him, he had a young woman with straight black hair. She was wearing a short, orange dress with sparkles all over it.

Mr. Clayton in a low but gentle voice began, "Tomorrow we'll be getting many books, looking at the stars, and start learning about Ceylon."

"Well, we'll try to see if we can see Ceylon though. Anyway, you'll be very pleased with universal class. We'll see you tomorrow." said Lori Linda in the highest voice Julia ever heard, but also just as friendly.

"It was nice to meet you both."

They nodded and went into the other room.

Julia looked to Carson drained, "Now that I've met everyone, can I go to sleep?"

"Yes you may. If you follow me, I will show you to your room." said Carson waving her on.

"Thank you." said Julia as she followed Carson to a narrow hallway.

The hallway exited outside and it was made out of the stone castle. In there, inside were candles lighted and many wooden doors. They came up to giant, green, wooden door at the end of the hallway surrounded by gargoyles and candles.

She stepped inside and there was white everywhere. There was a gigantic window with white curtains, white bed, tables, chairs, white walls, and white wood floors in the bedroom. The only thing that wasn't white in this gigantic room was the silver lining on the walls.

In the bathroom on the other hand, there was a another door to the closet, white and silver tile, an island bathtub in the center, white marble sinks, mirrors everywhere, a side door for the toilet, and another window. Then she went in the closet. It was just like the bedroom but without the bed, but instead of the bed there must have been hundreds of articles of clothing and a set of white nightgowns for her to choose from. There was also at least the same number of shoes as the outfits, and instead of white wood, there was white fur on the floor.

"Well, I should get going. Be prepared tomorrow." said Carson leaving and sighed.

"Thank you Carson. And I will be prepared."

He stopped at the doorway, thinking that he was about to let a human stay under his custody, but then said, "If you can, try to figure out a way back home. Goodnight."

Then Carson left. Julia shut the door and put her one of her nightgowns on. She set the book, fairy dust, diary, and the silver bell on the table next to the bed. She reminisced over Carss words, confusing her and silently shed tears to herself over the loss of her parents. She wanted to avoid all the reality in her mind and lose herself in this new fantasy land that she would dream of when she was a little girl. While she was thinking about the day, she finally fell asleep from tears, dreaming of her improbable desires...

In her dream she dreamed of a light, and then she saw herself in the forest, wearing her black dress and her black shrug, from the funeral, with her curly reddish-brown hair over her shoulders. She saw herself writing in her diary and crying. There was a speck of light coming out of the diary when she flipped the page. A tear fell in the light, like a droplet of water falling into a full bath. Out of nowhere, came a light that seemed like a wave all over the world and sucked her into the new world she was now in.

She woke up in such fright and was panting. She patted her head and felt a sickness in her stomach. Julia was having a fever and felt like she was going to vomit. When she came out of the bathroom, she saw Cassidy waiting on a chair in her bedroom.

"You should have rung the bell."

"I was fine."

"No you weren't."

"Yes I was and now I would like to go back to bed." Julia said putting down the sheets and climbing in, feeling almost as though she was being scolded like a child.

"Fine. No classes today. But tomorrow you better be up bright and early and not sick."

"All right."

"Oh, and if I were you, I wouldn't go looking for Ceylon either."

"Why would I want to see Ceylon?"

"Because of what it can do. But don't go looking for it."

"I won't." she said a little frustrated from her attitude towards her.

Then Cassidy left glaring because she could see right through Julia and knew she would look for Ceylon anyway even if she wasn't sick.

After the day of reading in the book and learning basic spells, Carson eventually came. He knocked on the door and came in with a concerned look painted across his beautiful face. Julia fixed herself as he closed the door behind him and smiled when he walked toward her.

"How are you feeling?" he asked sitting next to her on the bed.

"I'm better now."

"Well that's good. You're not a sickly girl are you?" she didn't answer and put her head down, "If you don't answer my questions, how am I supposed to find out more things about the person I saved?"

"Well, I'm trying to figure out a way to leave this place, so what does it matter?" Julia looked away.

Carson sighed, "Look, I'm sorry for my rude behavior yesterday. If you can forgive me, ask me anything." he slightly smiled ever so charmingly.

Julia turned back from being lured by Carson's countenance, "Ok then, here's a random question. Why is Cassidy so...so...well I don't know how to explain it?"

He laughed, "She just knows what's best but puts it in a protective way. I'm sorry if you got a bad impression of her."

"That's all right. But, she said not to go looking for Ceylon. Is there a reason for that?" she asked because she really wanted to know why she couldn't see it. Her curiosity was taking over her and itched to know what secrets lay ahead of her.

"Well, I guess Cassidy thinks it's too early for you to see it and learn about it."

"But why?"

"Because..."-he paused a moment to think if he should tell her- "it is the life source of many of us and once you see it and get a piece of it, like all of us, it takes part of your life and keeps it. And it usually only works for the people and creatures of this world, but we think it can work on humans too. It's just that we're not supposed to have humans in this world."

"Why?"

"Some things are better left unsaid...you're too curious," he looked at her for moment and started to get up to leave, "Anyway, you should get some more rest. You have a big and long day ahead of you tomorrow and-" he stopped and turned around, "Before I leave, I have one more question."

"Ask away."

"Why do I get the feeling you're reluctant to leave? Don't you want to back to your family and home?"

Julia thought of her parents and the funeral and knew for that very reason she didn't really want to go home, "Carson I...I don't have much family left." tears were coming into her eyes.

"What do you mean?" he came back to sit next to her concerned.

"My parents died recently. The day I arrived here in the Kingdoms, all I can remember is that after my mom and dad's funeral, I was upset so I ran into the forest behind my house and wrote in my diary. Then there was a big wave of light out of nowhere that sucked me in. Now I've ended up here. That was my dream last night as well. I was and still am scared," she rubbed a tear away, "And I'm sorry that I'm crying, but I'm still trying to get over my parents and this whole new place-"

Carson held Julia in his arms, "Hey, I know what it's like to lose your parents, believe me. My parents passed away a couple of years ago. Just give it some time. You'll be all right, I'm sure of it. Don't be ashamed of your tears; cry as much as you need to. I'm here for you."

She held onto his comforting hug, "I know you want me to go home, but I don't know how. I'm sorry."

"Julia, I will do whatever I can to help you. Just give me some time. I promise." he broke away.

"Thank you Carson, I just don't know how you can help."

"Well for right now I think you need some rest and I'll see you tomorrow. Goodnight." said Carson getting up and walking towards the door.

"Goodnight Carson. And again I thank you, but...for everything."

"You're welcome."

Then he left with a smile on his face. But this wasn't a slight smile like before, but this was a real, genuine, and sincere smile. As soon as Carson left, Julia got out her diary and started writing. It was a small, dark green diary from which her grandmother had given to her as a child, yet she never said where she had come to find it. Only the initials **K.F** were given to her and written on the first page.

Julia's Diary: March 22nd, 2000.

Dear Diary,

After I calmed down yesterday, I went on a walk to find some food. When I found some, I started to relax. While I was relaxing, there was a sudden explosion sound from the forest so I went to go check it out. Unfortunately, I got into some trouble with some bandits. Luckily, I was saved by a handsome young man by the name of Carson. He was mysterious and rude at first, but led me to a castle which is his work, a magic training place, a home, and a lab for scientists, weaponry hold, and a library in one magnificent castle. He introduced me to his team of trainers and gave me a room to stay in. The room is very nice. I met three pixies by the names of Veronica, Cassidy, and Lori Linda. I also met three other men who know magic by the names of Christopher, Mr. Doddsworth, and Mr. Clayton. Today I got sick, but I think it was because of the food I ate when I first got here, and I had a dream last night which confused me, so I told Carson. He said that he would do anything to help me, so for right now I will wait and see what happens. He's very charming, but I can't let any feelings get in the way of me trying to find a way home because humans are not allowed here. I still wonder why that is. What did humans ever do to them and how did they arrive here? The other thing is that no one wants me to see the life source named Ceylon because I'm a human, but I'm going to find it in this castle...tonight.

Chapter 2

CEYLON

Then she closed her diary and put it on the table next to her and grabbed the sack of fairy dust. Julia also put on her black shrug from yesterday, since it was cold, and went out of the room to find Ceylon just as she said. Her curiosity took her completely over and had to see for herself why everyone was keeping this from her.

She came into the stone hallway with the gargoyles staring at her with their piercing stone cold eyes almost as if they were watching her like a security camera in malls or stores back in her world. She walked past the meeting room while thinking of everyone she met having trouble remembering each one, but thought of their individual traits. Christopher had a suspicious look to him with a black twinkle in his eyes, Veronica seemed as sweet as sugar, Mr. Doddsworth was fascinating with his smile that almost said *I have many secrets that I will gladly share*, Cassidy was elegant and uncouth, Mr. Clayton was down to earth and ready to talk about anything, and Lori Linda seemed short, sweet, and tangy to make the best candy. She walked all around the castle to think of where she might find Ceylon, but finally decided to go to the library to find a book that could tell her.

When she came up to the library entrance, she looked around to see if anyone was following her and opened the heavy door, but she didn't notice Carson's sparkling arrangement of stars following her secretly. She looked around and found the C section at the corner of the library.

There was no book that said anything about Ceylon, yet there was a book out of place. So instead of just leaving it like that, she picked up the book and opened it. Inside was a note that said to go push significant markers on the wall to the left of her. On the wall were eight markers, each one with a symbol on them. When she pushed the combination that was on the paper, the wall split into two, revealing a long, dark staircase. She looked behind her one more time and went inside.

It was so dark that she had to step with caution, but there was a sliver of blue light to guide her. She walked more and more, closer and closer to the light and finally was amazed at what she was looking at when she got to the bottom. It was Ceylon, with blue light surrounding the whole room. A blue crystal in the center broken up into millions of pieces and the ten elements surrounding it. The only problem was that there was no way to get to Ceylon and get a piece of it, so she got out the sack of fairy dust thinking quickly and rationally-at least for this world.

"Julia! What are you doing?"

She turned around frightened, with her hand over her heart to try and control its pounding, "Carson...I just wanted to see it."

He shook his head coming up to her, "I knew you'd come looking for it. Luckily, I came prepared," he brought out a small piece of Ceylon on a necklace chain from his pocket, "I didn't want to risk anything," he placed it in her hands for her to look at for a moment, "You should've waited until tomorrow."

"I have to warn you, my curiosity is my worst quality," in her hands, it glowed as it turned purple for a split second-so acute that neither saw; it was normal for it to glow when a new person held it anyway, "Thank you." she replied.

"Would you like me to put that on for you?" he asked in a friendly voice.

She handed it to Carson, "Why not?"

"Here you are." he said tying it around Julia's neck for her.

"Thank you." she said again, turning around to see his dimly-lit face while she blushed into a crimson red and hoped that he didn't notice.

"You're welcome. Now, if I were you, I'd go to bed for tomorrow."

"I would too. Goodnight Carson," said Julia going up the stairs.

As she walked away up the stairs, Carson took a deep sigh and mumbled to himself, "I just hope the **Remora** doesn't find out about this."

She turned back around at the top of the stairs to face him, "What was that?"

"Nothing. Just have certain things on my mind," he replied.

She left to her room and wondered why Carson didn't tell her what he had said. She kept thinking about it until she finally fell asleep in deep thought. Nothing came into mind of what he might have said except *Why does my curiosity always taunt me?*

Chapter 3

FIRST DAY OF CLASSES

That night, after Julia fell asleep in her troubled mind, she dreamt about herself as a little girl. She was about eight-years-old and was sitting in her father's office. It was raining very hard and all of the lights had gone out.

Julia stared at the lightened candles put in a row in front of her as she sat in one of her father's comfy armchairs. Her parents were away at a fancy party with their friends and Julia's grandmother was watching her. Suddenly, thunder and lightning struck. The young Julia became scared and held onto her legs curled up in a ball. She was cold, but was soon comforted when her grandmother came in and put a blanket over her as she patted her back.

"Did the storm scare you sweetheart?" asked her grandmother kindly.

Julia nodded with her head still down, "Will mommy and daddy be ok?"

"Of course dear. The weatherman said the storm would only last a couple of hours. Your parents will be home safe and sound."

Julia hugged her grandmother as they stared out the window into the stormy night, "If you say so. Thanks grandma."

They stayed together for several moments until her grandmother got up saying, "I have something for you."

"What is it?" Julia asked sitting up straight.

Her grandmother reached into her jacket pocket and pulled out a small, dark green book, "This was given to me by my grandfather. He told me nothing was written inside, but to **never** open it. I'm giving it to you, and I want you to do the same. But when you're older, if you *absolutely* have to open it with your curious little mind," she dotted Julia's small nose with her finger, "open it when you feel you have the need to."

"But grandma, what's so special about this diary?"

"You'll have to figure that out for yourself. But remember what I said. When it was given to me, my grandfather said it was a **warning**."

Julia stared at the diary. When her grandmother died soon after that, she forgot about it. She only found it when she was looking for her usual diary to write in after her parent's funeral. In the forest she barely saw a light, and found out what was so special about it…

Around 10:00A.M in the morning, Julia finally awoke. She walked down the stairs and up the corridor, looking for anyone else who was awake. She only found Carson.

"Good morning. You slept in a little late." Carson gave a small laugh, but only for a second. "Julia, remember when I told you how I had certain things on my mind? Last night?"

"Yes. Is something wrong?" she still had a tired look in her eyes.

"I need to talk to you about something. It's called the Remora."

They walked into the meeting room and sat down.

"What is the Remora?" Julia asked inquisitively.

"It is a cult who betrayed the Kingdoms and now takes their revenge on them. They're the reason you can't be a burden- why I didn't think it was a good idea for you to be here in the first place."Carson said a little solemnly.

"But why do they want revenge on the Kingdoms?"

"I don't know exactly what they did, but I know that we can't trust them and the rulers before didn't trust them and that's why they banished them. Now they want revenge."

"What exactly do they want to take revenge on?"

"I don't know. All I know is that they hate humans." he said sadly because he hated not knowing things and not being able to give answers.

25

Then Cassidy came barging in on them.

"I've been looking all over for you. Sorry Carson, for barging in, but Julia is late for her first class with me. Hurry up; we need to go get some things."

"Goodbye Carson. I'll see you after my classes." said Julia being scurried out of the room.

"Goodbye Julia."

Then Cassidy closed the door shut tightly and rushed her into Julia's bright room.

"Here is the book of *Elements*, put it into this book bag," said Cassidy handing them to her.

"Am I going to get a lot of books today?"

"Not in my class, but in your other classes. Anyway, I'm going to tell you your schedule for every day except for the weekends because people in town work on the weekends."

Julia sat down to listen. When she sat down, her silky, green dress she picked out that day spread out like a patch of newly, blooming flowers.

"Classes start at 10:00 am. Your first class is with me. I will usually pick you up in here, but if not, go to the laboratory. Second class is with Christopher. He will teach you magic in the garden, which is downstairs and to the right. Third class is with Mr. Doddsworth. He will be teaching you government in his meeting room. From this room, it is downstairs to the left and then right with a sign saying Mr. Doddsworth. After those classes, it's lunch." Cassidy spoke in haste.

"Is everyone going to be at lunch at the same time?"

"Yes." said Cassidy while nodding. "After lunch you'll meet Veronica in the Ball Room for social class. There is a door in the weaponry room that leads to the Ball Room. After you have class with Veronica, outside the Ball Room is a balcony which you will meet Mr. Clayton and Lori Linda for universal class."

"How long is your class?"

"It's about...oh...thirty minutes."

"Is every class thirty minutes?" Julia asked out of her many questions she had for her.

"Well, at least one class before lunch, maybe about forty-five minutes."

"Oh."

"Anyway, we better get down to the lab. Hurry up get your things."

They went out of the room and headed towards the lab. When they were in, Cassidy put a metal suit, weird, steel goggles, and gloves on a table.

"When you come in, you put this equipment on. It's all part of the procedures."

Julia tried her best to puzzle the pieces of the suit over her dress and put on the goggles and gloves. Cassidy was doing the same, but used magic to place each piece of the suit over her gold dress by themselves individually. She stared at Cassidy envious for wanting to learn magic since there was none where she came from.

"How did you do that?"

"Well, *everyone* knows magic." said Cassidy smirking.

"Oh…of course."

"Shall we get started with the class?" asked Cassidy while putting her hands up by her head and spinning in the room towards the cabinets with much grace.

"I would like to." Julia said rolling her eyes.

"Good. Let's start by explaining the procedures."

She opened the cabinet to reveal a large piece of parchment that had the procedures listed.

"Number one put on a suit, eyeglasses, and gloves but we've already done that. Number two, get out a mixing bowl, lab ware and tools, ingredients, chemicals, and water from Ceylon."

"Why do you need water from Ceylon?"

"You have to mix things in something to get it started. And it helps with every potion you make."

"Should I write this all down?"

"I would. Here is a journal you can use to write in and a quill with ink to write with." said Cassidy handing Julia papers that were held together by ribbon and the quill with ink.

"Thank you." said Julia as she sat down with everything.

"You can start your writing with the procedures."

As such, Julia wrote down the procedures and Cassidy got out everything they needed out on the table.

"Have you written everything down?"

"Yes." Julia announced.

"Then let's get started with class. Today we're going to learn the basic potions."

Julia turned to the next page in the journal and titled it *Basic Potions.*

"The easiest is the teleportation potion, and then it is the light potion, and finally the healing potion."

Again Julia was writing in the journal in a neat way so she could be organized. At her college, she used to write Cornell Notes all the time. School was nothing new to Julia in her eyes.

Cassidy listed all of the ingredients out for her, and she mixed them together and put it into a glass sphere.

"Thank you." said Julia holding and gazing into the sphere in her hand. It shimmered with a dusty, gold substance buzzing inside it.

Cassidy smiled and continued with the lesson. "There are two ways you can make light, one is to use Ceylon the other is to make the light potion."

Julia put her piece of Ceylon behind her necklace because she didn't want Cassidy to know that she had a piece of it just in case Cassidy would say something. She seemed to about everything else. So she didn't see any reason of why not to now.

"This non-terminating light, except until ten years when it finally fades, consists of three things," she told her the ingredients and waited, "Now; mix everything but the ball of camilico butter."

As Julia was mixing, Cassidy went to go get ten wooden sticks of brushwood. When she came back with them, Julia watched as her mixture turned into a sticky wax.

"Are you done mixing?"

"Yes. Here you are." said Julia handing the mixing bowl to Cassidy.

"Thank you. Now take some of this potion and put it on the lighting brushwood and say *luminescent* while blowing your breath onto it."

Julia put the wax on the brushwood.

"After you're done, go take these to the cave of Ceylon. As you know it was dark in there so it needs some new lights."

"What are you talking about? I wasn't in there." said Julia in her most innocent voice even though it wasn't very convincing.

"Listen everyone knows you have a piece of Ceylon. You don't have to keep it a secret."

Julia had no reply, she had nothing to say; she felt like a little girl who was proved wrong.

"Anyway bring the brushwood after you've done the spell."

Julia said *Luminescent* while blowing her breath and saw that this potion was brilliant because it flared up in a second as what seemed to be white fire surrounding the end of it. When she decided to go to the library, she found Cassidy pushing the markers on the wall. She went inside when the wall opened and signaled Julia into the darkness of the cave.

"Just put them in the candle holders on the wall." said Cassidy trying to see Julia.

"All right."

The stairs were lit by the brilliant light. When they got out, Cassidy was surprised at the chime of the bell. "That bell tells you it's time for your next class. You have five minutes to get there. I shall walk you to the garden to meet Christopher, but tomorrow you should know the way."

"So, I guess that means we'll do the healing potion tomorrow."

"Yes. Now, let's go back to the lab and take off our suits because we have to go."

They walked to the lab and took off the suits, goggles, and gloves. Once this was done, Julia followed Cassidy to the garden. There were flowers flourishing everywhere. From daisies, to roses, and all sorts of color washed painted flowers. The blooms were all neatly arranged in terracotta boxes with shimmering water.

"Ah. There you are." said Christopher to Julia. "Thank you Cassidy, for bringing her down." she nodded to them and left.

"Well, there isn't much to say because we're just getting some books. But tomorrow I will show you how to make plants survive with just water and magic." said Christopher with a smile.

They went down to the library and Julia followed Christopher around trying to find books. She climbed most of the stairs while holding onto the rail. Julia sometimes even went on one of the sliding ladders and found it very fun. She squealed with delight when Christopher 'accidentally' pushed her over to the top of the M section.

"Let's see. *Witch and Wizardology*, *Magic Basics*, and *The Book of Creatures*. You can start reading these books tonight." he handed her the books after Julia had gotten down from the ladder and she went to a table and started reading *Witch and Wizardology*.

She was halfway through the book when the bell rang.

"If you could just read those books tonight that would be great."

She nodded and walked out the library and up the corridor. When she was the opposite from her bedroom door she turned right and then left to see the door saying 'Mr. Doddsworth' and she knocked on the door.

"You can come in." said Mr. Doddsworth in a rusty tone of voice through the door and coughed.

She went in and saw a desk, light blue walls with golden candles flying around the room, a maple table with chairs, a hallway, and a wooden counter holding a book titled *The Rulers of our Kingdoms*.

"Start reading that book for today." said Mr. Doddsworth coming through the hallway, holding another book.

She picked up the book and started reading. There were fifteen Kingdoms, each with a King or Queen or both. In the Felpierre Kingdom, Robert Felpierre was the founder and became King. In the Pierre Kingdom, Passerine Pierre found the Kingdom with her husband but when she found that her husband killed their son for the crown in all of the corruption, she turned him in. She did many great things after that, so she became Queen. She read about the other Kingdoms and Julia heard the bell ring the last time before lunch. It was a never-ending soft melody that went through her head like Church bells.

"Cassidy should be coming to pick you up for lunch." said Mr. Doddsworth looking up from the book with tired gray eyes.

"Are you not coming?" asked Julia.

"I will. I just need to do something first."

And as though on cue, Cassidy came in.

Julia gave a weak smile. "Hi, Cassidy."

She sneered back at Julia, "What are you doing?"

"Well, you were supposed to be picking me up for lunch."

"Oh, right." as Cassidy responded, she frowned at Julia.

"Is there something wrong?" Julia asked to Cassidy because she didn't know what she was missing in the situation.

"Not at all. Julia can you wait outside the room for a second? I need to talk to Mr. Doddsworth."

Julia stepped outside the room and put her ear to the door and listened. She heard Mr. Doddsworth grunting, as though he just had a shot of medicine put into him. She folded her eyebrows uncertain and listened more attentively.

"You're going to be fine. Eat a small lunch today. You should be more careful about your health." Julia heard Cassidy whisper.

Then Julia heard footsteps behind her. She stepped back from the door just in time so the person coming wouldn't see what she was doing. She leaned up against the white wall and sighed.

"Julia?" said Carson around the corner near her.

"Yes?"

"Where's Cassidy?"

"She's in there with Mr. Doddsworth."

"Oh, well, let's just walk to the Dining Hall."

They came to two tall and wide, wooden doors and opened them. Inside was a long room with redwood floors, long tables, chairs, and a wide table at the end of the room with all the food on it. Julia held her stomach realizing how hungry she was.

"I guess we'll just sit down." said Carson looking towards a table.

"Aren't we going to get our food?"

"Cassidy does that. She wants us to be 'healthy', so she'll pick the meal."

"Oh." Julia replied longing to get her own food.

They sat down and Carson reached into one of his pockets and he pulled out a black box. He slid it across the table to Julia. She caught it in both hands and wondered what could be inside it. "What's this?"

"Open it."

She opened it. Inside was a business card and three gold coins. Julia smiled, blushing from her surprise.

"It's just to get you started here in the Kingdoms with a job and money. The business card is to Adrianna's pet shop, you have your interview for the job on Saturday."

"Thank you Carson."

As this was happening, Cassidy came in with Mr. Doddsworth. She also noticed that Carson had given Julia something, and thought of her dream she had frowning. Then Cassidy went to go get everyone's lunches as Mr. Doddsworth headed for the table while looking at everyone else coming in.

They greeted each other as he sat down and waited a moment, "Julia…I want to apologize for not telling you anything so I'll explain now." he paused another moment, "I'm very sick, and Cassidy is helping me, but I may have to quit this job. It's only a matter of time before I do quit."

"I'm so sorry. Is there anything I could do to help?" Julia asked concerned.

"No, and I'm sorry for not mentioning anything."

Then everyone else came to the table. They all greeted and sat down. Julia forced a smile even though she felt a great sympathy for Mr. Doddsworth.

"So, I was thinking that on Saturday we could go into town and to the market. It could be a good chance for you to get to know the Kingdom better. Would you like to do that?" asked Veronica to Julia.

"I would love to do that."

"I'll go too; I have some people I need to meet up with there on Saturday." said Carson coming into the conversation.

"Great." said Veronica.

"I would like to point out that on Sunday is the premier of the play *Dancing with the Prince* at the *Aceline Theatre*." said Lori Linda.

"That's great. I'll make arrangements to go." said Mr. Clayton laughing because he loved taking his care-free niece to plays.

"What is the play about?" asked Julia.

"It's about a Prince who is fascinated with dancing but his father does not approve of it. So he goes looking for a dance partner behind his father's back and falls in love with her and his father finds out. When he does, the father is so enraged and bans him from the Kingdom. But the mother doesn't let him, so the Prince comes back with his true love and becomes the new King." said Cassidy spoiling the end coming to the table with everyone's lunches floating beside her.

"Thank you for telling me and thank you for the lunch." said Julia the first part a bit sarcastically as Cassidy set the lunches down.

"You're welcome." Cassidy sat down herself.

Everyone ate their lunches as they laughed and talked to each other with smiles all over their faces. To Julia, everything seemed to be in place and nothing could go wrong. Nothing at all.

Then came a whooshing sound from a tall window at the end of the room and came in, what seemed to be, a large black bird. It looked like a hawk. When it came to a halt at another table with people, it looked like a handsome young man. He had messages all over a belt that he was wearing, long, black hair, tan skin, broad shoulders, dark eyes, and had black wings. Then he started walking towards the table and Cassidy went up to him.

"Julia this is my brother Bade." said Cassidy hugging her brother.

"Nice to meet you Bade."

"Nice to meet you too Julia." said Bade giving Julia a smile. "I have a message for Carson and you Cassidy."

"Thank you." said Carson getting the envelope and reading it.

"Try to stay out of trouble sister." said Bade giving an envelope to Cassidy.

"I will."

Then Bade winked over to a blushing Veronica and spread out his wings to take flight as the bell rang. He swooped through the glassless window with no problem. Julia was indeed fascinated with the seemingly shy, strong, and attractive Bade.

"You can come with me Julia, after all you're in my next class." said Veronica who seemed extremely happy.

"All right. Goodbye everyone."

"Goodbye." said everyone else at the table.

"Julia, if you don't mind, I have more people in my class. Is that all right?" Veronica pleaded in the hallway.

"That's fine."

Julia and Veronica walked into the hallway to find two young men and one other young woman as they walked up to them.

"Everyone this is Julia. Julia this is Elaine and the two twin brothers Darcy and Aaron."

"Nice to meet you all."

"Nice to meet you too Julia." they all said simultaneously.

"Anyway let's get to class." said Veronica.

They walked up the corridor to the weaponry room and went to the side door inside the room and into a long hallway. It was dark and was only lit by the burning embers on the candles.

"There's another way to the Ballroom but this is the easiest way to get there." said Aaron to Julia.

"Good to know." Julia replied.

Chapter 4

HUMANS

They came to a halt at a gigantic, wooden door with many locks on it at the end of the hallway. It was magnificent; rich wood, gold locks and candles beside the door that made it seem like a mirror. Casting all their reflections, Julia couldn't decide to look at everyone or just at the grand door.

"Ready everyone?" asked Veronica and they all nodded eager to look inside.

The Ballroom was an extraordinary room because it was the most magnificent in size, color, and architecture. It expanded a long distance and could hold enormous amounts of people. The marble was a rich, cream of white with royal blue for the pillars and the floors. The ceiling was made of glass and there were many arched windows on the sides of the Ballroom. In the center were five chairs set up in a circle.

"All right class. Take a seat and we'll get started."

Then Julia started to think. *I wonder what everyone is doing back home. I wish I knew. If only they could see this wonderful place!*

"Now, I want you all to go around in the circle and tell us what you can do and why you think we need social class. You go first Elaine."

"I'm Elaine, I'm an elf, and I think we need social class to know what's around us in this world."

"Good job. You next Darcy and Aaron."

"Well we are shape-shifters." said Aaron.

"We can clone into anything or anyone we want to." said Darcy.

"Can you show the class?"

"Sure." said the twins together.

They cloned themselves into Julia but then quickly cloned themselves back.

"I've never cloned myself to whatever Julia is. It hurt." said Aaron.

"What?" asked Veronica surprised?

"He's right. It did hurt." said Darcy.

"How so?"

"Well, when you clone someone, you have to go inside of them and copy their DNA. While I was doing that, it made me feel like my head was about to burst." when Aaron said this, he sounded exhausted.

"Exactly. So what are you Julia?" asked Darcy equally exhausted.

"I'm a human." Elaine, Darcy, and Aaron all had the same look of shock on their faces, but before anyone could quarrel, Veronica cut-in.

"And that brings me to my next subject. We have to learn our classes in this world. Can you name any Elaine?" Veronica said sitting up strait.

"Yes. There are six classes. There is fighter, hunter, mage, rouge, creature, and spirit."

"Very good. But now in today's world we have a human. We've had humans in world before, but the last time we had a human in our world that the Remora didn't find —at least for a while-, was 120 years ago by the name of **Kahlil Flores**. Did your family know him Julia?"

"No. Is there any way I can talk to him? I'm sure there's some magic that you can use."

"I'm afraid that he was murdered by the Remora. Even in spirit, no one can talk to him." said Veronica upset.

"But why?" asked Elaine.

"No one knows. Many believe it's because of his protector."

Darcy and Julia must have been thinking the same thing because they both looked up and asked, "Protector?"

"Yes. When he came, a woman became his defender, so her family has been granted the title of being any human's guardian."

"Does that mean I have a protector?" asked Julia happily.

"Yes. You just have to look."

Chapter 5

PRINCE NATHAN

Meanwhile, Carson was in the meeting room when Cassidy came barging in. Her face was about as red as her hair and it frightened Carson. She closed the door, to his relief, but soon looked back.

"Oh my goodness! I can't believe you're in love with that-that *girl*!" screamed Cassidy.

"What girl? Julia?" Carson was stunned.

"Yes, Julia! Who else could I possibly be talking about?" Cassidy turned bright red and filled with anger.

"I don't think it's a big deal. She is a girl from another world, universe, or something in that manner. Can't I be nice to her? If you ask me-"

"Well, I didn't ask you anything!"

"Then I'll just tell you my opinion! I think you're being awfully rude *and*- and I think you're jealous!"

"I'm not jealous!" she screamed at the top of her lungs.

"Than what are you then?"

"Worried."

"Worried about what?"

"You!"

"*Me*?" Carson asked truly taken back.

"Yes you."

"Why?"

"Because…because of the vision I had last night." her voice tuned down now.

"What was in your vision that could possibly worry you about me?"

"You dying to protect Julia- and you could only do that if you love her!" she started sobbing.

Everything went calm and quiet. Then Carson got up and walked towards Cassidy. She only dared to look up.

"I won't die protecting Julia. I promise." as he said this in a kind voice, he gave Cassidy a handkerchief.

"All right. I'm sorry for disturbing you."

"It's fine. I better get back to work."

Then Cassidy nodded and walked out the door. The bell rang as Mr. Clayton stepped in. Carson gave a quick smile in greeting.

"Ok. See you tomorrow class." said Veronica waving the class goodbye.

"Goodbye." said the twins.

"Julia, your next class is out those glass doors over there." Elaine pointed to the corner window with much yellow light shining through it.

"Thanks Elaine." said Julia heading for the doors.

She opened the doors and the sun was blazing in the scenery in the distance. There were green mountains with the sun that rose high above to make the waterfall glisten in the sunlight. There were also white birds flying across this still moment in time.

"Good. You're here on time." she heard a familiar high voice speaking and turned around. It was Lori Linda.

"Yes I am. Where's Mr. Clayton?"

"He's coming. He went to go get permission from Carson to see Ceylon today."

"Oh."

"Anyway we better go get some books from the library."

As they were in the library and Lori Linda went to find some books. Once she found them, she strutted towards Julia. Lori Linda gave them to her with a smile.

"Here are you're books, put them in your book bag because here comes Mr. Clayton."

She looked at the four books and turned around to ask a question when Lori Linda had already went over to Mr. Clayton.

"Can we see Ceylon?" asked Lori Linda.

"Yes." said Mr. Clayton.

They walked up to Julia, who was looking at the books.

"Are you ready to see Ceylon again?" asked Mr. Clayton.

"Yes."

Lori Linda began walking towards the C section in the library.

"What book does she need?"

"Usually it's out of place so we can find it, but if it's not, we look for *Creatures of our world*. That way we can get the combination."

"Oh." she said feeling a little guilty that she had put the book back in place.

Then Lori Linda went over to wall to the left of her and pushed the markers in a random order that was on the paper and the wall split into two again. For a second, the librarian looked up and then back down again noticing Lori Linda. She waved Julia and Mr. Clayton over to the split wall.

"You go first Julia." said Lori Linda once they came to her side.

"Ok."

She walked over to the entrance to the cave and headed down the now lightened stairway. When they got to the bottom, there were three men looking at Ceylon. One was a handsome young man dressed in the finest looking fabrics and wore a silver crown with long brown hair running down from the bottom of it. The other two were talking to this man and wore draping red robes with gold shirts and white pants with a belt holding a sword.

"Mr. Clayton?" asked Julia in a surprised whisper.

"Yes."

"Who is that?"

"That is Prince Nathan and his two guards. He is soon to become the next King of the Felpierre Kingdom."

"Oh." she stated fascinated by this fact.

Once their conversation was over, Prince Nathan walked over to Julia, Mr. Clayton, and Lori Linda with the two guards following.

"Hello Prince Nathan." said Mr. Clayton bowing.

"Hello."

"What brings you to the Tabor's Castle?"

"Well, before I become King, I wanted to look around my Kingdom and since this is on the border, I came here first. I also wanted to meet everyone too."

"Ah, well, this is Julia."

"Nice to meet you Julia." he nodded to Julia, captivated by her with his eyes shining brightly for a moment with his liquid gold voice putting her somewhat in a trance and looked back to Mr. Clayton, "Where would Mr. Tabor be at the moment?"

"Carson is in the meeting room. My niece, Lori Linda, can show you to it."

"Thank you."

"Not a problem your highness." said Lori Linda while Mr. Clayton and herself bowed to him and Julia soon bowed too.

"I hope to see you all again." said Prince Nathan, making Julia blush a tint of pink.

"Us too." said Lori Linda and the two of them, including Prince Nathan's guards, headed upstairs.

"He seems nice for a Prince." said Julia after the four were out of sight.

After a moment Mr. Clayton replied, "Yes he's very nice. Anyway, let's look at Ceylon. Inside are many little crystals that glow when someone gets a piece and it's surrounded by Ceylon water that is held together by the elements. Of course you already know what the elements are, so we don't have to cover that. You also have a piece of it so I don't have to get another for you."

"But Ceylon is basically life you can hold." said Lori Linda at the top of the stairs.

"Exactly."

"You can make potions with it, heal, and use it as a light."

"Now that you know everything about Ceylon, we can learn about the stars." said Mr. Clayton starting to go upstairs.

"How are we going to see the stars at 1:10pm?" asked Julia looking at a watch she wore that was set to the time of this new world.

"I'll have to show you." said Mr. Clayton looking back at Julia smiling.

In the meeting room, Carson was doing taxes when Prince Nathan came in and Carson rushed to his feet and bowed.

"Good afternoon Carson."

"Good afternoon sire. What brings you to my family's castle? Looking for anyone?"

"In fact I am." Carson bowed his head; he did not exactly want to hit *that* target.

"Who?"

"Last night, this started glowing. Who is new to my Kingdom?" asked Prince Nathan showing his piece of Ceylon to Carson and sat down in one of the comfortable chairs.

"A girl." Carson smiled lightly and shyly as he stared at the piece of Ceylon that Prince Nathan put on the table.

"Who might be her? Where is she? What is she? Tell me everything." said the Prince leaning forward in his chair curious.

"Her name is Julia." he ruffled his hair with bright eyes.

Prince Nathan paused smiling charmingly, "I just met her."

"Really?" he asked looking up worried.

He laughed, "Yes."

"Did she tell what she is?"

He shook his head with a hint of confusion in his expression, "No."

"Ah…well…that's good." said Carson both relieved and uncertainly.

"What do you mean by that?"

He hesitated, "Well…she's…a human." then the Prince fell silent.

"Carson, do you realize what you have done?" he emphasized the done.

"No."

"If she is human we need to send her back now." he whispered.

"But…why?"

"You must have an alter ego. Of course you know why!" he rose angrily from his chair.

"Well, I don't."

41

"Think of the Remora...do you what they would do to her if they found out a human was living here?" he stretched his arm to the doorway as if Julia was standing just outside of it.

Then Carson had a horrible image and then he fell silent. Nothing was worse than the Remora. And he would *never* want to see her get hurt.

"Exactly. We need to send her back now."

"But I don't know how."

"Well think of it soon." said Prince Nathan heading out the door and Carson bowed one last time and thought. *How do I tell Julia?*

Chapter 6

LONGING FOR HOME

When Julia, Mr. Clayton, and Lori Linda were back on the balcony, Mr. Clayton started moving his hands around in formations. Lori Linda stepped to the side and seemed to watch Mr. Clayton's peculiar movements very carefully. Julia followed Lori Linda's example.

"He's going to show you how you can see the stars at this time of day." said Lori Linda never looking away.

Then Mr. Clayton started talking in a different language and the sky above him looked stormy, and became black for a moment. Then stars appeared and Mr. Clayton began to relax. He looked at Julia then looked back up.

"That was time travel." said Mr. Clayton in a tired voice.

"Am I going to learn that?"

"Eventually."

"It takes practice. I haven't even mastered it yet." said Lori Linda glumly.

"What you are looking at now are our constellations. The noble Adelio, Channer the wise, Asha of hope, the talented Dorinda, the sympathetic Kayla, and the great fighter Pallaton." said Mr. Clayton pointing out and looking at these constellations.

"And they are all part of the Kabira galaxy with us." said Lori Linda.

"The Kabira galaxy?"

"Yes. Is something wrong?"

"If I'm in a different galaxy, then I'm very far from home."

"What galaxy do you live in?" asked Mr. Clayton putting his hands in another formation.

"The Milky Way. It's a small blue planet."

"All right. I'll do my best to find it."

"Thank you."

Mr. Clayton moved his hands around in movements and the sky above had different galaxies traveling around until the familiar alignment of planets was seen. Then she saw Earth and Mr. Clayton relaxed. He looked up at the blue planet.

"Is that your world?" asked Lori Linda.

"Yes." Julia stated bemused with small tear droplets in the corners of her eyes looking at her home.

"Well that was just time travel. I don't know how to get you back. I'm sorry." said Mr. Clayton with sad eyes.

"I'm sorry for giving you all such trouble, but I don't know if I even can go back."

"Well, you don't have to worry about that." said Lori Linda and the bell rang for the last time for the day, "Now you are free to do whatever you wish for the rest of the day."

"Thank you. I'll see you two later."

Then they nodded and Julia headed for her room but ran into Carson along the way.

"Hi Carson."

"Hello Julia. Where are you headed?"

"To my room."

"Oh…well…can I speak to you before you go? In the garden?"

"Sure."

They walked into the garden and sat down on a bench.

"I wanted to talk to you about you being here."

"What about it?"

"Prince Nathan wants you to go back to your own world." he said sadly looking straight into her jade eyes.

"Why?"

"He doesn't want the Remora to get suspicious. Do have any idea of how to get back?" he put his hand on her shoulder, slightly turning her to look at him.

"I'm sorry, but, I don't."

"That's all right. I didn't expect you to." he brought his hand down.

She sat in silence for a moment and then asked, "But if the Remora found out I was here, what would they do?"

"Julia, you have to understand that the Remora is merciless. If they caught you, they would try to kill you."

"But why?"

"When Kahlil Flores came to our world, the leader of the Remora killed him because he turned her in. They hate humans. We could have stopped the Remora if the leader hadn't escaped and killed him. When that happened, a war started. It was the worst ever. That's why we don't want them to get suspicious. They'll start another just like all of the others since him. The last war we had was twelve years ago."

"I'm sorry." she replied with much remorse.

"It's fine. We just have to find a way to get you back." he paused looking forward solemnly and then looked down and saw all of her books, "Well it looks like you have a lot of reading to do so I'll leave you to it."

"Then I'll see you later, Carson."

"Yes, I'll see you at dinner."

Then Carson got up and left while Julia thought for a moment.

If the Remora finds me, I'll be killed? What if all of these people die with me because they kept it a secret? I need to find a way back.

Then Julia looked at her books, sighed deeply, and headed towards her room. She opened the first book that Christopher gave her and started where she left off and then read all of the other books she had gotten that day. All were somewhat short texts and she herself was an avid reader, so it didn't take her too long to read them. Julia also wrote the name of the human before her who had made a significant change to their world in her diary: Kahlil Flores. When she was done reading and writing, she lay down on her bed and took a nap while having a vision during her dream.

Chapter 7

CASSIDY AND MR. DODDSWORTH

She dreamed of her sitting on the ground and Carson in front of her and jumping but she couldn't see what he was jumping at. Soon, a sword was drawn right into him. He then died as Julia reached for him and woke up with a scream and someone knocking on the door.

"Julia, it's me Cassidy. Are you all right?"

"Fine."

"Can I come in?"

"Yes." said Julia feeling her head.

Cassidy came into the room and sat by Julia, "Why did you scream?"

"It was something I saw in my dream."

"What did you see?"

"Carson."

"What about him?"

"Nothing."

"Julia you can tell me."

But Julia didn't say anything and just looked at her.

"Look I know I can be a little protective but you can tell me." Cassidy said looking into her eyes intensely.

"He…he died right in front of me."

"I see." Cassidy looked down.

"Just don't tell him. Ok? He's probably already worried about how to get me back before the Remora finds out."

"I won't."

"Thank you. But, Cassidy?"

"Yes?"

"Why are you protective? Not that it's a bad thing." Julia said catching herself.

"Well, I've known Carson all of my life. Since we were kids, I've seen him at his best and his worst. I was always there for him. I helped him in any way I could. When his parents died...that was the worst. The only reason why he got out of that was because of Mr. Clayton and I. His siblings always thought of me as another sister. Even now, they still do. I just know what's best for Carson." she lifted her chin proud with a little tint of red from resentment resting on her cheeks as she gazed at Julia with envy.

"Maybe he knows what's best for him as well." her heart raced as new information about Carson was told to her and even a hint of jealousy that Cassidy had always been at Carson's side.

She breathed heavily and stood, "We should head down to dinner." and cleared her throat.

They headed out the door and to the Dining Hall and saw everyone at the table. Cassidy went to get everyone's dinners and Julia sat by Veronica.

After a greeting, Cassidy came back with the dinners. Everyone enjoyed the meal and had a great time as friends with Mr. Clayton quoting books as he fiddled with a coin in his hands, Lori Linda talking about different plays, and Mr. Doddsworth telling funny stories from his childhood. And after dinner, they all headed back to their rooms and got ready for bed.

I really like them all. I hope I don't have to go back soon when I'm just starting to enjoy myself here. But I do have to go back because my friends and the rest of my family might worry, and people might die on my very own account.

She had a good night of rest, other than the tears of the loss of her parents still lingered into her sleep and woke up the next morning and headed to the lab to meet Cassidy. When she got to the lab, there was a note on the door. The note said that Cassidy was in the Dining Hall with breakfast.

As such, Julia went to the Dining Hall and saw Cassidy eating her meal, and waved to her. Julia walked to her and sat down.

"Where is everyone else?"

"Work. You're a little early for class, so eat."

"Ok." they ate and then went to the lab.

They executed all of the preparations and got out what they needed.

"We're going to learn the health potion."

After a couple of minutes of stirring the items she had told her, she said, "I'm done mixing."

"Good. Now put it in this bottle." Cassidy said while settling it down.

She put the potion into the glass bottle and the concoction was a sparkling purple.

"The next thing we're going to learn is nutrition."

Julia learned about nutrition until the class was over and she went to the garden to find Christopher.

"Hello Julia. Are you ready to learn how these plants grow so well?"

"Yes."

"All right, the first thing you do is put Ceylon water in a stone bowl. It can be any shape you want and whatever size. Second put the plant seeds you want into it. And last say this spell and the plant will start growing and last 100 years. Here's the spell." he handed her a piece of paper telling her the spell, "I'm going down to the library to get a couple more books for you to read. You can practice the spell while I'm gone."

"Ok." she read the spell and was confused of how to pronounce but soon figured it out and Christopher came back with two books.

"Did you figure out the spell?"

"I did eventually."

"Ok. Now say the spell and only concentrate on the plant. Look straight at it."

She did this and began to say the spell, "Rasheria gerna hearo." and the plant started growing out of the water. Its green sprouts grew roots and climbed up until it was at least a foot tall. Then it stopped growing.

"It takes three days before it's fully grown."

"Oh."

"Good job with your first spell though. Now you can read these books and be done with class." he handed them to her.

"Thanks Christopher."

"You're welcome."

She read the relatively short books and was done just in time to head down to Mr. Doddsworth's class. But when she came into the last hallway, she found Cassidy very upset.

"What's wrong Cassidy?"

"Mr. Doddsworth isn't getting any better. He asked me to give you these books to read." she handed her the thin fifty page collection of books and Julia went to her room to read them.

She read a book telling her how their government worked; another telling her what types of land was around the Kingdoms, and the last one telling her the history of this world. After reading, she went to find Cassidy in the same hallway as before.

Julia only asked her where the kitchen was and followed her instructions on the path to get there. Once in the large, brick kitchen with a fireplace, she had one of the chefs to point out all of the ingredients she would need to make soup, hot tea, and find any herbs that could help soothe Mr. Doddsworth's sickness. When her remedies she knew from her mother were prepared and ready, she smiled in delight and brought it to the table in his setting. Looking up, she saw Carson with him and strolled over to help guide the weak, elderly man to his seat. Mr. Doddsworth beamed gratefully.

Chapter 8

THE LETTER

It was near lunch time at the Tabor's Castle as Bade sat in his small office room, fastening his belt full of letters to deliver around all of the Felpierre Kingdom. If someone needed a letter delivered right away, they would travel to town and to the old Bell Tower that was newly reconstructed to hold offices for mail deliverers like Bade. It was old, but large and beautiful in its antique russet color. The large, golden bell rang twice to signal the mail deliverers that it was time for duty.

Bade gave his belt one last tug before stepping outside. Once he saw the vivid light of the sun, and closing his eyes from the immense illumination, he spread his wings as far as they could go and shot off into the sky towards the dazzling sun. The air brushed against his face coolly and he smiled. Opening his eyes, Bade soared over the vast, stunning landscape with clouds wandering and hovering overhead. He loved to fly- it was a form of freedom to him.

Soon, he was above the forest before the Tabor's Castle and heard a rustle underneath him. Bade folded his eyebrows into a questioning look. But before he even had time to think, a shot rang out and an arrow pierced through his delicately feathered wings.

He let out a gasp of agony and was soon falling. Suddenly, it wasn't air between him and the ground. Bade was falling and hit many obstacles painfully, such as large trees before crashing hard to the forest floor.

Bade yelped out in exasperating pain and looked to his wings- his poor wings. They had been crushed and the wet with blood feathers twisted in all directions. He sighed in suffering. *This is not good,* he thought, *Not good at all.*

Rain started to pour down harshly and drenched Bade's face with mud from the ground. He tried with all of his might to get up, but failed. Bade put his head down wanting to give up.

Then, someone lifted Bade half up from the mud. It seemed to be a tall man, dressed in all black armor, covering his face. When he talked, it was an eerie echoing and mischievous voice.

"Give this to Carson Tabor as a warning." the man said shoving his back onto the trunk of a tree and forcing the envelope into Bade's fists.

The man disappeared and Bade fell onto the tree for support. Ghostly laughter then filled the sound in his ears and all around him. Bade was determined, so he limped to stand and tried to fly as difficult as it was. The warning was vital and needed to be known.

They went into the Dining Hall and it was raining. Cassidy went to get the lunches while Julia, Carson, and Mr. Doddsworth sat down at their regular table with everyone else. They talked and ate their lunch, until Bade came swooping in and crashed to the floor and Cassidy rushed to him. He looked a mess and as if he needed much help.

"What happened?" asked Cassidy while everyone else came.

"Bad flying." he said as Cassidy helped him stand, wincing.

"Tell me the truth." she said stern trying to hold back her gasps of breath, for she was worried.

"My wing broke."

"How?" Cassidy was shocked and outraged.

"I was shot down by someone and they gave me this letter to give to Carson." he said this while reaching for the letter with a white seal with a black dot in the center of it and gave it to Carson.

"Did you see who shot you down?" asked Carson receiving the letter in shock.

"No. I didn't see his face." he said looking back at his blood stained feathers sadly.

"Come with me. I'll mend your wounds." said Cassidy helping her brother walk towards the exit.

Passing Carson, he whispered, "The man said it was a warning to you." then as he passed Veronica, he grinned at her and she smiled back behind tears swelling into her eyes.

After Bade and Cassidy left, Carson looked at the letter with the white seal and black dot and knew who it was from: it was the Remora. He opened it and was petrified at what he read. It said *I know your secret.* Furthermore, the bell rang on cue.

"Veronica can you take Julia to your class now?"

"Sure. Let's go Julia." she said trying to keep her voice from breaking.

When they left, Christopher walked up to Carson, "What was written on it that got you all quiet?"

"Take a look at it." said Carson handing it to him.

He fell silent and looked at it again to make sure what he read was correct. "What…how?"

"I don't know how they found out."

"Carson, what happened?" asked Lori Linda.

"The Remora found out." said Christopher in a hurt tone that made him want to give up the peace that had finally come to their world.

"We have to tell Julia." said Mr. Clayton remorsefully.

"But who's going to?" asked Carson and everyone stared at him in response, "What?"

"I know who could tell her." said Cassidy coming back in.

"Where's your brother?" asked Christopher.

"Resting. And I think the one to tell Julia, is you Carson."

"Why me?" then everyone stared at him again, "What?" he asked for a second time.

Cassidy walked up to him and stood. "Because you know her best."

"Not exactly."

"But you were the one she met first, and she has feelings for you."

"What?"

"But I didn't say anything." then she and everyone else left but Carson hurried after Cassidy.

"Cassidy wait. Why did you tell me that Julia has feelings for me? It's – it's not true is it?"

"Are you really that blind? Anyone can see that she is. Why? Do you have feelings for her as well?" then she folded her arms across her chest in annoyed way and waited impatiently for him to tell her yes.

"Just because I asked about Julia doesn't mean I-"

"So you do love her?"

"Cassidy I…yes, I have feelings for her." he sighed.

"Fine. But don't say I didn't warn you because she had that same vision I had and that's when I found out that she's developing feelings for you." then she walked away and Carson started to think.

*Why? I can't think about this. I need to concentrate on getting her back and keeping the Remora from her. Then Cassidy says Julia had the same vision as her. Am I really going to **die**? I at least wanted to tell Julia that I…but I can't. She has to go back.*

Chapter 9

THE REMORA TAKING ITS TOLLS

Out of all the confusion Veronica and Julia had, they went to the Ballroom to have class. They learned about the other kingdoms and their culture until class ended and Julia met Lori Linda and Mr. Clayton on the balcony. They all had half-hearted smiles across their faces.

"Hello Julia."

"Hi Mr. Clayton."

"Today we're getting books."

They went to the library and got three books. One was about the different galaxies, another was about the theories of how the universe was created, and the final one was about the different planets in the Kabira galaxy.

"Just read these for today." said Lori Linda.

When Julia was done, she was now an experienced reader in a diminutive amount of time, she said goodbye and headed for her room but the bell didn't ring until five minutes later. Sometime after the bell, someone knocked on her door. Julia, curious, opened it to find Carson. He sighed asking, "May I come in?"

"Of course," she said kindly, noticing his expression; he looked somewhat hurt, "What's wrong?"

He breathed deeply, first looking to the ceiling and then handed her the letter, "We got a message from the Remora," he gazed at her with glistening eyes, "They know you're here."

Julia's hands shook as tears came to her eyes, "I can't just sit here and watch as people sacrifice themselves for my account, I have to find a way back…I have to. If any of you were hurt, I would just die."

Carson grasped her in his arms tightly, "Please don't say things like that. No one is going to get hurt. Only I will if you leave. I want you to stay. Please don't go."

She shook her head, "Carson the moment you rescued me, I knew I'd have feelings for you. But as much as I do, I can't let these emotions get in the way. You told me not to be a burden. You knew all of this. You should've just sent me away." she tried to break away.

"I couldn't do that."

"Why?" he didn't answer. "Tell me."

He waited, "I had to bring you here. I couldn't just leave you there."

"You knew I wasn't supposed to be here. I was selfish not to try to find a way home. Why would you let me be so self-centered?" Julia separated and stormed out of the room into the garden.

She sat on a bench, sinking her face into her hands as she sobbed. *Why did I do that? I know I over reacted, but, why did he bring me here when he knew I wasn't supposed to? He's going to make people suffer for my sake. To protect me.*

Julia looked up from her hands to a pool of Ceylon water in which she could see her reflection in, "But what can happen? How will they know who I am?" she dried her tears and saw someone else in the reflection.

Turning around, Julia saw a tall, broad-shouldered man dressed in dark grays, blacks, and blues from the top of his head to the bottom of his feet. His hair was shaven, but the color that still barely showed was a peppered color. He smiled enchantingly.

"Excuse me miss," he sat down next to her, "but why is a stunning young girl such as yourself, crying on a beautiful night such as this?" he stretched his arms up to the sky.

"Selfishness." she replied; he seemed trustworthy.

"Oh my child, everything happens for a reason. We can never please everyone, no matter how great our thoughts and ideas might seem. Just be sure that whatever you think is best to do for you, comes from your heart," he spoke so softly and gently, and pointed to her heart, then put his hands on her shoulders, "Now tell me, what did you do that was selfish and which is troubling you now?"

"I'm endangering everyone I know here. All of my new friends. I'm not supposed to be here," she couldn't keep the truth inside even though her thoughts told her it was dangerous; "I'm a human. They're all hiding me to protect me. All I want is for them to be safe and not jeopardize their lives from my account."

The man nodded, keeping his hands on her shoulders, "A human you say…"

Carson came from the shadows of the trees calling Julia's name. He stopped to find her with the stranger and eyed him viciously. The man smirked and maneuvered quickly to grab Julia while putting her hands behind her back. She struggled in his hurtful, tight grip.

"Let her go."

"Why? She's a human. She's the cause of all this mess."

Julia thrashed about, "Carson I am the cause. Let me take care of this. I can protect myself."

"Well that's the understatement of the year."

She brought herself up into a strong stance, "Nokotuo." she said as the ground then shook beneath her feet and up to hit the man in the face, breaking his nose and falter backwards, releasing her as she tried to make her way to Carson.

He spat out blood, "You little brat." and began running towards her.

Carson blocked his way and spun around him to take hold of his right arm. He painfully crushed it up against his back, hearing the bones splinter. The man gasped as his arm broke.

All of a sudden, an immensely deafening roar was made. It thrashed through Julia's heart, making her panic, having trouble breathing and even seeing. She looked up to see a slender, dark blue dragon on a tower, using its talons to hold itself up with another man in black armor riding it.

The dragon then started to climb towards the Bell Tower. Along the way, its claws and pointed armor made bricks and large stones fall. Julia ran to Carson, trying to avoid being hit as the dragon made its way to the Bell Tower.

Then, the beast grabbed hold of the massive bell with its jaw and used its neck to hurdle it down to the ground. Smoke was all around them, making it difficult to see. The bell chimed solemnly as it fell, with them trying to avoid the falling debris with it.

As if in slow motion and echoes, Carson reached for Julia, "Get down!"

Falling closer and closer was the bell. Julia screamed and tightly held onto Carson as they got on their knees. Just as they bell was about to crush them, she heard him say a spell. The bell then shattered into millions of pieces with a last earsplitting chime. Shrapnel spread all over the floor of the garden.

They looked up to find the man from before being helped up onto the beast by his good arm from the man in armor. Black eyes smirked themselves as he made the dragon go faster. Everyone ran outside and heard in a short distance away, "That was your final warning." Mr. Doddsworth's hands turned into fists at these words.

Carson looked around and then held Julia's shoulders, "Are you all right?" he asked checking to see if there were any injuries and helped her stand.

"I'm fine," she looked into his eyes and hugged him, "Thanks to you."

Veronica's soft voice was heard, standing next to the bandaged up Bade, "Mr. Doddsworth, what's the matter?"

He looked more pale and sickly than ever, "That...that was Aldrich."

"Who?" Julia asked.

"A traitor," he paused looking down, "He used to be my friend. But because of him, we lost the war twelve years ago. We could've defeated the Remora once and for all...it's all because of him that I lost my wife in that war. I can never forgive him."

She shook her head, "I'm so sorry."

He turned away, pale as the moon with red eyes, "I have to go." and left them all.

Mr. Clayton looked to Veronica, "Tomorrow when you three go into town, I'll arrange someone to clean all this up." they all nodded and Mr. Clayton left with Lori Linda on his right and Veronica helped Bade inside.

Julia separated from Carson looking down, and then noticed blood on Carson's neck and shoulder, "Carson you're bleeding!"

"It's nothing."

"It's not 'anything'."

Cassidy interrupted, "Julia, I'll bandage him up. You should try to get some rest."

Julia sauntered inside with Christopher putting one hand on her shoulder. As he walked her, his expression was of lost hope. He tried to smile once they came up to the door.

Saying goodnight, she waited until he was out of sight and went in search for Carson's room. She had to apologize. Thanking him for protecting her was another contribute to her wanting to see him.

Finding his door at last, she was about to knock but heard him talking to Cassidy. The expression 'curiosity killed the cat' escaped her mind. She put an ear to the door to listen.

"Do you really think she should be here?" asked Cassidy.

"What's done is done. It's too late now." he sighed but then let out a small grimace of pain from the bandaging.

"May I remind you of your duties? She's interfering with life-long friends. There are Coronations coming up and weddings. She's meddling with love and your status. Not to mention another war is going to start now."

"Enough Cassidy."

"I'm just saying I think it'd be best if she left."

Julia had heard enough. Her curiosity unfortunately didn't last long enough to hear Cassidy mention an arranged marriage; especially with Carson's status…

Making her way to her room, she held back tears. In her heart, she knew Cassidy was right. Her mind did not let her wander from the events that were caused by her being in this new world that night. Not even a minute's worth of sleep came until the next morning when she had to get ready for her day with Veronica and Carson.

Chapter 10

SATURDAY

The next day Julia woke up and started getting ready for the day and met up with Veronica. She put on a beautiful day dress, shoes, and jewels. Julia went down the steps and put some of her reddish, brown hair behind one ear.

"Are you ready to go?" asked Veronica.

"Sure."

"The carriage is ready." said Carson coming into the hallway surprisingly not looking at Julia.

"Great. Let's go Julia." said Veronica and they headed downstairs to another hallway and to a black, wooden door.

Carson opened the door, and it was a lightened underground tunnel.

"What's down here?" asked Julia.

"It's a tunnel that leads to the town in the mountains." said Carson eyes shining brightly at her.

"Oh. Is there a reason why we're going this way?"

"It's for your safety Julia." then Julia looked at Carson somewhat surprised and went down first.

Veronica and Carson soon followed for about five minutes until they came to a black carriage. Carson hurried to another man who came out from in front of it with the horses and talked to him. When they were done talking Carson walked back to them.

"He said ten silver for each trip, so time to go."

They got in and didn't say a word until they came back up from underground. There were many mountains and a small town coming up. When they got there, the carriage stopped and the man walked to the carriage door.

"We're here."

"Thank you sir." said Veronica.

"That will be ten silver for the first trip."

"Here you are." said Veronica handing the money to the man and he held the door open for them.

"Our first stop is for you two to look around while I do some business. Then I'll meet you two for lunch at the Inn." said Carson.

"All right. See you later." said Veronica waving goodbye and he waved back. "Julia, why are you mad at him?"

"He knew I wasn't supposed to be in this world. He put everyone in danger for me."

"That's not true. He brought you here because you would have died without his help and he loves you. Everyone has a purpose in life but you have to find it. And I think he knows *you* have a purpose of being here, so try to find it and return his feelings if you can."

"Thanks but-"

"But what? You're not going to have a good time because he saved you and it may cost some lives? But just let me say that you are worth fighting for Julia."

Julia fell silent. Could she return his feelings? Or rather, should she? She did care for him but thought it would be best if she didn't...

"Now, please try to enjoy yourself here."

"I will."

They walked around laughing and having a good time. They soon sat down at the Inn and drank.

"So I was wondering, who you love?" asked Julia.

"Well...Bade and I are engaged."

Julia was surprised, she had noticed they were close but didn't guess this, "Really? Have you told anyone?"

"No. Just you because he proposed last night."

"Wow. I'm very happy for you two."

"Thanks."

Then Carson came into the Inn and sat with them.

"Anything interesting happen?"

"Well…Bade proposed to Veronica last night." and Veronica showed them the gorgeous diamond ring.

"That's wonderful."

"Yes it is, and Cassidy is going to be my sister-in-law."

"I'm sure you're happy about that." he stated sarcastically.

"Of course I am." she said holding her chin up proud.

They talked, laughed, and had their lunch. Then Carson looked at the clock. He quickly put his drink down with 15 silver.

"We better be heading to Adrianna's pet shop because you have your interview in five minutes." he looked to Julia.

Finishing up, they walked to the shop and saw a young lady at the counter. She had, amazingly, blue hair and ten gold hoop earrings on each ear. She also had on a uniform and a white apron.

"Hi. I'm looking for Adrianna." said Carson.

"Is Julia here?"

"Yes."

"Um…she'll be with you in a moment." and she walked into a small room.

"Julia, what animals do you like?" asked Carson turning around.

"Well, I really like wolves." she smiled.

"Julia?" asked Adrianna from a distance and came out. She had rich burgundy hair, pale skin, and wore a purple dress with an apron over it.

"That's me." she almost raised her hand as though she were in school.

"Come with me." she waved her in.

"We'll see you after." said Veronica.

"Good luck." Carson encouraged.

They came into a room with many animals all around and a desk. Julia thought this was Adrianna's office. Julia loved the fact that this world was very different and the same in some ways as hers.

"Sit." said Adrianna sitting at the desk, "Why do you want this job?"

"I would like it because I love animals and I work fast and hard so you will learn to love me."

"And you're strait with answers." she said with her eyebrows raised. "What days are you willing to work?" asked Adrianna feeding a small, brown rabbit and pet it.

"The weekends."

"How much an hour?"

"Ten silver an hour."

"That's fine with me. You can start next weekend. Pick up your uniform at the front desk and be here at 11:00am next Saturday."

"Thank you."

"You're welcome." she grinned.

She went out of the room and saw Carson and Veronica standing behind a white wolf and holding the uniform.

"What...what's this?"

"I thought you might want a pet, so we got you Annabelle." said Carson.

"She's beautiful. Thank you." Julia said petting Annabelle's ears.

"You're welcome."

"I'm going to go get the carriage ready." said Veronica.

Once Veronica was gone, she looked up and said, "Carson, I'm sorry."

"I'm sorry-"

"No...don't be. I over reacted. I'm the only one that should be sorry. Thank you for all that you've done for me." then she gave him a kiss on the cheek, took the uniform, and started walking towards the carriage with Annabelle following her obediently.

Chapter 11

THE PLAY AND THE CRY

She got to the carriage and heard a cry for help. *What was that? It sounded so much like Peter. Could he come here?* Julia thought.

"Did you hear that Veronica?"

"No. What did you hear?"

"I just heard someone yell…help."

"It might just be your imagination because I didn't hear anything."

She trailed off still worried, "You're probably right."

Then Carson came and they went inside the carriage. They didn't speak a word until they were back inside the tunnel they were in at first and Julia kept thinking about the cry. *It sounded so much like my neighbor's son Peter. Could it be him? Could he have come to this world like me? How?*

They got out of the carriage and Veronica gave the man ten more silver when Carson noticed that Julia looked upset while petting Annabelle.

"Julia, is something wrong?"

She looked up at him and smiled. "No. Everything is fine."

He wasn't fully convinced, but thought it best if he dropped it. They went through the tunnel back to the castle and found out it was 6:30pm already, so they quickly put Annabelle into Julia's room and went to the Dining Hall for dinner. Everyone was already at the table with their dinners, including Bade. Veronica went to sit by him while Carson and Julia sat together.

"Did you have fun?" asked Cassidy.

"Oh yes. Did you tell your sister about us?" asked Veronica to Bade.

"Tell me what?" Cassidy inquired.

"No. I didn't tell anyone because I waited for you." said Bade thoughtfully and held her hand.

"Thanks. Well, tell them." her eyes sparkled.

"Um…Cassidy…everyone…Veronica and I are…getting married."

Then Cassidy squealed with delight and jumped to hug her brother, "I'm so happy for you." then she hugged Veronica.

"Thanks Cassidy." said Veronica.

Then everyone else gave them hugs and enjoyed the rest of their evening together. Before Julia left to her room, Carson gave her a beautiful red rose that smelled divine. She placed it into her diary to keep it forever.

The next day, they all got ready in colorful clothing and jewels for the play *Dancing with the Prince* at the *Aceline Theatre* and met downstairs by the black door again. The first ones down there were Carson, Lori Linda, and Mr. Clayton. They all smiled as she came down to them.

"Where's everyone? Is Mr. Doddsworth coming?" asked Julia coming down the stairway.

"No, but everyone else is." said Lori Linda.

"You look…wonderful Julia." said Carson.

"Thanks. You too."

Then Christopher, Cassidy, Veronica, and Bade came. Everyone had smiles on their faces and stood together. It was as though everything was set in the right place, without the worries of the Remora for a while.

"Are we ready to go?" asked Carson.

"I think we are." said Cassidy looking around.

Carson opened the door and walked down with everyone until they came up to a longer, white carriage that seemed to be pulled by a large white horse that a short man was petting. Carson walked up to the man and spoke to him, yet couldn't be heard because he was far away. Julia stood in amazement at the majestic horse.

After they talked, Carson waved Julia and everyone else over to him. They shuffled in and sat. Conversation started when Christopher looked to Julia.

"So have you been to many plays?"

"Well, yes, but in my world we also have shows called movies."

"Movies?" asked Bade.

"Yes."

"That's an interesting name."

"Very." she tried not to laugh.

They talked for about fifteen minutes and Julia was wondering why it was taking so long to get there.

"Where is the *Aceline Theatre*?" asked Julia.

"It's in another town a little farther from here." said Carson.

About ten minutes later they came to a bigger town and saw a giant building that looked big enough to hold over a thousand people. The driver stopped and held the door open for them for them to climb out. Carson talked to him and came back to everyone waiting.

"He said that he's going to look around the town while we're watching the play and he'll meet us back here when we're done. And the play doesn't start for another hour so let's go eat our lunch next door."

They went into the Inn next to the theatre and had a wonderful lunch and then went back to see the play. They walked in, and it was a place lightened by candles and mirrors lighting the fountain in the middle and the front desk. The cool breeze from opening the door, made the candles flicker, changing the light.

Carson walked to the desk with a woman writing something down, "Eight for *Dancing with the Prince*."

She handed him eight slips of paper without looking up and he gave her two gold coins.

"All right, let's go in."

They came up to another desk with a man taking the slips of paper and the people that gave him the slips walked into the doors up ahead of them. When they came to the man, Carson handed him the slips. The short man with no hair looked at the slips and pointed while saying, "You can go. It's to the left and then go in the third door to the right."

"Why do they need to look at the slips?" asked Julia on their way to the room.

"If you're in a play, he'll direct you where you need to go and if you're a customer like us, then he'll tell you when and where you can go in." replied Christopher.

"Oh. That's a little like in my world too."

They went inside and sat on the benches closest to the stage. The stage was brilliant because of the architecture. There were two marble columns on either side of the oak wood stage with a red curtain in front of it and many paintings on the candle lightened walls. Then the curtain opened.

"It's going to start." said Lori Linda excited and the woman from the front desk came out. Now seeing her face, it was old, she had glasses, and her white hair was put back into a tight bun.

"Welcome. I hope you will enjoy our premier of *Dancing with the Prince*, which was inspired by the story of King Trevor and Queen Kimberly of the Pierre Kingdom. They are now living *Happily Ever After* in their castle with their daughter Princess Theodora. So, again enjoy and thank you." then everyone clapped and the first actor appeared on what seemed to be the scenery of a garden.

Dancing with the Prince

Prince Trevor waited patiently in the garden hoping his father would arrive soon. His father called this meeting however; he was late. He wondered where his father could be. Was he hunting? No. Was he talking to someone? No. Did he forget that he called his son to talk to him? No. He was just simply late and after fifteen minutes of waiting, he finally showed up.

"My boy, I'm sorry I'm late." a fat King adorned in brilliant-colored clothing apologized.

"Did you forget?"

"No. I just wasn't here on time. Sorry."

"It's fine. Why did you want to meet me?"

"I wanted to talk to you."

"About?"

"You. I wanted to tell you how I felt about some things."

"Such as?" he asked trying to get to the point.

"Well, you are going to be King soon, yet you haven't found a bride? This dancing that you are doing is getting in the way. So, I forbid you to dance until you have a bride."

"But father! Dancing is the only thing that makes me happy and-"

"That was my final word." he said holding up a hand.

Then the King left, leaving the Prince to think while the servant, Kimberly, worked. Kimberly and the Prince were good friends and she always helped him. Maybe she could help him this time.

"Is everything all right your Highness?" asked Kimberly in a soft voice.

"No."

"Can I do anything to help?"

"I'm sorry Kimberly but there is nothing you can do."

"Are you sure?"

He was silent for a moment and then looked up at her, "You know what? There is something you can do. Come with me."

They walked into a pavilion in the garden that you couldn't see with all the trees. It was hidden, but if you found it, it was beautiful. White oak and small, pink flowers covered every inch of them.

"Do you know how to dance?"

"Yes."

"Good, because that is what you are going to do with me."

"But how are we going to dance without music?"

"Listen to the birds."

They took the dance position and she let him lead. They twisted, twirled, and hummed to their own song with the birds and finished with a kiss.

"I'm sorry." said Kimberly.

"It's fine."

"No...it's not. I'm a servant."

"Does it matter?"

"But...your father."

"I don't care what he thinks. He's not going to be King much longer."

"What about my mother?"

"Are you really scared of what might happen?"

"Yes."

"I promise nothing will happen." he held her hand in both of his.

"Alright. I trust you."

"Good." and they kissed again. "Meet me here tomorrow."

"I will."

They went through several days of dancing under the pavilion, until one day when Prince Trevor asked Kimberly to meet him at the Crystal Cave. She met him there and went inside. Kimberly was dazzled.

"Why did you want me to come here with you?"

"I wanted you to do me a favor."

"And what might that be?"

"To pick out any crystal of your choice." he said showing her a room full of different color, shape, and brilliance of crystals.

"Me?"

"Yes. Pick one."

She picked out the most brilliant, and green crystal. "I love this one."

"Really?"

"It's a remarkable gem. Who is it for?"

"For the one I should ask to marry me."

"Oh." she looked down hurt.

He got on his right knee, "And that person just happens to be you. Kimberly, will you marry me?"

Then she started to cry tears of joy. "Of course I will. Thank you."

He swept her off her feet and kissed her. "No. Thank you."

They went into town and made the crystal a ring for her and married three days later. But, the King soon found out and barged into the Prince's room one day.

"You married a servant! Have you completely lost your mind?!"

"Father! I-"

"No! I will not have it!" he interrupted and crushed his fist against a desk in the Prince's room.

"Father there is only three things in this world that make me happy. One is Kimberly. Second is dancing. And third is this Kingdom!"

"Well think of which one you want to give up!"

"But I don't want to give up any of them!"

"Then you lose your Kingdom! I hereby banish you!"

"Fine!" the Prince fled the room full of rage.

He got Kimberly and left the Kingdom. A couple hours later, the Queen heard and became very angry with the King. Before they went to bed, they *were in the hallway with three guards and she demanded answers out of her husband.*

"How could you banish our son?!"

"I had no choice."

"Of course you had a choice! He is going to be King tomorrow. Can't you sympathize for him? He married the one he loves. Can't you see that?"

The King didn't say a word.

"Well, I can. Guards, find my son and bring him here by morning."

"Yes my lady." said the head guard and bowed.

The next day was the coronation. It had begun, but the Prince and Kimberly were not there. The crown just sat on the pillow on a cushioned chair. Five minutes passed and the Prince finally came out. When the ceremony had finished they clapped and went in the Ballroom.

The former Prince went to his parents, "Thank you mother."

"You're welcome."

"Father?"

"I'm sorry. Where is Kimberly?"

Then Kimberly walked down the stairs in a beautiful gown, tiara, and jewelry including her ring, "There she is."

"I'm very happy for you." said the former Queen.

"Thank you mother." he repeated.

Then Kimberly came up to Trevor who was now the new King, "Hello."

"Hello."

"Why don't you two go dance? I would appreciate it." said the King.

"Thank you father."

Then King Trevor's favorite song came on, "Go." said Trevor's father.

They took dance position and started dancing. They twirled, bended, danced in the air, and finally kissed at the end. It was the most magical thing the former King had ever seen and was glad his wife brought their son back. He finally understood why his son loved the three things he did. The wonderful Kingdom, his beautiful love, and his impressive dancing.

The End

The curtains closed, everyone clapped, and the cast came out on the stage and bowed. Most people had tears in their eyes and clapped louder than necessary when the handsome actor who played the Prince walked out- mostly young women who idolized any good looking and sensible man. When it was done, Julia and everyone else strolled out of the theatre and went back to the carriage, but Julia heard that same cry again.

"Carson, did you hear that?"

"What?" he turned to her.

"That scream." and she heard it again.

Carson paid close attention and then he heard it too, "Yes. I just heard it."

"I think I know who it might be. We need to hurry if we're going to help him."

She ran.

Carson stayed where he was. *What was going on?* he thought. *Who does Julia need to help?*

Chapter 12

PETER

Everyone looked back to see Julia running away. They stopped and hurried to Carson. *What was going on,* they thought.

"Carson? Where is she going?" asked Cassidy.

"She heard something. I need to go with her." and he ran to follow her but when he caught up to her, she was crying at the feet of a young boy lying on the ground with a back-pack. It was Peter.

"He was like my brother I never had, but always wanted." and she started crying more.

Carson grabbed her shoulder, "We need to get him to the castle," and then everyone came up from behind them and gasped, "Bade, help me bring him into the carriage."

"All right."

They carried him into the carriage and put him near Julia.

"Julia, who is that?" asked Veronica.

"In my world, he's my neighbor's son Peter Acton."

Then he started waking up.

"J...Julia?"

"Peter it's me."

"How?...Where am I?" he asked looking around a little scared.

"It doesn't matter. What happened to you?"

He sat up strait and held his head, "I was building a tree house with Heather so I was bringing some supplies to it," he showed her the back-pack, "But I stopped at the creek because there was something weird about it. It was glowing green in an area so I went to go see it."

"What happened then?"

"I fell. Then I just saw white and then something black went over my head. It didn't come off until something hit my head and I was knocked-out. Next thing I know, I'm here screaming my head off and was brought into this. So, where are we?"

"You're in the Felpierre Kingdom." said Carson.

"I'm *where?*"

"Your not...home." said Julia.

"Well I knew that." he said agitated and rolled his eyes.

"You didn't change a bit even with shock, did you?"

"Nope."

Then Carson whispered to Cassidy, "When we get back to the castle, make sure he wasn't hurt in any other way." and she nodded.

"So, Peter. How old are you?" asked Christopher.

"Twelve."

"Oh," and then he whispered to Julia, "Don't let him get too attached to anyone."

"Why?"

"He's old enough to go to war."

"I won't let him."

"It doesn't work like that." he replied shaking his head.

"How does it work?"

"If war comes, it is stated by law, that ten and older men go to war."

"I don't want to discuss this. He's only a boy. He can't go to war."

"All right. I'd just thought I'd warn you."

"How do you even know if there is going to be a war?"

"If a human comes, the Remora pursues them. And they've waited a long time for another war. I don't see why they wouldn't start a new one."

"I see your point."

"Good."

"Where are we going?" asked Peter.

"To my castle." said Carson.

"I'm sorry, who are you?"

"Carson."

"Oh. Thanks. I'll have to remember that."

After a while, they finally arrived at the castle and Carson paid the man 30 silver.

"Peter, can you come with me?" asked Cassidy.

"Sure. What's your name?"

"Cassidy. Follow me."

"Ok." he shrugged and followed her.

Julia watched him go with Cassidy, and turned to Carson, "Where's he going?"

"I wanted Cassidy to make sure he wasn't hurt or anything else."

"Should I go with him?"

"I wouldn't. Cassidy will take good care of him."

"All right." and she headed for her room and slept with Annabelle on her bed until a knock on the door woke her from her slumber.

"Julia? It's me Peter. Are you awake?"

"Yes I'm awake. You can come in."

He came in and had different clothing on. It looked like the clothes that Carson wore but to Peter's size. Julia giggled to herself.

"What are you wearing?"

"Well, after Cassidy…I think that's her name…took care of me, Carson gave me a room and it had these clothes."

"I see. Are you feeling any better?"

"Yes."

"Was anything else wrong with you?"

"Nope." he said with a pop on the 'p'.

"That's good. Anything else?"

"Carson wanted me to tell you to come to dinner with me."

"All right, give me a minute."

She got ready and went to the Dining Hall with Peter. Everyone, except Mr. Doddsworth, was there and had their dinner in front of them that Cassidy prepared for them. Peter smiled with delight at the food.

"Peter, you can sit next to me and Bade." said Julia.

"Ok." he sat in between Julia, who was sitting by Carson, and Bade, who was sitting by Veronica.

"So…what do you do?" asked Peter to Bade.

"I'm a messenger."

"Wow. Do you go all over the world? What is this world called anyway?"

"No. Just in this Kingdom. And this world is called **Renata**."

"Why is it called *that*?"

"Many believe that this world will be reborn into something else just as it's been done in the past and the name Renata means that." said Carson.

"That's interesting. What was the last thing that happened in Renata?"

"We don't know, but there were many creatures before us."

"What about your world?" asked Cassidy.

"I don't know."

"Sure you do."

"Well, I do, but I just don't know all of the facts or the time order." he tapped his fingers on the table.

"So, back in the carriage, you said something about a tree house. What is that?" asked Veronica.

"Well, a tree house is a small version of a house in a tree and you usually make a ladder to get up to it."

"Maybe you can show us how to make one someday."

"Sure. How about after this dinner?"

"Well, it's still light out. I don't see why not."

"Perfect. The only things I need are some rope, wood, nails, a hammer, a saw, and a tree." he counted the number of supplies off with his fingers.

"I think we have all of those things." said Christopher.

"Cool." said Peter and everyone but Julia, who was giggling, stared at him, for they had never heard that word before.

Chapter 13

TRAINING AND THE PRINCE'S REQUEST

After dinner, they all went outside to the garden and saw the most magnificent oak tree that over looked a glistening blue lake while Christopher went to go get the supplies. Peter studied the tree and the angle to look at the scenery. He then went to Carson and Bade.

"Perfect. Although, I am going to need some help." said Peter.

"Bade and I will help." said Carson.

"What do you need me to do?" asked Bade crouching down to Peter's height.

"I would like you to build three walls but one with a window to look out at the lake when Christopher gets here with the supplies."

"All right." said Bade getting up.

"And Carson, I would like you to build the roof and the ladder."

"Ok. What are you going to do?"

"I'm building the front of the house and the base."

"That sounds like a lot of work. Are you sure you don't want me to do anything else?"

"No. I want the work to be split evenly."

"All right. Thanks."

Then Christopher came with all of the supplies.

"Here you are Peter." said Christopher piling the supplies neatly.

"Thank you Christopher." then Carson, Peter, and Bade went to work. After almost 30 minutes of working, Julia was curious to know what things Peter had brought with him from their world.

"Peter, what things did you bring from back home?" asked Julia.

"You can look into my back-pack. It's by the supplies."

"Thank you."

Julia looked inside it. It had an MP3, a book, food, bottles of water, clothes, candles, matches, flashlight, headphones, decorations, and medicine. The specific medicines that were in there were for headaches, fever, cough, sore throat, and asthma.

"Cassidy...come here. Quickly!"

"What is it Julia?"

"Peter has medicine from my world. It can help Mr. Doddsworth!"

"Come with me Julia. Bring that with you." and she brought her to Mr. Doddsworth's room rapidly.

She knocked on the door, "Mr. Doddsworth, it's Cassidy and Julia. May we come in?"

He coughed and wailed a little bit and then spoke, "Please do."

They went inside, "Mr. Doddsworth, Julia has found medicine from her friend in her world that can help you."

"Really?"

"Yes Mr. Doddsworth, it's right here," said Julia getting the cough and fever medicine out of the bag. She looked at the labels to see how much of each medicine to give, "Cassidy, this is the cough medicine. Give him this whole cup of it once a day for two to three days. And this is the fever medicine. Have him swallow two of these pills with water."

Cassidy gave him the amount of medicine he was supposed to have and left the rest of the medicines on the table next to his bed.

"Feel better soon." said Cassidy.

"Thank you. Hopefully, I will feel better by the morning. Thank your friend Julia. He may have saved my life."

"I will tell him."

They went back to the garden and found that Peter, Bade, and Carson were almost finished and Julia put the bag by the rest of the supplies.

"You've all done a fantastic job."

"But it's not finished yet." said Peter coming over to her.

"Will it be finished tonight?"

"I think so."

"That's good."

"Ya…it is."

"I'm happy you're enjoying yourself here."

"Why? Are you not? It seems you would be."

She arched an eyebrow, "Why do you say that?"

"All of these people care about you a lot. Especially Carson. What are you so worried about?"

"Something you don't need to know." and she started walking away.

"What? You think I don't know about the Remora?"

"You know? Who told you?" asked Julia turning around.

"When we were working, we were trying to think of who first saw me. Then Christopher told me about them because he thought it was them. But if I want to get finished with this tree house tonight, then I better not stay and chat."

"Fine." then she sauntered off. She walked around the rest of the garden to see it and the tree house was finally finished after five more minutes of work. Then Carson went to get Julia.

"Julia, it's finished. Come and see it."

"All right." then he grabbed her hand and walked towards the finished tree house.

She looked at it; it was the most beautiful tree house she had ever seen. The color of the wood complemented the wood of the oak tree, it looked like a small version of a house, and had a wonderful view. Julia wanted to be the first person inside it.

"Can I go in it?" asked Julia to Peter.

"Why not?"

She hurried up the ladder and went inside. It had an excellent view of the castle and the lake. It was sunset and she wanted Carson to see it with her. Then she heard someone come up.

"Mind if I watch the-wow! It's a great view up here!" said Carson coming up.

"Ya…it's really beautiful up here." she tried not to laugh.

"So...what I really wanted to do was look at the sunset with you. May I?"

"Sure."

They looked out into the distance of the lake and watched the orange sun descend into the red sky. When the moon came up, the white light glistened on the blue water. The sight was both calming and beautiful.

"It was nice watching the sunset with you. I hope we can do this again, now that we have the tree house." said Carson.

"I hope so too." and they gazed into each other's eyes, slowly leaning in as their hearts pounded, but were interrupted by talking from below and they went down to see.

There was a white rabbit in front of Christopher and Bade but soon changed into a woman with beautiful, almost white, blonde hair, magenta eyes, and a white suit of armor.

"Ahh...good to see you Bade. I'm looking for Carson." said the woman fixing herself.

"Good to see you too Amorita. And Carson is-"

"Right here. What can I do for you?" said Carson coming out from the darkness which Julia still stood in.

"I have a message from the Prince for you." she said handing the envelope to him.

"Thank you."

"Thank you, that was my last one for the day." then she changed back into her rabbit form and scurried off.

Carson opened the envelope and read the letter and thought for a moment. *The Prince wants me to help people train for war? Is the Remora planning on starting another? I thought we were at peace, but I guess not, now that they know about Julia and Peter and the Prince is starting training. I just hope Julia can handle Peter, Christopher, Bade, and I going to war. There's no stopping the Remora now.*

"What did the Prince want?" asked Bade.

"For me to teach and train for war."

"Carson..."

"It's fine. But I'm not the one to be worrying about." then he walked over to Julia and brushed her cheek lightly, "I'm more concerned about you."

Tears swelled up in her eyes. "I'll be fine. It's only training, right? I mean there won't be any war soon. Will there?"

He looked at her with concerned eyes, wiped a tear that had fallen, and hugged her, "I don't know. But please, try not to worry now."

"How could I not?" she asked letting go of his hug.

"I don't want you to get hurt to try to keep me or anyone else away from this if there is going to be a war. If there is war, I shall not die in it. We've all had the experience of war at twelve years old. Isn't that right Bade?" he said looking to Bade for support.

"Sure is. Julia, we can take care of ourselves. Please don't worry; Carson is the best trainer in Renata."

"Thanks Bade, but I'm not the best."

"Suit yourself." and he walked out of the garden with a sincere smile for his concern for Julia.

"I best be getting to bed." said Christopher yawning.

"All right. See you tomorrow," said Carson, "What about you?" he looked to Julia.

"I'm going to go to bed. I'm tired."

"I'm sorry that you disagree with Bade and I about war."

"Carson, the only reason I disagree is because war is meaningless. It hurts many families and hearts. If you died in a war..." she stopped, "goodnight."

Chapter 14

GOING HOME

Julia went to her room and Carson went to his and didn't think, or say a word until he was in his room and got ready for bed. When he was done, he pulled out a dagger and looked into the shinning blade, for it was his communication with his brother and two sisters. They had this communication because they had one too and put a spell on it to talk to each other. Images flew onto the blade until Carson saw his younger brother.

"Carson? Is that you brother?"

"Yes, Lane it's me. Where are your sisters?"

"Rebecca and Gamelle are asleep."

"That's good. Have you been taking care of them with the money I sent?"

"Yes."

"Good. Then I shall check up on you tomorrow."

"All right brother. Goodnight."

"Goodnight." then Carson put the blade away and fell asleep.

The next day, Julia was awakened by Annabelle scratching the door because someone was on the other side.

"Julia? It's Carson. I need to talk to you. May I come in?"

"Is it time for class?"

"That's what I wanted to talk about."

"Come in."

He appeared from the doorway and sat next to Julia, "Training starts today, so you won't have the same schedule."

"How so?"

"Well classes start at the same time but all of your teachers are teaching us how to fight in battle so, you can still be in the class, but you won't have as much interaction with them as before."

"That's fine."

"You may want to get ready because classes start in ten minutes. Go to Cassidy's class first, though."

"Thanks. I'll see you at lunch."

"I'll see you before then." then he walked out the door and went to Cassidy's first class early.

"Carson? What are you doing here?"

"I came early."

"Is something wrong?"

"I...I don't know." he slouched into a chair.

"You don't know?" she walked over to him.

"Am I doing something wrong?"

"What do you mean?"

"Julia is upset about something, and she won't tell me. I would like to help her, but I don't know how."

"Did you tell her how you felt?" and Julia came up to the door and started listening once again.

"Yes."

"You did tell her about the training right?"

"Of course I did."

"Then that's it."

"Why do you think that would that be her problem? I mean I know that she doesn't like it, but why?"

"I think she's worried about the fact that, if there is a war, you and Peter have to go."

"What should I do?"

"Try to comfort her. But why are you so...unsure about your feelings for each other?"

"Well, for one, I don't think she wants to love me."

"If she didn't want to love you, the only reason for that is because she doesn't want you to get hurt when she goes back to her world. But don't worry, she wants to love you. Any other reason?"

He paused, "I still haven't explained to her about when my parents died, they told me to look after my siblings and marry Princess Theodora- the arranged marriage."

"Carson…"

"What should I do?" he pleaded.

Then she heard Julia gasp and almost cry, "Go tell Mr. Doddsworth so you can get advice and then tell Julia. Go now."

Julia heard him coming to the door, he heard her, and she ran outside. He opened the door, sighed, changed into his form of stars, and followed Julia. She came to the garden, took a seat on a bench, and wept. *Why didn't he tell me? Why is he going to be disloyal to his parents' request? I-*

"Julia?" he came out of the stars and sat next to her.

"Why didn't you tell me?"

He leaned in, "Because I do not love Princess Theodora. I love you."

"But…your parents, and her parents? What will they do?"

"They'll understand."

"But they won't forgive you."

"I know that. But…don't you love me? Don't you want to stay here with me?" Carson held her hands while asking.

"I do love you and I do want to stay but I can't. I need to go home, and I think I know how." then she got up and started walking towards her room.

He followed her, "You know how? If it's the way back, you're just going to go? What about Peter?" she stopped and then kept going.

When they got to her room, she sat down and grabbed her diary, "What is the point of going back? If we go into war against the Remora, we'll win and then there would be no reason to go back."

"Carson, there will be a reason and that is because of the rest of my family and friends. And what if you don't win? Will you die?"

"I don't think we'll lose. And trust me, I won't die in war. Please don't go."

She opened the diary, and saw a speck of light. Julia started crying. Then she looked at Carson, "You're not making this easy."

"Julia, I…I'm sorry. I just don't want you to go."

"Carson…"

"Are you going to come back?"

"I…don't know."

"Please do. For my sake." then the light spread out, almost blinding her and took Julia back into the familiar, dense green forest by her beloved house, avoiding all the conflicts soon coming to Renata which were being cause by the ruthless and merciless Remora.

Chapter 15

CHRISTINA AND RENATA

In Renata, there was trouble afoot. Now that the Remora knew their secret of the humans being there, there was no stopping them. The secret was out and they wanted to pursue their madness and acts of horrid violence.

Their first move was a small, rich village. It was the village where Carson's brother Lane and two sisters Rebecca and Gamelle were staying to go to school, but had to leave quickly. They had finished packing and were eating their last meal in silence.

What they hadn't noticed was the Remora slipping in like shadows of the night, silently killing people one by one. A clumsy Remora member murdered a man and his wife let out an ear-piercing shriek into the night. Lane dropped his fork and Rebecca and Gamelle looked up worried and scared.

More screams were heard and a fight broke out. Lane looked out the window and saw homes burning to ashes. A horn blew sadistically to get more men to fight.

The young Lane spun around to see his two sisters already standing, wanting to run for they did not want to fight.

"Lane, let's just run! They don't need our help. We should just escape."

"No. We'll help the others. You know they'd help us," he grabbed his sword and held their shoulders tightly, "I will do whatever it takes to protect you two. Follow me. Step where I step. We have to ring the bell. We have to get help. Do you understand? We have to warn others."

His sisters nodded behind tears. They crept though the back door and crawled on the ground. In the alley way next to their home, a man was begging a Remora member to let him live, but the Remora associate mercilessly slaughtered the man clean and Rebecca accidentally gasped when she saw the ghastly sight.

Lane quickly covered her mouth with his large hand and the twins sat very quiet. They all turned their heads when the creature curved to look their way. He began walking closer but stopped because of a crash inside their house and other Remora members telling him to join them. He jumped through the window, and they breathed once more.

Lane pushed his finger against his lips signaling them to be quiet and to follow his lead. They crawled a long way, hiding in the shadows as they tried to reach the Bell Tower. Then, out of nowhere, another Remora creature jumped in front of them.

The young, brave, and strong Lane fought him off with difficulty and then was helped by another boy the same age as him. It was Black Bem and then the Remora creature finally fell to the ground dead.

Black Bem was quite useful. He wasn't only called Black Bem because his name was Bem, or that his skin was as dark as night, but because his power was water. It wasn't your usual cool, blue, and clear water, yet his was icy and pressurized like the cold, dark, deep, black ocean.

"Black Bem!" shouted Lane grateful, "Thank you."

"You're welcome." then another fire broke out, making a loud crackling noise.

Lane soon thought of an idea, "Black Bem."

"Yes?"

"We need to stop the fires. Can you make it rain?"

"Of course!" and so Black Bem looked to the sky. His eyes went all black and rain started pouring down from the sky in sheets. It was difficult to see, but it was helping to put out the small flames to rest, for they must have put on a special chemical to keep the flames burning.

"Thanks." Lane said.

"No problem." he looked to Rebecca and Gamelle, "We'll fight off anyone who comes near you. We'll protect you. But you must promise to ring the bell."

"We will." they said bravely together.

Lane, Black Bem, Rebecca, and Gamelle ran to the Bell Tower. Both Lane and Black Bem were excellent fighters and protected Rebecca and Gamelle just as they said they would. Then they finally reached the Bell Tower together almost undetected.

Black Bem and Lane fought off the Remora members that had followed them with cold water whipping at them as well as the harsh rainfall and Lane's superior fighting skills he'd learned from his brother Carson. Rebecca and Gamelle climbed up the tower hurriedly. Once at the top, very high up from the ground, they rang the large bell seven times for the signal of help and war in their village as a warning.

The sky soon became darker and thunder clapped. Startled, a werewolf that they hadn't noticed, jumped up and tried to drag Gamelle down. Rebecca reached for her as she sent wind to hurt the werewolf down at him.

The werewolf fell and Black Bem killed it with an arrow he shot. He smirked, but then a mysterious, overly-large figure stabbed him in the back while Lane was busy fighting. Gamelle screamed and Black Bem fell to the ground, clenching his teeth and trying to stop the never-ending flow of blood.

Once he saw this, the creature did no more harm to him. Another clap of thunder and lightning struck and revealed a Remora member behind Rebecca who was still trying to pull Gamelle up. Gamelle shouted for her to look out and also for Lane because the large figure was coming towards him then.

Rebecca pulled Gamelle up quickly and missed his attack by a split second. On the Bell Tower, Rebecca and Gamelle tried with all of their might to fight off the Remora member with their power of wind. Surprisingly, Black Bem still had enough energy to help them and, wincing, he cast the water up and it sliced his arms very deeply. Rebecca and Gamelle finished the rest.

Lane grinned at his two sisters. Then he noticed the large Remora creature as he tried to attack him. With much obscurity and precision, Lane tried to fight him off, but fell from the man's supremacy in fighting. The Remora crowded over him like a giant, pointing his sword at Lane's neck and laughing. Then the man screamed in sharp pain. A courageous villager helped Lane in his most crucial moment. He smiled in return as the man left and looked over to the wounded creature.

However, the large Remora mortal had one last thing to say to Lane before his last breath, "You should embrace the other side. Become a Remora member. You'll soon find out it's better. You fight well for a boy of your age."

"I'd rather die than be part of your cult!" Lane shouted against the rain and the creature fell dead.

He then ran to Black Bem. He was coughing and very hurt. Lane forcefully took off his piece of Ceylon.

"Where'd you get that?" Black Bem asked slowly, for he felt as if his own life was slipping away with each word.

"My brother." he replied as he blew on the Ceylon piece and held it near his wound.

It healed immediately, "Thank you." Black Bem said.

"Listen, you need to warn the other villages as well. The bell isn't enough. We need a reinforcement to hold the Remora back for a while. Can you do that?"

"Yes. But…what will you do?" he asked getting up.

"I'm going to fight." Lane said.

Rebecca and Gamelle came down from the Bell Tower and Black Bem whispered tensely, "You're mad! You'll die!"

"I shall not die in vain! I'm doing this for Renata and my family. I'll hold them off as long as I can. Please take Rebecca and Gamelle with you. For me."

Black Bem held them close saying, "I will. I'll keep the rain going for you. At full force."

"We'll be in the wind dear brother." Rebecca and Gamelle said hugging him.

"Thank you. Now go." he said surely.

"Good luck my friend." Black Bem said shaking his hand and then running with Lane's two sisters to the next village.

He watched them slither into the night. Lane then felt the rain become harder and wind that made it blistering cold and pierced the Remora's skin like a thousand needles. He smiled in satisfaction.

Lane then used his powers of light while shouting out his anger, and fought the Remora in a circle with the men of the village and him in the middle. They fought long and hard, working together until Lane was the last one. He picked up a Remora flag, which was black with their white symbol, and burnt it.

The flames licked at his wet skin as he fought off Remora with the burning flag. One member snapped it in half, so Lane improvised. He threw one piece into a man and the other, he stabbed into another with the burning flag at the end of it, making him catch on fire.

Soon, Lane picked up another sword and started fighting with two simultaneously. His eyes gleamed with furry as he fought them off, but slowly they began to cease. The Remora stopped fighting when one man mounted his horse, "Fight me!" shouted Lane, "Fight me!" and they fought.

In the morning, the carriage to pick up Lane, Rebecca, and Gamelle came. The old man stepped off of the front and saw all the dead bodies. His foot quivered in all of the ash.

———

Julia sat on the forest floor, carpeted with leaves. Looking up, she saw a line of houses a little farther than the trees in front of her. She was so happy to look around and see the forest that was behind her house and started crying tears of joy.

"I'm...I'm back." she looked at the diary and the light faded to nothing.

She sat on a rock and started thinking. *I'm back! I can't believe it! I need to see Christina! I need to tell her everything! What happened, why I was gone for almost a week, and tell her about Peter. Peter...I left him there. I'll go back to get him after I tell Christina...everything...even Carson. I wonder what he's doing.*

Then, Julia ran to her house and dialed Christina's number. The phone rang three times and she answered. She sounded anxious.

"Hello?"

"Christina, it's Julia."

"Julia?!" Julia then almost dropped the phone from the fret in her voice, "I've been calling there for two days strait. Where have you been?"

"I was gone two days?"

"Yes. I started calling after the funeral. I wanted to see if you were all right."

"Christina, I'll tell you everything if you come over."

"All right."

They hung up, and after five minutes of waiting, Christina rang the doorbell.

"Julia?"

"Coming!" she ran to the door and opened it.

Christina came in, and looked at Julia's extraordinary outfit, "What are you wearing?"

"A dress that came from Renata."

"Ok, you sound crazy." they sat down on the couches in the living room, "Where's this *Renata* placing you're talking about?"

"It's another world."

Christina gave her a strange look. "Are you feeling well?"

"I'm fine! Now, are you going to let me tell you the story?"

She leaned back into the couch and folded her arms across her chest. "I'm listening."

Julia told her. She talked about everyone she met, what happened, and Peter. Christina didn't say a word; she just sat there and listened for about an hour while Julia imitated and interacted with her weird story. When Julia was finished, Christina looked down and said nothing until a few moments later.

"Are you telling me the truth?"

"Yes."

She looked back down and then up, "Then it sounds like you should go back. Bring some things with you, especially your diary."

"Do you think I should? You personally?"

"Whatever makes you happy. I won't get in your way."

"Thanks Christina."

"You're welcome, but I better be getting back home. Frank will want dinner." said Christina getting up and heading to the door.

Julia got up and held the door open for her. "Goodbye Christina."

"Goodbye Julia." said Christina hugging her and then walked out the door.

Julia went to her room and started packing things that would be beneficial to her when she went back to Renata. She packed her diary, medicines, clothes, and family pictures. When she was done, she went out the door and started walking towards the forest.

I think I'm doing the right thing. I do want to go back. But when I get there, I'm going to get Peter back here and say sorry to Carson. Because... I'm so happy there in Renata and in love.

Julia came up to the creek. She looked at it and could have sworn she saw leaves coming out of it. Then she walked up to it and put her hand to it. It felt like it was raining. Looking back, she decided to go.

A white light came, and then it was rain blinding her. She took one step, and accidentally collapsed to the ground. It seemed to rain like cats and dogs in Renata too. When she got up, she ran out to the open space and saw a black carriage. It was small, but looked like it had gold on it, which meant someone important was in it.

The carriage stopped, and Prince Nathan rushed out, becoming soaked to the bone immediately, "Julia? What are you doing out here?"

"I came back from my world. Can I get a ride?"

"Of course. Come in." said Prince Nathan waving her to come.

She walked up to him and he helped her in with a warm hand and smile, "Thanks," they sat down and she looked out the window and then at Prince Nathan, "So how is everyone?"

"Well, everyone except Carson is fine."

"What happened?" she asked rapidly.

"His family's village was attacked by the Remora. His brother and sisters...passed away. No one was there to help them. Carson...has been lost without you and his family. It's good that you're back."

She was so shocked at the news that she couldn't speak for several moments. "I...I feel so sorry for him."

"At least you'll be there to comfort him."

"I hope so."

Then she turned to look out the window. It had stopped raining and it was a mixture of the colors of blue, white, green, and brown. Then the carriage came to a halt and she saw the entrance to Tabor's Castle.

"It was good to see you Julia. I'm sure we'll meet again soon."

"Thank you Prince Nathan and I hope to see you again." said Julia getting out and bowed when she was on the ground.

Then he closed the carriage door and drove off. She looked at the entrance and started walking towards it. When she came to them, she opened the doors and saw Cassidy standing right in front of her and was soon hugging her.

"I'm so glad you're back. We've been so worried about you, and, you're soaking wet." Cassidy let go of the hug and grabbed her hand, "Let's go get you dried off."

"Thanks Cassidy." said Julia being rushed to her room.

After Cassidy got Julia washed up and dressed, Julia sat on her bed and Cassidy sat on a chair. "Carson was very worried about you. What happened in the last three days?"

"I was gone three days?"

Cassidy nodded.

"It wasn't even a day in my world."

"Well, you're back. Carson is outside in the tree house with Peter. He doesn't know that you're here. Maybe you should go talk to him."

They went out of the room and Julia went straight to the garden and saw Peter and Carson sitting in the tree house staring at the lake. Carson turned and finally caught a glimpse of Julia and was stunned. He ran out and walked towards her.

Carson brushed her cheek and hugged her, "You're back. Please don't leave again."

"I won't." she said making it a promise she would always keep.

"Don't I get a hello?" asked Peter from the back.

"Of course you do." said Julia walking over a giving him a hug.

Peter looked at the clock tower. "Hey! It's time for diner. I'll go get everyone in the Dining Hall. I'll meet you two in there." he broke from her hug and waited.

"He really is like a little brother." said Carson thoughtfully, coming over to Julia.

"Carson...I'm so sorry. I-"

"It's fine. You're here." then he leaned in to kiss her, but was interrupted by Peter because of his hunger and they went down to the Dining Hall.

"Julia!" said Veronica coming to give her a hug with everyone else following her, even Mr. Doddsworth.

They sat down and Cassidy went to go get the dinners. They all had a great night. It was the last night with happy faces at Tabor's Castle.

When everyone was finished eating, they went to their rooms and got ready for bed, but, Julia stayed up a little later than the rest to write in her diary.

Julia's Diary March 30th (in Renata)

Dear Diary,

Sorry I haven't been writing. During the week I was training and during the weekend I went into a town for an interview and a play on Sunday. I also had come to know that Peter came into Renata (the world that I'm in). We brought him to the same castle I'm staying in and built a tree house. On Monday, I came back to my world and spoke to Christina. The way back was to use this diary. I just have to watch out for the page I flip to or use, otherwise I'm back to my world. But I'm glad I'm here in Renata. Training is going to be harder this week because the Remora (a group of people that want revenge on the Kingdoms) is planning on starting a war. I want Peter to go back home to our world, yet I don't think he wants to. What if he gets hurt? I won't be able to do anything about it. It's best if he doesn't go to war.

Princess Theodora and her head guard Soren were walking through the Royal Garden. They usually went on private walks together such as this almost every time that there was free time for the Princess. Together, they shared many secrets and Soren was always allowed to give her a rose, for he loved her very much, but she could not return his love because she only saw him as a guard and a friend, and her heart unexpectedly belonged to Carson.

"So," started Soren, "training has begun for the army against the Remora. What will you do when this is all over?"

"I shall fulfill my duties and become queen."

"And to do that, you must marry Carson?"

"Yes." she smelled the prettiest rose smiling.

Soren stopped walking, "You really do love him, don't you?"

Theodora looked at his saddened face, "Soren…"

He picked an elaborate, stunning red rose. Soren had never actually told Princess Theodora that he loved her. He thought now could be the perfect chance, since Carson claimed he loved the new human Julia. Soren stepped closer to her, giving her the divine red rose.

"My lady, what if I told you I loved someone? That my heart belonged to someone?"

"I would ask who." she smiled.

"And what if it were you?" he continued with his eyes shining intensely bright.

Theodora half frowned, "Soren, I think it's time we talked."

"We are talking." she started to slip away, but he lightly held her shoulders, "It's you. It's always been you. I love you. Only you. I always have. Why do you think I became a Royal Guard? I wanted to protect something that I loved and cherished with all of my heart. For once, I wanted to have meaning in my life and not fail. To not be useless. This is the first time I've ever felt warmth and happiness."

"I…I don't know what to say. Even if I can say anything." Theodora looked up to him.

Soren stared at her lips, "Then don't say anything." and he kissed her.

The rose fell from Theodora's fingers and onto the cold floor and received the kiss from the man who loved her. She indeed still loved Carson, but Soren was just something else to her. She enjoyed him and he loved her.

Soren and Theodora were too busy kissing to notice what was going on around them. They only stopped when a tall man covered head to toe in black metal armor stepped on the rose and they heard him breathing. Soren saw him out of the corner of his eye and moved Theodora behind him as he pulled out his sword.

"Who are you?! What do you want?!"

The man showed his glittering black eyes as he pulled out his sword pointing it saying in a deep, alienated voice, "The Princess."

"Never! You shall never lay a finger on her! Over my dead body!"

"That can be arranged." he signaled and more Remora members surrounded them.

"I'd do anything for her! I'd give my life for her!" Soren put a barrier around her and started fighting.

He was a great fighter and Theodora screamed when the tall man stabbed him in the upper part of his stomach. The barrier went away and she fell to the ground in tears and in shock. Soren was on the ground trying to gasp in precious air.

The tall Remora man grabbed Theodora by the wrists and dragged her as he started to walk off. Soren tried with all of his might to stand, and threw his sword at him. The man blocked it and was about to go back to finish him off, but another Remora member, which seemed to be a woman, stood in front of him saying, "Leave him. It isn't right. We've got what you wanted." she helped Soren off of the ground.

The tall man came back and lifted Soren's defender off of the ground by her collar, "I'm very disappointed. Then die here as well with him then!" and he dropped her and left with the Princess and the remaining Remora followers.

Soren's defender came close with her head bowed. She revealed a piece of Ceylon to him, which Soren abruptly took gratefully. Then the kind woman from the Remora disappeared into the night, just as the Princess.

Chapter 16

THE TRUTH

Julia put her diary down and went to sleep. She couldn't sleep well that night, though, because she kept thinking about Carson's arranged marriage. Tossing and turning, all she could do was think.

When is he supposed to get married to Princess Theodora? Is it any time soon? I can't love him; I wouldn't be showing respect to his parents or the Princess. Besides, he's not going to ask me to marry him.

The next morning, Julia woke up, got ready, packed her book bag, and went down to the Dining Hall for breakfast. She saw Carson, Cassidy, Peter, Veronica, and Bade talking to Prince Nathan at the table. When Carson saw her, he got up, walked, and stood in front of her. He looked at her with sadness in his eyes.

"We need to talk to you."

"About what? Is something wrong?"

"Yes. Come with me." he brought her to the table.

"Hello Julia." said Prince Nathan with a charming smile to ease the tense moment.

"Hello Prince Nathan. So what did you need to talk to me about?"

"I'll get straight to the point. Princess Theodora was kidnapped last night." said Bade.

Julia didn't say a word but looked at Carson who was looking at the ground below him.

"We're going to leave tonight. We wanted to let you know ahead of time so you wouldn't worry." said Prince Nathan kindly.

"Does Peter have to go?"

Cassidy nodded.

"Well, I'd best be off. Have a good day Julia." said Prince Nathan getting up and nodding to everyone.

"Goodbye Prince Nathan."

Carson looked up. He had a funny feeling that there was something between Prince Nathan and Julia. He left his gaze onto her eyes.

"Julia, your first class is with Christopher and Carson in the garden and after that you can just go to the weaponry room." said Veronica.

"All right." she said looking away from Carson's eyes.

They ate their breakfast and Julia followed Peter out because she wanted to talk to him. She stopped him in the middle in the hallway and turned him around.

"Peter, I don't want you to go to war. I can get you back home to your mom. I can…"

"No Julia! I want to stay here and fight for the people that protected and helped me. I don't want to back home until I know everything is at peace here from our account. I want to fight for us since you can't go to war."

"Why can't I go to war?"

"You're a woman."

"So!"

"Women need to stay out of war to care for the children not old enough to go to war, even if the women don't have any children, they couldn't go. It's one of the laws stated in the Felpierre and Pierre Kingdoms. Now, excuse me but, I need to get to Cassidy's class."

He walked off and Carson came up behind Julia, "Are you ready to go to class?"

"That's fine."

They started walking towards the garden and Carson started to think.

What kind of relationship does Julia have with Prince Nathan? Does she love him in any way? Are they just friends? I wonder how she's taking everything.

After a sort while, they came to the garden and saw many men and a few women looking at the tree house. Christopher was setting books on a bench and turned to see Carson and Julia, "Ahh. There you are. Julia you can sit on the other bench and Carson and I will prepare for class."

"All right." she did just as Christopher said and waited for the class to begin.

Carson and Christopher talked to each other in low whispers and turned around to start the class.

"Today's class is going to be a little longer because today we're going to cover how to defend yourselves, use a sword, and how to use your powers against your opponents. For example, I would like it if Aaron and Darcy would come up here for a demonstration." said Christopher waving the twins up.

"Sure thing sir." said Darcy.

The twins got up and Aaron changed into Christopher's form.

"Hi Julia."

"Hello Aaron."

He changed back into his regular form with his red hair glistening in the sun. "How are you sure that I'm Aaron, not Darcy?"

"Well I took a guess and it seems that I was right."

"Clever." he turned and walked the rest of the way up and stood next to his brother.

The two were exactly alike in size, tallness, red hair, green eyes, and everything else except for Aaron's tiny mole that was barely noticeable below his left eye. Carson picked up four swords and gave two to Darcy and Aaron, one for Christopher, and the last for him. "Now you two can take form of other people. How do you think you can use that power in battle?"

They shrugged their shoulders.

"Take my form."

They did and Carson looked at them nodding, "Impressive." he paused chuckling to himself, "Now, let's say that Christopher is one of the Remora. This will distract him and then someone can sneak behind him and give him what they deserve." said Carson pretending to strike the sword through Christopher.

Christopher pulled away from the position and straightened himself up, "Now make two lines, show us your powers, and we'll advise you on how to use them in battle."

Everyone did and Julia ended up at the back of Carson's line. The first person that came up to him was Elaine.

"Hello Elaine. You do know that-"

"I know. I can't go into battle, but I wanted someone to advise me on my powers anyway."

Carson chortled a bit, "All right. What can you do?"

"I have extraordinary healing powers."

"Do you need books or anything?"

"I would like to get better at them, and maybe a few books."

"Well, I have two books in the library that can help you and you can always see Cassidy for help."

"Thanks. I'll do that later on," she paused a moment, "Good luck in battle." she said it in a way as if she knew something, something that involved the Remora and someone among them.

"Thanks Elaine."

Many more men and women went to Carson so he could advise them on how to use their powers until Julia finally came up. They both smiled broadly and laughed a bit for being so amused by such tiny things, but it was good for them to lighten the sad and painful mood that surrounded them that would last until night came to take the men away to war. Yet, Julia also wished that she could have powers like everyone else in Renata.

"I don't think I have any powers, but I do know some spells."

"Good. Now, aim any spell you wish at that target."

A target appeared where Carson pointed and Julia got her hands ready. He backed up and Julia took one step forward and put her hands at a narrow position with her eyes.

"Rica Shinez!"

Then bright, orange flames shot out of her hands as she thrust them forward towards the target. It hit right into the center. Everyone was silent for a moment.

"That was very impressive." said Carson.

Julia came back into a normal position, "Thank you."

He walked in front of her and stood, "Now cast the spell at me."

Chapter 17

ALMOST WAR

Julia was nervous. She contemplated what to do. She couldn't hurt Carson, not after all that he had done for her. She had to know why he had asked that of her.

"Why would ask something like that from me?!"

"Julia, please. It's for the next part of the lesson. I won't get hurt."

"Positive?"

"Yes." he nodded and backed up a little more.

She got into position again, "Rica Shinez!", and stretched her arms out towards Carson.

In a fast move, he backed up again and moved his arms around while saying, "Xpencio!"

A blue, almost clear, shield covered Carson and the fire evaporated before him. Christopher was watching and was very impressed with Julia's progress. Her training in the castle had done her some good.

"Excellent," said Christopher, "I hope you all saw that. Now, we're going to learn how to defend," he said walking towards Carson. Christopher grabbed his shoulder, "How do you defend?"

He broke away and put his hands in front of him, "It's supposed to be a fast movement, so you put your hands eye level, make a circular motion in front of them and spread around yourself while saying *Xpencio*. Practice."

Everyone, including Julia, did as such. They kept doing it until everyone got it right. Yet, Julia didn't.

Carson and Christopher scrutinized everyone practicing the defense spell and noticed Julia wasn't getting it, "Keep your hands level to your eyes and try to do it faster." said Christopher putting Julia's hands eyelevel.

She tried it again and finally got it. The books were starting to pay off. Christopher nodded in delight.

"You finally got it."

"Thanks."

Carson left to pass out swords to everyone and Christopher looked back at Julia, "Can I ask you something?"

"Sure."

"How dedicated are you to Carson?"

"Very. Why do you ask?"

He looked Julia straight into the eyes, "You're not aware then."

"Aware of what?"

"The Prince seems to have feelings for you Julia." he said looking up.

"What? I'm not going to do anything about that. I don't love him."

"All right. I'm glad."

He walked off and Carson came moments later.

"What was that about?"

"Nothing."

"Well in that case, here you go," he said handing her a sword, "I hope you never have to use this against someone."

"Only if one of us were in danger."

Carson smiled as she grabbed the sword. He walked off to pass out more weapons while the word "ugh" came beside her. Julia turned to see the man and he had black hair with a tint of purple in it over his dark clothes and one long, skinny braid on his right side, but what really struck her was his amber colored eyes.

"I've seen better love stories."

"Who are you?" she asked angrily.

"My name is Alek. I'm here for training although I find it very unnecessary as I'm an excellent in battle."

"I'm sure you are. What powers do you possess?"

"My power is to create darkness."

"I'm human."

Alek stammered as he asked, "You're the reason we are going to war?"

"I'm not the main reason. Princess Theodora was kidnapped. Isn't that reason enough?"

A surprised Alek stepped forward but asked after a moment, "What is your name?" as he cupped her chin with his hand.

"Julia"

"Julia. That's a pretty name."

"What's it to you?"

Alek let go of her chin and replied as he walked away, "Let's be friends. Before we leave for battle this evening, join me for dinner. Bring your friends as well."

As Alek walked away, Carson called him and the other soldiers for training. The lessons of sword fighting went well. Afterwards, Carson instructed everyone to go to the Dining Hall for lunch. Everyone was in the Dining Hall including Prince Nathan. Lunch was quiet as thoughts of the upcoming battle weighed heavily on everyone's mind.

Suddenly, Julia thought back to what Alek said to her. Was she and Peter the main reason they were going to war? Why does Alek want to be a friend? Julia turned from her thoughts and began a conversation with Veronica. Julia whispered to Veronica, "Do you see that man over there?" as she pointed to Alek.

"Yes, what about him?"

"Do you know him?"

"A little. Why?"

"Well, he wanted me to sit at his table tonight at dinner. He said I could bring friends and I hoped you could come with me." answered Julia.

"Sure. Carson should join us too." Veronica replied. Carson laughed to himself before agreeing to join them for the dinner that night.

After lunch, everyone but Carson and Christopher went into the weaponry room. Cassidy went to the front of the room and stood until everyone was quiet. She called everyone by name, Julia, Veronica, Lori Linda and Elaine to stand with her.

"Now it is time to get your weapons and armor to prepare for battle. We'll help you select the right fit for your protective armor. Thereafter, you need to rest prior to battle. Understood?" instructed Cassidy.

"Yes ma'am." replied the soldiers as they pumped their fists in agreement.

They were all very brave soldiers. Prince Nathan agreed with Cassidy, to her surprise, and got into one of the lines to collect her armor. They knew that by doing this, they would go to war to protect Renata. Julia, Veronica, Cassidy, Lori Linda and Elaine stood by lines of armor and helped many men find their size. Afterwards, all the weapons were distributed to the soldiers.

Swords, daggers, bow and arrows, healing potions and transportation potions in glass spheres were handed out. Cassidy returned to the front of the room to admire the troops. "You're free to go."

The men nodded and left. Most went to see the castle or by the fountain in the main garden. Others went to their rooms to contemplate what was to come. Elaine and Lori Linda went to their room and bid each other farewell.

"Well, I'm going to meet with Bade. I'll see you two at dinner." explained Veronica.

"Alright" replied Cassidy as she looked at Julia to see if she was interested to visit the fountain. Julia wanted to join her, however; she needed to feed Annabelle first.

With that, Julia set out towards her room. She opened the door and spotted a young man feeding Annabelle. She tilted her curiously and he finally noticed her. He looked about 17 years old with blonde curls and he was wearing a servant's uniform.

"Pardon me ma'am. I was just feeding your wolf." he said, bowing timidly.

"Thank you. Please, there is no need to bow." Julia laughed as she looked over Annabelle who was lapping her plate clean. "My name is Julia. What is your name?"

"Jarvis."

"That's a nice name. What does Jarvis mean?"

"It means Servant" Jarvis answered.

"Oh" replied Julia. Jarvis immediately felt embarrassed and thanked Julia for speaking to him – a mere servant.

"That is very rude of others not to treat you kindly. I will always be friendly to you." Jarvis smiled as he left the room. Julia was pleased with herself that she could actually bring a smile to someone's face in Renata. Both Julia and Annabelle lay on the bed for a nap.

Julia awoke to total silence. Annabelle was still asleep and Julia figured that everyone was preparing for dinner. She quickly freshened up, dressed and quietly closed the door as not to wake Annabelle.

Carson was the only person in the hallway on his way to escort Julia. When they saw each other, they grinned and walked into the Dining Hall together. Cassidy arose from the table to greet them. "Julia, could you keep us company until you meet with Alek?"

"Of course." answered Julia.

Dinner was an enjoyable event. Julia gazed over to Alek and noticed him dining with Alek. Julia and the others walked over to visit with Alek. "Hello Alek. I would like to introduce you to Carson and Veronica."

"Glad to meet you both. This is my brother Jarvis. He's a servant here." said Alek.

"I know. I had the pleasure of meeting Jarvis earlier today." Julia responded and nodded at Jarvis as she asked, "You mentioned that you wanted to speak with me."

"Yes, I do. Please, everyone, be seated. I wanted to talk about you and being a human. "

"What about it?"

"Any human that comes to this world has a protector and I wanted to inform you that I am your chosen protector." "How do you know?" asked Julia.

"All the generations of our family have had these marks on our arms. The mark represents that we are protectors of humans." Jarvis explained as he lifted the sleeve of his shirt. Julia was pleased that Alek was her protector although she wondered if Alek would protect her with honor, love and friendship like the other guardians.

The sun was setting in the sky which meant that the battle would soon begin. Everyone began to move and hurry into their positions to prepare. Carson looked at Julia who was very upset. Carson gently kissed her to make her feel safe.

Julia regretfully walked into the Ballroom with Veronica, Christopher and Prince Nathan to say goodbye to the others. Julia saw the elder Mr.

Doddsworth and Mr. Clayton as they sat down with the girls as they were too old to fight. They all waited.

Chapter 18

FAREWELL AND THE ROAD TO BATTLE

The soldiers were ready for battle. Christopher, Prince Nathan, Bade, Peter, Jarvis, Alek and Carson convened in front of Julia's small groups to bid their farewell. Julia went to Christopher first.

"Thank you for being my teacher. Please return safely so that we can continue my lessons in magic. Good luck my dear friend." said Julia teary-eyed. Christopher nodded and smiled. Next Julia moved to Alek.

Alek grinned and said, "Don't worry Julia. I'll come back to protect you." Julia nodded in agreement as she bid good luck to the rest of the soldiers. Lastly, Julia approached Carson. Tears were spilling down her cheeks as she and Carson embraced each other tightly. Carson found Julia's lips and kissed away her tears. "Stay safe and come back to me. I love you." Julia cried. Carson replied, "I will come back to you and I will never stop loving you." as he left with the others.

Julia gazed out of the window watching the pained eyes as Carson and the others took hold of the reins of the waiting horses. The moon was shining brightly this evening as Julia dreaded to see those she loved and cared for riding to what she feared most. Now all there was to do is to wait.

Cassidy looked over at Julia and thought for a moment. *She's strong enough to go to battle. If she does, she will protect Carson and that's all that*

I want. She grasped Julia's arm and instructed, "Come with me and I'll help you get ready."

"Get ready for what?" Julia asked.

Cassidy pulled Julia to the weaponry room and asked, "Do you want to protect Carson and Peter? If so, you will have to pretend you are a boy. Would you be willing to do just that to protect the ones you love?" Julia responded with a yes that she would do what is needed to protect Carson. Cassidy then proceeded to cut Julia's long hair with protest from Julia. A few minutes later, Julia's thick auburn hair was now piled at her feet.

Cassidy mentioned there was one more thing to do for Julia's transformation. Cassidy needed to change the color of Julia's emerald green eyes to an amber color. This was to ensure that even Carson wouldn't recognize Julia. Cassidy cast the spell and Julia's eyes became the color of amber leaves in autumn. As Julia placed her helmet on her head, she marveled at the changes before her in the mirror. No one would recognize her. "I'm ready Julia announced."

Both Julia and Cassidy went to the stables to select a horse. Cassidy chose a black horse named Midnight. Tossing the reins over to Julia, she led them out of the stables and to the nearby lake.

"Alright, listen up. Your name is David and you're from the deep West Mountains. Got it?" Cassidy ordered. Julia nodded with understanding and thanked Cassidy for her help. "Head to the East Mountains and go to the battle ground. Don't get too close and observe what you can." With a quick hug to Cassidy, Julia rode off.

Julia rode on a hard earthy road for about an hour until the castle became nothing than a black speck. The road led to a steep rocky path on the edge of the mountains. Cautiously, Julia maneuvered Midnight on the road until they approached the waterfalls. She passed them and kept on a little longer until she came to a dark tunnel.

It was very dark and the only source of light was her piece of Ceylon. Julia suddenly recalled what her book of Elements had instructed. In order to make Ceylon shine more brightly, she had to say the word 'luminescent'. Focusing her energy, Julia repeated the word out loud.

The cave soon began to glow and showed the source of the waterfall. Julia came up to the waterfall and noticed that there is no way out of the cave. As Julia lifted her piece of Ceylon the stream of water parted as Julia went through it.

In front of her was a cliff. To her left, were smooth steps that led down to the battle grounds. Julia dismounted Midnight as she walked down towards the battle field. Julia made her way to the red and gold nestled tents on the field.

Julia breathed a sigh of relief as she tethered Midnight to a nearby tree with the soldier's horses. Julia looked around and noticed that hundreds of men had gathered around a bonfire listening to Prince Nathan. As Julia joined the other soldiers, she spotted Carson, Peter and Bade.

"Tomorrow at dawn we will crush the Remora for Renata." Prince Nathan exclaimed raising his sword. "For Renata!" all the soldiers excitedly shouted.

Carson looked at the ground and waited for the noise to settle down and said loudly, "It is very human-like that we continue to wage war to bring peace to our lands."

Julia watched intently as he arose throwing his cup to the ground. Julia longed to be the girl that she was to comfort Carson. He seemed deeply troubled. But she was now David and tried to quickly blend in with the rest of the soldiers as Prince Nathan approached her.

"Julia, is that you? I would know you anywhere. Why are you here?" Prince Nathan asked. "I'm here to protect Carson and Peter. Please let me stay." Prince Nathan agreed for Julia to remain with the soldiers just so long as she didn't go into battle. Julia thanked Prince Nathan and went to a nearby tent. As she lay down, Julia thought of her parents as she anticipated the next day. It was a restless sleep for Julia as she needed to remain anonymous to Carson. She loved him and needed to protect him. She would die for him and Renata.

Chapter 19

WAR

Dawn broke over the mountains and onto the battle grounds. Julia awoke with a start from the horn that announced the call to battle. Julia found Midnight and joined the other soldiers.

In the books Julia had read, she knew about battle formations. Julia saw that a circle formation was around the men. Julia went into formation with the other soldiers and waited. It was very quiet. The men were waiting patiently looking into the dim light over the mountains. The red and gold armor was shining brightly in the orange light until the sun was fully overhead.

Everyone observed the many small black figures running down the yellow stone rocks to the battle grounds. It was like watching an ocean of black about to take hold of you and suck the life out of you. It was the Remora.

The Remora outnumbered them with their goblins, demons, vampires, werewolves, dragons and other creatures of hate. The soldiers were apprehensive and began to lose heart.

All of the men and creatures in the army stopped in their tracks and watched as Princess Theodora were being dragged near a cliff as she hung from rope around her wrists. Everyone was outraged some started yelling. Then a dark sweep of arrows hurled towards them from the sky. The sun was blocked out by the dangerous swarm of arrows.

"Defenses!" shouted Prince Nathan.

The men in front as well as Julia cast the defense spell and shouted, "Xpencio!" A blue, clear dome covered them as it shielded them from the onslaught of arrows. The arrows did not penetrate the dome as they disintegrated as they hit the dome. The battle had begun.

Julia was horrified as the Remora fast approached the defensive line. Prince Nathan commanded the brave griffins with Bade take to the sky to fend off the attack. In a heartbeat, the griffins had snatched some Remora warriors tearing them apart limb from limb. The air attack continued with the Phoenix. He was standing near Julia with his fiery red feathers blowing in the wind. His companion with blue feathers wished him luck. The Phoenix burst into flames and breathed fire at the Remora.

The beautiful birds hurled rocks at the Remora as they breathed fire on them as well. Most of the soldiers cheered as they saw many Remoras perish. Unfortunately, a Remora in violet colored armor struck down the Phoenix. The Phoenix returned to a pale man covered in blood as he turned into ashes and died.

Outraged, Prince Nathan raised his sword and shouted, "For Renata!" The rest of the soldiers ran towards the enemy. Julia raised her sword as a Remora attacked her. Luckily, another Phoenix rose from the ashes to stop her assault. The Remora left a deep cut in Julia's left arm. Julia rode away to safety on Midnight. She caught a glimpse of Peter and Jarvis. She rode over to them to help but as she neared them, she was attacked by a werewolf. Julia screamed and Peter knew instantly that she was a girl and not a boy named David.

Peter rushed to her side to protect her from the werewolf. She was injured more now with painful bites to her torso. Peter exclaimed, "Julia! Let me help you." Peter removed a bottle of the healing potion and applied it to Julia's wounds.

"Peter watch out!" Julia screamed as she saw a fire ball aimed at Peter. She was too late. Peter flipped over and was scorched on his back. Julia crawled over to him and carefully rested his head on her lap while administering the healing potion to him. Jarvis witnessed the whole scene and came to both Peter and Julia. At this time, Julia decided to pull out her diary to send Peter home where he would be safe.

"What about you?" Peter asked. Julia replied that she wanted to remain in Renata. Peter agreed and happily was transported while thinking of his mother.

Jarvis stepped back next to Julia. A lightning bolt surprised them both. It was if Zeus had struck one of his lightning bolts at them. Jarvis warned Julia that he could not keep the barrier that protected them in place much longer. As the barrier broke, Jarvis fell to the ground. Julia screamed both in shock and in pain as a goblin struck her with his dagger into her neck.

"Keep still girly" said the goblin as he plunged the dagger deeper. Then the goblin gasped in pain as Alek told the goblin, "Thank you for keeping still as it is easier to kill you." Alek forced his sword into the goblins back.

"Alek! Thank you!" said Julia.

"No need for thanks. I'm happy to do it as it's my job." Alek said as he walked over to Jarvis.

"Is he...?" Julia asked.

"No. He's injured." Alek answered as he cast a protective barrier around him. "This should help him as he recovers." Julia breathed a sigh of relief.

After Jarvis had been attended to, Alek and Julia fought side by side; they were like one. Julia was attacked now by a demon. The ugly sprite pulled out a sword out of a swirl of tornado that surrounded him. As strong as wind, the demon ran towards Alek as they clashed with their swords. They fought long and hard with no clear winner. Soon the demon found Alek at a weak point and thrust his sword fiercely as Alek crashed to the ground. The demon wanted to fight more and lifted him up to only tear him down again.

Darkness now surrounded them as their powers clashed and spread in every direction. They both stopped fighting as they could not see what was before them. The demon soon found himself behind Alek as he pummeled him once again to the ground. Alek quickly regained his footing and shouted, "This isn't over and nor am I!" The demon fell to the ground from the force of Alek's sword. But this was not enough as the demon stabbed Alek in the stomach. Julia began to scream as the demon hastily approached her. The demon seized Julia and shot darkness straight into her body by piercing his nails into her arms and giving her a deadly kiss. Julia cried out Carson's name.

Carson heard his name above the fighting. He looked around at the thought of Julia crying for him. Then he saw her and nodded to Christopher to take his place fighting as he went to find Julia. He ran to Julia fending off any Remora. Carson saw that her eyes were blood shot as well as bleeding from her wounds. It seemed an eternity before Carson reached Julia.

Luckily, Carson was able to kill the demon by a surprise attack. Immediately, Carson gave a piece of Ceylon to Alek to help him. Then he looked at Julia and saw that she was filled with darkness. He held her close and shot his light into her by another healing and loving kiss. A protective barrier soon surrounded Julia.

Alek barely blew on the piece of Ceylon and it soon radiated healing light with its power. It was a wonderful feeling to heal the wounds. When Julia awoke she saw that both Carson and Alek were staring at her. Carson kissed her tenderly as she recovered. Now all three knew what needed to be done. They must save Princess Theodora.

Julia studied the cliffs and mountains near the Princess. She knew how to save the Princess. "Get the horses quick and follow me!" instructed Julia. Alek and Carson did as instructed although Carson took this opportunity to scold Julia for coming to the battle.

Julia led Alek and Carson up the mountain and past the waterfalls. They came to the cliffs with jagged rocks and Julia was able to fight off the Remora that was guarding Princess Theodora. "Carson, change into your star form and unlock the Princess. Alek and I will catch her." Julia said.

He nodded in agreement and transformed into a cluster of stars. He came up to the Princess and tied to unlock her from her shackles. Carson had some difficulty but finally freed her as Julia and Alek caught her below.

Alek put Princess Theodora on his horse while Julia mounted hers and waited for Carson. Once on his horse, they rode back to the battle ground. As they passed the cave, they heard a loud roar from a dragon. Julia looked up to see Bade being torn to shreds by the black dragon. "Bade!" she screamed.

Carson and Alek looked up and saw Bade falling to the Earth and the dragon positioning himself for a deathly strike. Julia quickly reached for the bow and arrow and shot the dragon dead through the heart. Both the dragon and Bade were falling. The dragon was falling directly over to where they were standing. As they moved away, the fall created a landslide.

Meanwhile, Prince Nathan was observing this scene and went quickly into action. "I'll be back. Have the healing potions at the ready." He struck his sword into the earth and cast a spell. He was soon where Bade would fall and caught him just in time with a barrier that prevented his crash to the ground.

Prince Nathan took hold of Bade and swung him over his shoulders, "Put your swords into the earth!" Prince Nathan commanded to his army as his cast his spell again. Everyone witnessed the landslide that killed many Remoras. Prince Nathan then looked to his left and saw Alek coming fast on his horse with Princess Theodora. Her brown curls were blowing in the wind as rocks from the landslide followed behind them. All cheered when Alek finally reached them.

Prince Nathan didn't see Julia or Carson with Alek. He asked Alek where were Julia and Carson. Alek had a look of sadness on his face and the Prince was terrified at what had become of his friends.

Carson and Julia were trapped by the landslide under rubble of rocks. Carson was unable to move. Julia was unable to move as well and it hurt for her to even breathe. She called out for Carson and he answered her with directions of not to move.

Carson then thought of the transportation potion. That was the solution! Carson struggled to reach Julia and when he did he was able to remove the potion. As he crushed the sphere, both Julia and Carson were safely transported to be with the others.

The battle was over.

Julia was relieved that Peter was safe at home, the Princess was saved and her friend's wounds would soon be healed. Julia was soon overcome with pain and darkness. Julia couldn't hear or see anything. She only saw fading colors that dwindled into a pool of black.

Chapter 20

BACK AT THE CASTLE

Mr. Clayton, Mr. Doddsworth, Lori Linda, Cassidy and Veronica had been waiting anxiously for everyone to return. They were especially anxious to see Julia. Mr. Doddsworth looked out of the Ballroom window.

"Are you okay Mr. Doddsworth?" asked Lori Linda.

"Not really." he replied. "I'm worried about Julia."

"We all are worried about her and the others." Lori Linda responded.

He stepped from the window and continued, "Women should not be in battle."

"Why do you say that?" asked Cassidy. "Julia is perfectly capable of taking care of herself."

"I know Julia is capable. It's just that my wife died in battle. She pulled the same stunt as Julia. The Remora had found out and captured her with the other men. The Remora pushed them to their deaths over the cliffs and into the shallow water below. I will never forget that day. I was about to rescue my wife… but a traitor prevented me. I will never forgive Aldrich." Mr. Doddsworth confessed.

"I'm sorry." was all Cassidy could say.

Lori Linda looked out of the window and happily spotted her friends coming towards the castle. Carson and Alek were carrying Julia into the main hall. Lori Linda was shocked but immediately ran to assist her friends. Lori Linda shouted, "They're here! Julia's hurt."

They all met in the main hall to help Julia. "What happened?" asked Cassidy.

"Let's move her to the infirmary – quick!" Alek instructed.

Cassidy said nothing and led them down the way to Ceylon and to the tunnel. The tunnel leads to a flight of stairs then up to the Infirmary. Carson and Alek lay Julia down on the bed as Cassidy came to her side. Cassidy then told everyone to leave as she needed to attend to Julia. After three days of fitful sleep, Julia awoke to see her friends by her side.

Carson asked, "How are you feeling?"

"Tired but better." replied Julia. They all laughed as they knew she had been asleep for three days.

"I'm glad that you are feeling better. Renata is indebted to you. How can we ever repay you?" asked Prince Nathan.

"There is no need for thanks. Renata is safe and at peace now. That is thanks enough." said Julia.

Everyone left the room with the exception of Carson. He wanted to speak with Julia alone. Although, they did not speak, no words were needed as they kissed.

A celebration banquet was planned of the victory over the Remora. Everyone was excited with the party planning except for Princess Theodora. The Princess approached Julia and said, "Even now I'm surprised that Carson would choose a human over a Princess. You don't deserve him."

"Why would you say such hurtful words? After all, I saved your life!" replied Julia. "Why would you think Carson wants a spoiled princess?"

The Princess lifted her chin haughtily and walked away making her plans to leave the castle. A furious Julia went to her room and slammed the door. Her room did not offer her the solace she needed and she desperately wanted to speak with Peter. Julia left her room for the library. Maybe she would find an answer there.

Julia found Carson in the library. Carson rose from his seat to welcome Julia. She asked, "What is the book that you are reading?" He answered, "*The Last Enchantment of a Songbird Warrior.* You should read it one day."

"Are you thinking of Peter? Would you like to communicate with him?" Carson asked gently. "Yes, I would like to talk to Peter." answered Julia. "I can make that happen. I gave Peter a silver wrist band and cast a communication spell on it. You have a silver watch. The two work together so you can reach out to him." Carson explained.

Julia lifted her watch as Carson cast his spell and soon Peter appeared in the face of her watch. Julia was delighted!

"Carson. Julia. Finally!" exclaimed Peter. Both Julia and Peter chatted about the events of the battle and they were both happy that everything turned out well. As Julia signed off from her conversation with Peter, she thanked Carson with a kiss.

Carson broke from the embrace to tell Julia that he was leaving the next day on business. Julia was disappointed as she didn't like being apart from Carson but he assured her that he would return the following day. Everything was fine. She was thankful for the new-found peace from the one she loved.

Chapter 21

A GOOD DAY

As Julia slept, she dreamed fondly of Carson. Suddenly, a black wolf appeared shattering her dream and becoming a nightmare.

"Wake up Julia" Alek's voice commanded. Julia awoke screaming as he playfully wiped tears from his eyes from laughter. I'm glad you are awake. Cassidy's class begins in five minutes."

"Then please leave my room so I can get ready." Julia said playfully. As Julia prepared for the day she walked out of her room towards class. Alek followed her down the hallway. Julia asked, "Alek, what's a *Songbird*?"

"Well, it's a bird…" he began but Julia interrupted him by saying, "No silly. It's in a book that Carson was reading last night.

"Oh, I know. The *Songbird* is a group of selected knights that protect the Kalama Kingdom and Renata. I'm planning to join that group as soon as I can. Not many are able to join as it a prestigious group." Alek explained. Julia wished him luck as she went into the class.

They went into the laboratory and Cassidy instructed everyone to put on their goggles, gloves and protective suit. Alek decided to observe class today instead of participating.

"Today, we're going to create a Love potion." said Cassidy.

"As if she needs a love potion." Alek mumbled.

"The ingredients are listed here in this notebook." Cassidy continued as she handed Julia the notebook. Cassidy provided a mixing bowl, bottle, and the ingredients and handed them to Julia. "Once you are finished mixing the potion, you must say, "Let the one I love drink this wine so in return my lover will love me."

Julia nodded with understanding and proceeded to mix the potion. Alek chuckled to himself that he needs to give this potion to Jarvis as he needs a girl in his life. Cassidy overheard his remark and asked, "Do you always speak about your brother in such a way?"

"Yes, most of the time." Alek smiled his reply.

After a reproachful glance to Alek, Cassidy told Julia to finish and begin her studies with books. Cassidy gave Julia two books on love potions. Julia was excited to read this subject. Alek soon tired of watching Julia read so after class he and Julia met with Christopher in the garden.

Christopher greeted both Julia and Alek. He told them that he was learning how to create protective barriers. "Those are very useful." said Alek.

"How do you make one?" asked Julia.

"The first thing to understand is that there are two separate ways to create a barrier. The first is to use your natural power. Alek, show her." Christopher instructed.

Alek obliged him and raised his hands above his head to cast this spell. Alek then put his hands by his heart and said, "Lycia ternio."

A black barrier appeared and covered him. Julia took a step back. Christopher was astonished at Alek's power even if he wasn't a noble.

"Would like to try now Julia?" Christopher asked.

She nodded in agreement and said, "So, since you have no powers, lucky for me there is another way to make barriers. You say this spell and the recite the element you want to use. Which element would you like to use?"

"I would like to try water."

"That's an easy spell. All you have to say is *l'eau viennent autour de moi avec votre protezione*. Got it?"

"You call that easy?!"

"Say it a couple of times and you'll get it."

Julia sighed and tried her best to say the spell. Alek laughed at her the first time she tried to say it. After the sixth or seventh time, she stopped.

"Close enough." said Christopher, "Now you do the motion while saying both spells. Say the water spell first though."

Julia did as she was told as best as she could and came out with a small barrier around her that glimmered with reflected light just like water. Alek was impressed and so was Christopher. He nodded in delight, "See." he said.

The bell rang and Julia looked at Christopher and Alek. *Time flies by fast in Renata*, she thought. Alek nodded to Christopher and signaled Julia to come along. Apparently, he knew Julia's whole schedule.

"We'll see you at lunch Christopher." said Julia and then followed Alek to Mr. Doddsworth's room.

She went inside with Alek and learned about all the groups in the government. Julia learned about things such as the Songbirds and reviewed the Remora. All were interesting and then they went to lunch.

Everything was in the right place, but only one thing was missing: Carson. Julia couldn't help but think about him. They had a nice lunch anyway and Prince Nathan was the one to bring up the last subject before lunch would be over.

He looked over to Julia as he spoke, "I should hope to see you all on Saturday for the Ball."

"Are you leaving your highness?" asked Lori Linda.

"Yes. I have to return to my family for the preparations."

The bell rang as Julia was about to say something but decided not to when Mr. Clayton said, "Well, it was wonderful to have you here Prince Nathan."

"Thank you."

They arose from their seats and said goodbye to the Prince. Veronica led Julia and Alek to the Ballroom and met Aaron, Darcy, and Elaine there. Julia noticed there were no chairs set up in the center of the room and stood beside Alek and Elaine.

"What are we doing?" asked Darcy.

"Today and tomorrow you're going to learn how to dance for Prince Nathan's Ball on Saturday. All of you are welcome to come."

"I don't know. I'm not much of a dancer." said Aaron.

"Well, then take dance position with me. Maybe you'll learn that way." Aaron stood in front of Veronica and took dance position as Darcy laughed at him, "You're the boy so you have to lead. I'll follow." said Veronica.

Aaron tripped on his own feet, for he was not just, not much of a dancer, but a bad one as well. Darcy kept laughing through the whole demonstration from his brother. After they were done, Veronica stood for a moment and then said, "Aaron, you stay as my partner. Darcy and Elaine, you're partners and Alek and Julia, you two are partners. Get in dance position."

"No music?" asked Darcy.

"Hum to your own tune."

Darcy and Elaine, Veronica and Aaron, and Julia and Alek took dance position. Alek led Julia humming a song that Julia did not know. Fortunately, Julia had taken dance class in her world and did very well with Alek. Alek was an excellent dancer himself, to Julia's surprise. Aaron was still learning, counting by threes in his steps, but everyone else was fine.

For the most part, everyone enjoyed dancing and couldn't stop. When the bell rang, they stopped and smiled at one another. Julia got out of dance position and out the balcony with Alek to meet Mr. Clayton and Lori Linda for universal class.

"Hello Lori Linda and Mr. Clayton." said Julia as she looked at the chairs and table next to the on the broad balcony.

"Hello Julia and Alek." replied Mr. Clayton.

"What are we doing today?"

"The time spell. I know Christopher was going to teach you it, but I wanted to."

"Oh. All right then."

"Now, so you can know everything you need to know about the difficult spell, we brought you a book to read about it. It doesn't take that long to read."

"All right." said Julia getting the book from Lori Linda and sitting down to read it.

Julia read going over how to do it again and again until she decided she could figure it out. She closed the book and stared at the cover. It was black and had stars on it with the title *To See the Beginning*. Lori Linda looked at Julia, "Are you ready to try it?"

Julia nodded, "First, take your position." said Mr. Clayton as Julia took position and Alek sat down.

"Then do the movements while saying the spell." said Lori Linda.

Julia did as such and whispered the complicated spell to herself. She raised her hands towards the sky above her for the last movement and saw the stars shining brightly. She smiled at herself knowing that she had done it.

"Well done." said Lori Linda and Mr. Clayton simultaneously.

"Thank you."

The bell rang and Julia nodded to Lori Linda and Mr. Clayton. She started walking towards her room as Alek followed her. When they came up to the garden door, Alek stopped her.

"Would you like to go to the garden?" he asked towards Julia's smiling face.

"Sure."

They walked into the garden and Alek immediately took Julia's hand and dance position, "What are you doing?" asked Julia flabbergasted.

"You have to practice dancing for the Ball, right? Well, I'm here to help."

She laughed and took dance position as well. They laughed and twirled around the whole garden for quite some time. When they came up to the tree house, Alek stopped and looked at it curiously.

"I've been meaning to ask you, what is that? Peter, Bade, and Carson built it, am I right?"

"You are and it's called a tree house. Do you want to go in?"

He shrugged his shoulders, "Why not?"

Alek and Julia went up the ladder and into the tree house. They both looked out into the distance in their own thoughts. Then Alek said, "You see that ridge over to the right?"

"Yes."

"That's where the Kalama Kingdom is."

"You really want to go there don't you?"

"Well, yes. That's where my home is- but don't worry. I'll stay here to protect you. It's my job isn't it?"

Julia giggled and smiled at Alek. He was a true friend. Then, Alek heard footsteps.

They looked towards the ground and saw Jarvis, "Ah! There you guys are. Want to go swimming?" Jarvis called to them.

"Sure." said Alek getting down.

"Swimming?" asked Julia as Alek helped her down.

Jarvis nodded and Julia continued, "But I don't have a swimsuit."

"A what?"

"A swimsuit. You know…something you wear when you go swimming."

"Do you mean a bathing gown?"

"Huh?"

"You know…something you wear when you go swimming." mocked Alek.

"Very funny Alek."

"Well, I don't see why Carson wouldn't give you a bathing gown, but I'll go help you look for one."

"All right."

Julia and Alek went into her room and straight to the closet. As she was looking, she didn't have any luck finding anything. Alek came over and shuffled his hands throughout the clothes.

"Not here. Not here. Hmm. Ahh!" he said pulling a white gown out and Julia shook her head, "Fine! Well, there's this red one. Do you want to wear it?" he showed her a beautiful red gown and she grabbed it out of his hands immediately.

"Perfect!" she exclaimed and then looked at Alek, whose eyebrows were perfectly arched.

"I'll be waiting outside."

Julia nodded and watched Alek leave her bright room. She quickly got ready and pet Annabelle as she stepped outside. They looked at each other and went out into the garden again.

Alek led her to a small iron gate and stepped out. The lake was glistening beautifully in the afternoon sunlight. Julia hurried down with Alek to Jarvis, who was in the water waving them to go in.

Soon, Alek jumped in and Jarvis was coming over to Julia. His blonde hair seemed a fading yellow with the sun behind him. It was an enormous lake, greenish-blue, and looked deep.

Julia thought the scenery was so great, that, she dared not to take another step. Jarvis was closer now, and smiled at Julia. He reached his hand out to her with the water shimmering on it, "Come in! The water's great!"

Before Julia could answer, two hands came up from the water and pulled Julia in. She screamed and when she came up, Alek was laughing and pointing at her. Jarvis was trying with maximum effort not to laugh with his brother, but failed by throwing his head back and laughing hysterically.

"You planned that didn't you?!" she yelled.

"Sure did!" said Alek still laughing.

"You're too easy to mess with." admitted Jarvis who controlled his laughing; *He seems to be more mature than Alek, even though he is younger*, thought Julia.

Enthusiasm was all around her. Julia swam all around and enjoyed the cool water surrounding her. When she came into the deep part, she went down and tried to touch the bottom, but couldn't.

"Careful. It's deep over there." called Alek.

"How deep?"

"Very." said Jarvis coming over with Alek.

"What's down there?"

"I don't know. Want to see? Surely, Jarvis knows a spell that can let us breathe down there." he said hitting Jarvis playfully on the shoulder.

"Yes I do." Jarvis assured, "Just say *Lavone etore ai soen*."

They said the spell and put their heads under water together. Julia's curious eyes were running wild, as if she was spinning on a top. Ruins, deep and wide water ways, and what looked like a green castle were in the distance.

"That's the Waldoboro Kingdom." informed Jarvis with his voice echoing under water.

"It's amazing!" she looked over to one of the ruins and saw gnomish writing on it, "Jarvis, what does this say?" Julia beckoned him over.

"It's a spell to get through this wall. This must be where Carson keeps his inheritance. Nice place to keep it. Look through that crack in the wall to see if I'm right."

Julia looked through and saw many gold, silver, and other expensive treasures, "You're right Jarvis!"

"Don't get too surprised. Jarvis is always right." said Alek in annoyed tones.

They all turned around towards the castle because they had heard a strange noise. Julia watched incredulously at the sight she was seeing: a pirate ship under water. Without turning she asked, "You're kidding me, right?"

"No. Not one bit. Pirates are coming to the Tabor's Castle." replied Alek bewildered.

The ship turned and made another scratchy noise. Soon, very soon, they would be coming. "Well, let's not sit around and wait for them." said Jarvis.

Alek, Jarvis, and Julia came back up above the water and to the surface. She looked up at the clock tower and saw that she should get ready for dinner. They got out and went to their rooms to get changed.

After Julia was done, she found Alek and Jarvis standing outside her door, "Are you ready for dinner?" asked Alek.

Julia nodded and they walked down to the Dining Hall. Everyone enjoyed their dinner and talked mostly about the Ball. It felt strange to not have Carson or Prince Nathan with them, but nonetheless, they were pleased to have each other's company.

Once dinner was over, Alek started walking Julia back to her room, yet saw the Ballroom more interesting, "You feel like dancing again?" he asked.

"Sure."

Inside the Ballroom, Julia and Alek danced wonderfully together. What they didn't know, was that Jarvis was standing outside the door to make sure Alek said what he had to say correctly and if he needed his brother's help. Alek stopped twirling Julia and productively made its way to a slow dance, shoulder to shoulder.

He looked down and Julia noticed asking, "What's wrong?"

After a moment he said, "Having two older sisters, one younger brother, and another younger sister tortures you, you know. Teasing you each time you like someone or you do something wrong. I never... really liked...girls." Alek trembled at the last word.

He started mumbling and Jarvis rolled his eyes while Julia tried to get the information out of his eyes even though he kept turning away, "What are you trying to say Alek?"

He tenderly placed his forehead on Julia's forehead and sighed until he was finally able to whisper his words compassionately to her, "Julia, what I'm trying to say is…I love you." he lifted his head, staring into her eyes, "And I know it's unfair to do this now because you love Carson, so I'm sorry. It's just that… nothing can help these feelings I have for you."

Julia stood there open-mouthed. She couldn't believe what she was hearing! Everyone seemed to love and care for her in this world. She grasped his hand and said, "Alek, you're a good friend but-"

He closed his free hand over hers, "But…you don't love me." his amber eyes looked pained.

"I'm sorry." Julia let go of his hands and promptly walked out of the Ballroom.

Taking no notice of Jarvis, she went straight to her room. Annabelle was inside and sitting close to the window. Julia opened it and let the cool air rush inside. She pet Annabelle and then got ready for bed.

After she was done, Julia subsided into her bed. Thinking content, she longed to write in her diary again. *Oh well. My diary is with Peter* she thought.

Chapter 22

A FRIEND IN NEED IS A FRIEND INDEED

The next day, Julia awoke and there was only silence. She looked out towards her window and saw Annabelle still sleeping. Smiling, Julia got out of bed and got ready for her classes.

When she stepped out of her room, the hem of her pink dress soared across the floor. Julia walked towards the laboratory and found that Cassidy was not there, and then saw that she was in the Dining Hall having breakfast. She sat down in her seat and started eating with Cassidy.

Cassidy stirred her tea without touching the spoon and drank a sip, "Good morning. Did you sleep well?"

Julia uneasily thought back to what Alek said and nodded while looking down.

"Is something wrong?"

Julia looked up, "No."

"All right. Finish your breakfast and then we'll head down to the lab."

She ate the rest of her breakfast and they went down to the lab together. Cassidy brought out the suits, goggles, and gloves and they put them on. Getting the supplies, Julia asked, "What are we doing today?"

"The invisible and deathly sleep potion. There are many types of deathly sleep potions. The most common one used is *Pedicu*." said

Cassidy putting everything down on the table, including two pieces of paper.

"Why is that?"

"Because it's not a liquid. It's more like a small, round tablet. When people poison each other, they don't want to leave any evidence. That's why most people use Pedicu- if they have to."

"I see. What exactly does it do?"

"Makes the person you poison, sleep for however long you want them to. You can't get out of it until your true love comes and kisses you."

"Oh."

"Now, the invisibility potion is not really a potion. It's more of a dust you put on things to make invisible."

"I've always wanted to be invisible."

"Fun, is the only word I can think of for it."

Julia giggled to herself and looked at the pieces of paper, "Those are letters from famous warlocks. They tell how to make these potions. Quite useful." said Cassidy.

"I bet."

"Start mixing." Cassidy said giving her the ingredients and mixing bowl.

She started mixing and noticed how the mixture slowly became round tablets. Looking over Julia's shoulder, Cassidy nodded. While Cassidy was getting a glass bottle, she said, "That's good. You're done mixing. Put it in here." and she placed the bottle down lightly.

Julia put the potion in the bottle and gave it to Cassidy's held out hands. Cassidy handed her another bottle and said, "Next, the invisibility potion." Julia set the other bottle down and handed Cassidy the other letter.

Julia picked up the items as Cassidy listed them off and started dropping them into the mixing bowl. Then, after mixing, it started becoming into a chalky, silver substance. Putting it into the glass bottle, it glittered when the light shown brightly onto it.

Some of the dust fell onto the table and it soon became invisible. Cassidy came over when she noticed, "Do you know the spell to make it visible again?"

Julia shook her head.

"It's, *decompsio a liron*. Try it."

Julia tried it and the table was visible again. Cassidy clapped her hands in delight.

The bell rang and Cassidy and Julia took off their goggles, gloves, and suits. They said their goodbyes and Julia headed for the garden. When she came out, she noticed it was another beautiful day and how her sparkly, pink dress matched the pink roses. She noticed Christopher by the benches and said, "Hi Christopher."

"Hello Julia. I have something for you." said Christopher reaching into a bag on the bench.

"What is it?"

Christopher pulled out a gold comb with green gems at the top, "It's a comb. I wanted to give to you. Everyone misses your long hair and this...this is a special comb. It can make your hair longer again." he handed it to her and she carefully held it in her hand. She stroked her short hair and was grateful to have something to make it long again.

"It's beautiful! Thank you." and they hugged.

Then, out of nowhere, Julia shrieked in pain like nails on a chalkboard. Christopher had long, sharp nails, like the demons' in the war, digging into her arms. Her blood was spilling red down her arms, staining her pink sleeves into a tainted red.

Christopher bowed his head, and when he came back up his face showed pain. It was bright red and the veins pumped wildly. Almost shouting, he commanded, "Get Mr. Doddsworth. Hurry!"

She tried pulling away, yet he screamed in agony pushing her down and cutting her bare chest. Abruptly, someone pulled her up. She noticed terror on Alek's face when she looked above her.

"Get Mr. Doddsworth!" he shouted again.

Julia and Alek ran to get Mr. Doddsworth, leaving a long trail of Julia's blood on the floor. When they came to the door, Alek knocked violently. Julia held her chest as she began breathing heavily, and Alek grabbed her while holding her close, staining his dark clothing with her human blood.

"Mr. Doddsworth! Hurry! It's Christopher! He needs your help and Julia's hurt!"

Mr. Doddsworth rushed out of his room and was running (jogging for an old man) down the hallway. Julia fell and Alek swept her up and carried her in his arms. He held her as Carson did in the war and placed his black jacket on the wound.

When they came to the garden, everything was torn. The bark on most of the trees and Christopher's skin as he held onto himself in a pool of his own blood. Julia gasped, turning away into Alek's chest, and Mr. Doddsworth darted to aid Christopher.

He helped Christopher get up; fighting off any non intentional punches and cupped his hands into one of the pools of Ceylon water. He made him drink it and said something, almost like a spell, to him. Christopher finally relaxed and managed to make out barely more than a whisper, "Thank you Mr. Doddsworth. Tell Julia that I'm sorry. It was an accident. Forgive me. Please lock me away so I can do no more harm."

"Of course. Alek, I'll be right back. Take care of Julia."

Alek nodded in agreement and Christopher, who was limping, and Mr. Doddsworth headed for the black door in the Tabor's Castle. He settled Julia on a bench while kneeling beside her and pressed a rag on the wound to try and stop the now less flowing blood. She looked away as he did this.

"Are you all right?"

"Better now. Thank you." and she looked away again.

He paused a moment, "I'm sorry about yesterday."

"It's fine. You don't have to be sorry. I'm the only one who should be." she closed her eyes and was silent.

"J-Julia?"

"I'm...I...I'll be fine." and did the same again.

Alek quickly gave her some of the Ceylon water, "Julia?" she didn't answer, but opened her eyes thankfully. "You're going to be fine." he brushed her cheek and her hair back. It almost looked as if he were going to kiss her but repeated, "You're going to be fine."

Mr. Doddsworth came back shortly after that and knelt beside Julia. She looked pale and was having trouble keeping her eyes open. "Bring her to the Infirmary."

Alek carried her to the Infirmary and laid her on a bed. Mr. Doddsworth came in with healing potion and stitching utensils. Wide-eyed Alek sat her up and stood behind the bed. Mr. Doddsworth had her drink the healing potion and take her arms out of her dress without him or Alek looking.

"Christopher is locked up in one of the dungeons. He's very sorry Julia." he said stitching Julia's right arm.

"I forgive him, but, what happened?"

"It's his powers. During the week of a New Moon, his powers make him crazy. He doesn't do anything bad intentionally."

Julia nodded and endured the pain of the needle piercing her skin so the wound wouldn't become infected from Christopher's powers.

"So this happens every month?" asked Alek.

"Yes. Every month since he was born. I was the one who found him hurting Carson when I first met them both." he paused a moment, "I still wonder why Christopher was in that old cottage by the creek. I think I remember him saying he was looking for something..." he paused again but continued, "At that time Carson had his parents so I brought Christopher to the Tabor's Castle to see Carson's father. Cassidy was in healing class back then and helped her dear friend out. They've all been good friends ever since."

"I'm happy for them. I still just can't believe someone like Christopher has to go through this suffering every month." said Julia, eyes glittering from the triangular light made by the blue and green curtains on the tall windows.

"Yes, well, not all powers are good." said Alek looking away.

After Mr. Doddsworth was done stitching Julia and cleaned the blood stains from her dress with a spell and said, "Let's take a tour of the castle today."

The three of them walked out of the Infirmary and to the hallway near Mr. Doddsworth's classroom. He opened a tall, wooden door with steel bolts and saw an amazing site. Stone doors traveling all around in all motions across the great room.

"What is this?" asked Alek reading Julia's thoughts.

"This is the transportation room. Carson has been doing some research, and apparently," he said tapping the end of a door with a blue mark, "this door leads to Ceylon on," he pushed the door until it was in the left corner, "that side of the room." said Mr. Doddsworth.

"Amazing!" exclaimed Julia.

"How did it get that way?" asked Alek leaning against a wall with his arms folded across his chest.

Mr. Doddsworth shrugged, "No one knows."

They walked around the castle and to the main entrance. While Mr. Doddsworth and Alek talked to each other near the fountain, Julia stood at the edge of the courtyard and leaned onto the yellow-stone wall surrounding it. Looking down at the ground below her, she noticed a dandelion puff and picked it up.

Holding it close, Julia took a deep breath. She thought of everyone she knew and wished them for their happiness. Blowing on it, little white and brown puffs left the green stem and soared into the air lighter than feathers into the golden light of the sun.

The bell rang and interfered with the silence. Julia turned around to see Mr. Doddsworth and Alek smiling. Their eyes were friendly, saying: let's go to lunch together.

Everyone, with the exception of Carson, was in the Dining Hall when Julia, Alek, and Mr. Doddsworth arrived. They had a good time with one another in their big group of friends. When the bell rang, an interesting tribute for Julia's courage took place.

A man and a woman arrived wearing strange and rugged clothing. They walked in speaking in low tones and, if they were heard, it was the woman's voice and she sounded excited. They kept watching Julia in amazement.

"I cannot wait until Prince Nathan's Ball tomorrow! Can't you Captain?" asked Marina.

"It'll b' fun Marina. I'm jus' glad that Carson let us stay 'ere."

Marina looked from her Captain to the rest of the Dining Hall and caught a glimpse of Julia. She turned back to her Captain, still eyeing Julia in amazement, and said, "Is...that...Julia Myers?! I never thought we would ever get the chance to see her, but there she is Captain! Look!"

"My, o' my. It is her!"

"Shall we go meet her?" asked Marina hopefully.

"All right."

They walked up to Julia and bowed. She stared at them incredulously. *Why would anyone bow to me, what did I do?* she asked to herself.

"Good 'ay miss Julia." said the Captain, "M' name is Timothy West, or better known as Captain West of the *Pirate's Knave*." he then turned to the woman next to him, "This is m' wife, Marina. We're staying 'ere this weekend for Prince Nathan's Ball."

"It's a pleasure to meet you." said Julia looking at the young Captain. He had light, blonde hair and purple eyes. Marina also had blonde hair, but had red eyes. Marina took Julia's hand and shook it.

"No, the pleasure is ours. We never thought we would see the woman who saved Renata." she said rather loudly and people stared.

"Thank you, but, I didn't save Renata."

"What are you talking 'bout?" asked Captain West. "Weren't you the girl who went t' war, pretending t' be a man t' protect the ones you love, and while doing so, defeated the Remora? Your accomplishments have traveled far. No one, not even a King should disrespect you! So don't say that you didn't save Renata. I believe the words of others an' even Carson Tabor says that you saved all of us."

"You really are too kind, but…wait. You know Carson?"

"Of course! He's letting us stay 'ere. Why do you ask?"

"Do you know where he is?"

"I'm afraid we don't Julia. We saw him earlier, but lost track of him." said Marina.

"Well, all right. Thank you for your kind words. I hope to see you both again."

"Indeed you will." said Captain West starting to walk off with Marina.

After a moment, Veronica and Alek came up to Julia and Alek touched her shoulder while Veronica said, "I know you're worried about Carson, but let's just get to class. All right?" Julia nodded and went to the Ballroom with her friends.

Chapter 23

COUNTING SHEEP

In the Ballroom, Darcy and Elaine were already dancing and Aaron was sitting on a chair waiting. Julia looked at Alek and he smiled back at her while stepping into dance position. Veronica walked over to Aaron and they too, took dance position.

As Julia and Alek were dancing together, she couldn't help but worry about Carson. *He was supposed to be back by now.* she thought. Smiling, Alek pulled her to him and let her twirl away as she closed her eyes at the thought that she might fall.

Coming back to grab his hands again, Julia noticed that they didn't feel the same. When she opened her eyes the sight that she was seeing was not Alek, but revealed a familiar blue-eyed young man: Carson.

She put the widest grin on her face and began to dance with him (for the first time). He smiled back and danced with her greatly. It was one of the happiest moments for Julia since she arrived in Renata.

After the bell rang, everyone stopped dancing and said their goodbyes to one another. Carson and Julia walked out of the Ballroom and to the balcony. Realizing that Mr. Clayton and Lori Linda were not there, they headed for the library.

When Julia and Carson came to the main hallway, Mr. Clayton seemed as if he was hurrying and held a book in his hands. They walked up to him and Carson asked, "Is everything all right, Mr. Clayton?"

He looked over to Julia and said, "Lori Linda and I have an

appointment right now, so if you could just read this," he handed the book to her, "that would be great."

She took the book from his hands and then positioned herself closer to Carson. Mr. Clayton smiled, "Why don't you two go into town tonight? It'll be fun, and anyway, you have to work at some point Julia."

"I bet it would be fun, and I'd love to go to work but," she looked to Carson, "aren't you tired from traveling?"

He stood up strait, put his head up high, and said, "I feel fine."

Mr. Clayton smiled and said, "Well then. I'll arrange a carriage for you two. You should go pack your things." he said waving his hands at them and then walked off.

Julia and Carson smiled at each other and headed down to their rooms. As they were passing the garden, Carson touched Julia's hand noticing the blood in the hallway. He asked, "What happened here?"

"Oh, well, Christopher," she paused a moment, "During class he went crazy and-" she pulled part of her sleeve down to reveal the stitched wound.

After a moment of silence, she pulled the sleeve back to its place and Carson said, "I'm sorry that happened. Who stitched it for you?"

"Mr. Doddsworth."

He nodded without a word until he dropped Julia off at her room, "I'll meet you by the entrance."

"All right. Where are you going?"

Carson started to walk down the stairs, "To talk to Christopher."

"Carson don't," she pleaded following him, "He feels bad enough as it is." Julia held onto his sleeve, slightly pulling him back.

He held her face in his hands, "Julia, even though it's not my job. But Alek's, I still want and will protect you." he then stepped down to the last steps, but Julia still held onto him, trying to follow.

"I'm fine. Just please let it be. I mean-" she accidentally tripped.

Catching her, both Carson and Julia fell onto the floor. He groaned a bit as he laid his head back. Julia panicked, "Oh, I'm so sorry. Are you all right?"

Carson looked up at her and smiled, "Never better."

Julia shook her head chuckling. After a moment, she lightly kissed him. Beaming, they both got back up onto their feet.

As he helped her up the stairs, Julia looked to Carson, "Please promise me you won't go to Christopher."

"If you say you're fine, then I promise," he smiled as he paused and then asked, "Will you meet me at the entrance soon?"

"Yes."

Julia stepped inside her room quietly and saw Alek and Jarvis standing next to each other speaking in low voices. Annabelle paused from her eating and looked up. Noticing, Jarvis turned his eyes toward Julia and Alek turned his head.

Jarvis walked to her with concern in his eyes and put his hands on her fore-arms, "Alek told me what happened. Are you all right?"

She looked over to Alek, who smiled with his gaze still on her, "I'm fine."

"What are you doing here so early? Isn't Mr. Clayton's and Lori Linda's class right now?" he said letting go of her arms.

"They had an appointment. I'm getting ready to go into town with Carson."

"I expect you don't need me to go with you then." said Alek turning to leave.

"I'm afraid not."

He nodded and all three smiled at each other. They left without another word and Julia looked for any case that could fit her belongings to pack into. She eventually found a light wooden case and packed her things into it, including the comb Christopher had given to her.

Giving Annabelle a last look, she pet her head and walked out of her bedroom door. She looked around at the surrounding walls and gargoyles in the hallway as she made her way to the entrance. Julia held the book Mr. Clayton gave to her close when she saw Carson by the doors with a similar black, wooden case.

They smiled at each other and opened the doors. It was still a bright, sunny afternoon and made Julia feel warm. She put a piece of her hair behind one ear with one hand while holding Carson's hand with the other.

He led her down the yellow-stone pathway that meandered in a zigzag form down the mountain. They came to a smaller courtyard halfway to the bottom which had their carriage waiting for them. It was a normal black carriage, pulled by a gray horse.

Carson let go of Julia's hand as he walked over to a tall, gangly, and thin man. Julia stepped to the side and looked back to the Tabor's Castle. She remembered the valley the lake rested on and the wondrous feeling she had when she went swimming with Alek and Jarvis. She would want to do it more often because of the weather warming up.

Carson beckoned Julia over to the carriage when he was done talking. He helped her inside and slid in himself. The man smiled a crooked smile while he closed the door behind Carson. After a moment, the carriage started to move and Julia pulled out her book to read it.

Along the way into town, Carson read with Julia until the book was finished. She fell asleep with her head on his shoulder the rest of the way. Julia dreamed of everything that happened to her since she first arrived in Renata. Some things were good and some things were bad. It played like a movie in her head; watching how she grew in the ability to do magic, the lessons she learned, the war, and her love she tried to give everyone.

"Julia, we're here." said Carson.

She slowly opened her eyes to reveal that Carson was carrying her out of the carriage. He set her down and went back to get their things from the man. Carson paid him ten silver and took his place by Julia's side. She took her suitcase and book from him.

Carson led the way to the Inn with a strut in his walk. Julia giggled as they stepped inside. They walked to the front desk which was occupied by a man with tanned skin, a squared, strong jaw-line, and curly dark hair.

"Hello. What can I do for you?" the man said in a rugged, raspy voice with a glint in his eyes.

"One room please." Carson said with enthusiasm, a smile which showed one of his dimples, and a golden glint in his eyes. It was as though they were doing a *charm* contest.

"That will be one gold." he never let his grin fall.

Carson paid him and added a wink over to Julia. The man retrieved the luggage and guided them to their room. As soon as he left with an even broader smile on his face, Julia turned to Carson and had to ask one question; she was only human to ask.

"What was all that about?"

"I did business with him once and we did the same thing back then. I guess he hasn't forgotten."

"Oh." she set her things by the bay window and turned to see Carson smiling at her.

He grabbed her hand and said, "Let's go have dinner." he led the way and they both sat heartedly in their seats.

The atmosphere in the inn was exhilarating. People laughed, drank, sang, and danced to fast music; it reminded Julia about Irish Pubs her mother used to tell her about when she went to Ireland one summer. It all was thrilling and exciting with people celebrating that Renata was at peace. Several times men and women looked to Julia and started speaking to their partners in cheery voices and then smiled at her. *How can one person be so appreciated for doing one thing? For the ones she loved?* Julia thought and looked to Carson. Secretly, Julia liked the attention.

The waitress came over to the side of the table and asked, "What would you like to drink?" she asked to both of them, but sounded like she was asking Carson more than Julia.

The waitress had spiky, striking, spunky, and seductive black hair into a Mohawk style. She also wore a blue sleeveless blouse, khaki pants, exotic black boots with gold laces, and a gold apron. Her gold eyes struck Julia with wonder.

Carson replied, "Your finest bottle of white wine."

She fluttered her eyelids and promenaded away. Carson and Julia enjoyed their discussions together after she left. In deep conversation, the waitress returned with two glasses and a bottle of their finest wine. As she poured Carson's portion of wine into his glass, she smiled and asked if they were ready to order. While Carson stated that Julia and he would have the lobster, the waitress never glanced at Julia or the glass as she poured the wine into it.

"By the way," she started, "my name is Paige in case you," she looked to Carson, "need anything else."

"Thank you." said Julia unenthusiastic, mostly irritated and Paige sauntered away.

As the dinner progressed, Julia and Carson celebrated among themselves. Paige never spoke out of turn and disregarded Julia even more. Yet, Julia didn't mind because Carson ignored the girl.

Near the end of their dinner, Carson held up his glass of wine and said, "A toast to us." Julia gave him a questioning look, "Well, to you Julia." he said grateful, "Without you, no one would be celebrating that Renata is at peace tonight."

"I didn't save Renata." she said sheepishly.

"Are you ashamed of your sincerity?" he asked putting his glass down with an astonished look and she shrugged, "It's one of the things I love most about you, but every time someone congratulates you or says that you've done something great, you deny it or say you don't deserve it." his clear, blue eyes stared deeply into Julia's green eyes and said in a lovely whisper, "You do deserve it. That and much more." and he drank a sip.

Julia shook her head from his perfect words, "I don't know. I guess it's because I've always been shy. Now everyone notices and gives me attention that I'm not used to."

"Didn't your parents give you attention?" he asked settling his glass inside the palm of his hand in the air.

"Of course! I'm talking about people I've never met before," she put her gaze on a man who had talked about her with his wife across the table, "and my friends. I was always the quiet one in my group."

"I don't see that." they both laughed and he set his glass on the table, "It's almost sunset. I wanted to watch it with you from the window."

"Then let's go."

Carson put five silver on the table as he stood from his chair a little off balance, "Too much wine." he said.

This wasn't like Julia, but when she saw Paige coming, she laughed and kissed Carson on the cheek.

They walked into the room, and looked out the window. The sun had much beauty with its redness descending into the sky. Its fiery orange flames as arms stretching to the gleaming white brightness of the stars above.

"Carson, remember the war?" he nodded as he stood in his position next to her looking out the window, "Hold me as you did then."

Even though he had a quizzical look on his face, he smiled as he held her next to him as they watched the sunset together. At one point, the sun was fully set and the moon smiled at them in a pool of white light as they stood in one form. They stayed like this for several minutes until Julia let go.

"I'm going to go get ready for bed. I'll see you in the morning."

"Goodnight Julia." and she fled into the bathroom.

After she was done preparing for bed, she stepped out of the bathroom quietly and found Carson already asleep. He lay across the cushion of the bay window with one arm over his head and another across his bare chest and a soft blanket. She tip-toed over to his side and gently pressed her lips against his.

"Goodnight Carson." she whispered and then got into bed.

Julia quickly fell asleep and awoke just as fast. She had woken up because she had heard a familiar lullaby being sung by a beautiful voice that sounded just like her mother's. When her eyes opened, Julia blinked several times; she couldn't believe what she saw.

The room wasn't there anymore and neither was Carson. Instead, white light almost blinded her and had flowers growing each time she moved on the ground. Ahead of her, she saw something she thought she would never see again: her mother.

She was dressed in brilliant white robes and stood before her on a patch of pink, yellow, and blue flowers. Her mother never stopped singing the lullaby with her red hair and colorful butterflies blowing in a wind that Julia didn't know was there. Julia's heart raced and she started crying tears of joy. She ran to her mother with every step growing the same flowers and tears spilling down her cheeks.

Julia ran and ran until she was in her mother's open arms. She held onto her mother and kept crying while her mother stroked her head, singing the lullaby. Feeling as though she was being a baby, Julia let go and her mother stopped singing to wipe her daughter's tears.

"Mom! I missed you so much! How can you be here though? Aren't you-"

"Dead? Yes, I still am. I missed you too sweetheart. And I'm here because you need me."

"Thank you mom." and she hugged her again.

Her mother let go of the hug the next time and held Julia's forearms, "I also came to tell you something."

"Go ahead."

"How much do you love that boy?" and Carson appeared to where she motioned her head and smiled.

Julia smiled even greater, "Enough to marry him mother."

Her mother sighed and became completely serious, "Julia, listen to me. This might be hard to bear." Julia sat on her knees with a quizzical look on her face, "You can't love Carson."

Julia sat in silence and open-mouthed until she finally managed to say, "What?! Why?!"

"This is why." said her mother putting a hand to Julia's forehead, making her have a vision.

Julia saw herself dying on the ground and Carson yelling something. She tried to see who he was yelling at, but everything was black for a moment and then saw a spray of blood when her sight was normal again. Yet, on the ground was Carson…dead.

Julia screamed and saw her mother in front of her again. She cried into her hands, not very silently either. Her mother touched her shoulder and she looked up and practically yelled, "Why?! I won't let it happen! Mom, I can't- I won't stop loving him!"

"Julia listen to me, just this once. Would you rather die knowing he's safe, or die of a broken heart?" Julia remained silent, "Now, I have to go. Listen to what I said. I love you." and her mother melted away in the white light.

The gorgeous scenery disappeared and left Julia watery-eyed on top of the bed. She thrust her face into a pillow and started sobbing. Her mother came to see her, but with tragic news. Only the sound of her weeping could be heard until an arm was wrapped around her waist.

"Julia, are you all right? What's wrong?" asked Carson sincerely.

She let her tears become silent and replied, "I can't say."

"Please tell me. What's wrong?"

Julia turned to her left and saw his blue eyes sparkling in the dark, "I saw my mother." and turned back remembering what her mother had told her.

"Oh. What did she say?"

"Nothing." she forced her face more into the pillow.

For a moment everything was silent, "Some say when they see their parents, it's for a good cause." she started sobbing again, "The morning I met you, my father came to me saying that it was of great importance that I would go to the Pierre Kingdom. He said destiny wanted me to look for someone extraordinary. And I found you. My father was right; you are someone extraordinary who changed my life. It was good that

I finally listened to him." Julia turned to face Carson, who wiped her tears, "So please, don't be upset. Your mother had good reason for coming back to you."

They kissed affectionately. Julia couldn't stop loving him; it was too much for her mother to ask. Then she said, "Stay with me tonight."

Carson nodded and kissed her lightly on the forehead. He lay down beside her with his arm still wrapped around her waist. Julia had trouble getting to sleep, but eventually did.

Chapter 24

MORNING

Julia awoke from the light shining through the window. She found Carson was already awake and dressed, for he was sitting on the cushion on the bay window. Julia could have cried, but decided not to. She thought that she would inform him what her mother really said to her after Prince Nathan's Ball that evening.

Carson looked over as Julia was getting out of bed and said, "You're awake. Are you feeling better?"

She walked up to him and hugged him tightly with a broad smile on her face, "I am now."

Several moments in this position, Carson stated, "I'm glad." and brought up her chin to kiss her.

After he kissed her, Julia let go of his forever-loving grasp and said, "I'm going to go get ready for work."

He nodded and she sauntered away into the bathroom. She got ready for work and put her chic little uniform on. When she came out, Carson was making the bed.

"I'm ready." she announced once he was done putting a pillow on.

"Great. Let's go have breakfast."

They ambled their way down the stairs and found a table to sit at with their packed bags. Carson and Julia didn't talk much, because both were thinking about the Ball later that twilight. Opposite feelings were put forth to it; Julia dreaded it because of what she had to tell him and Carson couldn't wait for it because of a question he had for her.

After their silent breakfast, Carson left money on the table and walked up to find the Inn Keeper look-a-like and paid him another gold coin. The man smiled and Carson grinned bigger than ever before. Julia couldn't help but smile as they stepped out of the inn. Carson led the way to Adrianna's pet shop and was blissful. Julia was glad that at least *he* was happy.

They came up to the shop and Carson turned to face Julia, "I'm going to go around town while you're at work. I also need to pick something up while I'm here. Is that all right?" he held her hands.

Julia never took her eyes of his hands covering hers while she said, "That's fine. I'll see you then."

He gave her a kiss on the cheek and left her teary-eyed looking at the sign above the shop. Clearing her eyes, she walked inside and noticed Adrianna. Surprisingly, Adrianna hugged her immediately after she saw Julia from the corner of her eye.

"Julia! You're here! Oh thank you, thank you!"

"For what? Coming to work?" she asked confused.

"No. For saving Renata! Thank you!"

"You're…welcome." said Julia awkwardly because she could barely breathe and pat Adrianna's back so she could stop.

Adrianna let go of her hug and pulled Julia towards the front desk next to the girl she, Carson, and Veronica had first seen at the store, "Julia, this is Anna, my niece. She's been working here for a long time, so if you need anything, ask her." and Adrianna left.

"I can't believe I'm standing next to Julia Myers." Anna said.

Julia blushed and said, "I can't believe I'm standing next to my boss's niece."

Anna then blushed as well and pointed to a large box with air holes in the front of it and said, "That is to be picked up today, so I'll let you do it for your first customer." she then walked to a cart with food on it and said, "Make sure they get this with the animal." she scrutinized everything to come up with a price and then looked at piece of parchment in one of the drawers in front of Julia, "Yes. They should pay you eight gold for the total."

"All right. I'll make sure that happens." then Anna left the front desk.

About fifteen minutes later, Julia was astonished to see Prince Nathan with his guards walking towards the shop. Julia flushed red as he gazed at her with equal astonishment in his eyes and smile. Then he asked, "You're here too?"

"Yes your highness." she bowed.

He brought up her chin and said, "After tonight, I would like for you to start calling me just Nathan."

Julia smiled and asked when he let go of her chin, "So what business have you come here today for?"

"I believe it's the large box in the back." he said pointing.

"Let's go check." she said leading him inside.

Julia was having difficulty opening it and then Prince Nathan pulled out a short, emerald encrusted dagger, "Allow me." and slit open the box along its edges.

The box's faces began peeling off to reveal a clothed beast wearing glasses and reading a book. He looked up from his book and said, "It's about time. It was getting a bit stuffy and it's hard to read without the proper light." he closed the book and held it up as he said this.

Julia laughed in amazement and happiness. Never in her life, had she seen a beast. It was fully grown, and apparently, very intelligent.

Prince Nathan's guards pulled the cart outside and the beast followed by walking. Julia looked back to Prince Nathan, who was putting the dagger back into its sheath. She smiled when he looked up and asked, "How much do I owe you?"

"Eight gold." and she placed her hand out tenderly.

He smiled and gave her the gold and happily said, "I'll see you at the Ball tonight."

"Yes you will." she alleged and then gave him a hug.

After Prince Nathan and his guards left, Adrianna and Anna walked up to Julia, "You know the Prince?" they chorused.

"Yes. Is that bad?"

"Oh no!" Adrianna started, "It's just that you know many important people. The Prince, the Princess, and you're in love with Carson Tabor."

"Any girl would be jealous." stated Anna and Adrianna gave her a pat on her back.

Julia smiled and continued to manage the front desk. There wasn't much business, but before Carson would come to pick her up, Julia sat and talked with Adrianna and Anna in her wild office. Many animal's noses ran wild and scurried about the room playfully. There were stacks of straw, food, and crates that the animals used; it was a little messy.

"Try not gaze at the mess." said Adrianna.

Julia smiled and asked them, "Are you both going to the Ball tonight?"

"Yes! I've already picked out a fantastic dress, yet, aunt Adrianna here hasn't." Anna said excited and motioned her head to her aunt.

Then Adrianna started defending herself, "I do have a dress! In fact, I have many dresses! I just can't decide." she said solemnly.

"We can help you pick out one. Do you have them here?"

"Thank you Julia. I have them in the back. You two decide which one I should wear."

Adrianna left the room with a delighted squeal. Anna mouthed *thank you* and Julia mouthed back *you're welcome*. In a heartbeat, literally, Adrianna came back inside but with a pink dress that had gigantic ruffles, sparkles, and puffy sleeves on. Speechless, both Anna and Julia shook their heads rapidly.

The next dress was a tight, a little too tight, blue dress that wasn't very complementary to Adrianna. They criticized the next couple dress crucially, yet Adrianna didn't have the right dress. Finally, Adrianna came out in a beautiful, silky, purple dress that was the best fit.

Anna and Julia both exclaimed, "Perfect!"

Adrianna clapped and went back to change into her uniform. Anna and Julia smiled and went back to the front desk. When they got there, Carson was leaning his back onto the desk.

"Carson?" asked Julia.

He quickly put something away in his pocket and asked, "Did you have a good time working?"

"Very."

He nodded to Adrianna who had just come from the back and asked, "Are you ready to go?"

"Yes." she looked back to Anna and Adrianna and said, "I'll see you at the Ball tonight."

They nodded and Julia looked to Carson. He led her to the carriage with a smile, yet Julia was still upset. How she dreaded the Ball.

They got to the carriage and Carson paid the man with another smile. He helped Julia get inside and closed the door behind himself. A tired Julia went to sleep holding Carson's hand as soon as the carriage started moving.

When she woke up, Carson was getting down and about to carry her out. Thankfully he still did, because Julia's legs felt like jelly. He set her standing on the ground and grabbed the suitcases as he handed the man the money they owed him.

Once Carson was done, they made their way to the entrance of the Tabor's Castle. Julia had always wanted to live in a fairy tale, and thought her experience in Renata was a little bit like one. Only one exception; the *Happily Ever After*. She looked back to Carson and was upset, for he was the only one to make her *Happily Ever After* come true.

Carson noticed that Julia had a sad look in her eyes as she stared at him and he asked, "What's wrong?"

"Nothing."

He walked up to her and held her hand, "Is it about the Ball tonight?" she nodded, "Don't worry. When we dance together, I won't let you fall." Julia smiled- if only that was her worry!

When they came to the entrance, Cassidy and Veronica were talking and waiting for them. They rushed to Julia and said, "Hurry Julia! We have to get you ready for the Ball!" Veronica laughed when she noticed Carson's surprised expression.

Julia looked back and said, "Well, it looks like I have to go."

"I'll meet you downstairs."

Cassidy and Veronica pulled Julia throughout all the hallways in a hurry. They came to her room and Annabelle looked up from the sudden opening of the door. Cassidy pushed Julia into her bathroom and said, "While you bathe, Veronica and I are going to get dressed and then we'll help you. So go as fast as you can!"

"All right."

Julia did exactly as Cassidy said and put on a robe once she was done. She saw that Cassidy was putting a last shoe on and Veronica was fixing her hair when Julia stepped inside her room. How beautiful they looked. She cleared her throat to get their attention. Cassidy looked up and smiled. Veronica swept past the floor and grabbed Julia's lean arm and pulled her to the closet.

Cassidy followed them into the closet and started shuffling her hands throughout the clothes. Veronica found two dresses and set them on the bed and Cassidy did the same. They came back and quickly grabbed a corset.

Julia stared at the corset wide-eyed. Never in her life had she worn one and didn't want to start now. Ignoring Julia's objections, Veronica and Cassidy tied the corset onto Julia without leaving her much room to breathe. Julia then chose a dress and the others were quickly put away.

Then Cassidy and Veronica sat Julia down to put her make-up on and fix her hair. They made her face pale with pink cheeks, light pink lips, and misted her eyes in royal blue and silver complemented by black eyelashes. Next, they took the comb Christopher gave Julia and grew and cut Julia's hair into a layered, long cut. Julia smiled when they curled her hair half up, tied with a silver ribbon, and put ivory beads into her hair. Finally, they helped her into her dress and tall shoes.

All looked into the mirror and smiled, "Carson is going to love you in this." Veronica said softly.

Cassidy hugged her from behind and whispered, "It's going to be a very special night."

Someone knocked on the door, "Is Julia ready yet?! I have to take her down to Carson." said Alek's irritated voice through the door.

Cassidy rolled her eyes and she and Veronica stepped out of the room to find him standing outside waiting impatiently, "You look nice Cassidy. You too Veronica." she heard Alek say politely.

Julia took one last look at herself. She loved the way her friends did her hair and make-up. She especially loved the ivory and royal blue dress with laced ivory sleeves they helped her into. Yet, something was missing; she needed a necklace. Deciding that she had no time, Julia walked out of the room to find a handsomely dressed Alek staring at her.

"Is something wrong?" she asked.

He straitened himself up and gently put his arm to her, "Not at all. You look great."

"Thank you. You too." and put her arm through his as they started walking to the long staircase.

Looking down before taking a step, Julia noticed everyone down there in exquisite fabrics staring at her. She noticed Carson was intoxicated when he looked at her. He was originally talking to Mr. Doddsworth, but trailed off and had forgotten what he was talking about as he gazed at her. Julia blushed as she stepped down to him in his impossibly handsome form wearing black, silver, and royal blue.

"You look beautiful." he said brushing her cheek lightly and then lightly kissed her.

"Time to go." said Alek starting to walk to the entrance.

As everyone headed for the carriage, Carson stopped Julia in the hallway and said, "I have something for you." and he pulled out a long, blue box.

"What is it?" she asked as he handed it to her.

"Open it."

She did and gasped. Inside was a silver choker necklace with a piece of Ceylon in the center. She started at it in disbelief. He was making the truth so hard to tell him after the Ball. She finally managed to make out a whisper stating, "It's…beautiful." and looked up at him teary-eyed.

"Not as beautiful as you though." he said gently clasping it onto her swan-like neck.

"Thank you." and she kissed him.

They walked to the entrance hand in hand and he led her to the carriage. It was a wonderful long, white carriage pulled by three white horses. She smiled as he helped her inside.

Julia tried her best to keep the smile on her face, but was deeply hurt inside. She didn't want to tell Carson that they couldn't love each other. It already pained her just thinking about it, yet she had to tell him soon before anything drastic happened.

The way to the Ball was long, since it was at Prince Nathan's castle, and everyone was happy. They pulled up to the main entrance to the castle. There were many excited people in stunning wears stepping inside the grand entrance. It was time for the Ball.

Chapter 25

PRINCE NATHAN'S BALL

They all got out of the carriage and gazed in awe. It was Prince Nathan's castle and it was magnificent. The castle stood tall, had many doors, balconies, widows, bridges, turrets, a tall iron gate that led to a flamboyant courtyard, and a large amount of land around it.

Carson, Julia, and all the others walked slowly to the gate. Guards stood in positions and many candles lighted the way past trees, statues, and fountains and the large, and the thin candles moved from their path as they passed them. They came to the main entrance doors and only dared to look inside. Prince Nathan stood with a guard in the middle of the entrance and greeted his guests. When the others before Julia came up, he smiled and said, "Hello, and welcome my friends. Thank you for coming." when Julia came, his face lit up and said, "Julia you look wonderful. Hello Carson. Thank you for coming."

Julia smiled as Carson nodded and stepped inside. A great deal of people had come to the Ball and all stood and gazed at the details in the Entry Hall. Julia looked around herself with Carson.

Red curtains hung high next to paintings of the former rulers of the Felpierre Kingdom. Gold columns stood around the room and stopped towards the end of the room where there were a short flight of stairs led to a giant wooden door. There were many doors and gold furnishings aligned in the hallway. The ceiling had a rimmed, gold star painted onto it.

After several minutes of looking around, the Prince was done greeting his guests and went up to the door at the end of the hall. He waited for everyone to pay attention. Julia and Carson put their eyes towards Nathan as the Prince began saying, "Thank you all for coming tonight. Now if you please, our next activity is the dinner waiting on the other side of this door. Take a seat wherever you would like. During our meal, a play will be performed to us for our entertainment. Enjoy the celebration." and he opened the door with a wide grin on his face.

People shuffled in and quickly grabbed whatever seat that they could. In the Dining Hall, it was enormous in size. It held a Head Table for the King, Queen, and Prince Nathan, more long tables of rich wood for other seating on the east side, a built stage at the west side of the room, a painted roof that changed scenes every several moments, and tall windows instead of a wall of the north side of the room.

Julia, Carson, and the others took some seats next to the Head Table, which Prince Nathan sat at with his mother and father on either side of him. His mother was beautiful because of her thin face, lovely short hair that was white, was placed back in a cropped bob and a thin, golden crown, cheek bones, and pink, heart shaped lips. His father was quite handsome as well because he too had a thin face, faded brown and a little grey hair under a gold crown, and the finest fabrics he had on him.

From what Julia knew about Prince Nathan, she sort of expected this. Carson didn't seem too surprised himself either. Julia tried to smile to him and he held her hand excited for what would happen next.

At the stage, a young girl stood and waited. Once everyone looked her way, stained glass appeared on the stage. It shaped itself to say *Beauty and the Beast* in beautiful cursive writing. Then the girl said in a soft, kind, and shy voice, "Tonight's entertainment will be the play Beauty and the Beast. I am your narrator, Mary."

Mary then began telling the story of *Beauty and the Beast*. It started with the stained glass capturing the scenes until Belle came on the stage. When the song *Be Our Guest* was starting to be sung by Lumiere, waiters and waitresses served the food as well and sung too.

Julia laughed and watched the play with great interest. The part of the Beast, was the beast she had given Prince Nathan earlier that day. Beauty and the Beast was her favorite animated Disney movie. Carson smiled and enjoyed everything as well. It was truly *A Tale As Old As Time*.

Once the banquet of food was finished, the play finished as well. The cast came out while bowing and everyone cheered. After the noise settled down, champagne was handed out and a faint ring came from the Head Table. The King stood and said, "I would like to make a toast." Prince Nathan blushed when his father put his hand on his shoulder, "Son, twenty-five years ago today, your mother had you. She held you in her arms and cried the most tears of joy I had ever seen anyone cry. Then, she put you in my arms. One look at you, and I knew you would be great. You have done so many immense things for this Kingdom. I cannot wait until your coronation; you'll make a wonderful king. Happy Birthday my son. Cheers." he said holding his glass up and everyone followed suite, drank, and clapped.

Julia looked to Prince Nathan; he was indeed in high spirits from the happiness in his eyes and a broad smile. His mother kissed his cheek and his father hugged him as though they were leaving. His mother stood and said in a soft, lovely voice, "The next activity will be dancing in the Ballroom. I'm afraid the King and I have to depart though. Enjoy the rest of your evening. Goodnight." everyone cheered and the King and Queen left.

Soon, all guests were in the Ballroom. As Julia and Carson stepped in, she was amazed. The walls were ivory with gold lining, the floors were red with tiny plants painted on it which grew as real ivy on the gold columns, and the ceiling seemed to be the ivy used as a canopy before the glass roof. It was stunning.

Fast music started playing and everyone got into two lines. Men on the left and women on the right. Julia turned to Carson and he smiled, "The first song is always the best." and he grabbed her hand to pull her along and dance with him.

Julia jumped into the right line with many women's bright smiles showing. Carson jumped into the men's line, most with crooked smiles like himself. They all dipped their heads and began dancing. Most of it was jumping around and twirling, and Julia found this fantastic.

As soon as the music stopped playing, everyone bowed and Julia turned to see Alek and Jarvis right in front of her. She jumped a little from being scared and they smiled. *Of course* Julia thought.

"Would you like to dance with us Julia?" asked Jarvis.

"Both of you? At the same time? I don't think I can."

Alek and Jarvis smiled, "Of course you can. And if not, it's about time to start learning." said Alek pulling Julia into position between him and Jarvis.

More fast music started playing and Julia caught a glimpse of Carson laughing as Alek twirled her. Her hands landed in Jarvis's and she started dancing between them. She was dancing with two men at the same time and felt as though she had accomplished something. Julia could never do this in her dance classes back in Rochester.

Once Julia smiled at the end of the dance, Alek and Jarvis did as well. Then, Julia saw Marina and Captain West. She nodded to Alek and Jarvis and walked to their side by the drinks.

Getting up to them, Marina almost spat out her drink as Julia got closer to them and blushed a crimson red, "My word it's Julia again. You look lovely. How have you been?"

"Good. You?"

"Wonderful! How are you enjoying the Ball?" asked Captain West.

"Very much. Have you been enjoying your stay at the Tabor's Castle?"

"Of course. Carson treats his guests' t' the highest respects."

Christopher came to join them, "Well, it looks as if Alek and Cassidy are having a good time." he said holding his glass of wine in the direction of them dancing gracefully.

"It does." she looked around the room and noticed Jarvis dancing with Lori Linda and Bade with his beloved Veronica dancing together, "Seems as if everyone is." she said smiling.

Christopher put his glass on the table holding the drinks and asked, "Julia would you care to dance?" he held out his hand.

"Sure." and she nodded to Marina and Captain West.

They got into dance position and Julia let Christopher lead. Julia noticed that Alek, Christopher, and Carson were all great dancers. Near the end of the dance, Christopher turned the far distance between him and Julia closer. Then he asked, "Do you forgive me for what I did to you yesterday morning?" he gently touched the part of her skin where he accidentally cut her with glittering black eyes.

"Yes I do. I'm sorry you have to go through that kind of pain." only silence for a moment, "I can't believe it was just yesterday."

"Neither can I." the music ended and Christopher looked from Julia to the table with drinks to find Adrianna and Anna.

"I'll see you later." Christopher smiled a crooked smile as she fled to her boss and friend.

Julia hugged them, "It's good to see you both here. I love your dresses."

Adrianna smiled and Anna looked down at her short, silky blue dress and blushed, "Thanks. Good to see you too."

Alek soon rushed over to Julia's side, "I just can't seem to stop dancing." he said to her and started babbling on again.

She sighed mockingly, "Do you want to dance with me Alek?"

He blushed, "Yes."

Julia looked back to Adrianna and Anna laughing, "It seems I have to leave." and they laughed even more as she was scurried away by Alek.

Julia and Alek smiled as they both took dance position. He led the way and productively made it into a slow dance and made their shoulders touch. They danced greatly together and Julia could have sworn she saw him blush once. He was truly happy that evening.

She looked over across the Ballroom. Julia noticed Cassidy and Carson dancing together. Some moments both were smiling, and others were very serious.

At the end of the song, Alek smiled broadly and Julia grinned as she looked over to Carson and Cassidy again. He was pulling out something, but she couldn't see what because Alek then left and was replaced by Bade. He smiled in dance position and asked, "May I have this next dance?"

"Indeed." she said laughing.

After a moment of dancing gracefully together, Julia asked, "So how are things between you and Veronica?"

"Great. Why?"

"I just want to make sure there's still going to be a marriage that I'm going to attend."

"Oh, you'll have more than enough to attend to." Julia stared at him blankly. *What could he possibly mean?* she thought.

Prince Nathan and Princess Theodora were dancing together on the other side of the Ballroom. They danced wonderfully with each other-bending, twirling, and grinning at all the right moments. It seemed as though Princess Theodora was trying to keep Prince Nathan's attention, and impress him while doing so.

She blushed when he twirled her close to him. Then Prince Nathan turned to look at Julia with both admiration and longing in his eyes. Princess Theodora seemed to be hurt by this, but perked-up her spirits and asked while brushing his chin toward her face, "So have you been thinking about us?"

"*Us?*" he asked shocked.

Princess Theodora laughed, "You say it so cute. Of course! Once Carson marries Julia, I won't have a betrothed. The agreement between our parents was that if Carson didn't agree to marry me, you would be the next betrothed."

Prince Nathan stared at her open-mouthed. He was speechless in astound. Princess Theodora was beautiful, but he couldn't possibly fall in love with her. He loved Julia!

Bade and Julia hugged at the end of the song. Next, they walked to the drinks where everyone was together. Carson smiled when they came up and asked to Julia, "Having a good time?"

She nodded. Everyone enjoyed talking to each other for a little bit until Mr. Clayton went to dance with his niece Lori Linda and others started leaving to dance some more. Soon, Prince Nathan went to Julia's side when a slow melody began playing and asked, "May I have the honor of dancing with you, Julia?"

She grasped his hand that he held out and said, "You may."

The melody was slow and was calming. They started dancing and Julia kept looking towards Carson lost in thoughts that spun around her in every direction. She had to tell him the truth at some point.

Prince Nathan looked to where Julia was and sighed, "Why do you seem so upset?"

"It's nothing."

"Well it's obviously something. Julia we're friends aren't we?" she nodded, "Then you can tell me."

"My mom...last night she came to me saying that I couldn't love Carson anymore."

"Why?"

"She said that he would die if I continue to love him."

The Prince sighed once more and whispered softly, "No matter what happens, just know that I'll always be here."

The song ended and Julia hugged him, "Thank you."

He then left. Two small girls went to the end of the Ballroom. One started playing a soft, sweet, and kind melody on a piano while the other girl sang in just as sweet of voice, never skipping a beat and remembered not to take too many breaths.

Carson came and stood in dance position in front of Julia. He didn't need to ask, and they started to dance. Out of all the dances, this was the most magical. They danced together magnificently, sweetly, and dotingly.

After the song ended, Carson kissed her and whispered into Julia's ear saying, "I need to ask you something in private."

Julia nodded and he grabbed her hand. They walked slowly across the Ballroom and to the windows. He opened one, which entered a balcony outside. Everyone stared at them smiling.

It was still and quiet. There was a rail to hold onto before looking out into the distance and a white bench to sit on. The clouds were rimmed with white from the moon's light, a tall fountain stood in another courtyard in the center of a garden, and a forest with clearings surrounded the castle.

Julia walked and held onto the rail while looking at the beautiful night setting. Carson came up behind her and embraced her as he did the first time. *If only time could let us stay like this forever* Julia thought, closing her eyes.

Carson then kissed Julia's cheek and settled his head on her shoulder. He also brushed his hand gently up and down on her arm and put his other hand on her free shoulder. As he did this, she asked, "So what did you need to ask me?"

After a moment, he replied, "How much do you love me?"

Julia almost cried, for it was the same question her mother asked her and knew she couldn't love him, "So very, very much." she managed to whisper while opening her eyes.

"That's all I needed to know." he sighed and walked off.

"Why...do you ask?" Julia asked after a moment of being alone in her own thoughts.

Turning around, she gasped at something she didn't want to see, at least not that moment. Carson got down on his right knee and pulled out a tiny black, velvet box. He opened it to reveal a gorgeous encrusted diamond ring with a silver band, "Will you marry me?"

Chapter 26

AFFECTS OF ANSWERS

Heart skipping beats and hands shaking, Julia stared at Carson in shock. She faltered back into a bench behind her and looked down. Julia started crying silent tears, knowing she couldn't love him and didn't want to tell the truth, yet she had to-now.

"Julia? Are you all right?" asked Carson coming up in front of her, still on his right knee.

"I can't." she alleged.

"You can't marry me? Why?" he asked with concern in his eyes as he lifted up her chin, "Give me a reason."

Julia contemplated what to do. She didn't want to tell him the real reason. So, she quickly thought of another excuse, but Carson interrupted her thoughts, "Is it our age?" he asked uncertain.

She took this as the other excuse, "Yes. Yes it's our age. I'm too young to get married." she tried to manage saying with an innocent, confused tone in her wavering voice.

"What? I'm twenty-four and you're twenty-two. It's the perfect age to get married."

"Really?"

He nodded looking deeply into her eyes and said hesitantly and sure, "But that's not the real reason, is it?"

She shook her head, "I…I didn't want to tell you until later."

"Tell me what?" he held her hands that were cupped in her lap.

Julia looked down at their hands, "Do you want to know what my mother really said to me last night?"

"What did she say?"

"She...she said that if I continue to love you...you'll die." he stood and turned away, "Carson, please. I'm so sorry." she pleaded.

"I...I'm just trying to make sense of all this." he turned around as Julia stood behind him and scared her from the confusion, a little anger, and sadness in his eyes, "If...if you don't love me, then just say it. Don't make up excuses." and he turned away to hold onto the rail.

She came up behind him once more, "Carson, what I'm saying is true. If I could change this, you know I would." he was quiet, "I'm doing this for your protection. I don't want you to die- especially if I can prevent it. I'm sorry." Julia said this with genuine sorrow and remorse.

Carson never looked back as he said, "I would rather die than go on living without you."

"Carson, I...I'm so sorry. I'll say it a thousand times if you want me to." he still didn't look at her or say a word, "I'm so pathetic. You shouldn't even have to look at me." these words melted Carson's heart.

"Julia!" Carson cried out with watery eyes as she fled across the Ballroom and to the gardens. Both hearts were being torn away from each other and broken into a thousand pieces.

Julia ran and ran, never stopping to cry. Her tears flew behind her as she ran, trying to outrun her troubles but couldn't because of the weight of her heart and unsteady knees. In the garden, there was a fountain, so she fell to the ground before it and wept. Alek came up behind Julia, knelt, and embraced her. She held onto him as she wept even more.

"Why did I do that?"

"It had to be done."

"But I wish I didn't."

Cassidy looked to the balcony in which Carson stood in after Julia whipped past her. She walked up to him and saw that he was pained. His eyes were wet and clenched onto the gorgeous ring in a fist.

"Carson..."

"How could she?!" he slammed his fist onto the rail making his knuckles red and burn from the diamond.

"Julia didn't say yes? Why?" Cassidy asked truly taken aback.

"She said she couldn't because I would die."

Cassidy was silent for a moment, "You know she's only doing this for your own good." he looked away forcefully, yet she continued, "To me, it's the way she can show you how much she **really** loves you."

"Look, it may make sense to you, but it still doesn't to me."

"I know you're mad Carson, but you can't stay angry. You need to go to her. All right?" she asked putting a hand on his shoulder.

People started leaving the Ball and got into their carriages with the helping hands of their partners and short goodbyes of others. Looking past the canopy of leaves from the trees and other beautiful plants in the garden, Alek noticed Lori Linda, Mr. Doddsworth, and Mr. Clayton leaving. Then Jarvis came up to Lori Linda and hugged her.

Alek stopped embracing Julia and said, "I'll be back. I'm just going to go tell Jarvis that I'm going to stay here," he looked into her wet eyes and wiped a tear, "with you."

Julia nodded and Alek made his way to the entrance. She sat alone on the ground before the fountain. She had finally managed to stop crying from Alek's helpful embrace, but was still upset. It seemed as though she would never get a *Happily Ever After…*

"Julia? Are you all right?" asked Prince Nathan coming from the shadows.

She slowly stood, "I…I-" she turned away.

He paced up to her side, he hugged her as she put her hands on his chest, and asked, "You told Carson the truth. Didn't you?" he wiped more of her tears from her eyes.

Julia nodded. She held onto their embrace more. After a moment she looked at his shirt with her tears on it, "Oh, your shirt."

"It's fine."

"No…it's not. I'm probably ruining your evening. It's your birthday; you should get back to the festivities. I don't want to be a burden to you."

"Julia, I'll stay if you want me to. You're not a burden."

She shook her head, "Go back to the party. I'll come back eventually."

Prince Nathan looked at her sympathetically. He nodded while walking away very slowly. Julia stood there for several moments, now knowing Prince Nathan meant when he said that he would always be there- for her.

Julia went back to the fountain. She lay down on its cold, stone rim. Looking into the waters, she saw her reflection, and then to her surprise, Carson's was behind her.

She dared not to move or breathe as he said in a hurt, but firm voice, "I understand."

Carson set the beautiful ring before her eyes. She let out one silent tear that fell into the fountain's waters while he slowly and regretfully walked away. Julia didn't want him to leave though, so she stood up from the fountain and called in a weak voice, "Wait."

He turned around in his stance. His eyes were hurt and he tried to force a smile because he loved her. She was glad he at least understood why they couldn't marry and ran to him. They embraced each other for the last time, he put the ring on her index finger, and they kissed. "I'm sorry." were the last words she said to him before he left.

Alek came back and grabbed Julia's hand, "Everything is fine with Jarvis." he looked concerned at her red eyes and cheeks from crying, "You don't look so good. I think you should lie down."

He took her to a tree and they both lay beneath it. Alek tried to stay awake, yet fell asleep while Julia cried silent tears as she held onto Alek. Then, a twig snapped. She looked up to find Prince Nathan standing there before her.

"It's late. You two should stay the night." he helped her get up and called Alek's name, careful not to be too loud.

"I swear I didn't do it!" he mumbled loudly as he started gaining his consciousness.

Julia gave a small, almost forced, laugh, "Didn't do what, Alek?" she asked when he opened his eyes.

Alek blushed and yawned as they made their way inside Prince Nathan's castle. When they got inside, he showed Alek to his room and led Julia to the one next to his. They stopped at a rich brown, wooden door.

"This is your room. Alek is right next to you and I'm just down the hall if you need anything. All right?" he brushed her cheek.

"Thank you. I'll see you in the morning."

Prince Nathan nodded and left. Julia quickly went into the room without glancing around first. The only thing she seemed to notice was the huge, brown, red, and gold fabric for sheets on the bed. Julia sauntered over to it and sunk her face into one of the soft pillows, while hugging another. Ignoring everything else, she cried herself into a deep, heartbreaking slumber.

The next morning, Julia awoke to find only silence. She opened her eyes to see white curtains silently blowing away from the opened windows. She slowly sat up on the comfortable bed.

Looking around, it was a huge room. *Well, I am in a Prince's castle* she thought to herself. The floor was a rich brown wood, ivory walls, complementary gold antiques and decorations, tables with chairs, a fireplace, and a stack of books settled on a sofa. In the bathroom, there was another window, small white and gold tiles, a large bathtub, side door for the toilet, ivory colored marble counters with sinks, mirrors, and a door to the closet. The closet had many clothes, shoes, and a dresser at the end with boxes of jewelry, and golden carpet on the floor.

Julia went back into the bathroom and then got ready for the day. She chose a natural colored gown to wear. Trying not to think of the night before, she sank into the cushion of the sofa and put her head back. She looked at the stack of books, chose one, and started reading, ignoring the beautiful ring that was still on her finger. It would be a long day trying to forget…

Carson hadn't slept all night; he only lay inside his bed with his eyes closed. When he decided to wake up, he opened his eyes and pushed the hair out of his face with a hand. He slowly sat up in bed and hung his legs over on the side.

Carson looked into the nightstand and found the blade he had used to communicate with his siblings. He rushed into his bathroom and set the blade down on a counter before a mirror. Looking at himself, he took off the shirt part of his night-wear.

He took the sheath off of the blade and stared into the cold, shinny iron. Carson looked back into the mirror, held his breath, and closed his eyes. The blade was put diagonal to one side of his heart and pierced into his skin.

It sliced downward and cut his skin deeply. He gasped at the pain and sighed at the end of the first cut. He looked at the blade and saw his blood at the end of it. Carson closed his eyes once again and did the same as before, except on the other side of his fast beating heart. The second cut was even more painful to Carson and he cried as he gasped for air thinking that the cut made his heart skip a needy beat.

He opened his eyes to find his blood trickling down from the blade onto the counter and running down his bare chest. Carson cried from the pain, dropped the blade, washed the wound with the water spell, and placed a rag onto it to stop the bleeding. After a moment, he took the rag away to find an *X* for his wound where his heart was.

Carson put the sheath back onto the blade and into the nightstand after he had picked it up and swiped the blood from it. He went back to the mirror and was angry. Angry at himself, his family for leaving him, and Julia because he couldn't have her- even though it was saddening to think someone was to be had. Carson subsequently got ready for swimming to flush out the wound. He went from the gardens and dove into the lake when he came up to it.

Coming back up from the cold water, the sun was high up in the mid-day sky. He looked at his wound and saw that it was getting a little better from the cool waters. When he looked back up, he surprised to find that Princess Theodora was standing before him.

"Sorry. I didn't know you would be out here." she said turning away.

"You can stay."

Princess Theodora looked unsure, but calmly came into the water. She stayed by the edge and let Carson come over. Immediately, she noticed his wound and asked, "What happened?"

Carson looked away, "Nothing."

She shook her head in disappointment. Then, she placed a hand on his chest were the wound was and waited a moment. Ice appeared on it, and then melted away, leaving two light-pink scars.

Carson took her hand away, "I didn't want it to heal."

"Why? Why did you do that anyway?"

"I wanted to keep the memory of something that pained me, so I can never go back."

"What do you mean? Back to what?"

He looked deeply into her eyes, "I never want to fall in love again. It's happened twice now. Four years ago, this girl named Ashley, I knew she never loved me, but I loved her. She was a little like Julia, always needed all her questions answered and cared for everyone. Yet, she fell in love with another man, ignoring all the things I did to try to show her that I loved her." he paused for a long time and continued in a quiet, loving, and hurt voice, "Then Julia came. I don't think I need to go into that too much. Everyone knows that I loved her with all my heart. Last night when I proposed to her, she said no." Theodora was surprised by all this information that Carson had never told anyone else fully about, and he continued getting out of the water, "I never want to fall in love again. Every single time I do, it all falls apart. I can't bare it any longer! That's why I can never love you Theodora."

She stared at him blankly and was sad. She now knew that he could never love her and why he always seemed so distant, confused, and sometimes hurt. Theodora pitied him and now wished she could hide the feelings she had for him.

Carson saw the sadness in her eyes and said, "Sorry. I never should have said anything." and walked away as fast as he could through the corridors until he came to his room and shut the door fiercely behind him to get ready for the rest of the day.

Princess Theodora still stood at the edge of the water in momentary shock. Her head guard, Soren, then took off the invisibility spell and they stared at each other. She quickly ran to him and started crying.

"I can't believe this. I just can't." she stated through her tears.

Soren pat her head and wiped her tears when she looked up, "Do you love him that much?" she nodded and he sighed, "Very well." and he then left.

After Carson finished getting ready, he went down to the Dining Hall for a late lunch. He was not alone, for he found Soren in there with him. He sat down across from him with a glass of wine already there.

"Come to join me?" Soren asked.

"I guess. Soren, why aren't you with Princess Theodora right now?"

"I didn't feel like seeing her so upset."

Carson looked down, "Great, now I feel guilty."

"Oh, sorry." and he drank a sip of his wine.

Then Bade came in to give everyone their letters. Carson left Soren to sit and walked up to him. Bade and Carson started talking about Bade's wedding coming up soon and took no notice of Soren. Now that neither Carson nor Bade were paying no attention to Soren, he took out a tiny packet and dispersed it into Carson's wine. Little did anyone know that it was ***poison***.

Soren saw that when Bade was leaving, and Carson was on his way back to the table. He quickly put the empty packet away before Carson was in front of him again and said, "Well, I feel pretty guilty about making Theodora upset. I'll talk to her in a little bit." he gulped down the wine.

Grinning, Soren said, "All right. I'll see you later."

Carson then left feeling a little tired. He walked from the Dining Hall to his room a little off balance and hit his shoulder on the wall once. He put his hand to his head and felt sweat, found that his mouth was dry, and was light-headed because he couldn't see clearly. When he was in his room, he fainted and collapsed onto his bed.

During the day, Julia did not let anyone into her room. She only read the books that were left for her and slept. Once dinner came, she told them to leave it by her door and picked it up when they left. Night came and Julia got ready for bed and went to sleep. Alek and Prince Nathan left her alone because they were concerned and thought that she wanted to be unaccompanied.

A couple of hours later, Carson awoke. He stood from his bed and felt as though his strength had been replenished. Carson also felt the need to see Princess Theodora again.

He opened his door and walked down the hallway. On his way to the library, because that's where that he thought he'd find Theodora, he felt a significant surge of power that he never felt before. To him, it felt wonderful.

Carson came up to the library and noticed Princess Theodora sitting in a chair and reading. Looking at her, he suddenly had the feeling that he had when he saw Julia, and went up to her side. She looked up and felt a little awkward from the conversation they had had earlier, but he looked deeply into her eyes, brought up her chin, and kissed her.

What Carson hadn't noticed, was that Cassidy was also in the library at the moment. She gasped when he did this and waited in the shadows to talk to him afterward. *What is wrong with him?* she thought.

After Carson kissed Theodora, he said, "I'm sorry about earlier. I don't know what came over me." and he kissed her again.

"Apology accepted. Thank you." she was about to lean in to kiss him, but from the corner of his eye, he saw Cassidy trying to hide and stood up fixing himself.

"Sorry, I have to go." and he left.

Cassidy walked slowly passed Princess Theodora, trying to not get her suspicious. When she was out of the library, she ran after Carson. Then she saw him, "Carson!" he turned around to face her, "What was all *that* about?"

"What?"

"Why did you kiss Princess Theodora? What about Julia?"

He grabbed her wrists and crushed her back against a column, "Does it look like I care about Julia anymore?" Cassidy yelped from the pain he was causing her, "Never mention her name to me again!" he let go of her, walked away, and she collapsed to the floor below her. She was shocked by all of this. *How could this happen?* she thought.

Cassidy started crying. She had never seen Carson like this. She became scared and went to Christopher for help. Surprising, he was in the laboratory when she came in.

He noticed that she had been crying and embraced her asking, "What is wrong Cassidy?"

"It's Carson. Something's wrong with him. It's like he changed into another person. He kissed Princess Theodora, said he doesn't care for Julia, and hurt me." she showed him her red wrists.

He stared at her in disbelief. This wasn't Carson at all! He went to the cabinets and started looking for potions, "It sounds like he's been poisoned. I don't know with what, but," he showed her a round, red tablet, "this may help him."

"How do I use it?"

"At any cost, he has to swallow it. I would recommend Princess Theodora to kiss him to get it into him, but she probably won't do it."

"So what you're saying is…I have to…"

Christopher nodded. Cassidy left with the potion in hand to Carson's room. *This is the only way.* she thought to herself.

She knocked on the door and waited. Cassidy put the potion in her mouth without swallowing it and knocked on the door again. Her hands started to shake uncontrollably. After a moment, Carson's voice said, "Come in." she slowly turned the doorknob and opened the door.

Carson stood by the window and stared at Cassidy when she came in. She felt awkward doing this, because deep down, she knew that he still loved Julia. This poison that someone had given him was changing everything about Carson, and Cassidy couldn't stand it. Luckily, she was the only one who could have done what she was about to do.

"What do you want?" he asked crudely.

Cassidy slowly walked up to him, "I need to know why you're acting the way you are. This isn't you." she said with a hand movement that signified him, "What has come over you?"

Carson took a couple of steps toward Cassidy with his hair rimmed by the moon's light coming from the window, "Nothing has come over me except greater interests. I'm in love with Theodora. Why can't you accept that?" he placed his arms around her as he said, "But if *you* want my love…" he leaned in to kiss her.

Her heart beat burst out of control and had hoped Carson didn't notice and closed her eyes almost out of fear. Slowly, Cassidy kissed him, forcing the potion beyond his perfect lips, but he quickly backed away and took the potion from his mouth, "I knew it! Poison!" he almost went to hit her, yet something held him back from doing so.

"It's not poison! It can make you-" but he shoved her fiercely against the floor, holding the potion in one hand.

"Why?! I have more power now, and it feels great. Why are you trying to take that from me?" he picked her up as shot light into her body and she gasped in pain as she fell to the floor again.

"What is wrong with you? This isn't anything like you!"

"You're right. It was time for a change. This is what I've always wanted to be. This is who I **really** am." he picked her up, brought her out of the room, and pushed her back to the wall again while putting more light into her.

Cassidy was in immense pain; physically and her heart was breaking from what was going on with Carson, "Just take the potion. It'll make you better." she said through tears, cupped her hand on his that held the potion, and fainted in his arms.

"I am better."

Carson paced throughout the corridors and hallways to Cassidy's room. He placed her on her bed and sat on a chair staring at her. He couldn't believe what he had done, because the old Carson was starting to come out, little by little.

Quickly leaving, Carson thought he could still obtain his new surge of power if he left. In the hallway next to his room, he stared at the little red tablet. Thinking, the old Carson made him take the potion automatically at the thought that it would make him better. He traveled through the hallway in a sort of daze.

When Carson was in his room, he felt drainage of power. He yelped in pain that was coming all throughout him. *What did Cassidy do?* He thought while he held his head in pain.

In fact, the potion hurt him so much, that his nails were longer; tearing at his skin and clothes, his eyes turned from pacific blue to red, and his light became eerie and unnatural. He was being changed to something worse than before. He screamed for Cassidy and Julia. If only Christopher had known the potion would've make him worse…

———

The next morning, Julia woke up again to find Alek in her room. He smiled, but his eyes looked concerned for her. Julia forced a small, weak smile.

"You don't have to force yourself." he said kindly.

"I'm not." she said lying through her teeth.

Alek shook his head while giving her his hand, "Get dressed. I'm dying to see the rest of this royal castle."

Julia got up, made Alek leave to get ready, got ready, and walked outside of her room. They gazed around the Entry Hall, Ballroom, Dining Hall (which they had a quick breakfast together in), and the rest of the castle. Soon, they found the library; it had bookshelves all the way to the ceiling and around the room, a rounded lounge at the end that was surrounded by tall windows, chairs, couches, tables, stairs, sliding ladders, and a round ceiling that was a painting of a Phoenix in the clouds breathing fire with its wings stretched out.

Alek tried to make Julia have a good time by sliding the ladder while she was on it, reading funny books with her as he animated with different voices, and skipping, almost falling down, as he told her jokes on the stairs. Julia was happy that her dear friend was trying to make her feel better. Prince Nathan surprised them as he rounded the corner of the library.

"Would you care to walk with me in the gardens?" he asked Julia.

She looked at Alek, who nodded, "Sure." she replied.

Prince Nathan and Julia left the massive library. They paced from the library, to the Entry Hall, and finally to the courtyard. It spread out into gardens, then a tall maze, and finally the Royal Garden with many trees, flowers, and stone statues and fountains set up in a labyrinth style. There were even waterfalls, river walks (but not actual rivers), and ponds with colorful fish inside them. Alek watched them without being seen.

Passing white, yellow, and red roses, Prince Nathan talked of his childhood with Julia. She smiled at his stories. Some of them reminded Julia of her own. When they came to some fruit trees, Prince Nathan picked the luscious fruit carefully and handed it to Julia. They walked around eating them for their lunch with satisfaction.

A small child, who looked about the age of eight, came in a little white gown with light brown hair under a thin, silver crown. She stretched her arms to him. Nathan picked her up with a wide grin on his face, "This is my youngest sister, Samantha."

"She's precious."

"I have two other siblings. Philip is twenty-two and visiting the Eckhart Kingdom. The other is-" but he was cut-off because an eighteen-year-old with blonde hair under another thin, silver crown came rushing through the leaves calling Samantha, but he said, "This is Paiton."

"Sorry brother. Samantha ran off when the guards came. They said a bandit has come, but it's not their leader Killian. No one recognizes him!"

"What?!" he asked astonished, "Get back inside the castle and I'll see who it is." he handed Samantha to Paiton and they rushed back in, passed the shocked, still unnoticed Alek.

"A bandit?" Julia asked terrified remembering the bandits she had first encountered when she first arrived in Renata.

"They're not supposed to be here. We gave them the land that they wanted. What could they want now?" he asked turning towards the castle and then back at Julia, "You need to go. Far away from here."

"Why?!"

"I don't know what they're here for, but if it involves you, I want to keep you from harm's way." he said putting her back gently against the trunk of a beautiful tree and his hands on her shoulders.

"But-" Julia kept her eyes open in alarm at the fact that Nathan was kissing her.

"I've tried to hide my feelings as best as I can, but...I can't any longer. I love you. If anything happens, go find Alek and leave as fast as you can." and she let him kiss her again, wrapping her arms around him.

As they kissed an *almost* familiar voice was heard, except that it was layered in cold, hard, rustic, mocking, and evil tones, "This is why you couldn't marry me?"

Julia gasped and both she and Prince Nathan looked up. Alek came from hiding in the shadows. Carson was standing on the wall with a black cloak on. He jumped down and took off his hood to reveal scars, darkened hair, and his beautiful blue eyes that had changed into an evil blood-red tint.

"What happened to you?" she asked practically crying as she stood well behind Prince Nathan.

"This is why you couldn't marry me?!" he repeated shouting and pointing his finger at Nathan and Julia.

"Carson, what is wrong with you?" Alek asked reading everyone's thoughts.

Carson shouted while pulling out his sword, "Nothing is wrong with me! The question is, what's wrong with her?!" he pointed his sword threateningly at Julia.

Alek and Prince Nathan pulled out their swords. Since Alek was Julia's protector, he pulled her next to his side as he held his sword outward. Prince Nathan was confused; *Doesn't Carson love Julia? What happened to him? It's as though he's changed entirely.* he thought, but held his sword high saying, "If you touch Julia-"

"Oh how sentimental." he laughed, "You'll do what? Kill me?!"

Carson swung his sword, but Prince Nathan blocked it from hurting her.

The guards were heard from the other side of the wall, "What was that? Was that the bandit? Last time I saw him, he was heading for the Royal Garden."

Another guard's voice was heard, "Then we have to hurry! Prince Nathan and Julia went in there!"

Carson thrust his sword out and shot light into Nathan. It wasn't his normal light though; this light was an eerie yellow rimmed with orange, unlike his old light which was white and rimmed with blue. Prince Nathan stumbled back from Carson's painful light. As Nathan was distracted, Carson used his light to make a barrier when the guards were about to round the corner into the Royal Garden.

Julia couldn't stand the sight of the three of them fighting. Carson was combating because he couldn't help it from the poison, Nathan loved Julia, and Alek was Julia's protector and he loved her. Alek then tried to fight Carson off for a short while as neither showed any mercy. She couldn't stand another moment of the battle between them all.

As Carson propelled his sword at Nathan, he stopped because then Julia stepped in front of him shouting, "Stop this Carson!" yet he swung his sword at her, but Alek took the blow and stumbled back holding onto a deep cut in his arm.

Julia cried and helped lean him against a tree as Prince Nathan and Carson fought. She lifted his hand from the wound and saw the horrible, bloody gash. Crying more, she lifted her wrist and snatched her piece of Ceylon that she wore. She blew on it and gently placed it by the wound. It started healing and Alek said while pushing her hair from her face and wiping her tears from her pained eyes, "Thank you Julia."

Carson and Nathan met swords. Muscles giving in, Carson kicked Nathan in the stomach. He fell to the ground as Carson took advantage of the moment by jumping into his fall, sword first. Julia screamed when Nathan tried to get up. Carson had gotten distracted by her scream, and didn't notice Nathan's blade forcing into his chest, near his ever so needed heart.

Time seemed to stop as Carson fell to the ground with the sword inside of him and Julia screamed again. Everyone gasped and Julia ran to Carson's side. He first pushed her away from helping him, but the old Carson was coming back because the wound was deteriorating his new, evil power.

Julia cried as she pulled the sword from his body. He yelped in pain and they ripped his shirt to get a better look at the lesion. It was indeed a mess. She took her piece of Ceylon and did the same as she did with Alek. After a moment, they realized that nothing was happening; the wound wasn't healing.

"Why isn't it healing?!" she asked shouting through tears.

"I don't know." replied Prince Nathan dumbfounded.

Julia turned back to Carson, who was having trouble keeping his eyes open, and put her hands on either side of his head crying, "Carson stay with me. Don't leave me." whispering, she said, "I love you." and she kissed him.

Julia's kiss made Carson's hair turn back into his gorgeous golden-brown color, his eyes turn from red to his beautiful pacific blue, and the barrier turn back into its normal color. The old Carson was back! The barrier went back down and the guards were shown.

Even though the old Carson was back, his injury did not heal. Prince Nathan ripped his sleeve and pressed it to the wound to try and stop the enormous amount of bleeding. Carson was having a lot of trouble keeping his eyes open.

"Carson, look at me. Look at me!" shouted Julia repeatedly.

"It...won't heal." he managed to whisper through his cries of pain.

"It will Carson. Just wait and see. Stay with me!" but he closed his eyes much too soon.

Then, Bade and Cassidy rushed into the Royal Garden. They ran to Carson's side and Cassidy took his pulse. Surprisingly, he was still alive. Standing up, she said, "Alek and Prince Nathan hold onto Carson."

Bade grabbed Julia when Cassidy stepped back from everyone. She surrounded herself with fire, and upright walking Phoenix stepped from the orange flames. It was beautiful; it had Cassidy's red colored hair for the color of its feathers, elongated, scaly legs, a short, yellow beak, and larger feathers flowing in the wind like large and thick red ribbons and large pieces of fabric. The Phoenix sang a short melody aloud. Holding onto each other, Prince Nathan, Alek, and Carson changed into a multi-colored star form that was lifted and then sparkled all over

Cassidy's feathers. Then, stepping about another foot away from Bade, it shot into the sky.

Looking at the far distance between them on the ground, Julia turned back to Bade who said, "Hold onto me."

Julia wrapped her arms around Bade's neck. He spread his black, hawk-like feathered wings as far as they could extend and jumped into the dark, cloudy sky. Julia closed her eyes, and when she opened them, she saw that she was flying and was scared. She was scared for Carson.

Chapter 27

AT SIXES AND SEVENS

The Tabor's Castle was seen in the distance. Bade maneuvered his way downward and flew through an open window. Julia was then set on the wooden floor of the Infirmary.

Julia let go of Bade and watched as he walked over to the window. He waited a moment until the Phoenix was in front of him. Bade reached into the multi-colored lights that were dusted from Cassidy's feathers. A hand came, and it was Carson's with a loose grip. Bade pulled the hand outward in a tight grip and Carson was pulled from the cloud of multi-colored lights.

Helping Carson onto a bed, Alek and Prince Nathan jumped from the lights. They came up to the bedside next to the crying Julia. The Phoenix came through the window and surrounded itself with fire.

Cassidy walked through the fiery orange flames and quickly came up to Carson. She removed Carson's hand from his wound and felt his head, eyes still closed and shut tightly. Cassidy then placed her hand over his bloody wound and closed her eyes. After a moment, her tears fell from her dark, sparkly lashes and onto his torn skin. First, the wound healed itself and faded away, then the scars he inflicted on himself, with the exception of the *X* on his heart, and the blood that had stained his clothes and that had traveled with him. Cassidy lifted her hand from his wound and watched as his blood disappeared.

Carson slowly opened his eyes. Julia wept tears of joy and everyone smiled with their eyes and lips. Then, the doors to the Infirmary thrust open and Jarvis, Mr. Doddsworth, Mr. Clayton, Lori Linda, Veronica, and Christopher rushed in. They all came and stood beside Carson's bed and smiled as they noticed he was fine.

Cassidy explained what had happened to Carson to the others. They all spread themselves about the room; Alek leaned his back onto a wall in the corner, Julia stayed by Carson's side, Prince Nathan and Jarvis sat beside the window, Cassidy, Bade, and Veronica sat on the bed beside Carson, Christopher paced with Mr. Doddsworth, and Mr. Clayton and Lori Linda sat on the other bed next to Carson. All were shocked and asked many questions. Some answers made no sense.

"So do you have any idea of who did this to you?" Mr. Doddsworth asked to Carson even though he didn't remember much.

"I have one theory. And that is that it was Soren."

"He and Theodora left early this morning. Why do you think it was him?"

"After I talked to Bade in the Dining Hall, I drank a glass of wine that Soren had seemed to have left for me or maybe someone else. Soon after, I fainted and everything seemed to be disconnected and a new..." he hesitated, "power of some kind came over me. I had no idea what to do. Theodora was suddenly the only thing that I seemed to think about." he looked to Julia with sad eyes, "I'm sorry."

Julia placed her hand into his by his side, "It's fine. At least you're back."

Carson gently grabbed and placed her hand on his heart where the faded scar was. Then he kissed her other hand. Alek and Prince Nathan looked away with a gilded pain on their hearts. Julia lifted her hand from his heart and traced the lines with her index finger, "What happened here? Why didn't it fade with all the other scars?" Prince Nathan and Alek looked back curious.

He ruffled his fingers through his golden hair, "Because I inflicted it on myself before I was poisoned. And then Theodora healed it."

"Why would you do that?" she asked hurt.

"I couldn't stand living without you. All I wanted was you." Julia blushed but was still confused and sad, "It's obvious that I really can't live without you. So please," Carson looked deeply into her eyes with

173

a pleading, desperate look while he brushed her cheek, "please marry me."

Alek and Prince Nathan were desperate to hear Julia's reply. The others anticipated her answer as well. Julia didn't know what to do or say and all of her thoughts confused her.

What am I to say? If I say yes, mother says that Carson will die. If I say no, Carson won't die and I'll…I'll…I don't know. And what of Alek and Prince Nathan? They both love me and…and nothing. This decision is too hard for me to make.

"Carson, I…don't know what to say."

"Then say nothing. Nothing now, at least. Just stay here with me for the night Julia. You can tell me your true answer tomorrow."

"All right. Thank you." and she caressed her lips against his perfect, pink lips again.

Once she saw Alek and Prince Nathan turn their heads away from Julia's hurtful kiss, Cassidy left the Infirmary. She left everyone confused as they stared at her leaving and Carson looked to Julia. She helped him get up and he followed her. In the hallway, he called after her and she turned around watery-eyed.

"Cassidy, what's wrong?" he asked her.

"You should go back to Julia and get the rest that you need." and she started to walk away, only to find Carson's hand holding and gently pulling her own.

"What did I do when I was poisoned? I barely remember anything."

Cassidy's eyes swelled with tears becoming red, "What you did… you should be glad that you don't remember well."

"What happened?"

"You fell in love with Theodora, betraying Julia, didn't want anything to do with her, hurt Alek, tried to kill Prince Nathan, and you…you hurt…me. Physically and mentally." her tears fell to her cheeks.

"I…I-" he struggled to find the words he needed to say while he was in a slight stage of shock, "You…I never meant- Cassidy, I'm so sorry. I never- ever wanted to hurt you."

"I know that. That's why it hurts so much, because it was you, though almost forced to. At one point, I vaguely remember you saying that this change made you better…but it made you worse. So much more than anything that you had ever done. It was like you changed into another person, completely ignoring the others you used to care about." she was silent for a few moments and whispered, "And you kissed me." she felt her lips while looking down and then back at him almost yelling, "Then you hurt me again!" she wept as she forced her face into Carson and he embraced her.

Carson let Cassidy cry all of her tears into his shirt. Once her weeping became silent, he held her head as he did when his sisters used to cry in his arms. At least he wasn't hurting Cassidy, but rather helping her feel at ease from his behavior.

<hr />

"Let's walk home." Carson said to his brother Lane and sisters Rebecca and Gamelle starting to walk away from their parent's burial site on top of a hill.

Leaving, Carson went over their names in his mind over and over again. *Owen and Matilda Tabor. Owen and Matilda Tabor.*

As they silently walked through the flowered fields in the valley, the seven-year-old twins, Rebecca and Gamelle, walked to the young, eighteen-year-old Carson's side and tugged the bottom of his shirt. Seeing their sad faces, Carson put Gamelle on one shoulder and then reached for Rebecca. She shook her head and just held his hand.

"There not coming back, are they?" Rebecca asked in a voice that strummed Carson's heart strings painfully.

"No. I'm afraid they're not." he said fighting back his tears.

Gamelle cried into his muscular neck and Rebecca swiped a tear away that had seemed to have traveled down her cheek. Carson stopped, put Gamelle on the ground, and bent lower. His sisters forced their small figures into his and wept as he embraced them and held their heads. The ten-year-old Lane also came over and crawled into Carson's arms; weeping as a family.

"I'm going to miss mommy and daddy." Gamelle gasped through tears rubbing her eyes forcefully.

"We will too." stated Lane coming out of the bunch.

They all laid their backs onto the fields, coving their figures with colorful flowers and watched the clouds passed as they cried silent tears. It was such a beautiful day in its tranquility, for such a sorrowful time for the Tabor family. Time stood still, transfixed in one emotion. Lane reached into his belt and pulled out four blue, violet, red, and purple colored boxes with silver locks and their individual initials on them. He handed them out with a sorrowful expression.

"Mom and dad left these in my room for safe keeping. They said if anything happened to them, I would give these to each of us. Now's the time to do that." he also pulled out four silver keys and gave them to his siblings, "Open it with this."

All four emotionally drawn siblings did as they held their breath. The boxes had a letter in each with their name on it and a small, brown sack that was held together by a gold ribbon. They took the letters out first and opened them. Carson's letter:

Dear Carson,

Your mother and I know what you must be feeling. Despair, anger, and sadness. But do not put these feelings in place of us. We love you and will always look after you, even if you can't see us. Take care of the Tabor's castle in our place. Your inheritance is in the lake and the spell is written where it is. If you remember, the spell is our secret phrase. We have some favors to ask of you: most of all look after your sisters and brother and, since it was in our agreement with you and Theodora's parents, you must marry Princess Theodora. As you know, that has already been arranged. There are spare keys to the Tabor's castle, your father's badge, and your great grandmother's wedding ring in the box. The best of luck to you! We love you.

Sincerely,

Your Mother and Father

Owen and Matilda Tabor

Carson wiped the tears from his eyes and pulled out the gifts. The keys were many and were held together by two pieces of leather sewn together by gold thread. His father's badge was beautiful with a golden eagle in the center of a ruby in a 14-karret gold frame. Finally, his great grandmother's ring was a silver band incrusted all with both tiny and large diamonds. Little did he know that he would soon give it to the love of his life, Julia…

He looked over to Lane and saw him reading his letter over and over again, trying to find its meaning because their parents always challenged him because he wanted to become a scholar and find hidden riddles or secrets. He also had a beautiful quill and ink set and their mother's old key of different languages resting by his side. Lane was just like his brother Carson. In looks, powers, and interests. Carson always called him his little clone.

Looking over to Gamelle, he found her staring into a glass sphere. To Carson it looked like nothing, but to Gamelle, it showed different colors of smoke as it told her favorite story that only she could see and hear. It was one of the most precious things anyone had given her because she loved to listen to different stories because she wanted to be an actress.

Carson finally looked over to Rebecca. She held a tiny book in her hands, and after she said a certain spell, the book grew large. He thought this was an exceptional gift to his sister because she wanted to be a writer. His parents were marvelous at giving the right gifts. It made him miss them even more. But instead, he would only carry-on good memories of them instead of sorrow...

Carson loosened his embrace as he thought back to his family and said, "I...had no idea. Like I said before, I'm sorry. If you want, I'll say it as many times as you need me to. Never let me become poisoned-ever again. It brings the worst out of me."

Cassidy lifted her head and nodded, "I'll make sure of that."

Carson hugged her once more, and after a minute he asked, "Do you want to go back to the Infirmary with me, or should I just walk you to your room?"

"I'm a little tired, so you can just walk with me to my room." and so they did.

After Carson and Cassidy left the Infirmary, Julia stepped out onto a balcony with Alek. She held onto the rail and looked out into the afternoon sky. Earlier, the sky had seemed a little darker than it was at that silent moment; as though it had changed too.

In her deep thought of what she was going to say to Carson the next day, Alek asked Julia, "So...are you going to marry him?"

"I really don't know Alek." she said turning around to face him, but he had a look of shock in his eyes.

"I can tell you why you *shouldn't* marry Carson, Jules." said a lost, but oddly familiar voice.

Julia spun around quickly from the nickname only her father called her. She gasped at what she saw, because she thought she would never see this person: her loving father. He was really there too, like her mother, in Renata.

"What? B-but-" Julia stuttered because she was bewildered.

"Julia, who is this?" Alek asked.

"My...my father." after a moment of being stunned by his loving smile, she asked, "What are you here for dad?"

"The same reason your mother came to you." he studied her, "You look a bit more mature than I last saw you." Julia laughed and he hugged his daughter thoughtfully. She was very happy to see her father again; maybe for the last time.

Julia let go of his hug and gestured towards Alek, "This is Alek. He's my protector here in Renata." she was trying desperately hard to try and change the sad subject because she knew what was coming next.

Alek brought his hand out to shake her father's. Even though he could barely see him, Julia's father's touch was warm as if he were alive. But, he was not and a sort of version of *Mister Cellophane* because you could look right through or walk right by him and never knew he was there unless you knew his voice to direct you to his transparent, faded figure.

"It's a pleasure to meet you, sir." said Alek with a smile.

Julia smiled when her father did saying, "Good to meet you too Alek. Thank you for protecting my Jules. I'm happy to see that she's in good hands no matter where she is in Renata." he looked to Julia when he said *no matter where*.

"Dad-"

"Sorry, but we need to continue with that subject. You can't love Carson. The first vision you had, already came true." Julia thought back to the vision he was referring to and gasped at his accuracy and new information; now she definitely knew that she couldn't love Carson. "Now, listen to me because I'm only going to say this once." she nodded and looked down, "They say when someone you love dies, a part of you dies with them. As your father, I don't want you to die of a broken heart. If it's too tempting to fall in love with him by staying here, then leave."

"Fine."

"Well, I have to leave now." he looked to Alek and gave a nod, "It was a pleasure." Julia's father turned back to her and embraced her, "Goodbye darling." and he faded in the afternoon light.

After a long, awkward pause, Alek commented saying, "At least he was nice about what he had to tell you."

"Nice." Julia said without enthusiasm and turned to go back inside the Infirmary.

Mr. Clayton quickly came up to her before she could go through, "Sorry, but I couldn't help over-hearing you and your father's conversation." he paused, "He's right, you know. You can't stay here. You'll just fall in love with Carson even more. None of us want you to leave, but it seems that you may have to."

"But where can I go?"

"I'm leaving for the Kalama Kingdom soon-" Alek started to say, but was cut-off by Julia.

"Why?! I thought you said that you would stay with me. You're my protector!"

"Well, I'll just be going to my house for a little while. Then, I'm going to the Kalama Kingdom to become a Songbird. It's what I've always wanted. I told you that Julia." Alek said starting off strong and then trailed off at the last sentence.

"Alek..." Julia said as though she was losing her dear friend.

Mr. Clayton cut-in, "Stay with Alek for the time being, and when he leaves, we'll think of something."

She looked to Alek with sad eyes, "Sounds like I wouldn't have much of another choice."

"Or you could ask to stay with Prince Nathan." he said hurt because he had seen Nathan kiss her-twice-and wanted to kick himself for even bringing that option into the conversation.

"I wouldn't want to be a burden to him."

"Then the only choice left, would be for you to go back to your own world." Mr. Clayton said heavily.

"I don't want to leave Renata. Besides, the diary was the only way back. And Peter has it." Julia said in an as-a-mater-of-fact tone and all too casually.

"Then it's settled. You'll stay with me." said Alek with a smile and a wink.

"What time are we leaving tomorrow?"

"I'll give you enough time to get ready and say goodbye to Carson."

"How?"

He pointed to his head, "In your dreams."

"That's really comforting." she said sarcastically but looked to Mr. Clayton with a pleading look for a moment, "When I'm gone, please take care of Carson."

He nodded, "Of course Julia. Of course I will."

Julia, Alek, and Mr. Clayton paced back into the Infirmary. In the same groups, they talked amongst themselves. Julia noticed Prince Nathan sitting by the window alone and walked up to him quietly.

"Prince Nathan?" she asked unsure.

He turned to face her smiling, "I take it that you need somewhere to stay-"

"No." she interrupted him, but careful not to sound anything close to mean, "That's already been taken care of."

Prince Nathan stood, "Then how can I be of service to you?" he straitened his shirt and she noticed his ripped sleeve on his right arm.

She took his right hand and held it. There were many cuts and scratches left on his hand from his fight with Carson. Julia was very grateful of how persistent he was to keep her safe. She also thought of his kiss.

"I'm sorry." she said.

"For what?"

Julia looked deeply into his chocolate-brown eyes, "You were so... determined to protect me because you say you love me. We kissed and now...with Carson the way he was and where I am...I'm just sorry."

He quickly embraced her, ignoring the others who were too preoccupied in conversation, "You don't always have to say sorry for the things that aren't your fault."

"But it is."

"It is not." she looked up, "Believe me, it's not your fault."

Awkwardly, she replied, "Thank you." and let go of his kind embrace.

To their surprise, Carson was waiting by the door and staring at them. After a moment, Carson went back out the door to leave. Without a second thought, Julia followed him.

In the cave of Ceylon, she found him going up the lighted stairway and called, "Carson, wait."

He stopped and waited for Julia to get to him, "Can we take a walk for a while?"

Julia nodded. They walked out of the library in silence. However, in the hallway, she was the first to speak.

"Carson, what you saw in there…it meant nothing to me."

"Nothing? Right, and I suppose those kisses he gave you meant nothing also." he said sarcastically.

Julia stared directly into his intense blue eyes, "I swear I never meant for that to happen. Please don't be angry."

"Well, believe it or not, I'm not angry. I'm just…upset, afraid, confused, or whatever you want to call it. I only have those feelings because I'm pretty sure of your answer that you'll give me tomorrow." he saw her about to say something, but quickly hushed her, "But don't give me your answer now." he placed a piece of her hair behind her ear, staring at her lips, held her in his arms, and ended the quiet moment with a kiss.

"I'll wait for tomorrow, but until then can we do something fun?"she chuckled as she made the last steps of the way down the hall to her room.

He smiled, and after a moment he asked by the door to her room, "Do you want to go swimming?"

"Sure." she opened the door, "I'll meet you out there."

Carson nodded as Julia stepped inside her room, closing the door behind her. She quickly went to her closet and chose a green bathing gown to wear. Dressing herself, she noticed that the fabric glittered as the same color of her eyes.

After she put it fully on, she pet the smiling and hyper Annabelle and headed down to the lake. Julia found that Carson was already in and popped out of the water when she came. He stretched his arm out, giving her his shimmering hand, and helped her in.

They enjoyed swimming together very much. The temperature of the water felt cool to the mid-day spring heat. When it was time for dinner, they came out and went to their own rooms to get ready for their meal.

In the Dining Hall, everyone except Cassidy was there. Everyone smiled as they ate their different meals that Cassidy hadn't prepared with the healthy food they needed. In fact, when Cassidy finally showed up, she gasped at this sight. Immediately, she went to Bade and gawked down at his all-protein meal (no veggies!). Her cheeks immediately turned red.

"How many helpings of meat is that?!"

"A lot." he said chewing while looking up at her blushing.

Cassidy took his hand and playfully smacked it, "Shame on you." she looked to everyone, "Anyone else?" when everyone shook their heads, she said, "You all should have waited. None of you can be healthy without me!" she said raising her chin proudly.

Everyone laughed as Cassidy sat down. Julia looked to Carson while laughing with a questioning look. "I told you. She wants all of us to be healthy." he prolonged the word all.

At the end of their meal, Prince Nathan said his goodbyes to everyone, especially Julia. In the hallway, Julia and Carson were walking together and Alek whistled. She looked back and saw Alek pointing to his head and mouthing the words *Remember, in your dreams*.

Julia smiled. Of course Alek was going to remind her. How could she forget? But a wave of sadness came when Carson held her hand as they began to walk.

Carson smiled to her, pretending like nothing was wrong, when indeed there was. Julia only smiled back because his was contagious. They walked throughout the hallways aimlessly, until Annabelle was spotted ahead of them.

"What? What are you doing out here?" Julia asked petting her spontaneous wolf.

"She was probably tired of being cooped-up in that room all the time." Carson looked into Annabelle's amber eyes, "Maybe she'll enjoy a walk with us in the garden."

"All right." she smiled and led the way with Annabelle to the garden.

As Julia and Carson walked around the garden hand in hand, Annabelle caught sight of a toad by a small pond. Annabelle stood guard in front of it and stared at it. When it croaked, Annabelle jumped and barked at it. Frightened, the toad hopped about the rest of the garden with Annabelle, equally as jumpy, running after it.

Julia giggled and Carson chuckled. They came up to the tree house and stared at it. Her stomach fluttering, they looked to each other grinning, and grabbed the ladder to get inside.

They climbed the ladder being vigilant with every step. Once inside, they sat holding each other's hands and Julia leaned against his warm chest, hearing his steady heartbeat. Thinking contently, they watched the beautiful sunset together.

The sunset settled in the late horizon and was striking. It was as though someone had painted a picture with nectarine colored water colors. Yet, the top was a wet royal blue with glittery white stars. Sure enough, a kiss was shared afterward.

"I love you." he whispered sweetly.

"I love you too."

Carson kissed her hand and then noticed the watch she wore, "Would you like to talk to Peter?"

"Sure."

He cast the communications spell and Peter's face flickered onto the face of the watch, "Hey Julia. Hi Carson. What's going on?"

"Just checking up on you. How are you doing?" asked Julia.

"Good. My birthday is tomorrow."

"Well, happy birthday." said Carson and Julia simultaneously.

"Thanks."

"Anything else?" she asked.

"My mom. She…after what happened…she wants me to start going to counseling in a couple of days."

"Oh."

"I guess she just doesn't want to believe the truth."

"I'm sorry Peter."

"It's ok. I'm glad I came back when I did. Things could have been a lot worse. Thank you Julia for sending me home when you did."

"You're…you're welcome."

Carson smiled with his eyes glittering and Peter continued,

"Well, I'm going to bed. If I get the chance, I'll come to see you both. Goodnight."

"Sweet dreams Peter." said Julia.

"Goodnight Peter." Carson said in a brotherly voice.

"Goodnight you two." and his young image disappeared.

"Thank you." Julia said kindly looking up at Carson.

"The least I can do." and she giggled.

"Hello?! Anyone up there?" a woman's voice called.

Carson looked down. A familiar woman stood beneath the tree house. Julia went down with Carson and found that it was Amorita waiting for them.

"Hello Amorita. Were you looking for me?" asked Carson.

"In fact I was. I have a letter for you." she handed it to him with a slight smile.

"Thank you." he said taking it gently.

"You're welcome."

Amorita changed from her regular, heroine form into her rabbit body. Her funny, white, and furry rabbit self scurried across the garden with her pink nose smelling everything. The last thing they saw was her fluffy, white tail through the bushes.

Carson stared at the seal on the envelope. The blue and silver coloring on the bluebird indicated that it was a message from the Pierre Kingdom. He started to walk as he opened it up to the letter. His eyes trailed to the bottom to find it saying: *Love, Theodora*. Then Carson folded the letter back in its place in the envelope and then in his hand by his side as they walked together.

"Aren't you going to read it?" asked Julia.

"Later. First, let's find Annabelle."

She nodded and they began searching. At the end of the garden, they found her. Annabelle was trapped by a thick ring of frogs surrounding her. She wined and Carson and Julia couldn't help but laugh. They got Annabelle out and finally brought her to the safety of Julia's room.

They walked hand in hand to Carson's room. When she stepped inside, Julia realized that it looked exactly like her room except it had gold lining. She stepped over to the window as Carson read his letter. Julia gazed at the silver and white twinkling stars in the Paris Blue colored sky.

"Princess Theodora is coming tomorrow. She wants to talk. That's all that she said," Carson said when he had finished reading. Julia nodded and Carson embraced her from behind as he handed her the letter, "You can read it. I'm going to go get ready for bed. All right?"

She took the letter and smiled, "Sure." and then she read it.

Dear Carson,

*I am so sorry for what happened. I would like to talk to you about what happened though, because I'm still not entirely sure what **did** happen. Tomorrow at noon, I shall be waiting for you by the entrance of the Tabor's Castle. We can talk then.*

Love,

Theodora

Princess Theodora of the Pierre Kingdom

Julia folded the letter up and crossed her arms over her chest as she stared out the window. She was thinking of how Alek was going to be in her dreams tomorrow morning. Hopefully he wouldn't try to scare her again.

She stood gazing out the window until Carson was done. He kissed her cheek as he told her and then took the stance in the window himself. She took one look at him before she went to get ready for bed.

When Julia was done, she found Carson half asleep in his bed already. As she kissed him goodnight and turned to leave, he held her hand saying, "Stay here."

She sat on the bed. Then he took her in his arms and embraced her. Julia fell asleep in his Carson's embrace that evening as if to keep herself from leaving.

Early in the morning, Julia found herself still in Carson's embrace. She also noticed that it was sunrise and how his hair glowed in the light and lightly kissed him on his cheek. Alek had not woke her up yet, so she decided it was too early and closed her eyes once more.

Julia dreamed of different ways she could say goodbye to Carson when she woke up. She saw herself writing in her room. Soon, Alek came through the door in her dream saying, "Julia, it's time."

She woke up to find that Carson was gone. The sun was brightly shinning through the window and hurt her eyes as she stared at it. Julia quickly got out of bed and then to her room.

Julia saw Annabelle, pet her, and got ready for the day. After, she started packing silently and Alek came in with a sincere smile on his face. She forced a smile herself and packed a picture as her last item.

"Those are your things?" Alek asked looking at the bag that was in front of her on her bed.

She nodded holding the picture and Alek picked the large, heavy bag up in one sweep into his arms, "Go say goodbye to Carson and meet me down at the entrance."

"I was thinking that I should write a letter for him."

"Whatever you think is best." and he left with Annabelle following.

Julia picked up some paper she left out and her pen and started writing her letter to her beloved Carson.

Dear Carson,

*Goodbye my love. I'm leaving with Alek, but I promise that I will never forget you. I'll write to you whenever I get the chance. I love you. My only wish is for you to be happy. **Peace, hope**, and **love** make life. I'm doing this just for you- to protect you. Again, I love you. Never forget that.*

Love,

Julia

Julia Myers

She folded the paper and slipped out of her room. Julia paced through the hallways and corridors in a hurry to say goodbye to Carson. When she came up to the door, she knocked slowly as she held her breath.

Carson's hurt voice called saying, "Come in."

Julia shuffled through the door and saw Carson on his balcony, clutching onto the rail. She stepped forward quietly as Carson looked over his shoulder. He quickly ran to her and held her close.

"I...I thought you had already left." his voice began strumming Julia's heart strings as though a harp and saddening her more than ever before.

Julia paused. She didn't want to leave him, not in any way whatsoever, but thought it was best, "*Never* without a goodbye."

Carson sighed heavily, "You really are going?" she nodded.

Looking down, she added, "I...I just wish..." she stopped and looked up at his wet eyes, "just read this." she handed her letter to him saying, "I can't seem to think of any word other than sorry. But I truly am."

Julia stepped away from Carson as he took the letter. But soon, he came up behind her, turned her around, and kissed her. She held onto his loving embrace once again and was miserable. She let tears fall onto her cheeks as she reached for her engagement ring.

Once Carson saw her trying to take off the ring, he clasped his hands over hers saying, "I gave that to you for proof that I will always love you. Keep it." he placed the ring back on her polished finger.

She kissed his cheek saying goodbye. He kissed her forehead and stole a light kiss from her lips before she left hastily. When Julia stepped in the hallway, she slumped to the floor below her by Carson's door and cried into her hands.

Then, Julia felt like she was being lifted. She slowly opened her eyes to find Alek carrying her to the entrance in his strong arms he and Carson always seemed to carry her in. He helped her in the carriage, with Annabelle patiently waiting and fell asleep in his arms. Being on the road always put her to sleep when she lived in Rochester...

Chapter 28

CARD SHARP

Julia slowly opened her eyes when the carriage came to a stop. She barely noticed Alek kindly, getting her out of the carriage still in his strong arms. He smiled when he saw that she was awake.

Alek cautiously set her down on the earthy, brown soil when Julia smiled back. She looked around as Alek grabbed the last bags and Annabelle before the carriage drove off. Nearby, was a large, frayed house in the middle of the tall, grassy plain fields- the country land.

"Is that your house?" she asked earnestly.

Alek laughed, "It used to be." he crouched down to Annabelle's height and played with her furry ears, "But that was a long time ago. My family home." he paused a moment and then got up as he looked to Julia, "This is my parents house. I just need to pick up a few things. Is that all right?"

Julia nodded. Alek picked up the bags and they walked up to the door with Annabelle following in the midday spring heat. He reached for his key and put it in the lock.

"Do they still live here?"

"Yup." he said unlocking the door.

"Are they home?"

"I don't know. They always lock the door." he unlocked it and took the key from the lock.

"If they are, should I be scared?" she asked in a joking manner.

Alek grabbed the doorknob and placed his amber eyed stare on her emerald eyes, "I would be." and she giggled as he opened the door for her.

Heart pounding, Julia noticed the dark rooms that lay before her. Alek came in and set their bags down while Julia studied the outlines of the furniture. Feeling alone, she closed the door quickly and followed Alek to the cabinets in the kitchen.

Adjusting her eyes to the darkness in the house, because there was only the light from the tiny kitchen window and living room, Julia looked back to the living room at the delineates of the furniture. Suddenly, she noticed an outline move quickly. She put her eyes back on Alek as he reached for something in the tall cabinet.

"Alek, what was that?" she asked pulling on his sleeve.

"Hmm?" he followed to where Julia's eyes were and saw nothing as he said, "Probably just your imagination. No one's here." then he went back to trying to find what he was looking for.

"All right." she looked back to him, "What are you looking for?"

"Honey. I forgot to get some last time. I was going to use it for the dinner I was going to make you tonight."

Julia smiled as she thought, *So he was going to prepare dinner for me? He really is sweet. I'm so lucky to have a friend like him. One that can protect me if any danger comes.*

Alek mumbled because he was starting to get irritated that he couldn't find the honey, "Honey? Honey. Honey. Where are You?" he finally grabbed the glass jar labeled Honey and cheered, "Yes." he brought it down and closed the cabinet door that was filled with many jars and cans, "All right. I got what I needed. Let's go."

Alek and Julia turned to leave, but stopped because all the lights suddenly turned on and a crowd of people in the house shouted, "Surprise!" as they raised their arms in joy and Alek and Julia almost fell on their butts from being frightened so easily.

Alek regained his balance, noticing that it was his family who had terrified him. An elder woman, probably in her late forties, dressed in tattered clothing, fuzzy, faded brown hair, amber eyes, short and stout, and wore a broad grin on her face. She stretched out her arms and tightly hugged Alek, which he gladly hugged her back smiling and blushing.

She broke away from his hug and placed her palms on his cheeks, "Oh, my son! You're back!"

Alek laughed as he placed her hands in his between them, "Good to see you too mom. You look great." he giggled at Julia's bewildered expression decorated onto her face and held her hand saying to his mother, "Mom, this is Julia."

Alek's mother shook Julia's hand politely in her eagerness, "It's an honor to meet you Julia. Will you and Alek be staying for lunch?"

Julia looked to Alek who just shrugged, "It's up to you Julia."

She glanced back to Alek's mother and said, "If it's not too much trouble-"

She waved her hands, "Oh no trouble at all! And you can call me Ella." she looked back to the young women behind her all wearing fine, colorful silks, "Come and welcome your brother and Julia."

A young woman from the other end of the room put a wide smile from her glossy, heart-shaped lips and hugged Alek with her half black and blonde hair sweeping across his broad shoulder, "Good to see you made it out of the war, *alive* brother. So did Julia help protect you?" she winked at her with beautiful amber eyes.

"No. I protected myself *and* her. Thank you very much, Sofia."

They all giggled and another girl came up to hug, who was still laughing with large, luscious pink lips and her blonde curls bounced with her shoulders trying to contain her hilarity, "I have to say, I didn't think you could do it."

He sighed as she walked off playing with his hair, "Ugh! This family never gives me a break. Especially Emma." he mumbled looking at her standing next to Sofia with her brown eyes even chuckling.

The youngest looking girl at the other end of the room slowly came up to Alek and Julia. Her intense purple eyes and her thin, red lips showed anger. She gave a slight smile to Julia and placed her hand on Alek's shoulder, "Good to see you." and walked off with a flip of her jet black hair.

"Come now, Genevieve! Give them a greeting."

Genevieve gave a harsh glance to her mother, "I just did."

Julia looked to Alek as Genevieve and Ella spoke to themselves, "We had gotten in a bit of a fight before I left." he said and Julia then understood why her appearance was so negative towards her brother.

His mother then shouted to the man on the other side of the room, "Jefferson! Go and greet your son while I talk to Genevieve."

"As you wish, my love. I just wanted to wait until the mob of women were done saying hello. This house is dominated by them." this everyone laughed to because it was truly obvious.

I love how he called her 'my love'. It's the same thing my father used to say to my mother. I long to be called that someday. I was close with Carson, but... Julia had thought almost becoming teary-eyed once again.

"My son." said Alek's father hugging him, "How are you?"

"I'm fine dad. It's good to see you after all this time."

He chuckled, "Yes it has been a long time." he held Alek's shoulders, "You know, your uncle's been asking about you. He says he can't wait until you and your brother go to stay with him to become a Songbird."

"Really?" Alek laughed, "I never expected him to."

Julia cut in at the surprising news that Jarvis was going too, "Wait. Jarvis is going with you? To be a Songbird?"

Alek nodded and his father walked up to Julia, "So this is our new human? Welcome!" and he hugged her.

"Thank you sir." she said after his kind hug.

"You can call me Jeff." Alek rolled his eyes mumbling his name and chuckling to himself.

"Thank you, Jeff." Julia smiled and looked to Alek, "So why does Jarvis also want to be a Songbird?"

"He says he wants to follow in his brother's footsteps. I say rubbish. He probably just wants all the credit."

Ella came rushing into the room with pink cheeks, "Oh stop talking such childish things about your brother! Where is that troublesome boy anyway?"

"Right here." said Jarvis popping into thin air, scaring Ella so much that she jumped and he hung up his coat on the coat hanger next to the door with Lori Linda standing behind him.

They've been spending a lot of time together lately Julia thought as she smiled to her friends.

"Jarvis!" yelled Ella as she pulled one of his golden locks from the crown of his head, making him shriek in pain, "You know my poor heart can't take that anymore. It never mends."

"Oh, it doesn't?" asked Jeff in the sweetest voice and held Ella's hands as he reached to kiss her.

Alek sighed and muttered in an irritated voice, "Here we go again."

"Oi vey!" said Jarvis turning to Lori Linda who smiled.

Julia seemed to be the only one whom thought this was sweet and at the same time hurtful, like piercing her heart quickly, but indeed sharply. Her parents told her not to lose herself when things did not work out with another person, yet Julia couldn't help herself. It was as though some of the dreams she only dared to dream had left her to travel to a far away land beyond the horizon. Even a thought of Carson or love gave her grief that she had never wanted.

Annabelle chased another white wolf playfully around the house, sticking her wet tongue out in a smile almost as if they were old friends who had just found each other again. She looked around the house from where she was standing and saw that it was indeed a country farm home and was cold. Julia stopped scrutinizing when Jeff came up to Jarvis and rocked him back and forth by holding his shoulder in a grip asking, "So what took you so long to get here?"

"Probably sleeping." interrupted Alek and received a glare from Jarvis.

"Were you?" Jeff asked. When Jarvis nodded his head in agreement Jeff sighed and said, "Son, you're going to sleep your life away!"

"Well, unlike my brother who likes to kill time, I like to use time in a useful way."

"And not waste money, I might add." Jeff ruffled Alek's hair.

"Oh! Quit your yakking and help set the table!" Ella yelled to her family but looked up to Julia apologetically, "Except for you deary. Come sit yourself down though." she led Julia to the table and held a chair for her to sit on.

Everyone set the table as Ella asked and sat when they were finished. Ella severed the food in big pots and pans on top of towels to keep from burning their lacy, white tablecloth. Julia sat herself down staring at her white bowl.

Ella ladled what looked like soup from a large pot and asked, "How much do you want Julia?"

"Just a bit Ella. Thank you."

"Of course dear." she said taking the bowl, spooning the soup into it, and placing it down back in front of Julia again.

As Ella served everyone else, Julia gawked at the soup-or maybe it was stew- she could not tell. It seemed slippery and was mushy and brown. She couldn't tell what it was made of and smelled it. Surprisingly, it smelled delicious. When Ella sat herself down and everyone was served, Julia tasted it, finding it very delectable and told Ella as well, who smiled greatly. She took a small sip of her drink to her right.

"So I hear that you're in love with Carson Tabor." inquired Genevieve nastily.

Julia almost choked, slightly coughing. When she was about to answer, Ella became irate and said, "Genevieve, we don't ask questions like that. They may be personal."

Julia nearly whispered before Genevieve could protest, "How...how does word like that travel so quickly?"

Genevieve looked down smiling. Apparently, she'd accomplished what she had been planning on doing. She was trying to insult her guest as a way to get back at her brother.

Alek put down his spoon, making it clink, and said, "I'm sorry for my sister's rudeness Julia. Ignore her. I always do." he smirked and she frowned devastatingly back at him.

Thankfully, Emma tried to change the subject, "So how do you like Renata so far, Julia?"

It took Julia moment before answering, looking at everyone's curious faces and smiled, "There's always something around the corner."

Before thinking, Alek asked a question he had hoped his thoughts of Julia's reaction would be wrong, "If you could, would you go back to your own world?" everyone was apprehensive for her reply.

"I...There are times when I sometimes wish that I had a reason to go back to my on world, yet I can never find any." Jarvis, Alek, and Lori Linda looked to her eyes, knowing what things she was referring to that she have may wanted a reason to go back to her own world for, "I will admit that I loved it there, but I was never truly happy with who I was. I always felt like there was something missing. And one day someone told me, that there was something about me that said I wasn't supposed to live a normal life. Now that I think back, I believe him. I don't think me opening to that page in my diary was just any old coincidence- only that it was meant to be."

"I think so too, Julia." said Lori Linda, whom Julia had not heard speak in quite some time, so was a little jumpy from hearing it.

"There's one thing I don't get though." Sofia said.

"And what's that?" asked Jeff, giving Julia a chance to breathe. She almost felt as if it was somehow an interrogation.

"Julia, if you loved Carson so much and was only afraid of him being in danger *here,* then why didn't you just take him to your own world?"

"I thought of that-believe me I did, but I considered all the possibilities and came to two outcomes. One is that Peter has the diary, so there's no other way back. The other is that Carson wouldn't survive in that world. I barely did."

"But couldn't have he just adapted to it?"

"I highly doubt it."

Alek got up from his chair swiftly, "Excuse me everyone. Julia, can you come with me?"

Julia nodded stepping back from the table and followed Alek. He brought her down into a hallway with no angle to see the table. They could not see or hear them. There were more rooms down the hall that were dark. In the hallway, there was a beautiful painting of his family with everyone smiling.

Julia put her back against the cold wall and Alek looked down and into her eyes, "Julia, I'm so sorry. Are you all right? Do you want to leave?" he asked in his most sincere voice.

She shook her head, "No. No, I'm fine."

He placed his forehead on hers gingerly, "Are you sure?"

Julia looked down, "It's not you or your family. It's just...it's me." he clasped his arms around her thoughtfully, "I'm just so afraid of what will come in my future." she held tightly onto his hug, as though it was the only thing supporting her to stand.

"Don't worry. The future can always change as long as you're willing to let it." she looked up at his eyes, and he in turn looked at her as though he wanted to kiss her, yet instead, he released his hug and said, "Now, what do you say about going back to finish our lunch and make it a good afternoon?"

Julia giggled, "All right."

They headed back to the table and sat. Everyone paused for a slight moment and continued their lunch smiling; noticing Julia had not shed any tears. It was quiet, but amusing enough to pass the time.

After what was remaining of the scrumptious lunch, Jeff, Jarvis, and Alek devoured the last of it until only crumbs were left. *Men.* Julia thought to herself laughing.

Then, Emma brought out her cupped hands from under the table. She opened her hands to reveal a small, fuzzy animal. Only when Emma said, "Wake up Vivvy" was when it came up and looked like a miniature girl in the palm of her hand.

It yawned and smiled as she looked up to Emma, "This is Vivvy, she's like a pet- or a young girl." she chuckled.

"Am not!" she called to her master, then looked back to Julia, blushing, "Vivian Isabelle Valerie Victoria Yarbrough at your service." she bowed, then came up with dimples on the sides on her round face, "But you can call me Vivvy for short. *Tehe!*" she laughed high-pitched.

Vivvy was one of a kind. She had a sort of animal appeal to her, but also had similar traits to a young girl. Many blonde braids flowed downward as her hair, had a girlish, friendly face, big feet, a mouse's nose, large, fuzzy ears, and a furry costume for her clothing. Julia thought she was very cute.

"She's adorable!" Julia exclaimed.

"I'd prefer the term *fierce.*" she said jumping from Emma's hand onto the table and growled so charmingly with a hilarious face.

Julia snorted lightly, "Fierce it is then."

Vivvy shook her head energetically and started reaching for all the remaining crumbs from the lunch. She first took bread, then cheese, and finally an olive- which was all too much for her to carry by herself. She soon placed it down, and then stuffed it all down with one bite each by two cute buck teeth like a mouse's.

When she was done stuffing herself, she plopped down onto the table and let her small tummy bulge into a bubble shape. She yawned as she stretched and looked sleepily to everyone at the table who was smiling at her. Emma placed her back where ever she was first brought from under the table.

Julia smiled to Alek who said, "That's all Vivvy ever does: eat and sleep."

Ella brought dishes up from the table, "She's delightful, but a brat at times. Like some little girls of my own." she said eyeing her three daughters and Julia laughed for her own mother would have probably said something similar to that.

"Why do you all talk such nonsense about my Vivvy?" Emma smiled, but was also serious.

"Well…" Jarvis looked to Julia for a moment and said, "I'm sorry you have to be here Julia while we try not to scold her, but to give her suggestions," he emphasized suggestions as he looked back to Emma, "But, don't you think you're a little too old to have Vivvy?"

"I most certainly am not. She's like my own little companion. And why do you always try to sound wiser than you really are Jarvis?"

Ella came in from the kitchen, "Hush now Emma. We have a guest. Your brother is just trying to reason with you. He doesn't mean to scold you, it's just who he is. He spent most of his life in school. Now he works for Carson Tabor and is going to become a Songbird with his brother Alek." she said the last sentence proud.

Emma sighed into her seat while Sofia patted her head. Ella went back into the kitchen to finish cleaning up and Alek went to help her. Jarvis sat in his chair looking down not saying a word with Lori Linda staring at him equally as silent. Nonchalantly Jeff sat motionless as he thought deeply while Annabelle sat with the other white wolf next to her, playing with their ears.

"I didn't know Annabelle would be so fond of other white wolves." Julia said slightly smiling at her spontaneous wolf.

"You…you don't know?!" Jarvis asked shocked for some odd reason looking up.

Alek came into the room with Ella, "I don't think anyone told her."

"Told me what?" asked Julia confused.

Ella sat herself back down into her comfortable chair and said, "That other wolf she's playing with, Brianna, is her mother."

"What?" asked Julia surprised.

"It's true." Alek said with his eyes showing all truth and little sadness, "We had to sell her. Along with her siblings."

"Why? Was she not good?" asked Julia truly taken back.

Ella spoke in using her hands for gestures as spoke, "Well Julia, you can see for yourself that we are poor." she looked sorrowfully, "So we had to sell the lovable pups for gold."

"I'm sorry."

"Oh it's not your fault Julia! It could never be. And I can see you Love Annabelle very much." Julia nodded, she did love her dear pet, "But times are hard now. That is why Sofia and Emma are married to higher status gentlemen to help support us and Jarvis and Alek are going to become Songbirds."

"That's only the main reason mother." Jarvis cut in.

"Oh of course she already knows that Jarvis." Jeff said sitting up in his chair and reaching into his pocket pulling out a large deck of cards, "Who wants to play?" he asked smiling, waving the stack in the air.

"I do!" shouted Jarvis and Alek simultaneously.

They all moved into the living room and set up a playing place for their games on the round table. Jeff was obviously the dealer and handed out the cards while Lori Linda joined them all. Julia sat on the couch and observed.

"What is the game?" she asked.

"Ropes and Gnomes." replied Alek.

"How do you play? What's the point?" she asked after a laugh to herself at the title of the game.

"Well," Alek started to say laughing as he held his cards, "The game is quite simple actually. It is a game of bluff. All you have to do is catch the person bluffing of how many and what kind of cards they have. Each time they're caught bluffing or lying, they're called a gnome. If the person is caught three times, they get the 'ropes' and have to quit the game. The last person gets the last piece of mom's DELICIOUS pie!" he cheered.

"So it's like BS." she said realizing.

"What's that?" Jarvis asked.

"Nothing." replied Julia trying to contain her hilarity. Many things about Renata were similar to her own world.

"Come and play Julia!" said Lori Linda excited.

Ella came in holding the last piece of the yummy pie and set it on the Dining table while saying, "You know, I'm the one who made this pie. I should be the one to get it."

Everyone but Julia laughed outright and said, "No."

Emma held her cards close as she said, "But it's a good thing we only do this once a week. Us girls in this family watch our figures very strictly."

"That's even if you win to get the pie!" Alek said big-eyed to Jeff, "I swear, he always bluffs and never gets caught. I think he cheats." he waved his cards in his direction and only received a grin.

Jeff placed two cards faced-down in the middle of the table while stating, "Two aces."

"Gnome!" Alek sneered.

"Nope." Jeff replied laughing and showing him the cards for proof.

"SEE?!" and everyone laughed outright.

Julia then pulled up her own chair and sat. They started the game and she soon got the hang of it and enjoyed herself. The first person out was Sofia whom merely just shrugged her shoulders and walked to the couch to sit and admire the unique, funny game. She also added that she was always the first to get out, then with Ella following- which rapidly took place and she too sat on the couch as though it were a waiting area to watch and see how the game concluded.

Soon-almost too soon- Emma came out of the game as well by both Jeff and Alek seeing that she was lying. She simply chuckled and said she never liked the game anyway. The game continued and Genevieve called Julia a gnome when she had said that she had three 4s. Alek sighed in response and Julia said nothing. Genevieve's rudeness continued when she also called Lori Linda a gnome and had to quit because Alek and Jarvis did the same earlier in the game.

Julia continued to bluff and claimed she had four 7s smiling. Genevieve called her a gnome once more. She was beginning to become agitated with her. *Why does she have to be so rude?* Julia thought.

Alek almost growled, "Really Genevieve?" he asked, "Honestly? Do you have to do this now? It doesn't make things any better for you."

Genevieve said nothing and she also then bluffed. Julia was the first to call her a gnome. She smirked at Julia in response. The next to be called a gnome was, surprisingly, Jarvis by Jeff. Then Genevieve was called a gnome by Jeff also- he seemed to be paying more attention now that there was less competition and Jarvis laughed at this.

Next it was Julia's turn who had declared she had one 9, but

Genevieve called her a gnome for the last time and said she had to get the ropes. So Julia had to quit the fun game which irritated her. Alek was about to argue, but Julia quickly said, "That was fun, but I was caught." and smiled.

Genevieve grinned and Alek caught her bluffing so she too had to quit and smiled when she was leaving and Ella said to her, "Genevieve, I think it'd be best if you went to your room."

"Very well."

Now the competition was fierce. It was Jeff, Alek, and Jarvis left each with one gnome against them. Out of the three, Jarvis was the first to go and blamed Jeff for it saying that he agreed with Alek about their father cheating. Everyone laughed. Then, it was sudden death against Alek and his father. Each of them was trying desperately to win. It was not so much for the pie, but the title of beating Jeff at his own game. Julia found this hilarious and exciting at the same time. Everyone was glued onto the scene, until finally; Alek got the ropes with a bluff of two 6s.

"I swear every single time!" Alek said jokingly as he put down the cards. Ella got up and generously gave the piece of pie to her loving husband. Alek helped Julia up from the couch and said, "Well, instead of being tormented, I think it's time for Julia and I to head out."

"Us too." said Jarvis with Lori Linda next to him.

"All right," said their mother, "When will you come back?"

"Tomorrow, maybe, soon." replied Jarvis.

"Soon." Alek said.

"Did you at least somewhat enjoy yourself dear?" asked Ella to Julia.

"Of course. Thank you for your hospitality."

"You're welcome anytime you wish." she smiled and Jeff came over and gave her another kind hug.

"It was a pleasure meeting our new human. Come back to us soon."

Everyone else but Genevieve said goodbye to Julia and then she stepped out of the lovely home with Alek, Jarvis, and Lori Linda in now renewed spirits, trying to ignore the harsh pain in her chest as she tried not to think of Carson.

Chapter 29

DAY ONE WITH ALEK

It was lunch time at the Tabor's castle. After Julia had earnestly left Carson, he met Princess Theodora at the entrance as she had requested. They difficultly discussed about what happened and how Soren unexpectedly left. Theodora said he was probably ashamed of what he did- which he should've been.

While they were finishing up their conversation, Cassidy interrupted to fetch them, and brought them all down to lunch with everyone. Carson barely uttered a word to anyone as he sat there, not even touching his food. He was like a zombie among them and seemed not to care. After a while, Cassidy was tired of it.

"Carson, there must be *something* worth talking about today!" she said and everyone stared at Carson, who looked down.

He noticed he was wearing a silver band on his wrist and remembered Peter mentioning that it was his birthday that day, "Well, today is Peter's birthday."

"I think we'd all like to congratulate him." Cassidy alleged and everybody nodded in agreement.

Carson cast the communication spell and everyone saw Peter's happy smile flicker onto the silver. He was in a room reading a card with a pointed, blue hat on his head. Peter then looked at his wrist and saw everyone laughing; only Carson forced a smile.

"Guys! It's so good to see you!"

"Happy Birthday!" they all announced back to him and Peter laughed in enjoyment.

"Thanks. That means a lot. I miss y'all."

"We miss you too." Carson said truthfully.

"How old are you now?" Bade asked.

"I'm thirteen now. Oh! Look at what I got for my birthday! A new cell phone!" he showed the amazing little machine to them.

They all gazed in awe, "What does it do?" Veronica asked with her eyes shining brightly.

"Kind of like the communication spell. If you had a cell phone, I'd dial the number and be able to talk to you. Wherever I am. Although you can't see me." he said demonstrating.

"Even so, brilliant!" said Mr. Doddsworth excitedly and everyone laughed.

"Hey," started Peter, "I just noticed, where Julia is? And Alek, Prince Nathan, Jarvis, and Lori Linda?" everyone became quiet and watched as Carson looked back to the cold ground once more.

"Not here." Mr. Clayton replied sadly.

Everything seemed calm and peaceful. Everyone was thinking in their own state of mind- good and bad. Until Jarvis interrupted the silence.

"So how are you going to travel brother?" asked Jarvis in a mocking tone, "Are you going to be smart and use the transportation spell, like us," he held Lori Linda's hand and laughed at Alek, "or waste time and travel on the horses?"

Lori Linda laughed as she spoke, "Why do you always torment each other?"

"He always torments me!" whined Jarvis.

Julia smiled and Alek said, "I think we'll take the horses."

"Suit yourself." Jarvis said and snapped his fingers and disappeared, and then Alek looked to Julia, "Do you mind?"

"No." she said looking up to his sincere smile and friendly eyes, "I'm actually glad you like to waste time."

"Really? Why?" he asked curious.

"Gives you more time to think."

"What do you think about?"

"Certain things."

"Such as…" he tried to get to the point.

"Anything." she said casually, "I tend to think a lot about of what is going on in my life, my past, and what will be in the future." she looked up to him teary-eyed, "Although, sometimes it's better not to waste time. It can help you from lingering into your past." Alek was about to say something comforting, but she continued on with tears on the edges of her eyelashes and voice cracking from the harsh pain in her chest, "I'm trying…I'm trying so hard not to think about it. But I can't control it!" she sobbed into Alek's chest trying to contain the ache of the pain in her heart, but couldn't any longer. Luckily Alek was there; otherwise she would've curled up into a ball, holding her torso from splitting into two.

He let her cry for a good amount of time before she thought she was making a fool of herself in front of a kind man who loved her. *How can he love someone so broken? Someone who regretfully can't return his love?* She thought and released herself from the loving embrace.

Alek wiped the tears from her cheeks, wishing she would smile with all of her heart and truly be happy because he hated to see her so upset and said, "Let's not waste any more time." and lightly grasped her hand as they walked over past the wide farm, country land to a meadow where wild horses kept to one side of a fence and the tamed horses of Alek's family on the other side.

He chose two caramel colored horses, leading them and Julia to a small, frayed barn (which still had a faint little red and white tint for its color), put saddles on the calm, beautiful horses, and strapped their bags onto them. Annabelle came in and just examined the process as she sat and waited. When he was done, he handed a set of reins to one of the horses to Julia saying, "Hop on."

Julia did as he told her what to do and waited patiently for him. He was soon on the other horse at her side and made his horse go forward a few steps. Julia followed Alek silently and Annabelle followed them both with her tongue hanging out playfully on one side of her mouth.

The setting was stunning as they rode their horses to Alek's home. It was late afternoon and the golden sun was set high in the sky. The meadow was a yellowish tint on the tall, green grass that seemed like an ocean in the wind, butterflies of all shapes, sizes, and colors, and luscious apple trees scattered about before the forestry tree line ahead of them. They came up to it and Alek got off his horse and Julia did as well. Then he said, "We'll have to travel on foot from here."

Julia nodded and followed Alek as he maneuvered around the forest, casting quick glances at Annabelle to make sure she was following. Even though the forest was small, it was dense. Every leaf, branch, and vine seemed to want to play with Julia but sighed in relief when Alek guided her out into a wide open space with beautiful tall green grass, evergreen tress with their leaves scuffling throughout the wind, flowers of all the colors of the rainbow- roses, blue bonnets, blue flags, sunflowers, and much more, and a small house. Alek smiled to her as he said, "This is it."

"It's very nice." she said in reply truthfully, for it was in her opinion very pretty.

He smiled as he took off the reins of the horses. They galloped off after he'd gotten the bags and Alek motioned his head towards the house. Julia followed in partial excitement, for it was all she could handle, and Annabelle raced ahead of her and Alek.

They came to the front door and Julia thought he was going to unlock it, but when he turned the knob, the door flew open and set their bags on the left side of the darkness. Julia looked to Alek, "Don't you lock your door?"

"Na. No one ever comes to this place. Besides, it's enchanted. What good is magic if we can't use it?"

Julia nodded seeing his point from his eyes. He truly was an optimistic person. Then, she tried not to, yet couldn't, and lingered into a thought of *him*.

Alek caught her slight shift and said going into his house, "How about a tour? Shall we?"

Julia forced a smile. He went inside as she saw the lights turn on. She sighed and went in to smile at the comforting home.

The first thing she saw was a living room with a fireplace, couch, and many books on shelves. To her right was the Dining room with a round, red oak table and chairs with a chandelier holding ten candles. Alek guided her along to a door next to the Dining room that led to the kitchen. Then down a short hall was his bedroom and bathroom that was the same style as the Inn she had stayed in with…him.

"So," said Alek thankfully shattering her thoughts and hoped he hadn't noticed, for he didn't seem to, "I'm going to start making dinner. What would you like to eat?"

"Something light." she said as she walked over to the books, which Alek snickered at.

Julia chose one book and sat on the couch. Annabelle glided over to her, lay by her feet, and let Julia pet her soft head. Alek smiled and went to the kitchen.

Julia started reading something about the Songbird group and her curious mind made her ask Alek, "Do you have any books about the human before me?"

"No." he said coming out of the kitchen with, surprisingly to Julia, a contorted angry face and laughed with a hint of sarcasm in his voice, "All of the archives are unfortunately unavailable. Even to the family of the protectors." he shook his head and walked back into the kitchen- he obviously didn't want to talk about it.

Julia felt sorry for Alek, whatever the problem was, and continued to read. A couple of minutes later, she smelled a sweet, delicious aroma filling the air. Julia placed the book back in its place and turned to see Alek putting two plates with delectable food on them.

He smiled, "It's ready."

Julia smiled coming to the table and he helped her into a chair as she said, "Thank you. It looks divine." she waited until he sat down and took her first bite, "And it is!"

Alek laughed, "Thank you. A lot of people say I take after my mom."

"You do!" she then took another bite, "Where did you learn to cook like this?"

"Mom. But I can never make my foods healthy. Cassidy wouldn't be very happy about that." and they both laughed full-heartedly.

Julia smiled happily, if one person could make her feel comforted, it was Alek and said, "Thank you." she was truly grateful and Alek knew she was thanking him for everything he had done for her, and he didn't do it just because it was his job, but because he loved her with all of his heart- she was his first love.

"You're welcome." and he smiled as he ate in content with her.

Not too long after they finished dinner, Jarvis and Lori Linda knocked on the front door. Alek sighed and Julia laughed. He opened the door to find Jarvis with his arms spread to hug him, "Brother!"

"What are you doing here?" Alek laughed.

"And yet you still won't give me a hug." he said shaking his head laughing as he put his arms down, "Can't brothers just hang out?"

"No." Alek chuckled and let them come inside.

They all sat together in the living room and talked. Most of the time they exchanged stories and laughed. Several hours later, they had had enough fun and Jarvis and Lori Linda left smiling.

When Alek closed the door behind them, he looked back to Julia and they both burst out in laughter. It made Julia feel good to laugh. After a moment Julia composed herself, "I think I'll get ready for bed." Alek just smiled in response as she headed down the hall to get ready.

As she was getting ready, Julia mistakably thought of Carson by accident as she was thinking of the Ball. It had been one of the happiest moments of her tiny life and it had all been crushed by her. Her knees quickly gave up from beneath her and she fell onto the ground shaking. She almost screamed from the pain tearing at her inner chest. She held onto her ribs with one hand and the other to keep her from staying on the cold floor, yet it was not as cold as her heart. Julia tried to get up from the heart wrenching ache, but failed. She sank into her lap and cupped her hands around her face repeatedly saying, "Why?!"

Alek knocked on the door to the bathroom, "Julia, are you all right?" he asked concerned.

Julia gasped and said, "Fine. I'll be out in a minute."

"Are you sure?" he sounded fretful.

She quickly said yes and waited until she heard him quietly and slowly walking away from the door to let three silent tears trickle down her face. *Had he been listening the whole time? I need to learn to control myself. But...but...but my heart...it aches so much. How can I do it? What can I do?*

Julia got up from the ground and looked into the mirror. She thought she looked a mess. All of her tears drenched down her neck and chest and soaked into her night gown. Even some of her hair was wet with her tears, and her nose, eyes, and cheeks were flushed a tint of red. Julia pulled her hair back and wiped her selfish tears from herself.

She walked out of the bathroom and into the living room to find Alek had set a fire in the fireplace and he was sitting, petting Annabelle with a look of a saddened frown on his lips and an almost hurt emotion in his eyes.

"I'm done." she announced and felt horrible for the way she had acted.

He slowly got up with the same expression painted across his attractive face. This scared Julia, usually he was happy. *What is wrong with him? Is it me?* she thought and he came closer and closer. Julia was about to ask what he was doing, for he looked like he was about to kiss her, but there was no way she was ready for that yet. But he came even closer to her, and hugged Julia without saying a single word. He didn't utter a sound, but just held her in his arms just as he had earlier that day.

Julia became teary-eyed, "I'm being so selfish."

"No you're not." he caressed his fingers to wipe her almost tears, "Please, no more. I'm going to get ready for bed now. Just don't think Julia. Just remember the happy moments before coming to Renata."

Julia nodded to his advice and he left. She got the book that she'd been reading earlier off the book shelf and lay before the fire with it, a blanket from the woven basket next to the couch, and a pillow. Annabelle came and lay down next to her on the soft carpet. She read for some time becoming tired and was half asleep when Alek came back into the room.

He touched her shoulder lightly, "You should go ahead and go to bed. I'm staying out here on the couch to sleep."

She shifted slightly to see him smiling as the fire crackled, "I'm fine right here. This is your house anyway."

"But you're the guest."

"Goodnight Alek."

She smiled and he went over to the couch and made his bed saying, "Either way, I'm sleeping on this." and he got in smiling.

Julia went to slumber quite fast and left the book open next to her. Annabelle cuddled next to Julia. The smell of sweet flowers and meadows filled the night air as though it was a spell to help her rest well after a long day of tear-shed.

Chapter 30

TRY FOR ME

Julia woke up to a sweet, delicious smell floating in the air. It lingered and gave her a spark to wake up. She sat up to find Alek gone, her bed a mess, and the book still open by her side. To clean up, she placed the book back, folded the blanket, and replaced it.

Alek came out of the kitchen saying, "Good morning. Breakfast is ready."

Julia smiled as he brought the plates of food onto the table. He helped her into her chair and she blushed. Alek was truly sweet in every way. She saw Annabelle out of the corner of her eye eating her own breakfast Alek had also prepared for her.

After a couple bites of the scrumptious food, and complimenting Alek on it, Julia said, "I think I'll go to work today. I want to."

"Well, I have to do some preparations in town for my trip to the Kalama Kingdom, so I'll do that while you work." he smiled.

"Sounds like a plan," and smiled back.

Alek stared at her with a look of concern and love. She blushed and tried to look another way. He took the hint and drank a sip of his, what seemed to be, a fruity drink that looked and tasted a bit more pungent than the regular orange juice from her world.

When they had finished their tasty breakfast, they took turns getting ready. Once done, they headed out the door with Annabelle following. The day was a beautiful spring morning as they walked in the calming setting once again, but with puffy white clouds over their heads. They only walked for about fifteen minutes until they saw the town in front of them.

The town seemed full of life; everyone was shopping, having fun, and there was a smile upon every mouth. Drinks were being drained with much laughter. They smiled as they came up to Adrianna's shop, but Julia had made the mistake to look over to the Inn she had stayed at. The one where her dead mother told her she couldn't love Carson and she had to make the most difficult decision of her life. Thinking this, she knew the pain was coming inevitably.

Julia looked down quickly and tried to contain her heart. It was hurting her so much. She felt as though it wouldn't mend.

Alek caught this as quickly as she did and lifted her chin lightly, "Please Julia. Just...not today. Just try for me. No tears please." he looked deeply concerned, hurt, and serious and rested his hand on her cheek, "Have a good day." and left her silently with one silent tear left as a small line on her face.

Julia felt terrible. She hated crying and feeling sorry for herself. But even more, she hated making Alek feel like he did. Happy was the only thing she wanted to see as his emotion. *Try for me* is what he had said. To try for him would mean to not cry over *him* every waking moment and to become closer to Alek because he loved her.

Julia shook off her feeling and went inside the shop to start work. It looked like a mess. Anna rushed past Julia holding a large and seemingly heavy box.

"Oh Julia!" she said very happy and exhausted, "My goodness. We've never been this busy. Can you run the front desk please?" she pleaded with puppy eyes and Julia nodded happily over to her work space.

The day was indeed busy. Within the first hour, Julia had helped over forty costumers. When it came time for lunch, all three women had to rush and go straight back to work. Julia was happy for the end of the day when they closed shop and she saw Alek coming to fetch her.

She smiled as she said goodbye to her co-workers and walked off with Alek back to his home. Along the way to start conversation, he asked, "So how was your day?"

"Busy!" and he laughed.

Julia had decided that she would try for Alek from then on. She felt as though she could repay him a little by that. They walked the salient trail again and Julia accepted the new routine in her life.

Once back at his house, Annabelle hoped onto them and gave them wet kisses as soon as they had opened the door. They laughed joyfully and at each other from being so surprised. Julia thought Annabelle wanted to be fed, so she walked into the kitchen and asked where the bowls were.

"In the far right cabinet." she reached for it, "But maybe I should get it. You might not be tall enough." Alek said laughing as he compared their sizes and he was indeed taller.

Julia chortled as she tried to grab a small, blue bowl. Without a doubt, it was too tall for her and she slipped. Alek caught her in his arms and the bowl in a tight grip in his right hand.

They stayed in this position of him holding her in his arms until after a moment Julia uttered, "Alek." and looked down.

Even though she couldn't see his face, his eyes were sincere as he smiled slightly saying, "Told you." and released her.

Turning to him, Alek stepped away and brought out food and put it into the bowl for Annabelle. Without looking, he handed it to Julia. She placed it before Annabelle and she immediately started gobbling it down.

Julia left Alek in the kitchen in silence. As he started making a bigger dinner with the honey he had brought from his mother's house, she sat on the couch. She didn't think or make a noise as she sat in quiet peace.

Shattering the serenity, a knock came from the door. She got up and asked, "Who is it?"

"Who do you think it is Julia?" laughed a familiar voice.

She opened the door and saw Jarvis and Lori Linda, "Did you miss us?" Lori Linda asked.

"Of course we did." called Alek laughing sarcastically from the kitchen.

"Did you have a good day today?" Jarvis asked Julia as they came in.

She nodded. The three of them sat in the living room and talked as Alek prepared dinner. When it was done, Jarvis helped him set the table and helped Lori Linda into her seat as Alek helped Julia into hers and they all laughed.

The dinner was even more delicious and Julia tasted the scrumptious honey needed for the dish. After it was completed, they all did the same as the night before and sat in the living room to talk. Even more laughs were shared that pretty evening.

Towards the end, Lori Linda claimed her favorite book out of the book shelf and read the first few chapters aloud. Her voice layered over every word, almost making the story come to life and it was brilliant. They all clapped at the end and they merrily left with broad smiles on their faces into the night. It was a silky, royal blue shaded sky with twinkling silver and white stars.

Next, Julia and Alek took turns getting ready for bed. Doing as what Alek said, Julia didn't allow her thoughts linger to *him* and no tears were shed- Alek smiled as he saw this. As he went to get ready, Julia went to sleep reading Lori Linda's favorite book, which seemed very interesting to Julia.

Alek came into the room to go to bed and saw this. He beamed and walked over to her about to wake her up, but he thought she looked too peaceful. Instead, he reached to pick her up. Annabelle gave him a 'what are you doing?' look.

Alek ignored her smiling and carried Julia to the bed. He tucked her in sweetly without waking her up. He then turned to go to bed himself on the couch, but looked back at her in the doorway.

He thought she really did look at peace. It seemed as though her heart was just starting to mend. Alek thought it was best not to interfere with her needed healing. But he wanted to kiss her.

Everyone else has kissed her- Prince Nathan and Carson. Why shouldn't I? I do love her. But it's not fair to either of us. I'm leaving. And if I'm caught, I'll have no excuse. Only one. That is only that I love her. he thought.

Alek pondered over the thought. He walked to her bedside in the darkness. Only the light from the moon and stars illuminated the tiny room.

Scared, Alek gently, ever so gently, placed his lips on hers. He truly did love her with all of his heart. A protector loving the protected soul.

A perfect match. But she would never, regretfully, be able to return his inexhaustible love for her.

Taking their lips apart, he looked to her face to make sure she hadn't awoken. Alek was happy that she hadn't, in fact she smiled. He quickly left grinning and went to sleep a little guilty that he was happy- but he couldn't, like all others, control his heart.

Julia never woke from her deep, happy slumber until early in the morning she heard something. What she had heard was *his* voice saying, "Julia, I'm so sorry Julia. Please, please forgive me," and she woke up frightened, panting. Alek came into the room to make sure she remained safe. Julia was fine. But something about the way she looked up to him, some new look of concern, sadness, worry, and shock mixed into one emotion and scared Alek.

Chapter 31

HOW...

Julia was extremely afraid of *his* words said to her. *What could they mean?* she thought. Alek stood worried.

"What happened?" he asked coming up to her.

Julia threw herself onto him, embracing him crying saying, "I...I heard *him*."

"Heard who?" he asked confused because he didn't understand.

"Carson." she gasped.

"What? How? What did he say?"

"He said he was sorry and to forgive him. He never said those that before. Those words are new to me. Something has happened! I can feel it. I don't want to relive what happened before. What happened to him? What did he do?"

Alek had no idea what he could've done and said comfortingly to Julia, "Today when you go to work, I'll find out. Please don't worry. You'll be fine. Take as much time as you need to get ready." and he let go of his loving embrace for her.

She nodded as he wiped her tears away. He left back into the kitchen. Julia quickly got up and took a long time getting ready, musing over Carson's words and shedding silent tears so Alek wouldn't hear.

When she'd come out, Julia found that Alek had made breakfast and ate his. He then went to get ready himself. She ate her breakfast and once she was done, Alek was ready to go.

They walked silently on the trail to town. Along the way, Alek said regretfully, "Julia, tomorrow...tomorrow I have to leave."

Julia uttered in reply sadly, "For the Kalama Kingdom?" he nodded, and she continued, "I'll figure something out. I know it's your dream. I won't let myself get in the way."

Alek placed his hands lovingly on the sides of her face, "Julia, you're my priority. I'm your protector. I should stay."

"No Alek." she said taking his hands in hers, "You need to fulfill your dreams. It would make me upset *not* to see you go."

He placed his forehead on hers, "Are...are you sure?"

"Positive."

"Thank you." he did want to go, it was his dream, but he didn't want to leave her.

They came up to the town and it seemed to be even more full of life than the day before. Everyone was celebrating and, what seemed to be, confetti was sprinkled everywhere- a party. Drinks were gulped down one after another and dancing seemed to be in every alleyway with loud music coming from the Inn.

They came up to the shop, dodging the large crowds of people, "I'll see what all the fuss is about and what we talked about earlier." Alek said carefully choosing his words.

Julia nodded and he left. She thought this day would be even busier than the day before. She was correct. With barely a greeting, she was out to work.

At lunch, they finally got a chance to breathe and gave Julia her pay for the days she had worked. Julia thought mood was strange, people were celebrating but Anna and Adrianna seemed to look concerned to Julia.

Had they too found out about my troubles? she thought.

After a few customers were taken care of by Julia, surprisingly she saw Prince Nathan coming up to her. He was surprised as well. She bowed politely.

"Your highness."

He smiled, but his eyes were deeply anxious for her, "So this is where you ended up?"

"I would say chose to go."

Prince Nathan had the same emotion as Alek and it scared Julia, "Are you at least happy?"

"I've made progress." she looked up to him, "What's wrong?"

"I heard Alek is leaving tomorrow."

Julia looked down, "You've heard correct."

"That isn't the only news I've heard around here. There's much celebration over it."

"Over what exactly?" she asked curious from all of the celebration.

"There has been word that Carson and Theodora are engaged." said Nathan so sorry for her.

Julia looked down almost gasping tearing up, then looking up she asked, "So soon?"

"I'm afraid so Julia. I'm so sorry." he said as he placed her hair behind her ears and she held his hand.

Now she knew why everyone looked so hurt for her. She now knew the meaning of Carson's words so early the morning. Nathan came from the desk into the shop and held Julia close to him and let her cry. She had every right to.

Still holding her, he said, "Why don't you stay with me for a while? I wouldn't have to worry about you so much then."

He was worried about me? she thought and asked him that very question.

"Of course I was." he pulled away for a moment, holding her shoulders, "So will you stay with me for a while?"

"Prince Nathan-" she was cut off by him saying only and only his name, "I don't want to be a burden to you."

He wiped tears from her eyes, "You're not a burden. You never could be," he waited a moment, "Will you stay?" Julia nodded and he smiled, "I'll be here tomorrow at the same time to come and get you. All right?"

She nodded again with wet eyes looking at his sincere chocolate brown eyes. He kissed her forehead and left her in shock as he left the shop with his guards. Julia's heart seemed to stop beating at that moment and Adrianna brought her into her office, sat her down, and gave her a glass of water.

Adrianna sat, "I'm sorry Julia." she started crying and Adrianna went over to her and let her cry out all of her tears into her motherly hug. *How could he do this so soon?* Julia thought mournfully.

Once Julia recovered, she came out to see Alek waiting for her with that same expression that continued to scare her. Alek saw that she had clearly been crying and nodded to Anna Adrianna in the back. They started walking home in immense silence.

Julia admitted what she wanted to tell him, "I found out why Carson said those words to me."

He stopped, yet she shook her head, kept walking, and held his hand to guide him to her side.

"Are you…Do you need-"

"No thank you." she said solemnly.

They reached the house and he held the door open for her. Annabelle was being fed by Jarvis. Lori Linda was on the couch and looked up to see them walking in and hugged Julia.

Alek walked up to his brother. "What are you guys doing here?"

"Mom wants us to come over to talk and eat with the family before we leave tomorrow."

Alek looked to Julia who was being held in Lori Linda's arms. She was quiet, but slightly smiled to somewhat tell Alek that she wanted to go, "All right." he said.

"Good." Jarvis said, "But unfortunately," he smiled gleaming, "I forgot horses, so we'll have to travel by the transportation spell."

Alek rolled his eyes, "Whatever."

Jarvis said the spell all popped up behind Ella as she was talking to Genevieve by the front door. She jumped. Everyone laughed.

Panicking, Ella said in a furry, "Now all of you just go and pop up everywhere!"

They all laughed some more and Julia caught Genevieve's eye, who said, "Julia," her mother gave her a warning glance and Alek mumbled her name harshly, but she asked, "Can I talk to you in private?"

Everyone had seemed to hold their breath and sighed when she nodded. Genevieve brought her into a room down the hall. It was illuminated by candles with mirrors reflecting the light. There was a stone wall in front of them.

Genevieve said a spell and the wall broke into two revealing a stone staircase that led outside. They walked down outside to the splendid setting. Genevieve leaned against the trunk of a tall, green tree.

"I'm sorry."

"For what?" Julia asked from Genevieve's sudden apology.

"For being so rude the other day." she paused and smiled weakly, "I was just trying to get back at my brother. I crossed the line. I apologize."

"It's fine."

"But I'm also sorry for…for the news of Carson." she stopped as she saw Julia gasp from hearing his name, "It's been all over town. But just let me say it's not your fault. People are only celebrating because they knew of their arranged marriage. Losing to a human for her love cost much of her reputation that she barely had. They're just glad that their Princess finally took a stand. He still loves you- I'm sure he does."

"But Genevieve, I can never be with him." she cried mutely and Genevieve stopped leaning on the tree and came up to Julia.

"Why not?"

"It's me." she said loudly and Genevieve let her collapse into her arms crying.

Alek rushed down the stairs that led outside to them, "Julia?" he looked to Genevieve and as soon as she heard Alek, Julia tried wiping her tears away with no luck, "Genevieve?" he asked and she merely just held Julia. Alek touched Julia's slender shoulder lightly while calling her name once more.

She turned around to see his hopeless expression tinted onto is face. She didn't want him to give up on her. He brushed her cheek, "Do you wish to go home?"

"No!" Julia burst out hysterically.

This was Alek's and Jarvis's last chance to see their family before they left the next day. This night was for them and Julia didn't want to spoil it. She wouldn't let him leave on her account.

"But Julia, if you're this upset-"

"Alek, I don't want to leave."

"Julia, I can tell-"

"Oh, Alek," said Genevieve holding Julia, "You need a woman in your life to understand them. Just listen to the poor girl. I think staying here is the exact thing she needs- maybe a sort of remedy for her broken heart."

Julia was stunned by Genevieve's incredulous speech. She had taken what she was thinking and put it into a statement more than an argument. Julia nodded to Alek in agreement looking down as she did.

He thought about it for a moment. Alek looked at her vexed as he wiped her now less-flowing tears that were thankfully coming to a halt. Studying her condition and Genevieve's 'hurry it up' look, Alek said, "All right. If that's what you wish to do."

Julia lightly grasped his hand and let Genevieve guide them back inside the house, closing the wall behind them. With the exception of Genevieve being friendly, the night went as well as the other day they had been there. At the end was when it became saddening. Ella cried as they said goodbye to Alek and Jarvis with promises to write as soon as they could. They would never let those become empty promises to sadden their hearts.

Alek followed Jarvis's example by using the transportation spell to bring them back home. Once there, they took turns getting ready. As Julia got ready, she continued to run water to overshadow her grieving so Alek wouldn't hear her.

When she was done, she found Alek packing with his braid falling on the side of his saddened face. Julia saw her bag next to his and started packing like him with an expressionless face. After he was done, he helped Julia carry his and her bags next to the door. He came back into the room with a sorrowful expression that saddened Julia.

"Tomorrow's a big day," he said, "It seems as though this was a waste of time. Don't you think?"

"Of course I don't!" she said shocked, "Alek, you've helped me more than you can imagine. More than anyone else I know. You've healed me to my full extent. I can't thank you enough!"

He smiled, but his eyes still showed pain, "But you're still sad. And I'm…" he didn't continue.

"You're what?" she asked.

"Still in love with you." and then there was silence between them.

"Alek…" Julia had no idea what to tell him. She felt horrible for her self-centered tears. They soon swelled to her eyes again, "How…how can you love someone so broken? You deserve so much better."

"Look, I know," a pause, "I know it's unfair. But I've never felt this way about anyone ever before."

"Oh, Alek." were the only words that could suppress through her sealed lips, "If only there was time. But unfortunately, there's not."

"I know that now." he stepped closer and stared at her wet eyes, "You know how you always say you want to repay me?" she nodded, "Then at least do this for me. Kiss me. Just once so I can have the memory of your kiss no matter where we may go."

Julia understood. She owed him at least that much- one kiss. Nothing more would come of it though- she wasn't ready, not then.

"If it's the one thing that will repay you for everything, then I will."

Julia moved his braid as she wrapped her arms around him. Immediately following, she placed her lips on his. Surprisingly, tears flowed from her eyes and he wiped them away as he stood there kissing her. Unpredictably, they couldn't part. His love overpowered her and made her cry from his supreme passion, but was fine with it. Julia cared very deeply for Alek. It was love, yet a different form. She was happy she had shared a little memory of her cherished friend.

They stopped, "I've always loved you. I'm sorry," he said kindly in a whisper.

"You shouldn't be sorry. No one can control the feelings they have inside their heart," she said looking up.

Alek sighed heavily and smiled, "Goodnight Julia," as he kissed her forehead sweetly and stepped away to sleep on the couch.

"Alek…" she whispered, but he had already left.

Even though Julia was crying tears silently to herself as they traveled down her cheeks, they weren't only for Carson. They were for Alek as well. She was going to lose her dear friend who loved her the next day and dreaded it. She blew out the candles that were the only source of light and climbed into bed. Julia drifted off into a somber, fretful sleep with Annabelle on the floor next to her. Could she be falling in love, with more than just one person?

The night before, Carson was in his room on the balcony gazing out into the distance of the calm, silent night. After his talk with Peter and everyone, he only wanted to be left alone the next days. No one came into his room, but Carson could tell that Mr. Clayton and Cassidy were both watching over him carefully.

Carson heaved a large sigh. He was still upset and instead of feeling nothing and shutting down like he did before, he became numb and was drowned into his own thoughts. Succumbing to his feelings was something he did not want to do.

He thought of his family that he had loved so much, but Carson did not want to weep as his thoughts lingered to them. To distract himself, he ruffled his hair and wandered over to his nightstand to receive his blade again. Carson brought the blade back with him over to the balcony once more, throwing the sheath to the ground.

His eyes shimmered and beamed in the cold iron of the blade. Carson breathed back his tears. He didn't want to cry, and he didn't want to hurt himself again.

Carson held the blade outward. Closing his eyes, he whispered a spell softly. Shortly afterward, the sharp blade broke into millions of pieces. Carson finally opened his eyes as his mind tried to say goodbye to his family and Julia. The shards began to float away in the wind with Carson's peaceful heart and mind beginning to mend.

Finally feeling somewhat at harmony, he needed support. Carson gripped onto the rail on the balcony forcefully and shaking. Then he put his head down towards his chest, sighing deeply and giving his family honor.

After obtaining a moment to take a in a few profound inhales, he bowed down. Once he was back up, he saw the glistening shards of the blade blowing in the wind in all directions. He smiled.

Carson then had the need to go see Mr. Clayton. If there was one man he could go to for help or to talk, it was him. Mr. Clayton sort of became a father-figure to Carson after his parents passed away.

He hastily went to his door. Opening it, he found Princess Theodora looking as if she was about to knock on the door. Surprised, Carson slightly smiled, but her only response was an unpredictable anger in her eyes.

"Can I come in? I needed to talk to you." she said in the doorway fixing her hair.

"Sure." he let her in, licking his lips and eyes twinkling intensely as he watched her come in, "What did you need to talk to me about?"

"You," Theodora then started laughing a little sarcastically and then turned around to face him, "You want to know what I wanted to talk about?"

Carson was a little confused and stepped up to her a tiny bit closer, "Of course I do." he paused noticing her furry, "What's wrong?"

She put her hands to her lips but then calmly said, "Let's start when we were kids," she paced around for a moment, "Our parents agreed that for me to properly become queen, I would have to marry you. An arranged marriage. Am I wrong?"

"No, that was the plan."

"Exactly," she paused, but continued smiling, "Carson, my whole life I've adored the fact that I was going to marry you. I couldn't wait! And I thought in time, maybe you could learn to love me as I've always loved you."

Carson came up to her and brushed her arm, "Oh, Theodora-"

She pulled away slightly and continued, "Now, let's go a little forward in time," he nodded and looked down for a moment, "As you *clearly* know, a human came. Even though everyone strictly claimed that we were not allowed to have a human in Renata, you brought her. It was forbidden. People said you brought an awful omen. Some ran shrieking that the Remora would come to finish what they had started and set out to do," she looked up to him.

"I don't deny it." he replied.

"Do you know what they said about you?" he shook his head, "An honorable man with money, charm, and power throwing everything away. Finally letting his disappointing side show for once. A disgrace."

Carson somewhat put his head down in shame, "Seems a little harsh, but I understand. I didn't know they had said those things."

"But they were saying it," Theodora breathed nervously, she'd been waiting to have this conversation with Carson for a long time, "Now," she had a sign of tears in her eyes, "Now even though you knew it was forbidden to bring a human and did, you then did the worst possible thing. You fell in love with her!" Theodora was hurt and her hands became shaking fists at her side.

Carson then became faintly upset with her. He didn't think him loving Julia was the worst possible thing that could happen. He just followed his heart.

"Look," he started, "don't you think you're being a little too dramatic? Was it really the worst thing that could happen?"

"Yes!" she practically shouted, "Are you really that dense? After you claimed you loved Julia…everything started changing. First, people started saying even worse things about you. Next, the Remora found out. And that was horrible. Then things changed with me," Theodora paused trying to hold back her tears, "The night I was kidnapped, Soren declared his love for me. Half of my heart wanted him, but the other half belonged to you. Now I've lost him forever." she shed one sorrowful tear.

"He…he loved you?"

"Yes." Theodora swiped the tear away, "After the *war*, you still hadn't given up your feelings for her. As a Princess, I've done many things, but not much for myself. My friends and even servants told me of the horrible things people were saying about me, having lost to a *human* for my love," looking up harshly to him, she said, "I was humiliated."

She put her fists onto Carson's chest as he held onto her to support her. Next, Theodora cried. She could no longer bare it and had finally said what she needed to.

"It seems I've neglected everyone around me and their feelings just so I could follow my own heart. I'm sorry." Carson said sympathetically.

She looked up to him with wet eyes and he helped her into a soft chair to sit. Carson wiped her tears away feeling so apologetic for the way he had treated and ignored her. She held his hand at her cheek and he stared at her.

"I'm so sorry Theodora. If you could ever find it in your heart to forgive me, I'll always be here." he smiled.

Princess Theodora smiled herself with sparking eyes that reminded Carson vaguely of Julia, "I already have."

Carson went to his nightstand and hurriedly pulled out an expensive looking box with a golden lock. He said a spell and the box clicked open. He then took out what was in it and came back to Theodora.

"Then please, let me have the honor to marry you as it was originally planned. For me to love you." Carson got on his right knee and revealed a gorgeous gold, diamond, and sapphire ring from the box that was originally made for their arranged marriage together, "Will you marry me?"

Theodora gasped as she started to cry tears of joy, "Of course I will!"

Carson held her in his arms. He then wiped her joyful tears away as he kissed her. Putting the ring on her finger, Theodora laughed happily and Carson smiled.

Cassidy, Bade, and Veronica had been listening to the entire scene in the garden right below Carson's window. Cassidy picked up one of the shimmering shards that still remained from Carson's blade and held it close. Bade and Veronica held each other tightly feeling terrible for her.

"I'm sorry Cassidy." Bade said kindly to his sister.

"Don't be," she said surprisingly, "I only want him to be happy." she smiled back to him.

Early in the morning, Carson awoke alone to his own thoughts. He thought of the night before sighing. Touching his lips, he sorrowfully thought of Julia. Could Theodora mend his broken heart in time?

Carson breathed deeply, "Julia, I'm so sorry, Julia. Please, please forgive me."

Is it too soon? he thought.

———

The next morning, Julia saw that Alek had made breakfast, eaten, and was getting ready. She ate the scrumptious breakfast by herself and saw Annabelle chewing down her own. Julia saw Alek come out when he was done and got ready herself fast.

When she was done, Alek held their bags ready to go. Annabelle followed them out the door happily. Julia insisted that she'd carry her own bag, but he claimed it was lighter than air and carried it promptly.

They soon came up to town and it seemed to be a *normal* busy day. Julia tried to take slower paces as they came closer to the shop. Alek and Julia regretfully still came up to it and he set her bag on a wooden counter.

"So this is it?" Julia slowly asked choking on her emotions that were caught in her throat.

"I'll write to you as soon as I can- every day." Alek said wiping a tear that had accidentally escaped from Julia.

Soon they were embracing each other. She whispered tightly, "Goodbye Alek. I'll miss you." and indeed she would.

Alek released the embrace saying, "I love you." and he long-fully kissed her right cheek and left.

Julia cried more tears as she watched him go, silently whispering his name, but a sweet voice interrupted her weeping, and "Julia?" called Anna.

"Hi Anna." she replied.

"I know you probably don't want to, but could you please run the front desk for me, if you're up to it?"

"Of course." Julia said grabbing her bag and let Annabelle follow her as she went inside, wiping her tears dry.

She immediately went to work and was busy with the moderately concerned Anna and Adrianna. They had lunch together at the Inn and some people stared incredulously at Julia, almost waiting for her to cry in front of them. Adrianna made them finish quickly avoiding stares and they were soon back to work.

Just as he has said, Prince Nathan showed up at the same time as he did the day before. He smiled kindly to them all. They all bowed politely back to him as their response to his gentle smile that never seemed to fail.

"May I receive Julia now? Or do you still need her?" he asked trying to make Julia feel better.

Adrianna laughed, "Of course, your highness."

"Thank you." And Julia followed him and his guards silently to his carriage.

They climbed in and Julia looked up to Prince Nathan. *I wonder if he too is still in love with me.* she thought. By the sincerity in his gleaming smile, she knew the answer to her question was yes. She fell asleep in his arms calmly as they began the rode to his memorable castle once again.

Will it hurt my heart to go back to that place? she thought sleepily thinking of what would lie ahead of her on this new journey.

Chapter 32

A ROYAL TEST

Julia dizzily woke up to a sweet, pungent perfume. Surprised, she found she was still in Nathan's carriage. Even though it was a warm, spring day, she felt cold and cuddled in Nathan's strong arms who sat beside her.

He smiled and harmoniously kissed her forehead as the carriage came to a halt, "We're here." he said kindly.

Julia smiled but looked out the window. Prince Nathan helped himself out of the carriage and waited on the ground for Julia. When she started to climb out herself, Nathan swept her off her feet and swiftly twirled her onto the ground standing while laughing.

Prince Nathan stared at her with caring brown eyes as he chuckled. Then, the grand entrance to the castle opened. They both turned to see a thin man, the bottom half of his body formed by a goat's legs and hooves. A small, furry, green-eyed faun.

Nathan lightly touched Julia's back, "Julia, this is Mr. Roberts," he turned to him, "Would you be so kind as to help miss Julia carry her bags to her room?"

"Of, of, of course your highness." he smiled a little jittery while bowing to both of them before getting the bags.

"He's a little nervous. This is the first time he's ever met a human." Nathan whispered.

Mr. Roberts stepped in front of them before the entrance with the bags in his hands, "Would, would, you like, like me to sshoww the waaay in your highnesssss?"

"If you wouldn't mind." Prince Nathan said politely.

"Not at all!" he replied in a rush and guided them inside.

"You don't mind staying in the room you did before do you?" Nathan asked to Julia as they walked through the corridors.

"No. I loved that room."

He smiled. Now seeing the halls more in daylight, Julia thought they were marvelous. They were tall and ivory with gold furnishings, paintings, and mirrors.

"You know, this is the first time I *really* looked around here during the day."

"And how do you like it?" he asked.

"Splendid."

"Your highness," Mr. Roberts was calmer now, "We really weren't expecting you until later. Your brother and sisters are still in town."

"Yes, well, change of plans. And Philip is a bit of an embarrassment." Mr. Roberts nodded and they came up to the door.

Mr. Roberts set her bags down and they went inside where Nathan asked, "Speaking of plans, tonight my parents want the both of us to have dinner with them alone- seeing as my siblings aren't here. Would you come?"

"I'd love to." she smiled.

"I'll come to pick you up here when we're ready. All right?"

"Sure." and he kissed her cheek and left.

Julia turned to Mr. Roberts who immediately stood up straight the very second she looked at him, "Earlier he said that his brother is an embarrassment. Why is that?"

"Because there's a rumor going around that I'm gay." said Prince Philip in the doorway. His eyes sparkled a deep dark chocolate brown and long, shaggy brown hair like his brother Nathan, curling around the shape of his face, defining it.

He wore many neon, bright, and Easter colors in his expensive fabrics. He smiled largely with pearl-white teeth that seemed whiter because of his pink lips and dark skin. Philip laughed as he came from his position from leaning on the doorframe to kissing Julia's hand,

"I'm Prince Philip. Charmed, I'm sure." he said lightly with a gleaming smile.

Julia bowed as Mr. Roberts did, "Your highness."

Prince Philip turned gracefully to him, "Mr. Roberts, would you be so kind as to let me accommodate with miss Julia alone?" he smiled and winked playfully.

"Of, of, of courrrrrse your highness." he bowed deeply and left, shutting the door behind him.

Prince Philip came close to Julia as he studied her and giggled, "So you're having dinner alone with Nathan and my parents are you?" he asked with his eyebrows perfectly arched in amusement.

"Yes." she stated.

He ran his curious eyes studying her once more, "Well, you might want to find something else to wear." she looked down but he put his hands up and anxiously said, "Not that you bad. But my parents... they're quick to judge. And they judge on everything," he prolonged the word everything and his eyes grew large, for he was very animated in his speaking and gestures as he said, "And believe you me, everything. So, let's find you a dress. Shall we?" he guided her to the closet.

Julia laughed, "All right."

She shuffled her hands throughout the clothes and picked out a trendy, blue dress, "How about this one?"

"Honey, you *never* where blue the first time you meet my parents."

Prince Philip helped Julia pick out a white evening gown for 'innocence', as he put it, with silver as the trimming. He helped her do her hair, making it luscious, find shoes, and her makeup as he put some on himself to show the color and two bows in his hair. This made Julia laugh throughout the whole time, actually enjoying herself with the adoring Prince Philip.

He swabbed off the makeup and removed the bows. It was almost time for Julia to go to dinner. They stepped in front of the door so Philip could say his goodbye.

He leaned in forward to Julia almost as close as possible, "Prince Philip, what are you-" she asked but was cut-off by him silencing her with his lips.

Julia shoved him away, "Your highness!"

"I'm sorry Julia. But I wanted you to know."

"Know what?"

"That I like women of course. I'm just picky is all. I'm sorry Julia," he paused laughing, "My brother was right about you. You're beautiful. I'll need to find someone as pretty as you." he kissed her hand as she stood in shock, "Arrivederci." he said leaving and Prince Nathan was in the doorframe not a moment later.

Nathan gazed dazzled at her, "You look wonderful."

Julia slumped her shoulders, "Is that why you love me?" she turned away, "Is that the one and only reason why people love me?"

"Julia, I love you for your heart." Nathan replied back stern, without any hint of hesitation in his voice.

She smiled slightly, "I bet with just one wave of your hand, you could force me to love you."

"I would never." Prince Nathan touched her shoulder lightly, coming up behind her and whispered softly into her ear, "I know you're not ready to love yet. If I really want your heart, which I do, I have to earn it. I would never force you to love me. When you're ready, I'll be here. And I'll try my best to win your precious heart I've always wanted and waited so impatiently for."

Julia turned around from the honest confession of Prince Nathan's very own heart, "You're much, much too kind."

"I just hope one day that you'll think I'm more than just kind."

"You're highness…"

"But, would it be so much as to ask you to call me just Nathan?" Julia said nothing and he continued, "Well, before my parents start complaining, let's head down for dinner."

Julia nodded. He placed his hand warmly on hers as they left the room. They glided throughout the grand hallways until they came up to the ostentatious door to the Dining Hall.

She looked up and stared at the tall, luxuriant red oak door with gold glistening off of it. Nathan smiled slightly and then sighed. Julia had a feeling something of much importance would take place at the dinner with his parents as he opened the door, releasing his breathe he was holding, and she held hers in anticipation.

They stepped in to find his parents standing and talking in low voices with guards and servants positioned in the corners of the large room. It was the same Dining Hall at the Ball, but only the head table was left and set with an embellished, silky white table cloth and silver Dining sets of plates, cups, and silverware. There were also many pink roses in silver vases and basins. Furthermore, the stage had its curtain closed, which was a beautiful ruby red with golden stars.

"You're late," said Nathan's mother in a hard voice, shattering the silence of Julia's admiration, but then said sweetly, "Do sit down."

As they stepped to their seats and the servants helped them into their chairs, Nathan replied, "I'm sorry mother. The fault is mine."

The King and Queen sat on either end of the table, with Julia and Nathan taking the sides, "So you're The famous Julia?" asked the Queen, receiving a nod a little embarrassed, "And you're a human." she said coldly.

"Mother?" Nathan asked, trying to hide the appall in his voice.

"My son," the King interrupted, "it's just a simple…statement." He said kind at first but them smirked at the word statement.

Servants brought out delicious, delicate looking food and put smiles on their faces. They took a couple of moments to eat, Julia letting them take the first bite to show respect, and looked into each other's eyes. The King and Queen stared at each other as she looked to the Prince's somewhat confused expression and felt an unusual feeling of her having to answer every question they asked, truthfully.

The King put down his fork and clasped his hands together as he began asking Julia, "So, how exactly did you come here?"

"My diary. But my friend Peter has it now."

"Who's Peter?"

"The other human, dear." the Queen said thoughtfully.

The King continued, "Did you come here on purpose or by accident?"

"By accident, your grace."

"I see. Do you have any family back home that you abandoned by coming here?"

"Yes, but my parents died. The last time I saw them was when they were telling me not to love Carson so he…" Julia stopped.

Every truth, every barrier was broken. Every wall of her defense crumbled. She couldn't control the truth that passed her lips and brought her much ache and pain to her chest. The cause was his name.

Julia gasped and pressed her fingers to her lips, silencing them and closed her eyes to hold back the tears burning her eyes. The King sat back into his seat, placing his hands on his lap. Prince Nathan was perplexed as he watched his beloved Julia in pain by the words of his parents. *What's wrong with them? Why are they trying to hurt her?*

"Is that what happened?" the Queen asked genuinely.

"Yes."

"Do you still have feelings for him?"

As much as Julia wanted to say no, as much as she wanted to lie, she still had feelings for him and could not lie. An unbreakable energy seemed to force her to answer, "Yes."

"And do you love our son?"

Julia hid her face behind her hair. *Do I love him? I care for him, but…is it love?*

"Mother, please." Nathan pleaded.

"She must answer the question."

Then Julia's body and mind felt as if being pushed. She looked up. One tear revealed itself, "I…I know in time I will. Most surely. But now, at this moment, I…my heart…I'm just not ready. Not yet. I'm so sorry."

Prince Nathan looked to his parents with pleading eyes, "Mother, father, *please.*"

"Fine. I'll change the subject." his father said raising his hand then drank from his cup, "I'm curious to know, the war. You're a woman. A human. Why did you do it? How? Were you found out?"

"I was found out. By your son. He let me stay," she smiled, "Alek, my protector, helped me most of the time.," she whispered, "and Carson." she paused, "Together we rescued Princess Theodora. I did it because I wanted to protect Peter and send him home. Also to protect Carson." a heavy breath was taken.

"How courageous." the King replied happily and the Queen smiled in agreement.

For a few minutes, they sat in silence letting Julia have a chance to breathe. They only drank from their cups and thought to themselves. Julia only looked down trying to contain all of the mixtures of emotions flowing throughout her.

"Just out of curiosity, "the Queen began, "why were you two late?"

"Talking." Nathan answered.

"Hmm," the Queen mused, "It's just, I couldn't help but notice the smudging of Julia's lipstick on her face. What happened?"

Julia immediately looked up, feeling the smudge the Queen was referring to, and again the truth poured from her mouth, "It was Prince Philip."

"Philip?" everyone asked shocked.

"He was trying to show me that he wasn't gay as the rumors had said he was."

Prince Nathan rubbed his forehead, "What an embarrassment."

"What did he say then?" his parents inquired, eager to know.

"He's just picky." and everyone seemed to sigh in relief.

Out of nowhere, the most painful thing occurred for Julia. The King and Queen both asked her personal questions left and right, back and forth, one right after the other in all directions. Nathan protested and all Julia had the will to do was answer the questions while trying to contain her feeling while holding back tears. She felt as if her head was about to burst.

Wanting to get out of the situation, she finally said, "Excuse me." and as she got up to leave, a plate fell, shattering as it crashed onto the floor, "Oh no."

"Don't worry about it." Nathan said to her as she crouched down to pick up the pieces and a servant came to help, "You'll cut yourself."

Julia's eyes swelled with the tears or her emotions she had felt all throughout the horrid dinner, "No it's not fine. It's my fault. Ouch!" she said as a large shard sliced her finger, starting to bleed.

Prince Nathan brought her into the hallway in a hurry. The King and Queen just stood. Once in the hall, he took her hand in both of his. She cried and he kissed her hand, the blood and pain instantly dispersing.

Nathan still held her hand as she gasped through her tears, "What was all that about?"

"I honestly don't know Julia." he caressed her face where the smudge of her lipstick was. He held her held her close as she cried, which he was perfectly fine with. She needed to cry and had the right to; he felt it was somewhat his fault.

Prince Nathan led Julia throughout the halls once she was done weeping. They walked in utter silence, but Julia didn't blame him- she couldn't. After a little bit, they stopped at one door a short distance away from her room.

"This is the private library. I come in here a lot o think. You're free to use it at any time." he smiled trying to make her feel better as he opened the door for her.

"Thank you." she said stepping inside, forcing herself to smile and he left.

Julia looked around the room. There were a few book shelves, a fire place, table, comfortable looking armchairs, piano, small gold and youthful décor, and two other doors leading to other rooms. She spun around to see the King standing in the doorway in beautiful fabrics.

"Your highness," she bowed, holding the heavy emotions in the pit of her stomach.

Surprisingly, he clapped. Julia responded with a questioning look. He smiled and hugged her.

"I'm very sorry for our behavior Julia. But you passed the test." letting go, he smiled again at her.

"Test?"

"A Royal Test. To see who you are and how well you can handle things. You did very well. We were impressed. I apologize again, but it's our way of getting to know you."

"Did Prince Nathan-"

"No. My son didn't know anything of this. Did you feel as if you could only tell the truth?"

Julia nodded, "Yes. Very much. Like an invisible force."

"That was my wife. She has that power. Mine is to make sure you actually answer the questions."

"I…I'm actually relieved."

"Really? How so?" he asked sitting on the piano bench.

"Your grace and the Queen didn't seem to be that way."

The King laughed, "No we are not," he looked down, "Do you know how to play the piano?"

"Yes." Julia said thoughtful; it was the only instrument she could play.

"Sit."

231

Julia did. The King then taught her how to play a lovely piano version of the melody that sounded like Moonlight by Yiruma. He had her play it several times until she smiled in delight when she got it right.

"Perfect." he said leaving.

"Thank you." and she curtsied.

The King left and Julia sighed. She walked throughout the corridors until she came to her room. Julia got ready for bed and fell asleep peacefully with Annabelle next her.

That night was the first peaceful night of her dreams of just seeing the smiling faces of her family and friends. In the morning, Julia awoke feeling refreshed and got ready for the day with a new meaning. She slipped through the hallways and to the Dining Hall.

The servants served her a delightful breakfast with smiles all over their faces. Then, the Queen came in. She looked spectacular in gold and ivory as she grinned with pretty pink lips to Julia.

Chapter 33

DEAR NATHAN

The Queen glided across the across the floor. She was very beautiful with her smile and reminded Julia so much of her own mother. Then she stepped up to the chair across from Julia.

"Do you mind?" she asked kindly.

"Not at all. I'd be honored actually," a servant helped her majesty into her chair, "So my husband has told you the meaning of last night?"

"Yes your highness."

"The only reason we did anything of the sort to you is because we only have our son's best interest at heart."

"I understand." Julia beamed.

Breakfast was served to the Queen and she happily ate it. They sat in silence for a bit, eating contently. The Queen soon brought up small talk and spoke to each other merrily.

After a while, she stopped and smiled as she asked to Julia, "There's a room I'd like you to see. Will you come with me?"

Julia nodded. Both she and the Queen were helped out of their chairs by the servants. Then, they walked to the private library and through another large, dark wooden door.

Amazed, Julia gasped at the beauty on the other side of the door. She could almost hear the choirs and orchestras playing from them being needed for that moment in the room. It was a little cool, but the scent of roses made it warm. Iridescent white tiles trimmed with stunning emerald green. On the ceiling was a beautiful painting of angels in the clouds. Finally, the pearl white walls surrounded hundreds of statues with large paintings hanging gracefully.

"Wonderful, isn't it?" asked the Queen jovial.

"Absolutely!" she replied excitedly.

They both walked merrily around, taking in all of the astounding artwork. There were many fine pieces of art hanging all throughout the room. They stopped at a peculiar one that was very pretty.

The setting seemed to be the private library. A young, tall, and handsome man in brilliant fabrics was standing with a grin across with shining face. He held a gorgeous youth, who was wearing elegant robes and fabrics and she shared his joy sitting down.

She spoke ever so sweetly, "That's the King and I, before we had all our beautiful children."

"You both are still so young and charming."

"Why thank you child."

They continued walking cheerfully until the end of the room. The statues they had passed were some of great elegance and beauty. There was just one particular painting that hung high at the end, catching their attention.

In spring colors of an outdoor setting, painted an exquisite scene of two small boys with their mothers. The first boy wore a small, thin silver band at the crown of his head of wavy brunette locks and a red children's suit. He was walking with his arms out as far as they could go and laughing to his mother- the Queen.

Another smaller boy was being held close by his mother. She was extremely beautiful in a lovely blue dress, kind blue eyes, cherry cheeks, a loving, happy smile, and long, golden hair elegantly placed in a braid. The young boy was very cute. He was tiny in a blue suit, golden hair just starting to grow, an adorable smile with no teeth, and twinkling blue eyes as tried to reach for a miniature white and blue star joyously. The children were vaguely familiar to Julia and guessed that the seemingly older and brunette boy was Nathan.

"Ah! The memories," the Queen said both happily and with tears in her eyes, "Do you know who that is?"

"You and your son, his highness, Nathan."

"The other boy and his mother, dear."

"I have one guess."

She nodded, "That was Matilda Tabor and her son Carson," Julia flinched a little at his name, "His mother and I- oh! We were the best of friends. His father and uncle were in Parliament with the King and we always got together during the meetings and our free time," she paused for a moment, "Matilda loved her children so much. Carson and my dear Nathan were like brother. But when his parents died...that was the worst. He intended to keep his promise to his parents and kept the business running. Work became his life. Eventually he never had any friends unless they were around him at work."

Julia hated what she did next. She crumpled onto the floor at a slight loss of breath. The Queen rushed to her.

"My dear! Are you all right?"

She nodded her head vigorously. Anxiously, they waited a moment for her to compose herself. Julia tried with all her might and finally felt at ease.

"What happened?"

"I'm still in need of a little more healing my Queen. I'm sorry." she explained looking up to her.

In response, she nodded back saying, "I understand." and helped her up.

"Thank you."

"It's fine," surprisingly, the Queen hugged her and then let go after a moment, lightly holding Julia's shoulders, "We don't have to mention this to Nathan if you don't want to."

"I'd prefer if he didn't know."

Affirming her comprehension, she asked, "Shall we head back?"

"Sure." and they started walking away.

Heading out, Julia caught sight of yet another painting. Yet, this one was different. She gazed at it curiously.

It was a young woman laying on a bench in a charming pink dress that hung over the side at the end. Above her in the background was Renata's overture of beauty with a lake, forest, mountains, and a small tip of a castle revealing itself. Below her was the feather of a raven, a sign of sadness and sometimes death.

As she lay there, the half of her face closest to the Renata background seemed exuberantly happy. The other half of her face closer to the ground was crying. She held something in her hand as well, but she couldn't make it out. Yet, the most miraculous thing about the painting was that the girl had reddish-brown hair and green eyes.

"She looks very much like you!" the Queen exclaimed.

"Who is she?"

"It's just a story that's been told since the beginning of Renata. The legend is that one day the **Queen of Renata** will come and bring us to a new age. No matter what conflicts she faces, she strives through and she also comes to have all the powers of Renata as well. The artist *George Patterson* studied her very carefully and made a handful of these fascinating paintings of her. The legend also states that she will come to us in time."

"Amazing." Julia said genuinely.

Her majesty chuckled a bit and they started to head out once again. After a moment the Queen stopped walking and turned to a small statue. She smiled.

Julia came up to the petite figurine as well. It was Prince Nathan from his shoulders up. His features were defining and were very attractive. He looked proud as he grinned gently, humbly.

"My dear, dear Nathan," her highness sighed admiringly, "He is truly a King."

"He's very handsome."

"Oh yes indeed. He and his friends were always the handsome fellows," they both chortled, "I think I'm ready for lunch now. Are you?"

"Yes your grace."

So they both walked out of the brilliant room back into the private library. Servants brought them a tray of fruits and vegetables for lunch. They ate joyously and once they were done, the Queen said her goodbye. Julia stayed in the private library for some time. She thought about her morning with the Queen and smiled. The piano became her interest for a while, but then asked the servants to bring her writing and drawing supplies.

The first thing she did was that she began to write about when she arrived in Renata. It began very well and Julia was indeed happy with herself. Next, she drew a window setting of the private library with dazzling colors of paints the servants brought and made the picture turn out very nice. Then as a small inside joke to Julia, she wrote a speech titled **We Are One**.

Unexpectedly, a servant came in with a letter for Julia. Hastily, she opened it to see who sent it. It was from Alek. Julia sighed seeing that it wasn't from Carson. They promised to write each other. *Maybe it's best just to forget him.* she thought and read Alek's letting smiling.

Dear Julia,

How are you? I know it's only been a day, but I'm worried about you. I hope you are doing well. Jarvis and I miss you. We're doing fine here in the Kalama Kingdom. We arrived just in time. Right on schedule to meet our uncle and settle into our new home. Then there was a party- which was fantastic! I met many new people. They're all Songbirds and they're very enjoyable. The life here is thrilling and exciting. I cannot wait until training, although I won't need very much. Remember? I hope all is well and I get to see you soon.

Your Friend,

Alek

Alek

"Oh Alek." Julia said to herself missing him more than ever. Immediately following, she wrote a letter to send back to him. It wasn't hard for her, it was always easy to talk to him.

Dear Alek,

You shouldn't worry. I'm doing just fine. I miss you and Jarvis as well. I'm happy to know that you both are well and are enjoying yourselves. And yes, I remember that you don't need much training. Have fun accomplishing your dream and doing what you do best as a Songbird. Hope to see you soon as well.

Your Friend,

Julia

Julia Myers

Once done, Julia grinned and placed her letter in an envelope. She gave the letter to a servant to be delivered to Alek and they left with a broad smile. After a couple of minutes, another servant came, informing

Julia to come to dinner with the King, Queen, and Prince Nathan once again.

Julia laughed a little and left the private library. She quickly freshened up in her room. As she was about to leave, Prince Philip stood in the doorway smirking.

"Another dinner?" he giggled.

"No test this time."

Philip shook his head still chuckling, "If you wish, you can wear blue around my parents now."

She looked down at her pretty yellow dress and said, "I think I'm fine with this."

He beamed, "Good choice. Shall I walk you down there?" he held out his arm for her.

"You may." she replied linking arms.

They strolled down together chuckling and he joined dinner himself as well. It was a very nice with great food, conversation, and actual enjoyment. That night was one of the happiest nights for Julia since coming to Renata. But the only reason she wasn't happy was because she felt the only way she could be, was to forget Carson.

After dinner, they all remained at the table and continued to converse in high spirits. They even let Mr. Roberts, who was standing in the corner, join them. *They're just regular people. No wonder their whole Kingdom loves and admires them.*

Night soon came and they all said goodnight to each other. Both the King and Queen hugged her, Prince Philip lightly kissed her cheek and ruffled her hair at the top. All giggled and once everyone but Julia and Nathan were gone, he fixed her hair and embraced her, "Goodnight." then longingly kissed her other cheek with glistening eyes and left.

Julia's heart began to beat rapidly. Prince Nathan was becoming even more dear to her than he already was. Her mind thought that it was the beginning of love. He was always so kind to her and cared for her more than anything, as she thought of all the things he did for her. It was time to forget Carson.

Julia quickly went to her room and breathed deeply as she shut the door. Forgive and let die is what her father used to say. She let one tear fall and wiped it away.

Getting ready for bed, she surprisingly had no trouble remembering the times she had spent in Renata. No tears fell again and she was grateful for it. After she was done, she still wasn't tired and went to the private library with Annabelle.

Julia chose a book and sat in one of the comfy armchairs. Annabelle lay on the floor next to the fire. Only a couple of minutes into reading, Julia fell asleep with a smile on her face.

Sometime later, she was fast asleep and Prince Nathan walked in. Quietly stepping to close the door, he noticed Julia in her slumber. He smiled and fixed the blanket on his shoulders. A moment passed as Nathan stared at her with longing and compassionate eyes. Then, he turned away. His long, shaggy brown hair covered half of his defined featured face and lightly tanned skin, with golden radiance from the fire almost radiating off of him.

Looking back, Prince Nathan thought to himself. *I love her so much. Tonight was wonderful. I just want her to be happy. I hope I can make her feel that way in the future. But how long must I have to wait? Selfish is what I'm being, but even father wants me to become King now. And I can only do that if I marry. Julia is the only one I want by my side.*

Every feeling he was having and emotion showed in his expression. Stepping closer, Annabelle whined a little. Prince Nathan held a finger to his lips, quieting her.

The book Julia had been reading earlier was on the floor. He knelt to pick it up and set it on the table next to the chair. He also placed his blanket on her. Julia breathed and he froze.

Waiting a moment, he Breathed again and looked down. Finally, he couldn't take it any longer. Prince Nathan lightly grasped Julia's hands on the arms of the armchair, slowly closed his beautiful eyes, leaned in, and gently caressed his lips against hers.

Before the kiss, Julia was even dreaming of his highness. He was smiling ever so broadly and kissed her before he seemed to go away in the dream. She awoke in shock to find him kissing her in reality, but let him and was fine with it. Although, her heart beat sped up in an unforgiving manner.

The fervent kiss ended. Nathan quietly leaned back and slowly opened his eyes. What he saw a blushing Julia.

Almost shamefully, Prince Nathan looked down, "I'm sorry," he started to get up, "I-"

Julia held his hand, making him stay and said, "I am trying to forget Carson. Don't give up on me. Please."

The Prince was a little surprised, "Give up on you? I'd never. Julia, you're making the choice to live a life with a broken heart. So please, let me try to mend it with my love for you." Nathan whispered in a compassionate voice to her.

She wrapped her arms around his strong neck, "I think my heart is ready for love again." and she kissed him.

Magic. The only word to describe that kiss in that moment. It was the first time Nathan had kissed someone whom he truly loved and the first time Julia had kissed with a healed heart after everything that had happened to her.

Amazed, they both parted and Julia cried tears not of sadness, but of joy and said, "You've had my heart for some time now. But I just wasn't ready to give it up. I now can. And you have it."

He kissed her once more happily and replied, "Well, I think it's time I got some rest. I have business in the morning to take care of. Shall I walk you to your room?"

"Please."

Beaming, Prince Nathan helped her up. Annabelle rushed out into the hallway and he held the door open. Looking back, he snapped his fingers and watched as the book put itself away and the fire blew out. He loved magic.

They walked in the hallway holding hands all the way. Once at the door, he held that one open for her as well. There were no words to describe the happiness flowing through him.

Julia turned around to him, holding the blanket, "Would you like this back?"

"Keep it. I'll see you tomorrow."

"Goodnight you highness."

"Goodnight Julia." and lightly kissed her once more before he left.

Annabelle snuggled in her place on the floor below the window and next to Julia's bed. She wrapped herself in his warm blanket and fell fast asleep. She could not help but dream of Prince Nathan the whole night. Indeed, she was falling in love with him.

Chapter 34

YOUR HONEST ANSWER

Early in the morning, Julia awoke. She put an arm behind her head and smiled. Getting up after a moment, she noticed Annabelle lying on her bed.

"Good morning Annabelle."

Annabelle wagged her tail playfully and jumped off the bed. Julia went to her window and opened it. A breeze blew in and the sun barely began to peak up in the distance in a pool of pink behind the stormy, gray clouds.

Taking a deep breath, she asked, "Would you like to go take a walk outside?"

Annabelle let her tongue hang out in excitement and ran to the door in response. Laughing, Julia quickly put shoes and Prince Nathan's blanket on. Once she was done, she and Annabelle walked to the gardens.

The morning was stunning. Then Annabelle growled lowly. Julia looked to the sky and saw a small, dark speck in the thick clouds. Looking a little closer, she saw that it was Bade. He came down and he noticed her as well.

Julia grinned, "Bade!" she exclaimed.

"Julia," they rushed to each other and hugged, "How are you?"

"Just fine. You?"

"Wonderful," he reached to his belt and received two envelopes,

"This is the invitation to my wedding. One is for you and the other is for his highness. I thought you'd still be with Alek."

"No," she sighed, "He went to become a Songbird. I was surprised as well to know how soon he was leaving." Bade sighed deeply and she saw asking, "What's wrong?"

"There's more," he reached to his belt and pulled out two more envelopes, "I didn't want to be the one to tell you."

"Well, what is it?"

He looked down, "You know of Princess Theodora's and Carson's engagement, right?"

She swallowed, "Of course."

Bade gave her the letters looking into her eyes deeply concerned, "This is the invitation to their wedding for you and Prince Nathan. I'm sorry."

Julia tried her best to hide her feelings and hugged him tightly, "It doesn't matter. It was good to see you again."

"Are you sure you're ok?" they parted and she nodded, "All right. Goodbye Julia. See you soon." and he left.

What happened to her the following couple of hours, Julia did not clearly remember. Only that she had thrown the invitations on a table near her bed. The whole day she remembered as a sort of daze. Her feelings- she could not even begin to imagine.

Carson was really gone, almost wanting to get out of her heart as soon as possible. In seconds, the pain in her chest came back to her, but instead of wallowing in self-induced pain of heartbreak, she forced herself to become numb. To not feel the world or anything at all seemed more pleasing to her.

Surprisingly, she at least made her way to the private library thinking *How could he do this? So soon?* the entire way. Julia sat at the piano feeling nothing. She did not eat anything and asked the servants to leave.

It started to rain hard and it hit the windows loudly. Thunder and lightning clapped in sheets, scaring Annabelle. Julia lit some candles thinking of her grandmother, forcing all of her tears back.

The windows began to fog up, making it chilly in the small room. Her drawings were still where she'd left them. Without thinking- without feeling- she tore them up. Little shreds dropped to the floor as though her heart. The paintings were gone with nothing left; nothing but sorrow. Julia even made more and tore them up as well when she had finished them.

The weight of her eyelids holding back her tears became unbearable. Julia crumpled to the floor, holding some shreds of paper in fists. Annabelle whined in disapproval, and tried to lick her, but Julia only turned away.

Thankfully no one had come in to see her in that state the entire day. When night soon came, she was shocked. Still, she sat there but knew Prince Nathan was likely to come into the private library, so she got up, wiping the tears severely from her eyes.

Outside seemed more promising to Julia. Her steps were slow, but brought her to the gardens. She was soaked to the bone not even a minute after she stepped a foot outside.

Dripping wet, thunder roared in the sky as if it were a lion. Then she came up to a fountain- the fountain. Tears streamed down her cheeks like the rain and fell to her knees before it.

This time there was no Alek to hold her close. This time there was no Nathan to comfort her. She was all alone, in oblivion.

Suddenly, a soft slow beat of her mother's lullaby began to ring in her ears. Julia looked all around her with no sign of her mother anywhere. Then, she looked inside of the fountain. What Julia saw was a slight vision of her family. Then, Carson appeared. He beamed one of his smiles and held out a hand, a tanned, loving grasp, out to her.

In truth, what was really happening was that nymph creatures with the songs like sirens in the water, were taking Julia's most sensitive thoughts, luring her in. The song, his smile, were exactly the same as the originals. She received the hand.

The beat stayed constant, making her dizzy and her eyelids become heavy. She saw the last sparkle of blue in Carson's eyes before she became fully mesmerized and fell asleep. The nymphs smiled with glittering eyes and brought her almost lifeless body into the cold waters with them.

Their magic had made the fountain disappear and was now only a cylinder of deep, freezing, and clear water. They dragged Julia down, down, down, farther and farther still playing the lullaby. She didn't have the will to wake up, she couldn't.

She floated comatose in the water, making her lips a tint of purple, her skin pale, and her last breath surpass her lips. The nymphs left for a moment to let their prey settle in peace, even though her heart was broken. Only the soft melody played for several moments as she began to slip away as a lost soul forever…

As lost as Julia was, a faint echo shouted desperately, "Julia! Julia!"

Prince Nathan's blanket had fallen off of her when she cried at the fountain. Who was calling her? Was there any way to save her?

Abruptly, a dark figure jumped into the water. It swam down to the bottom near Julia. It was Prince Nathan! Yet his face was shocked when he saw Julia and then showed urgency.

Hurriedly, he came to her and received her wrists. The nymphs quickly came in a furry. They threatened him by being hostile with their teeth and claws.

Ignoring the threat, he held her close, trying to swim away as quickly as possible. The nymphs took action following them, and pulling them down once more. It was a difficult rescue.

"She is ours!" one cried out.

Nathan closed his eyes thinking of a spell. He then held Julia as close as he could. Barely more than a whisper, for that was all he could handle with the water trying to rush into his lungs, he said a spell.

Instantaneously, a wave spread out, making the nymphs freeze and then swim away in terror. He smiled faintly and promptly thought of another spell. They ascended rapidly to the surface.

Coughing, Prince Nathan swam to the rim of the fountain and brought both of them out of the water. He set her lying on the rim and sat on his knees beside her. Examining her, he held her head in his hand with a desperate look through the rain.

Her lips were purple and almost blue. Her eyes were shut tightly. Her body did not move.

Acting swiftly, he kissed her, and opened her lungs to cough up the water. Thankfully she did immediately. He smiled and held her face in his hands, pushing the wet hair out of her eyes, knowing she was safe and sound now.

Julia's lip quivered as she lay there wet and cold, "Your highness," tears came, "I'm so stupid!" and held onto him for support, yet fainted as he held onto her there in the rain.

Neither could believe what had happened. Nor fully understand it. But she was safe, and that's all that really mattered to him.

Julia slipped back into conciseness a little while later. She was in her room sitting on her bed, being tended to by servants who were trying to dry her hair, and in her closet. Prince Nathan was being dried as well, tended to a cut he had received from one of the nymphs, with a warm blanket over his shoulders.

He turned to see that Julia was aware now, "I'm fine. We're both fine. Everyone please leave." he gave the blanket to one and then they all left.

They first stared at each other with many questions in their eyes. It was the two of them alone. Both in their wet clothes. He turned away for a moment but then looked back.

Prince Nathan came up and knelt before her with a deeply concerned expression, "Are you all right?"

Julia nodded and then looked back up to him, lightly touching his scratch so she wouldn't hurt him, "And you?"

He gently pulled away and held her cold hands warmly in his own even though he was freezing, "Julia, you know I've always loved you. I've shown nothing but kindness to you. But I've never been hurt or even knew this new feeling of a little anger before until recently."

She put her head down with her lips quivering from the cold and her tears, "I'm sorry."

Nathan got up, releasing his kind grasp, "What were you thinking?" he pushed back his long, dripping wet hair ad sighed.

Julia faced him, "I don't know. I'm sorry. I honestly have no idea."

He shook his head- he still had no knowledge of the wedding invitations, "What happened? There has to be a reason."

She looked down once more. Then, Nathan took off the soaked and heavy royal dress robe that was draped over his drenched clothes and lightly threw it to the ground next to the table. He spotted the invitations and read them.

"Your highness…" Julia's eyes were scared and heavy from the tears.

Sighing deeply, he looked down closing his eyes and set the letters back into their place, "I see."

He turned to face the petrified Julia who only said, "I…I…" she couldn't utter another sound.

Slowly coming up to her he said, "I should go." and took one step.

She quickly grasped his hand in hers, "No. Please don't your highness," she begged and paused, "Yes I still have feelings for him but-"

"Well obviously if you're willing to drown for him."

"Your highness *please*."

Then Nathan wanted answers. He lightly pinned Julia on her back on top of the bed. Not wanting to hurt her in any way, he gently held her wrists. A small glimmer of anger was shown in his eyes, "Why won't you call me Nathan?" in shock, she turned away sadly, "Is it too difficult for you? Do you not love me?"

She turned back, "Of course I do."

"Then last night…didn't that mean anything to you?"

"Of course it did. I love you."

He exhaled, closing his eyes again as he asked painfully to Julia, "How do I know if you really love me if you still have feelings for Carson?"

"Kiss me."

And so he did, first taking a moment, then putting his lips on hers. He loved her immensely and his only wish was for Julia to return the same amount of love for him, eventually. Nathan wiped her tears that were escaping from her eyes onto her cheeks.

Ending the kiss, he looked away, "Your tears say enough." and got up.

"Nathan." she called sitting upon the bed as he turned around shocked with his eyes radiant.

With hopeful eyes he knelt in front of her once again, "Yes Julia?"

"It wasn't just his face," he held a questioning look as his expression, "I saw my parents." Nathan then realized it wasn't just *him* she was thinking of and felt ashamed of the way he had treated her, "Before I came to Renata, my parents died. It was horrible trying to get over it. I miss them so much…You have no idea what that's like." she shook her head and the tears away.

He held her face in his hands, "I'm so sorry Julia. If I had-"

"But you still have the right to be angry with me."

"Why?"

"I do still have feelings for Carson. And I'm trying, trying so hard to forget him. I have to."

"Why try so hard?"

"Because I love you," she shivered bit, the cold was getting to her, "I'm sorry for today, but thank you for rescuing me." she kissed his cheek.

He was stunned as he held her hands, but then embraced her, "I always want to be with you. I want to protect you. I'll make sure nothing will harm you- even though I myself am guilty of such cruel acts tonight."

"You didn't hurt me. You just didn't understand. But one thing is certain, I love you."

"And I, you."

Then, they shared another kiss. Luckily, no tears were shed and she was jovial, but also cold. Him holding her made her feel as though being melted. Julia shivered faintly.

"Julia you're freezing! You'll get sick like this."

"I'm cold, but I'm fine." she held onto him.

"No you're not." he carried her into her bathroom and set her on a chair, as she noticed the bathtub already filled, "The servants ran a hot bath for you. Now, for me, please make yourself warm. I'll be back later." he kissed her forehead getting up.

Julia called to him when he was at the door, "Don't forget to knock."

He laughed and went to his own room. She put her hand in the water to feel its temperature. It seemed to even melt her on the inside.

Julia ten wanted to be out of the misery of being cold. She took the bath and felt calm. Then she got ready for bed, but put a shawl over her shoulders since his highness said he would be back.

She lay down on the couch as she waited. Not too long after, a knock came and she replied saying to come in. It was his highness, holding something in his hands.

Julia was curious to know what it was, but smiled instead. The Prince grinned one of his charming smiles back. She sat up on the couch and he kissed her lips lightly, "Told you I'd be back."

She smiled and kissed him, "That you did."

"Would…would it be too much to say that I want to be with you every second of the day?" he paused laughing, "Well not every second, but just to be with you?"

"I would like to also. But I would have to stay here. I don't want to be a burden though."

"My parents adore you. Everyone enjoys you here. You're a breath of fresh air."

"Yet, I still haven't officially met Paiton or Samantha."

Nathan smiled, kissing her cheek, "You will soon," he looked down slightly, then back up, "Julia, I want to share and spend the rest of my life with you. Please do me the favor of making me the happiest man in the world," she was a little confused, but he pulled out a stunning ring that was a gold band with small diamonds set in a halo setting with rubies in the center, curling to make a red rose, with a sparkling diamond in the center, "Will you marry me?"

Julia gasped and put her hands to her face, "Oh Nathan! It's beautiful."

He gently took her hands in his, "I...I know maybe it's too soon, and that it's a big step, but I love you. I'll help you forget about Carson. I'll help you forget about all the pain in her life. You'll have no more worries. So please, will you be the Queen at my side when I become King?"

"I absolutely will! I love you." they laughed and shared a kiss.

Julia cried tears of joy as they kissed affectionately. Nathan put the ring on her finger and kissed her forehead so happy that he was going to marry the one he loved. As they were blissfully kissing each other, a knock came at the door.

Prince Nathan stood as Julia said, "Come in."

Mr. Roberts opened the door smiling with Annabelle at his side, "I found her wandering the halls and thought you might want her back." Annabelle ran into the room and up to Julia.

"Thank you. I was starting to wonder where she had gone off to."

He chuckled, leaving graciously. She then turned to Nathan beaming. The Prince smiled as well, leaning in to kiss her, "I'd best be off," he said lovingly, "We'll announce the engagement tomorrow. Goodnight my love." he smiled broadly, but even more charmingly as he got up to leave.

"Goodnight Nathan. I love you too."

He left with ever so thoughtful eyes and grin. Julia breathed and beamed giggling to herself. Annabelle let her tongue hang and her tail wag playfully.

Julia laughed outright merrily with joyful tears, "Annabelle, I'm getting married!" she exclaimed as Annabelle jumped on her in response.

Chapter 35

WEDDING BELLS

That night, Julia had been dreaming about the ocean. She kept staring at the rhythm of waves lapping up and down onto the shore. The white, cool sea foam stretched up to her feet in between her toes. Dreaming of being on a beach meant times or events were changing in your life. Indeed there was a big change upcoming soon for Julia, as she slowly remembered the night before opening her eyes to the friendly yellow sun gazing at her.

"Good morning." Prince Philip said above Julia.

She screamed in terror. Prince Nathan came running as fast as he could down the hallway to her room, still in his royal night robes. He looked as charming and sweet as ever with sleepy eyes in shock and a bed head.

"What happened?!" he shouted with his voice still groggy with sleep.

Julia lifted up the sheets and pointed at Philip, "You're brother! Oh I can't believe this! Sitting right there watching me-"

Prince Philip interrupted, "Sitting right here calmly!"

Nathan grabbed his brother, "What? Oi vey! Julia, I'll be back later," he took his brother out the door saying, "You're such an embarrassment!"

"My feelings are sincerely hurt." Philip yelled back at him.

Julia laughed at how at how wild a Prince and brothers could be.

She then got ready in a splendid white gown. After, she looked out the window to find that it wasn't morning, but rather mid-day.

About ten minutes later of her playing with Annabelle did Nathan come to get her. They walked around the hallways hand-in-hand and ever so merry. Soon, they went into the private library and shared a small meal the servants had brought. Prince Nathan cut and fed her some delicious pieces of meat, complimented by fruit, cheese, and tasty red wine to soothe the pallet in a sweet, loving gesture.

As the Prince and Julia laughed enjoying themselves, Philip came in, "What do you want?" Nathan asked jokingly with a smile.

"Well, mom and dad want to go get Paiton and Samantha from town today and eat dinner there. I came to help Julia get ready. May I steal her until we're ready to go?"

He had already made her get up, "Fine," Nathan replied.

Prince Philip chuckled and led Julia into her room, ducking into the closet.

"So what should I wear today? White for 'innocence'? Or maybe blue for 'calmness'?"

He shuffled throughout the dresses and found a spunky purple one, "How about this?"

Julia didn't think that purple was the right color for the mood of announcing her engagement, "I was thinking more of green or white." she handed him two dresses.

Philip spotted the ring, "Oh my! It's gorgeous."

She put her hand behind her back, "You weren't supposed to see until later."

"But we're practically related now! Let me see it."

She showed the ring to him, "Wow that's beautiful."

"We were going to announce the engagement tonight," she poked him, "So don't say anything."

Philip raised his hand, "I swear as Prince Philip I won't say anything. You have my word."

They laughed and he snatched the ring to find a perfectly matching green dress, accessories, and make up. Of course he tested them all on himself first, but told her that she was pale compared to him. Giggling, they finished just on time.

Nathan knocked as he came in the room smiling, "Well we'd best be off."

"Doesn't she look beautiful dear brother?" Philip asked twirling her into Nathan's arms.

"Yes." he replied grinning while she blushed.

"See ya in the carriage." Philip laughed going out the door.

"What's he on about?" he asked jerking his head to the doorway as if his brother were still there.

"He knows," his eyes became large and she giggled, "He promised he wouldn't say anything."

"Let's hope."

They both went to the entrance in high spirits, with Prince Philip coming up behind her and covered her eyes, "What are you doing?" she chortled.

"Look at the carriage."

He brought his hands down from her eyes to reveal a stunning black horse pulling the magnificent carriage. Julia gazed closer at the horse, thinking it looked familiar, and had a flashback to the war. It was Midnight- the trustful noble steed that she had used in the battle.

"How did you find her?" she went up to and pet Midnight.

"Well, it wasn't easy, but brother here insisted." Philip tugged Nathan's shoulder, then stepped into the coach.

She looked to her fiancée in delight, "Thank you."

"Oh let's get a move on!" called Prince Philip from the carriage.

"Yes, we don't have much time to waste." remarked the Queen coming up to them.

"Yes, yes. No time to waste at all," the King said in a hurried manner, "Oh boy! I hope there's going to be lots of *meat*!" and he quickly stepped inside with Nathan and Julia laughing.

"Well go on Chuck." the Queen called to the driver after a moment.

"Yes, make haste Chuck. But make the ride as scrumptious as possible."

"Scrumptious?" asked Julia.

"Dear Conan, you're frightening the poor girl."

"Sorry my dumpling."

The Queen held her hand, "Julia, my King is a half beast. He can turn into any beast he wishes, but his favorite is the wolf. He also *loves* meat- more than anything." she rolled her eyes.

"Not any more than you my little pumpkin." he kissed her cheek and they began laughing.

Nathan sighed as Philip said, "I prefer young love," winking over to Julia and received a glare from his brother.

In town, Princess Paiton and Samantha were coming down the stairs at the Inn to meet Julia and the others. Paiton didn't see Julia or the others anywhere so decided to get a drink while waiting. She spotted the charming Inn Keeper look-a-like in all of the business, "Samantha, why don't you go to the Inn Keeper by the piano? He'll play a song for you."

"Ok sister."

Paiton came up to the bar area where the waitress Paige was the bar-tender.

"What can I get you?" she asked with Paiton replying with red wine.

"Are you waiting for your family?" a man asked kindly.

Paiton turned to see a man with armor of the Pierre Kingdom, "How did you know?"

"I can read people's thoughts," he said with a drunken smile. Paige gave Paiton her drink and he said to her, "I also know that this girl has been thinking about her puppy for the last three hours," Paiton giggled, "And reflecting on the time Carson Tabor was here- which adds more shame to my pride." he drank from his cup.

"What do you mean?"

"I'm not entirely sure myself. All I know is I lost my honor, my job, and the only woman I have ever loved." his voice became higher in rage and threw his glass to the floor, then his hands were on Paiton's shoulders, making it painful for her, "Don't take your loved ones for grant it."

"Get your filthy hands off my daughter!" the King shouted with the commoners bowing around him.

Soren started to laugh, "My King, I was just warning your daughter to be careful of all her spoils!"

Suddenly, the King jumped at Soren, revealing his pointed teeth.

Paiton screamed. The townsfolk tried to break it up as the Inn keeper held onto the crying Samantha and Nathan holding Julia.

The fight was broken up leaving the King wiping the blood from his fanged mouth and Soren holding his burgundy stained shoulder. Samantha hurried to Paiton who was soon in the arms of her father. Soren cried drunken tears of rage, "Kick a man while he's down," he spotted Julia with fire coming to his eyes, "This was your fault! Filthy human. Enjoy your peace." and shoved people out of his way leaving.

The Inn keeper came up to them, "I'm so sorry your majesty. Please try to enjoy yourself with anything you should need." he then turned to the silent Inn, "Well don't just stand there people, the royal family is here. Play some music and enjoy yourselves!" he smiled enchantingly.

Music started and everyone sat down beginning to talk amongst themselves, "Are you all right?" Julia asked.

Paiton nodded, "I'm fine now. Thanks. I was just scared for a minute."

"You don't have to worry anymore sweetheart." her mother hugged her, then sat at the table.

"That's what papa wolf is for." she smiled sitting across from her mother.

Paige came up to the table with several mugs, "Creamed Cider on the house."

Samantha started to chug hers, with Paiton setting it back on the table. Chuckling, Philip grabbed his mug, and gulped while stepping on top of another table beside them. Upbeat music began and he made the entire Inn thunder in laughter as he sang a song about a pretty lass he once knew.

A long time ago, in a far away land
I was looking for a girl to take her hand
There was once a pretty little lass I knew
And her virgin name was Molly-Sue!
Down in town we'd get drunk and sing a song
By the end of the night we'd get along
I'd like an honest fight for that saucy maid
What I'm basically saying is I like to get – paid
Oh that pretty little lass I once knew

And her virgin name was Molly-Sue!
She'd fight with her clothes I was always mussing
What were clothes? Much ado about nussing!
She had bouncy blonde curls for her golden hair
Oh that lass was just so fair
When I had to leave that dainty town, she'd cry away
Then I asked, "Hey Molly-Sue will ya marry meh?"
She told me no, for she was too young
By the time I was gone, another boy asked for some fun
Ohhh that pretty little lass I once knew
Now her name is Legs in the air, dormez-vous!

He sat back down when it ended with a standing ovation for a slight minute. Giant bowls of food came with many roasted vegetables and savory ribs. The King's eyes twinkled, "Keep it coming!" he said with giggles from everyone.

Later on during dessert, cheesecake and fruit was brought, "Julia, could you pass me the fruit please?" Philip asked nudging his head to the left winking.

Julia looked at her ring finger on her left hand to see her engagement ring. Philip was trying to reveal it. She smiled, wanting to play his game.

"Here you are brother." said Samantha as she passed it instead.

He took an apple, placing it down, "Can I see your hand?"

"Oh but it has scratches."

"I just want to see one thing." he grinned.

She gave him her right hand, "All right."

"No, the other hand."

She gave him Nathan's hand, "Here."

"I don't want Nathan's hand. I want to see your left hand."

"Psst," started Samantha, whispering into Prince Philip's ear, "Say the magic word: please."

Philip sighed and laughed, "May I please see your left hand?"

Julia looked to Nathan, who nodded and she showed the bravura ring. Philip only held it up to his gasping family without a word. Prince Nathan cleared his throat and beamed, "Mother, Father, as you can see, Julia and I are engaged."

"My son!" the Queen cried tears of joy as she went to hug them both with everyone joining.

The King stood to collect everyone's attention in the Inn, "My good people, my son has finally found a bride. We are immensely honored to bring the human Julia into our home, Kingdom, and our hearts."

The Inn roared in excitement and clapping. Confetti was soon thrown from upstairs and music shook the walls. Drinks were gulped and everyone sang and danced to celebrate with smiles never falling-especially not the Inn Keeper look-a-like. Not even Paige frowned.

At the Tabor's Castle, Carson was in the library trying to conjure up a letter for Julia. He had been at it for an hour and still couldn't think of what he needed to say to her. What he wanted to say was that there was still a place in his heart for her, he thought his engagement to Theodora might have been too soon, and for some unexplained reason, he was somewhat angry that she was with Nathan. This was very odd to Carson, but he kept it bottled inside.

Bade came into the library in haste. There was confetti all over him-in his hair, wings, and armor. His hair was a bit damp as well, having come from flying in the clouds.

Carson scanned him, "I'm wondering if I should laugh, or be concerned about what you're doing right before your wedding."

"I just came back from town. I have news I'm afraid you won't like."

He got up, "Well, what is it?"

Bade tugged on his right shoulder, "Julia and Prince Nathan are engaged," he started to back away, "They just announced it."

Carson crumpled up his unfinished letter and threw it into the pile with all of the others, "I need some time to think." and stormed out into the main hallway.

"Don't think I don't know why you're angry," Carson turned around to see Theodora, "I have resources as well. A Royal Guard informed me a few minutes ago."

He looked to the ceiling breathing heavily, "We're not even married yet, and we're already fighting."

"We wouldn't be if you didn't lie to me about our engagement if you still love Julia."

"Theodora, I need some time alone. Maybe you should do the same."

They parted ways and she wound up in the garden. Theodora eventually came up to the roses, eyeing their beauty. Looking down, she saw a single divine, red rose with a small piece of parchment underneath. She picked them both up and read the tiny inscription. It said: *Farewell, my Princess.*

Theodora immediately looked over the wall to find a person making their way through the underbrush towards the forest. She looked closer. After a moment, she realized who it was.

"Soren." she called.

He turned around with glistening eyes, "Your majesty." and bowed to her.

"Soren please come here. I need to have a word with you."

He slowly walked to her, "How can you trust me after all that I've done?"

"I've always trusted you. Don't fail me this time."

Soren climbed the wall, receiving a hand from his once love to help him. He was brought over the wall, wincing from the pain of his shoulder. Noticing, she gasped, but he only kissed her hand.

"What happened to you?"

"I couldn't stand to see you upset. You loved Carson even though he didn't return your feelings. I poisoned him. I was afraid of losing you. Then something went wrong. The poison counteracted with something else. I knew you'd be upset with me. I knew that if I was found out, I would lose my honor, job, and you. If Parliament found out, I might've even lost my life. So I fled. I'm sorry my Princess," he noticed the engagement ring, "but I can see things worked out for the better." He started to leave, but Theodora held him back. He grimaced at the shoulder she was holding.

"Sit down," they sat on a bench with her hand remaining on the wound.

After a moment, the entire left side of his body was frozen. His breath became a fog in the air and the lesion stared to heal bit by bit. She lifted her hand, revealing that not even a scar was left.

Soren looked deeply into her eyes with his own saying all of his emotions of everything he'd been through and his love, "Thank you," he paused, standing for a moment looking around, "Where are the Royal Guards?"

"I sent them away."

Soren held her shoulders a bit worried, "Why would you do that? You need protection."

"Calm down. There's no Remora anymore."

"There are other things that could harm you," he waited an instant, "Including me."

"Don't be ridiculous-" she was cut off by a kiss.

One hand went to the side of her neck, making it feel warm with his touch, with the other meeting hers pressing against it. She felt weightless and couldn't part from him. They were light as a feather but also as stiff as a board. He parted from her and began to climb to the top of the wall.

"I must go. This is the last time you'll ever see me. Take care, my future Queen. Don't let me down," she reached for him, but he only smiled as he saluted her, "Farewell Theodora." referring his love as his equal and jumped down to the ground once more.

She watched him leave, never taking her eyes off of him. Looking at the rose again, she pressed her hand to her lips. Then she spotted her engagement ring.

All of a sudden, she heard soft clapping and Carson came from the shadows, "Wonderful scene, yet it leaves me confused. How is it that you can still love Soren, yet there can be no place in my heart left for Julia?"

Theodora began to walk back towards the entrance, "I've had enough."

Carson caught her by the waist, "Wait. This conversation isn't over."

She almost glared at him, "Then let me make this clear. Julia is going for more money, that's why she's with Nathan. She'll never go back to you."

"And Soren can never be with you," he smirked, "Now there's something we have in common."

"What's wrong with you?"

"We have to clear these things up before we get married. Assuming you don't want to call it off."

"Of course not, I have to become Queen."

"Is that why you're marrying me?"

"Carson, we may have our fights and differences, but I still love you. When two people care for each other, you have to try your best to make things better. In truth, I'm a little scared of the future and I want you by my side. Do you still care for me?"

He held her hands warmly in his, "Yes. I do care for you. I'll be there by your side. Count on it."

The next six days seemed to have flown by very fast. Close friends were attending Bade and Veronica to their wedding day that afternoon. During the time, no engagements were called off, yet stress was amidst. While preparing to be a bride's maid for Veronica, Julia grew closer to Nathan's family. Soon, she would have to learn the names of the servants since she was going to live there.

Carson unfortunately never got the chance to write a letter to Julia. He was too preoccupied in being Bade's Best Man. However, Alek wrote every day. Apparently, he hadn't heard of Julia's engagement, so she sent out an invitation as soon as possible, still waiting for a reply.

In the afternoon, both Julia and Nathan started getting ready. Philip came into Julia's closet holding Veronica's pretty turquoise colored dress for her bride's maids, along with servants. They did everything Veronica and Cassidy had done the night of Prince Nathan's Ball, she thought reminiscing.

When she was finished, Philip smiled and gave her his arm as he took her down to his brother, holding a gift, "You kids stay out of trouble."

"I'm older than you."

"Whatever. Ciao!"

Shaking his head, Nathan cast the teleportation spell to the Tabor's Castle where the wedding's preparations were being carried out before heading out towards the ocean where the ceremony would be held. He went to go meet some of the other guests and friends while she made her way to Veronica's room. She knocked and waited patiently until Veronica answered, leaping to hug Julia.

She came in to see the room a mess and Cassidy setting bottles of lotions, oils, and perfumes on the bathroom counter, "Here's the plan, you go bathe while we clean up. All right?" stated Julia.

"Sorry about the mess. I'm just so nervous," she fanned herself with her hands to get some cool air to her face, "Lori Linda is on her way in a little while. I'm so glad you're here. Now, show me that ring!"

Laughing, she placed her hand out for them to see, "Wow."

"It's gorgeous."

Cassidy began to push her towards the bathroom, "Ok, you've seen the ring. Now go start to get ready."

They began to pick things off of the floor, "How have things been?" Julia asked.

She chuckled, "They couldn't be any happier."

"Carson is the Best Man, isn't he?"

"Thank goodness too. No one but him knows how to organize things around here." she said as she put clothes away in a dresser.

After a long pause Julia looked to the window, "It's been a while. Hasn't it?"

"Everything's changed." Cassidy hugged her, "Promise me I won't be the last one here at this castle."

Julia pulled away laughing, "You can visit any time."

"Same as you."

A little while after, Veronica came out dressed in a silk undergarment.

"Where's the corset?" Julia asked still remembering the pain of it.

"She doesn't need one because of the type of dress."

"Lucky."

Next, they gave her an all natural look for her makeup. Her hair was then put in bouncy waves with a gorgeous white flower. The jewelry she wore were the shiniest and finest looking pearls Julia had ever seen. Soon, they got her in her dress with lovely shoes. Many giggles and stories were shared during this 'girl's' time and finally Lori Linda showed up at the last minute.

"Way to make an appearance." Veronica chuckled.

"Oh you know I love you," she hugged her friend, "I wouldn't miss this for the world."

A bell ran loudly and Veronica gasped, "It's time."

"Hold hands ladies." Cassidy said extending her hands.

The teleportation spell was cast onto a beach. It was a magnificent green pasture cliff looking over to the vast, clear blue ocean. Veronica set up with her father in a tent as Lori Linda, Julia, and Cassidy were given flowers and set up in the front.

Then, Mr. Doddsworth, Christopher, and Carson came as the grooms men all looking very dashing and handsome. Walking towards the front, Carson spotted Julia, stopping in his tracks. She held her breath thinking his eyes matched the ocean. Prince Nathan and Princess Theodora arrived, and he kept walking. She began to breathe again and saw people shuffling into the ceremony, taking their seats. Even Darcy, Aaron, and Elaine were there.

Music started to play from wonderful instruments and Bade came out looking the best he ever had. Veronica's little cousin was the flower girl and as cute as could be. Nerves pulsating, Veronica and her father walked down the aisle to the famous music.

When they ended up at the end, a dwarf entered, "Do you consent on giving this bride away?"

"I do." an aging man with a peppered mustache and an amiable grin replied, containing his small laugh.

He kissed his daughter and sat down. The wedding then continued with the speeches, the rings, the vows, the 'I do's', and finally the kiss. Everyone clapped and lit lanterns because it was nightfall. During the ceremony, Carson couldn't keep his eyes off of Julia. When the reception began, he made sure he was the first to speak to her.

"Did you do all of this?"

"As a matter of fact, I did."

She smiled, "It was beautiful."

"Thank you."

"What about yours? It's coming up in six days."

"Actually, we decided just to have a reception. We'll have a private wedding."

"Well, I'm sure it'll be fantastic." they laughed a bit with the cool breeze blowing, "You seem...different."

"We're both different." he backed away a bit when Nathan and Theodora came up to them, "Well I think it's time to celebrate."

The four of them of them walked into the reception, which was set up easily thanks to magic. It was almost like a festival with the scenery of the ocean, stars, colors, lights, sounds, and all the laughter shared. Food was assorted on tables of eight as they watched acrobats, and water and fire shows. Following tradition, Veronica's father made a toast to the bride and groom with a loving story of his daughter and Bade. The splendid evening eventually ended with dancing. Everyone then said goodbye to each other first, and bid the bride and groom farewell.

Carson and Nathan had planned all the weddings six days apart from each other. Over the next couple of days, Carson concentrated on the reception and left with Theodora on the fifth day to be wed. Twelve days away from her own wedding, Julia had Nathan's family, Cassidy, Veronica, Lori Linda, and the servants to help her with her own. From the theme, to the colors, dress, flowers, food, cake, etc.

In a rush, Carson's and Theodora's reception arrived. Accustomed to the schedule, Philip helped both Nathan and Julia prepare for the party. As soon as she was done, she met her handsome fiancée near the entrance. He held their gift smiling, "Only six more days until our own wedding."

"I can't wait," she replied wrinkling her nose.

Philip pouted, "Why don't I ever get invited to these things? I know how to party!" then snapped his fingers to bring them both to the entrance at the beach of Captain West's ship docked.

The sight was nothing short of amazing. It was night time and the whole vessel was illuminated by wonderful moving lights of different colors. They were greeted by Marina and Captain West inside to find an even more marvelous picture. As soon as they stepped in the interior, a grand ballroom was shown at the bottom of an elaborate staircase. On either side were tables for everyone with the bride and groom towards the left by the cake.

Everyone Julia had met in Renata (with the exception of Alek, Peter, and Nathan's family) was there. The delightfully greeted themselves to one another. Then they congratulated the bride and groom, whose eyes had never seemed brighter.

In an organized way, everyone sat themselves at tables and continued on in amusing conversation. When Carson and Theodora sat, a show began. It was an appropriate adventure story about pirates. During the show, everyone fawned over the scrumptious food served to them, along with drinks, the cake, laughs, gasps, and cheers.

Next, the dancing took place. First up were all of the couples. At the end, Nathan kissed her and went to Theodora as Carson stepped up to Julia.

They took position and began. She remembered the first time they had danced together and noticed that they'd gradually gotten closer every other beat. He sighed once, "I'm sorry I never wrote."

"We never got the chance. We probably won't be able to for a while."

Carson waited a moment at a slower pace in the music, "You can change the future, you know." he twirled her by her right hand where the ring he had given her was still placed on her index finger.

She looked down at the ring, but then back up to his almost desperate countenance, "Was that a double meaning?"

"Did you ever think that your vision of me dying was because we weren't going to remain loving each other?"

Julia backed from him a little by little, "My mother showed me that vision. Was I just supposed to ignore her? What about my father's warning?"

His heart was pierced by that last question, "Julia-"

"May I cut in?" Mr. Doddsworth asked beside them.

In a slight smile, he gave Mr. Doddsworth her hand and left. When they began to dance, she was surprised at how well he was doing for someone his age. He seemed to notice the astonishment on her expression and chuckled, "I may be old, but I'm young at heart." he looked down at Carson's ring she still had on, "You still have it? Julia, you have to let it go."

"I know, but how?"

"You can tell from his eyes that he thinks of you. Have you still been having those visions of him?"

"Truthfully now more than ever."

"Julia, I know this may seem harsh, but necessary. You must hurt him. Hurt him to save him."

She nodded sadly, "I don't want to, but I understand."

A hug was shared and they parted ways. She stepped out of one of the doors onto the deck. The moon illuminated down onto the water, making everything peaceful. Yet, there was a smaller glimmer of red around the rim.

Jarvis came up and stood next to her, "The red on the moon that you see isn't an Eclipse. It's a warning that a loved one of yours has had their bloodshed."

Her eyes grew wide, "Who's hurt?"

"Alek is. He's sick Julia. No one thinks he'll make it. He wanted to see you one last time though."

Julia could tell he had been crying earlier from the redness of his eyes, the tone of his voice, and his deep breathing, almost as if to calm himself, "There's not a moment to lose Jarvis. I'll tell Nathan. Please wait for me."

"I'll be down at the beach."

She ran inside and found Nathan as fast as she could. He got up and held her in his arms. Her eyes were almost near tears.

"What's wrong?"

"It's Alek," she gasped, "He's sick. I have to go to him. I have to make sure he's all right."

"Who's taking you?"

Jarvis is. I promise I'll be back no later than two days. Say goodbye to everyone for me."

"I will." he kissed her, letting her go.

Julia rushed out, only to find she was being stopped by Carson pulling her hand, "Julia, where are you going?"

"Let go of me Carson. I have to leave."

"It's my wedding reception."

"I know," she tugged away, "I'm sorry-"

"Wait Julia, there's something I need to tell you," she stop pulling, letting the tension fall as well, "Even though you're standing here," here drew closer to her, leaning in, "you're still so far away. Does Nathan make you feel as real as I did? Does he understand you like I did? When you loved me, it was one of the happiest times in my life. After…after everything that had happened to me, it seemed as though the pain was lifted. I loved you with all of my heart in return. Back then and still, love is all around you, and you give it back. Because of that, your universe is full with anything you desire. But in my world…my Renata…there is only you." he then tilted his face and lips to hers about to kiss her, but she stopped him.

"If there is any honor left in you, please never do that again."

"Does he really mean that much to you?" she nodded behind full eyes, and he breathed a heavy breath, "I won't ever kiss you again... unless you ask me to."

"And I never shall. Carson, I'm engaged. You're married!" she reached for his ring and gave it to him, "I don't love you anymore. Just forget about me."

He let his hand fall, letting her go. Watching her leave in Jarvis's arms into the carriage, he stood perfectly still. His hand moved over his heart. The ring he had given her was now in his possession, but he didn't want it.

Chapter 36

DIVINE ALEK

The journey to the Kalama Kingdom was a long, lingering one by coach. At that moment, Jarvis didn't know of the urgency needed to get to his brother, and he wanted to take time away from seeing him in such pain, so he road by carriage instead of using the teleportation potion as he normally would have. Jarvis and Julia tried to stay up during the night by conversation, but eventually fell asleep. Although, Julia was given another nightmare.

In the nightmare, she was holding Carson. Blood stains were everywhere- even on the grass is lay upon. Suddenly, all life of his was lost. Not even a glimmer of light had shown through. He was gone. She quivered with fear and awoke to dawn in the window of the carriage.

"Are you all right?" Jarvis asked.

She felt her forehead with the back of her hand, "Just a bad dream." she waited a moment looking out the window, and just as she was about to ask, the coach came to a halt.

"We're here." Jarvis said getting out first to help her.

Julia stood in amazement at the Songbird Keep. It looked exactly like it was described in all of the stories she had read. The tallest trees she had ever seen shot straight into the sky in a circle, and the center was an almost Aztec looking city with a large, pyramid made of stone steps in the middle, surrounded by a high wall- almost like a stadium.

A massive, golden bolted gate soon opened. Forcing it ajar was a knight- a warrior. The strongest armor was sealed onto him, a strong face, and grayed hair.

He came up to Jarvis with blood on his cheek and hands, hugging him, "Jarvis."

"Uncle." he replied holding him.

Parting, his uncle put his hand on the back of his head, "I'm afraid there's not much time left."

Jarvis nodded, "This is Julia," he brought her closer to his side and his other hand on his shoulder, "This is my uncle Hector," he looked into his eyes, "Now please bring us to Alek."

"Of course," he turned to Julia, "But I must warn you, what you see might be hard to bare."

"I understand."

Hector led them both through the gate into the bustling city. Many knights were walking around, a market created much noise, and citizens ran with metal and supplies for each other. He led them to a large tree with, what seemed to be, a tree house built on it. Next to it, other tree houses were being built as well.

Hector climbed the ladder first with Jarvis and Julia following, "Thanks to Peter's idea from your human world, we've found tree houses quite useful and started to build them. We got the first one."

"I'm glad it made a difference."

Hector then helped them both up into the great dwelling, that almost seemed like an apartment. Alek lay on his bed with a blue blanket over him. He sat up when he saw them.

"Julia-" he cringed in pain and forcefully turned to his side.

His uncle came up to him, "No too fast my nephew."

"Let me see her."

"Alek I think it would be best if she didn't. You're hurt."

"It's all right."

He got up from his side and brought Julia to him, "Alek I'm here."

Alek's wet amber eyes met Julia's. Blood dripped from the side of his mouth. His braid hung loosely from his head as though it weren't even supporting it.

His hand shook as he brushed her cheek, "I've missed you."

"I've missed you as well my dear friend. You've missed two weddings."

He tried to laugh, "I didn't really know Bade and I got sick."

"What happened?"

Hector cut in, "His lungs are giving in- he's drowning in his own blood as we speak."

She looked to their uncle and then back to Alek worried, "Isn't there any kind of medicine or something?"

Jarvis stepped one foot forward, "We've tried everything from herbs, to healing potions, to spells- everything. Nothing has worked."

"Or anything 'guaranteed' to work doesn't stay in me long enough." He coughed vehemently into a white handkerchief, in which became covered in crimson blood. She gasped and he shook his head saying, "I'm sorry you have to see this Julia."

"Alek…" she cried.

Hector pulled her into his arms leaving, "Jarvis take care of your brother. Tend to his every need until I get back."

He came up to his dying brother, wiping the blood as his uncle took Julia away. Once back on the ground, he embraced her in his arms with all the kindness he could muster with the emotions of his sick nephew. She cried into his embrace.

"I warned you." he said with his own eyes red.

"How could this happen? He was perfectly fine when he left."

He broke the hug, "I know. I know…let me take you away from here for a little while my dear. Lunch will be on me." he tried to smile.

He took her to a pub much like the Inn back in town of the Felpierre Kingdom. Trying to get their minds off of Alek, they made small talk. One topic brought up was that the famous Oracle of Renata was in the Songbird Keep for protection. It was said that she could see anyone's future and heal all wounds- both emotional and physical.

Julia was indeed fascinated by this; her curiosity making her itch to know more. She then walked back with Hector to the tree house. Jarvis was waiting at the bottom, "I need to talk to you Julia."

"All right."

"He doesn't have much longer. Maybe an hour and hour and a half at the most. He's dying. There isn't anything that can be done."

She looked down, "When did this even start?"

He paused, "The day he got your wedding invitation."

Julia gazed back up with eyes and cheeks already burning, "Are you trying to blame this on my engagement?"

"He loved you Julia!"

"Jarvis!" Hector yelled, "You were raised to be a gentleman. Saying anything like that to anyone is disrespectful."

"No…he's right. It's my fault." she ran back into the city with tears of guilt as she heard the both of them calling her name.

Julia stopped in an alley way and hugged her knees to her chest. She then cried. She felt so guilty and so sorry for her dear friend who loved her and who was now dying.

"Why are you crying miss?" a young five year old girl with black hair and black eyes asked.

"My friend is dying."

The little girl grabbed her hand, "Follow me."

She was led down streets, passageways, and alleyways all the way to a staircase that led underground. Nothing could be seen in the darkness. Soon, the little girl's hand was gone and she was left alone. A glimmer of a white robe appeared and a soft voice.

"You are the human Julia. A past of great sadness shows. In the present, a friend is dying. In your future…much chaos. Too foggy to tell most of it."

"Are you the Oracle?"

"Silence," she felt a chill, "But yes I am," she paused, "You came looking for answers as well as a way to save your friend." a veil was lifted in front of Julia's face.

It was the face of the young girl, but instead her eyes were an icy, almost white, blue from blindness, "That is true." she replied mesmerized.

The Oracle waited as her face changed becoming an old woman, "Beloved human Julia, I see a power in you that is very strong- one I've never seen before. I will give you an elixir that will erase your friend's *entire* death sentence. You must make sure he drinks it at all costs. But, you must answer one question for me…if no death was predicted in their future, no matter how wealthy or what their status was-all equal-who would you have chosen? Alek, Carson, or Nathan?"

Alek had been resting for an hour. Hector and Jarvis searched for

Julia, but came back to Alek worried. They sat next to him, hoping for a miracle.

"Where's Julia?" he asked.

"We don't know." Hector replied.

"I'll wait for her."

"Nephew-"

"Uncle you don't understand. I love her," he coughed violently, "I'll wait for her until my last breath. Every time I see her I feel alive. Especially when she's beside me." he coughed more and more crimson blood.

His back shivered and his hands became fists clutching onto the blanket and pillows. Jarvis touched his shoulder. Alek shook more, becoming pale and almost crying, "I will not die. I will survive. I'll wait here for her in my time of dying."

Julia came from the entrance holding a beautiful, elongated and jewel encrusted bottle. She came up to the blood drained Alek and slightly sat him up. Jarvis and Hector helped her as she took the cork out.

"Where did you get that?" asked Jarvis.

"At all costs he has to drink this. No matter what."

She tried to waterfall some of the clear liquid into Alek's mouth, but his body refused it. In the end after many tries, Julia ended up having to put some in her own mouth and make it surpass his lips into his system. It was the only thing in Renata that could possibly save him.

Uncontrollably, his body tried to fight it off as he took it in, making his muscles tremble and his veins pump wildly. He screamed as much as he could muster and then fell back. His body became cold as ice. Suddenly, he breathed. Life almost immediately flooded back into his body and turned into his natural color. He was healed. Alek beamed.

That night, Julia slept in one of Hector's guest rooms. She had no nightmares, but replayed her visit to the Oracle again and again in her dream. Julia woke up the next morning and remembered she's saved her friend's life. As a thank you and early wedding present, Hector had requested specially made Songbird armor for her. She put it on and smiled in a mirror dazzled by all the detail and the blend of the colors of blue and burgundy with silver and gold trimmings. It was stunning armor and couldn't have asked for more.

Julia eventually climbed up into Alek's tree house before she left. He was washing his wounds and put a blue robe on, taking out his braid onto his shoulder. He smiled when he saw her.

"Surprisingly, the armor suits you."

"It does seem strange for a girl who hates violence."

Alek laughed, "Thank you Julia. I don't know how I could possibly repay you."

"I know how," she fixed his robe smiling, "Remain my protector, continue your dream of being a Songbird, stay healthy, and come to my wedding."

Alek kissed her cheek, "I promise." they quickly embraced each other and she said goodbye to Jarvis and Hector, with Jarvis laughing as he cast the teleportation spell.

Julia was sent back to Prince Nathan's castle. Servants were everywhere and hurried her to Nathan in the private library. He kissed her and complimented her new armor, and then she told him everything that had happened. He was happy that Alek was now better and impressed that she'd gotten to see the Oracle. Then, his family barged in and stole her away for more wedding preparations.

Chapter 37

TI AMO

Stress was at its maximum level about to shatter as a vase would once it hit the floor. Julia's and Nathan's wedding was the last to be completed before the Coronation. No one could even get a quiet moment without remembering something that needed to be done.

At last the day came. May 3rd - a perfect spring afternoon. Philip was too busy helping his brother, so the Queen, Paiton, Cassidy, and Veronica arrived to help Julia. After many laughs, stories, and tears of joy from the Queen, she was ready.

They cast the teleportation spell to a great, dazzling antique Church. It was striking with glass-panned windows with tall columns to support it. In a vague way, it reminded Julia of her own Church.

The bride's maids Cassidy, Veronica, and Lori Linda, set up on the left side. Then the groom's men placed themselves on the right, which included Carson and Alek, with Philip as the Best Man. Julia waited in another room as many important people of Renata and the Felpierre Kingdom filed in. Many common folk waited outside, since they could not get in, to congratulate after the ceremony.

This was one of the happiest days of Julia's life. Her only regret was that her mother wouldn't be able to see it and her father couldn't walk her down the aisle. Instead, Mr. Doddsworth came in and had thankfully previously agreed to walk her.

The music then sounded. She felt as if her heart was about to beat right out of her chest. Mr. Doddsworth gave a comforting smile. Reassured, she wrinkled her nose in anticipation and linked their arms to walk down the aisle.

It was an ivory and gold wedding that looked spectacular. Julia saw Philip winking, all the girls so cheerful, Carson with eyes shining like the stars themselves, Alek grinning, and Nathan looking the most handsome he ever had. She begged that she wouldn't fall, wanting to close her eyes. The renowned music came to a halt when she got to the end.

A large, frayed old man came out wearing the colors of the Kingdom. He beamed greatly with plump, cherry red cheeks and twinkling eyes. Next, he looked to Mr. Doddsworth, "Even though you're not this girl's father, do you consent on giving her away?"

"I do."

Mr. Doddsworth then hugged Julia and went to go sit by Mr. Clayton, along with everyone else. She stepped up to Nathan's left side, lightly grasping his hand. He smiled contently.

The portly Priest continued, "Is there anyone who knows of any reason this couple should not be wed?"

Julia looked out of the corner of her eye to Carson, who only looked below him. No one answered his question. He then asked the bride and groom with no objections.

The ceremony proceeded, "Prince Nathan, wilt though have this woman to be thy wedded wife? Wilt love her, honor her, keep her and guard her, in sickness and in health? As a husband should a wife, and forsaking all others on account of her, keep thee only unto her, so long as you both shall live?"

"I do." he said with such sureness without even a hint of hesitation in his voice.

The Priest then asked the same to Julia, only changing the wording of 'as a husband should a wife'.

She replied immediately with, "I do."

Continuing the wedding were the vows, with Nathan first, holding both of her hands in his, "I Nathan, take thee Julia to be my wedded wife, to have and to hold from this day forward, for better, for worse, for richer, for poorer, in sickness and in health, till death do us part."

"I Julia, take thee Nathan to be my wedded husband, to have and to hold from this day forward, for better, for worse, for richer, for poorer, in sickness and in health, till death do us part."

They both bowed their heads and received the wedding bands. The rings were golden Claddaghs with a garnet in the center. A Claddagh represented friendship, honor, and love.

Nathan whispered as he turned to face her, "Garnet is your birthstone."

"Thank you." she whispered back.

"Exchange the rings please."

"I love you Julia." Nathan said proudly, placing the ring on her forth finger.

"I love you Nathan." Julia smiled greatly while placing the ring on his forth finger.

"You may now kiss the bride."

They shared their first kiss as husband and wife. Everyone stood and cheered in excitement. Bells and chimes rang through the now evening sky.

Food, cake, and dancing lasted until almost the next morning. This was the second most important celebration of the year, next to the Coronation. A party like none other.

The festivity was unfortunately ended by a sudden spring shower. Laughing, people said goodbye to the happily married couple. Afterwards, they set out for their seven day honeymoon on the beach to relax before the much anticipated Coronation.

May 8th. It was six days before Nathan's and Theodora's Coronation. Carson had fallen asleep very late the night before from packing to move into Theodora's castle. He awoke around 1:00pm to find his wife not next to him. Worried, he got up to go look for her.

After searching the entire castle in haste, he still couldn't find her. Luckily, Cassidy stopped him in the main hallway to tell him that she was in the Infirmary. Confused and troubled, he ran past all the corridors until he reached his destination.

"Carson." Theodora said when he arrived, out of breath.

She held onto her stomach, "What's wrong?" he asked.

Unable to contain her happiness and delight, she replied, "Absolutely nothing," she got up, holding his hands, "Carson, I'm," tears came to her eyes, "I'm pregnant."

Carson's eyes widened and flickered with such immense bliss than the most they ever had in his entire life. He lightly touched her belly and felt the warmth of a now growing child. Sheer exhilaration flowed all throughout him and held his wife in his strong arms as tears came to his eyes as well.

Julia and Nathan came back from their honeymoon to help arrange the Coronation. Carson and Theodora organized the ceremony and party while Nathan came up with a guest list. Julia and Philip decided on the garments to be worn.

The day before, Carson, Theodora, Nathan, and Julia all traveled to the palace where the Coronation would be held. It was in the Pierre Kingdom called the Hall of Renata. The architecture was much like the Church and the Tabor's Castle combined. Beyond it, the scenery was a hill top overlooking the infinite, cerulean sea.

Inside, everything was made of stone; the tables, chairs, benches, etc. At the end of the Hall, was a luxurious staircase leading to four large, polished ivory thrones. On the walls were paintings of past Kings and Queens of Renata. Statues of the same rulers were placed all around the Hall randomly.

Behind the thrones was a large water-colored painting of a map of Renata, with glass panned windows beneath, leading to a large balcony. The ceiling was an elegant art of all the constellations as if they were living with the characters of their stars on a jewel on the crown each wore on their heads. On the opposite far end of the Hall, was yet another image of the Queen of Renata. In this particular piece, she was on a throne wearing beautiful silk robes, bejeweled by diamonds, pearls, and rubies, and had a white wolf resting at her feet.

Each husband and wife then went to their own rooms after looking around. Julia was truly astounded by everything she had seen. She also anticipated for the next day when Nathan would become King and she would help rule the Felpierre Kingdom by his side as the new Queen.

Night came and passed quickly for all four of them for May 14th to come. In the morning, they immediately had a large breakfast, then went straight to their duties. They helped people arriving in setting up all attributes until Parliament and other guests started to arrive. When both sets of the Kings and Queens came, the men went to a room on the right and the women to the left.

As soon as the Kings, Queens, Carson, Theodora, Nathan, and Julia were ready, Carson and Julia were brought out by the heads of both their Parliaments. Carson was seated on the far right throne looking very handsome in the Pierre Kingdom's colors of blue and silver with a small blue, velvet robe. She herself was seated on the far left throne in the Felpierre Kingdom's stunning burgundy and gold colors, with a small burgundy robe placed on her shoulders. Guests then poured in, seating themselves with immediate family at the front, Parliaments, and then friends and other guests sitting according to their Kingdom. Pierre was on the right and Felpierre was on the left. A small Bishop waited in between the two center thrones.

Music seeped in through the walls and echoed amongst the audience and building. Coming out from the right, Nathan met his parents at the foot of the stairs, and sat next to Julia with them at their side. Then, Theodora came down from the steps on the left to meet her guardians and sat next to Carson, with at their side as well. The Parliament leaders bowed low at the foot of the stairs.

Looking to the Kings and Queens, the Bishop lifted his chin and began to say, "The first to pledge their allegiance. Do you condone your crown and your duties that follow with it to your own flesh and blood as your successor?"

Smiling, each pair looked to their children and individually said, "I do."

Nathan and Theodora beamed. This day was everything they had waited for since childhood. At that moment, both realized their dream was becoming real.

Gazing to Parliament, he said, "You are the second to pledge your allegiance. What say you?"

Both Parliaments said in chorus, "I pledge my allegiance to my majesty with trust and loyalty. I shall stand by every decision and only do and put forth what is best for the Kingdom."

Nodding, the Bishop turned to Carson and Julia, "The third and final pledge. Will you govern the laws of the Kingdom with fairness and justice? Will you stand by the decisions of your majesty for the better?

Will you listen, protect, and serve the people in their wishes? And will you have mercy in your judgments?"

Taking a deep breath, Nathan held Julia's hand as she said with Carson, "I will."

He then turned to Nathan and Theodora, "You have received allegiance from your family, your people, and your love," he stretched his hands to everyone, "I hereby present unto you, your undoubted majesties."

Music began to rise triumphantly into a slow, calming rhythm as the Bishop was given the crowns placed on purple pillows by the Parliament leaders, and then placed the treasured crowns upon their heads, continuing with the vows, "Will you solemnly promise and swear to govern the people of your Kingdom according to their respective laws and customs?"

Proud, they said with pride, "I solemnly promise so to do."

"Will you to your power cause Law and Justice, in Mercy, to be executed in all your judgments? Do you solemnly promise to love, honor, and keep and guard your Kingdom in both darkness and prosperity?"

Theodora was almost in tears and Nathan short of breath replied, "I solemnly promise so to do."

Trumpets began a glorious call in the sweet scenery of music. Embellished crowns on their heads and golden staffs, Nathan and Theodora rose from their thrones and began to stride down to the bottom of the stairs. Julia and Carson each came up to their spouse as the new Kings and Queens.

The Bishop raised his arms to the audience, "I now present to you, our new Kings and Queens of the Felpierre and Pierre Kingdom."

Everyone responded, "Long live and welcome the new Kings and Queens of Renata!"

Prince Philip, Samantha, Paiton, Alek, Jarvis, Christopher, Cassidy, Bade, Veronica, Lori Linda, Mr. Clayton, Mr. Doddsworth, and everyone else in the Hall cheered exuberantly. All four of them laughed from pure happiness. Everything seemed to be in place and Julia couldn't be any more content.

The reception began by magic. Stone tables and chairs rose from the ivory floors and was served a delectable dinner onto them and colorful masks on each setting to prepare them for the masquerade after. The beginning dance was the new Kings and Queens dancing the tango with brilliant bejeweled gold masks.

While switching partners, Julia saw Carson's eyes shining brightly through the mask. His breathtaking scent drifting off of him, making her dizzy, with each step he took with the music- to which his beautiful voice hummed to, mesmerizing her. He stooped down with her, arching her back as Nathan and Theodora did as well, twirled her, and made their shoulders touch. Her heart strings strummed with each move and became tangled. Her world then began to spin around her and turn upside down. Vibrant colors swirled and had to hold onto Carson's forearms for support, almost about to faint when the song ended. She kept her head down as he helped her stand. In her racing mind, all she could think was *Why does my heart cry? These feelings I can't fight... This is more than I can stand.*

"Are you all right?" he asked inconspicuously so no one could tell anything was wrong with her.

"I need some fresh air." she said breathing heavily.

Carson nodded and brought her over to Nathan, "My fellow King, I'm taking miss Julia outside for a minute. She's not feeling too well."

Nathan nodded still holding Theodora's hand, "May I have the next dance with your wife then?"

He smiled, "Of course."

As the next song began to play, Carson brought Julia out into the cool night air. The sound of the waves crashing against the rocks was calming. A breeze came, letting her relax as she stood gazing out into the distance of the ocean with the moon and stars.

"I'm sorry about in there." she said.

"What happened?" he asked standing next to her.

She shook her head, "I don't know."

"The pressure of being Queen isn't already getting to you, is it?" they laughed.

She smiled, "No."

He paused a moment, "Theodora's pregnant."

Julia turned to his smiling face and cheerfully said, "Congratulations! Is it going to be a boy or girl?"

"The doctor said it was going to be a boy."

"I bet he'll have your eyes," he chuckled, "What's his name going to be?"

"We haven't come to one decision, but we're thinking either Quentin or James."

"I like the sound of Quentin…it's different."

He nodded, "That it is," he looked back into the Hall, "Do you think you're ok to dance again?"

Julia grinned, "Yes. Thank you."

He brought her inside to Nathan, who kissed her. Much dancing, music, and singing then continued and lasted until almost the next morning. It was a historical, memorable, and wonderful night for everyone.

"I'm grateful that you came, Cassidy. I just don't know what's wrong with her." said King Nathan walking in the hallway with her towards his chambers.

"Of course, your majesty. After these first few weeks with you and Julia as our King and Queen, it's the least I could do. What are her symptoms?"

They came up to the door as he held it open for her, revealing Julia lying down in bed, "I'll let her tell you," he paused, "Please take care of her."

"I will you highness. You'll have nothing to worry about."

Nodding, he left and she stepped inside, closing the door behind her. Cassidy sat next to Julia on the bed. Putting a hand to her forehead, she felt a fever rising.

Julia awoke, "Cassidy." she helped her sit up and hug her friend.

"Sorry I couldn't be here any faster. Tell me what's wrong."

She felt the back of her neck with the long sleeves of her pink robe falling to her elbow, "Well starting a couple of days ago, I've just been incredibly tried, throwing up every morning-which is disgusting-, backaches, headaches, not to mention the horrible nightmares, and I've been craving food nonstop. I thought it just might be stress from the Kingdom at first, but now I'm starting to think it's something else."

"I think I know what it might be." she smiled and put her hand to her forehead again, resting the other on her stomach, having somewhat of a vision to see if her prediction was right.

"What do you see?"

Cassidy chuckled when she opened her eyes, "Julia, you're pregnant!"

She spoke not a word for a moment, "I'm...what?"

Laughing again, she said, "Well, you're not that far along, but you're definitely pregnant."

There were tears in her eyes, "I can't believe it. I'm speechless."

Cassidy smiled, "It's going to be a baby girl too. But this baby will make you very sick in your future. Make sure people and medicine are around you at all times."

With joyful tear coming down her cheeks, she tightly hugged Cassidy again, "I will. Oh I'm just so happy! I have to tell Nathan."

"Go." she grinned as she helped her up and into the hallway.

Julia quickly found Nathan in the Ballroom. She ran to him and into his arms. Unable to control her tears of joy, she made Nathan concerned.

"Julia? What's wrong?" he asked apprehensive.

"Oh Nathan, nothing is wrong. I'm just so happy." she smiled greatly.

"And why is that?"

Julia laughed, "I'm pregnant."

He stood perfectly still with bright eyes for a moment, "You're... pregnant?" she nodded and he smiled charmingly while wiping her tears with his thumbs from resting both of his hands on the sides of her face, "Congratulations my love." he touched her stomach, feeling the life inside, then laughing as he twirled her around carefully.

They kissed passionately in their joy. Julia finally had her Dreamland and didn't want to give it up for anything in the world. Laughing together, she cried more tears of pure elation.

Many months passed with her excitement growing more and more with each passing day. However, she got just as sick. On December 13th, almost the end of the year in her world, Julia lay on her bed calmly asleep bundled up.

In her dream, she was back at the Songbird Keep in Alek's tree house. She was in her handmade armor and stood in front of Alek. He smiled holding something.

"Julia, I need to see something," he held out a piece of Ceylon and placed it in her cupped hands, "I need you to think of all your experiences here in Renata."

She did, closing her eyes. Some things made her shudder and cry; others made her smile and blush. The last image she saw was her being crowned as Queen with the Oracle staring at her. Confused, something happened to Ceylon in her hands.

First, it rose from her palms into mid air. Then, it turned a shade of bright purple and shattered into tiny pieces, circling her hand.

When she looked back up to Alek, his eyes were huge and bright. He gasped, then she unexpectedly turned Ceylon back to normal. She wondered where she'd learned to do that.

"Alek, what happened?"

He started to vanish from her dream with his voice calling out, "Julia, forget what you saw."

All of the scenery in her dream then vanished. She woke up sleeping in Nathan's arms in the cold moonlight. Her curiosity pierced her and held onto Nathan, feeling like a child once more.

In the following remaining months of her pregnancy, she kept herself busy. Julia made it certain that she saw and visited everyone she met in Renata with her friends congratulating her on the upcoming baby girl. They also tried to come up with name for the baby Princess.

Each day she got sicker, but tried her best to pull through. In the palace, she met everyone at last and remembered their names from their individual acts of kindness. Mr. Doddsworth visited often to continue teaching her about the government. In Parliament, she learned that it was split up into three parts.

House of Commons were those elected by the people. House of Lords were unelected members whom inherited their titles. Finally, Monarch governed through Parliament- neither above or below it. The leader of Parliament is then elected by the monarch.

Julia also continued to write. Since she didn't have her diary, Nathan had her a specially made journal. Along with that, she wrote short poems that described some of her experiences in Renata.

Then on February 10th, 2001, Theodora's and Carson's son was child was born. It was an adorable baby boy with little brown hairs at the crown of his head and the bluest eyes- like his father. Carson laughed at this fact. They had finally decided to name him Quentin. Unfortunately, Julia was unable to see the birth of the young Prince from being so ill. Nathan stayed by her side at all times, holding her hand to comfort her. Cassidy and Alek arrived when they had heard the news of the babies being born. Alek stayed at his house and transported to Julia everyday to check on her.

The day soon arrived: March 6th, 2001. Cassidy was concerned for Julia's health so only allowed Nathan, the doctor, and herself to remain in the room. Nathan's family and all of their dear friends waited impatiently. She had much trouble from being so frail and fainted soon after.

Luckily, Cassidy and the doctor nursed her back to health. Julia opened her eyes to find her husband holding their precious little daughter. He smiled and let her hold her baby girl. The little one was so tiny with a fuzz of Nathan's hair color and Julia's pulchritudinous emerald eyes.

As she yawned, Julia cried tears of joy, "Oh our little Passatine."

"What a beautiful name." Mr. Clayton said with all of her dear friends standing in the open doorway.

No other sight was a beautiful or as cherished as this. Nathan's father held her in his arms with a large grin. Philip and Alek chuckled.

"Hush little baby, don't say a word. Papa's gonna buy you a mockingbird. And if that mockingbird won't sing, Papa's gonna buy you a diamond ring. And if that diamond ring turns brass, Papa's gonna buy you a looking glass. And if that looking glass gets broke, Papa's gonna buy you a billy goat. And if that billy goat won't pull, Papa's gonna buy you a cart and a bull. And if that cart and bull fall down, you'll still be the sweetest little baby in town." Julia sang to her little daughter Passatine, rocking her to sleep, then setting her in her crib.

In the open doorway, Mr. Roberts bowed and smiled saying, "A boy has come to see you my lady."

She nodded, "Bring him in quietly."

A familiar, yet taller Peter stood in the doorway. At the sight of her now older friend, Julia immediately stood. They hugged a little tighter than normal in their delight of their reunion.

He let go of the hug and care freely spoke loud without realizing the baby at first, "Hello Julia. 'Been a long time since I saw you last. How are you? Who's this?!" he asked happily and surprised, noticing the crib, looking over in it.

"Shhh," she laughed, "That's Passatine...my daughter."

Loudly, he asked, "Your daughter?" Where's Carson? And why are you at Prince Nathan's castle? Oh! Did I mention I'm thirteen now?"

Chuckling, she hushed him again, "No you didn't and that's exciting. Carson is with Queen Theodora. A lot has changed since I last saw you- a whole year! King Nathan and I are married now."

"What?!!!?" he almost shouted and Julia had to cover his mouth with her hand.

"I know...just stay here a little while longer so I can explain more fully."

"Don't mind if I do." he plopped down in a large red chair, folding his arms across his chest as a reply.

And so she explained everything to him in full detail. She began telling about the peace after the war, Nathan's Ball, and how Julia's mother came to her explaining why she had to refuse Carson when he asked her to marry him. How he was then poisoned and fought both Nathan and Alek. How she was told she couldn't remain with him at the Tabor's Castle and stayed at Alek's home for a few days. How she became closer to Nathan. How both she and Carson got engaged. Bade's and Carson's wedding. Julia curing Alek when he was sick and her own wedding. The Coronation. And finally Carson with his son Quentin and Passatine with herself.

Peter sat perplexed taking all of this information in. None of this was at all what he expected. He ruffled his hair and put his hands on his knees with large eyes and a crooked eyebrow, "Well, I can't ignore the elephant in the room. I really thought it was going to be you and Carson."

"Apparently a lot of people thought that."

He made a pop sound as he looked to Passatine then to Julia, "Will you go back to our world? Even if it's just a day's visit?"

"I can't Peter," she looked to the crib, holding a rod, "I have to be here for the Kingdom and my family."

Peter reached to his pocket a pulled a familiar, small green diary out, "What do you want me to do with this?"

"Keep it. You use it to visit again if you want. I don't want the connection to our world."

"Thing is Julia, I can't come back. My mom wants me to forget this whole thing, and maybe it's for the better. I came just to tell you that."

"I think it's best if you kept the diary. And safe," she turned back to him, "I'll miss you. How long are you staying?"

"I think I should be heading off now actually. I can't be gone long," he got up from the chair, "Don't give me a goodbye speech, and just hug me." he spread his arms outward.

Julia laughed and tightly hugged him for the last time. They smiled and he stepped back, opening the diary. The white light came, making him disappear, "Bye Peter."

He gave her the peace sign and faded away. She giggled remembering how silly he was. Being in Renata showed her how fast she had to grow.

One night fast asleep in Nathan's arms, she had a nightmare. On such a peaceful night, she thought this was odd. The nightmare consisted of Alek and fire.

She only saw his face crying with fire behind and beside him. He was in pain and his eyes were red from tears. Looking to her, he said, "Goodbye Julia." then screamed from the burning flames swallowing him.

Julia jolted up from the nightmare panting and sweaty. Feeling her heart rate, it was pounding. She felt an arm around her waist and Nathan sitting up, "Julia, what's the matter? Was it another nightmare?"

She breathed deeply, "Yes."

"What was it this time?"

"I saw Alek...burning."

"I'll send a letter out at dawn. All right?" she nodded and he kissed her forehead, "Try to get some sleep my love."

They lay back down again but she still had a troubled mind. Consequently, she wasn't able to sleep. What could have possibly happened to Alek?

In Nathan's castle, Christopher stormed down the hallways looking for him and Julia. His footsteps were like thunder to the floor. His hands were in fists and his stare was deadly. Mr. Roberts told him that they were in the library, so he slammed the door open.

Confounded, Nathan and Julia stood as he made haste to them and bowed, "I'm sorry my King but there isn't much time. I've brought urgent news."

"What is it?"

"We need to set up a trial with the Parliaments of the Pierre and Felpierre Kingdoms."

Nathan was confused, "Why?"

He bit the bottom of his lip while his expression became angry, "We have found the bastard traitor who told the Remora of the human Julia being in Renata."

Chapter 38

A MOTHER'S CRIES

April 19th, 2001. Over a year since Julia accidentally came to Renata. What started with a rescue, progressed into war. On that day in the courtyard of the Hall of Renata, both Parliaments, King Carson, Queen Theodora, King Nathan, and Queen Julia waited on stone thrones awaiting the culprit who betrayed the Kingdoms and told the Remora of the human Julia being among them.

Mr. Doddsworth and Mr. Clayton were part of the Pierre Kingdom's Parliament. Both Bade and Jarvis had been elected as members of the Felpierre Kingdom's Parliament. Christopher was more of a Supreme Judge, who just carried out their orders, and stood in the middle of them all. Surrounding the courtyard were large, green grassy hills that were a darker shade of lime green because of the sunset, which seemed more red than usual.

Julia grasped Nathan's hand lightly, "So this person we're to judge upon...they told the Remora I was here?"

"Yes." he put one hand against his chin.

"What are they going to do? You know that I don't like violence."

"I don't know darling. It's whatever they decide. Monarch has to rule through Parliament and not above it."

"So you're saying it's a unanimous vote?"

He nodded looking over to the infuriated Theodora and an angered Carson. The audience around the courtyard was small and only consisted of close friends and family. Julia saw that Veronica, Cassidy, and Lori Linda were anxious to see who the traitor was.

Christopher cleared his throat and raised his hands, "Your majesties," he bowed, "Parliament. And everyone else effected by this traitor," some of the audience clapped, "I will give you all my evidence first. Afterwards, you shall decide this man's fate," he paused signaling to someone, "Bring him out."

A large, cloaked man, kicked another man with a black cloth over his head into the center of the courtyard saying, "Get out there."

The man was handcuffed and sat on his knees panting. His knuckles were enclosed with blood, and his shirt was torn, clinging to the bottom of his arms. On his back were fresh, painful looking whip lashes.

Christopher removed the black cloth from his head. Dark hair with a tint of purple and a braid had shown, along with his amber eyes when he opened them. It was Alek.

Everyone in the courtyard gasped. Julia tried to protest, but Nathan quickly hushed her. Speaking out of turn was not of moral code for monarch.

King Nathan then asked, "What evidence could you possibly have on this man?"

"This, your majesty," his eyes twinkled and he looked to Alek, "Over a year ago, your brother Jarvis was a servant at the Tabor's Castle, was he not?"

"Yes." he sounded exasperated.

"I seem to recall your face lingering in the shadows, spying on Julia during class."

"That's a lie! I had never even seen Julia until we started training for war."

"What deceit. I remember your visage the night we were first attacked- by Aldrich for that matter. What was your purpose there? To stay long enough to find where Carson kept his inheritance to steal it?"

Alek looked to King Carson, "I won't lie to that. It was my original plan. My family was poor- still is. But then-"

"But then you saw a human here and sold her out!"

"No." he replied coldly.

"What about when Carson was poisoned? I knew exactly what

remedy he needed to become normal again, but someone switched it. You probably stayed at the King's castle just for an alibi."

"Never."

"Then you fought with both of the Kings you kneel before! Was it just to strike them down?"

"No!"

Suddenly conversation among everyone grew. It was as though they were under an influence of some kind. Julia knew in her heart none of this was true. Why was it even being speculated? She wanted to speak out against this. Nathan tried to calm her, but it only upset her more.

"If you can't defend justice in times like these, then when can you?!"

Christopher smirked with his mouth curling up to his scar, "That reminds me, you didn't even tell Julia that you were her protector until hours before we left for war. She stayed with you for a few days. For all we know, you could have her under a spell. Gain trust of the one you had to break."

A member of the Pierre Kingdom's Parliament spoke, "Which raises the question of Julia being a fit Queen. A woman must only love once in order to rule at a King's side."

Theodora spoke, "Now people are starting to see my point of view."

"Enough Theodora. You were in the same position yourself." Carson said harshly.

Christopher came back, "Let's stick with the task at hand," he looked to Alek once more, "Weren't you also a bandit?"

"A long time ago. Like I said, my family is poor."

"So you stole things?"

"In order to survive. It was all because of these damn taxes that we have."

"Those taxes...pay for the wars that people like you cause!" yelled Queen Theodora.

"How can you say that?" Alek asked hurt, "I saved your life in that war!"

"Only to gain trust. That's probably why you want to become a Songbird. To 'protect Renata'. You sicken me." Christopher spat at him,

"Isn't your power darkness? One of the many evil powers the Remora loved to use."

"You're a demon. That aspect makes no difference between you and me."

He punched Alek in the mouth, making him spit out blood, "There is a difference. I always had their trust. You had to trick your way through to partially get it."

Julia couldn't take anymore. She got up from her throne and kneeled next to Alek, looking into his eyes. Tears in hers as well, she yelled, "Enough."

Christopher looked to the Parliaments, "She's right. Enough. It's time for you to decide his fate. She's already made her choice."

Discussion roared in the courtyard. Julia brought Alek out of the crowd with the Royal Guards following. He began to cry as she did.

"I swear I didn't do this Julia. I'd give up my life before even thinking of doing something like this."

"I know. I'm so sorry Alek. I promise I will do all that I can in my power to save you. I know you're innocent."

About an hour after debating, they cast their votes in. Julia stayed with Alek, comforting him. He quivered at each ballot cast into the golden chalice.

Christopher counted each one an stood in the center once he was finished, "The ballots are in...both Parliaments find Alek of the Felpierre Kingdom, hereby guilty...and shall be burned at the stake for his crimes."

Chaos then turned into madness. Guards swept Alek away, setting up the fire. Nathan tried to keep the kicking and screaming Julia calm. They both knew he was innocent. Holding her, she struggled and cried out for justice to be made.

Alek was then tied to a ladder on top of the wood. He made a great effort to fight back and cried out with all of his might, but it was no use. No one could save him now.

Flames were ignited onto the brushwood. Terrified, Alek panicked. Julia had never seen such cruelty, malice, and horror. The fire slithered up to his knees. She thought back to her own parents dying in a fire and couldn't stand it, "Someone save him! Please!"

The arms of the flames stretched to lick the skin of his shoulders, "He's innocent!" Nathan finally shouted.

No one listened. He was almost consumed in the fire. Many tears seeped from his eyes, "Goodbye Julia." and was then swallowed by the flames as he cried out, screaming at the top of his lungs.

Suddenly, rain poured down from the sky in sheets and depleted the fire. Alek's face revealed and was both relieved and baffled. He was saved! Julia and Nathan let out a sigh of relief.

The rain was nowhere else but on the charred wood. Thinking this was strange, Julia looked around to see three people standing in the audience. One was a young boy with skin as black as night with white eyes, yet when they turned normal, the rain stopped. The other was the bandaged bandit she had seen when she first arrived in Renata. He was fine now, dressed in dark maroon and gold with his fiery orange hair framing his defined face and golden eyes. The final person was the Oracle.

People gasped and cheered. They came down to the center of the courtyard. Christopher was astonished, "Why did you save him?"

"He was innocent." the boy replied.

"Uh...thank you for saving me and all, but...do you think you could get me down from here?" Alek asked politely.

The bandit cut him down, "Watch yourself."

Alek accidentally fell down, but quickly got back up, looking to the boy, "If you knew I was innocent, why didn't you do that earlier?"

The Oracle cut in, "I wanted to put more emphasis on our dramatic entrance."

"You crazy old lady! I could've been killed!"

"No you wouldn't have. The potion I gave Julia to save you, made you immortal," everyone asked the same question of, "What?" and she looked to Julia, "I thought you knew." she winked and disappeared with her laugh lingering.

Coming in once more, Christopher asked, "So then who told the Remora of Julia?"

The bandit spoke, "I saw Julia with my men when she first arrived in Renata," he looked to her and bowed, "I'm sorry for all of the trouble that we caused. I'm the leader, Killian. One of my men was a traitor. He told the Remora and I haven't seen him since. I'm deeply sorry."

She hugged Alek, "I'm just glad no one got hurt," she went back into Nathan's arms and kissed him, "Thank you."

"And apparently, I'm immortal," Alek felt from his shoulders, all around to his torso, "Honestly I don't feel any different."

Julia laughed, "If you felt something, it was probably when I gave you the potion."

Carson then spoke, "Young man, what is your name?"

"People call me Black Bem your majesty." he bowed.

"Did you know my brother?"

"Yes," he looked down, "He and your sisters were dear friends of mine."

Carson sat forward eagerly, "Do you know what happened to them?"

"Your brother sacrificed himself to save your sisters, me, and the rest of the village," he paused, "I haven't seen Rebecca or Gamelle since the battle before the war. I have no idea what's become of them. I'm sorry, my King."

He sighed and stood from the throne, "Thank you."

Julia followed Carson to find him in a dark hallway. He was crying to himself, trying to hold back the tears. She touched his shoulder lightly.

He turned around and held her in his arms, "I'm sorry Julia, but I just need some comfort. For all I know, I could be the last of my family."

She held onto him, "I know how you feel. I'm so sorry."

About a month after Alek's trial, Royal Guards ordered by Parliament found Soren. He was poor and worked on a farm for his insolent mother. At this site, they confirmed it as poetic justice and left him there.

Soren continued to work indifferently, but let his heart linger back to the days of being the head of the Royal Guards himself. Chopping wood, each thrust of the axe made another memory reveal itself. Theodora's smile was what he missed the most.

Abruptly out of nowhere, a menacing laughter blew in with the wind. The tress rustled and the ground shook. He swung around to see if anyone was around him, but there wasn't. The laughter echoed through his head and punctured his heart. He couldn't even cry out. Something wasn't right...

May 15th, 2001 was not a day Julia was bound to forget. It started off wonderful with the servants watching the baby Princess as Julia, Nathan, and his family visited town. They were helping Julia's old boss Adrianna with her work and also the towns people by giving them food as they listened to their input of how to make the Kingdom more prosperous than it already was. Julia paid most of her attention to the children, with Nathan smiling with his love for her becoming even more noticeable every day.

Then, disaster struck. When they came back to the castle, blood was spilt onto the floors. Terrified, Julia and Nathan sprinted to Passatine's room. Julia screamed in horror at the ghastly sight.

The room was burned, torn, with dead, blood stained servants on the floors, an arrow with a note, and finally, the crib empty. Tears were already streaming down from her face, wanting to know what happened to their daughter. With shaking knees and hands, she made her way to the arrow, piercing the heart of her in a painting of Julia holding Passatine with Nathan behind her. Her blurry vision allowed her to pull the arrow out of the painting and open the note, as Nathan came up to her side, trembling as well.

The note:

If you ever want to see your child again, come to war. She will be waiting for you in the cottage by the famous creek, which you, Julia, appeared from.

Queen Julia kept reading it over and over again. She could not believe they had taken their daughter. Knowing Nathan, he'd probably enforce the war they wanted. She regretfully, had not killed them off in the first war. Her hands shook even more and her voice trembled and cracked as she handed the letter with the Remora's seal to her husband.

Nathan read it and became greatly disturbed. Indeed, as he suspected since Alek's trial, the Remora was back and had taken their daughter. They were also planning to start another war. He had to get Passatine back and keep Julia, who remained silent, safe.

"It's probably a trap." he said.

"It probably is. But I have to go!" she put her fists on Nathan's chest, "I have to go! I failed to defeat them last time. But now- Our daughter is…" she was sobbing now.

King Nathan embraced his wife.

Several hours later into the evening, Julia was still in Passatine's room. Frightened servants cleaned up the mess, but her baby was still gone. Nathan had gone to round up troops in haste as soon as he could. He was finally back, talking to his family. She only wept in her chair next to the crib, holding the letter and reading it. She memorized every word hours beforehand.

"Julia?" asked a familiar poetic voice from the doorway.

Turning around, she saw that it was Carson. Slowly getting up from her chair, she immediately ran into his embrace. He then let her cry as much as she needed to.

Only when Nathan entered, did she compose herself, "What news do you have my King?"

"I have managed to gather one thousand soldiers to be ready for battle tomorrow."

"As have I." Carson said wiping the last of her tears away.

She picked up the arrow, "Will you send the Royal Guards with me to rescue her?"

King Nathan held her shoulders, "I will not put you in danger. I'm sorry to say this Julia…but…for all we know…our daughter could be," he gulped tears back, "dead."

She forced herself away, "No! That's a lie! I have to save her!"

"Julia please calm down." Carson tried to soothe her.

"I'm a mother! I can't just sit here and-" she never finished her sentence; unfortunately all of the high stress took a toll on her, making her faint in her husband's arms.

Chapter 39

SHUFFLE OFF THIS MORTAL COIL

Julia awoke to the thundering noise of loud cheers and clanking armor in the Infirmary bed. She slowly got up to look out the window to find two thousand soldiers praising King Nathan and King Carson. He had already given his speech of loyalty, pride, and gratitude to them, and now they were ready.

Cassidy came in seeing Julia standing, so she protested, "What are you doing up? Lay back down before you hurt yourself."

She obeyed and noticed that Cassidy was wearing armor, "Why are you dressed like that?"

"Because of you, women are allowed to fight now. I wanted to help. In fact, many of those soldiers are women. And everyone is down there, except Mr. Doddsworth and Mr. Clayton of course. We just can't find Christopher or Alek."

"We're really going to war, aren't we?"

She sighed and nodded, "We have to."

Her eyes became red, "What about Passatine? Who's going to save her?"

"Julia, you can't go." she said sternly.

"Why?"

"Because you're pregnant...again. This time it's going to be a baby boy," she slumped back into the pillows, "Save yourself from harm Julia. Please. For Nathan."

She wiped the tears from her eyes, "I have to talk to him."

"I won't be here when you get back."

Julia hugged Cassidy with gratitude and all the love of her friend, "Goodbye."

Leaving the Infirmary, she found her King in the private library. Dressed in the new King's armor, he looked like a warrior. The Songbirds crafted it superbly.

Julia sauntered over to and hugged him from behind, "Nathan, please let me go."

He turned around and kissed her, "I will not risk losing you," he then kissed her forehead, "That is final, my love."

"I can't just sit here and do nothing. That's all I've ever done before coming to Renata."

"Please do it just this once. They want you, nothing else. And I certainly won't give you to them," he accidentally held her a little too close; making her shudder from the tight pain, "Julia...?" he felt life against the palm of his hand, "Are you...pregnant?"

"Yes."

Her kissed her once more. In those hard times, that was the only joy that came to him. He caressed her tears away, and held her in his arms, kissing her cheeks. But then he thought as he said, "I have to keep you from harm's way at all costs," Nathan pulled away sadly and left the room to lock her inside, "I will not let you go. For me Julia, please stay here and protect our child."

She slammed her fists against the door, "Let me out. Please. Someone has to save Passatine."

"I love you." were the last words she had heard him say before Nathan hurried out to the soldiers, not wanting to hear his love's cries; but he knew in his heart that he had to do it to protect her.

He met King Carson with his horse in front of the army, "Did you take care of Julia?"

King Nathan nodded and looked to his soldiers, "I thank you all once again. Let this day be the last of the Remora in Renata. Let this become a new dawn!" he then swung his sword to lead the two thousand soldiers to the battlegrounds once more.

"No! No! No! Please…" Julia cried out locked in the private library for a little over a half an hour.

Thundering footsteps were heard from the other side of the door with a short pause following, "Your highness, where is the King?" she heard Alek's scenic voice ask.

"He has already gone to the battle grounds." Paiton's soft tone replied.

"Damn." she heard them both leaving.

Pounding her fists against the door, she called out, "Wait! Alek, let me out of here. Please!"

Opening it, his face showed puzzlement. Her white gown flew as she promptly hugged and thanked him. Then, looking to the servants, she ordered, "Get my carriage and the Royal Guards ready," they bowed and she turned to Paiton, "I'm sorry but I must speak with Alek alone." and hurried him away.

In another hallway, they slowed their pace and he asked, "Why were you locked in there?"

"Nathan wanted to keep me safe," she shook her head, "but I have to save Passatine. And I insist on going alone." they made their way outside, where the Royal Guards waited with the carriage.

"Why?"

"Because I want you to protect Nathan."

Alek sighed, "Are you sure?" she nodded and he hugged her, "All right. I will protect him." and smiled when they parted.

"Am I crazy for wanting to do this?" asked Julia to Alek.

"A little, yes."

Julia smiled stepping into the coach, "You know something, and I used to be somebody else. Somebody entirely different."

He grinned back, closing the door and said into the window, "I wouldn't doubt it for a minute."

Alek then got on his horse and followed the tracks of the army to the war. Julia set a course to the forest where she first appeared more than a year ago. She touched her stomach, feeling the warmth of her new child, allowing her to gain the courage to save her other.

The carriage sped fast throughout the forest, never stopping, racing as fast as Julia's heart. Even the horses pulling the coach knew how important this mission was to Julia. The wheels dug into the earth harshly, smashing any obstacles that lay in the road. She needed to get her daughter back to keep her from any harm the Remora might put on her.

This request from the Remora was probably a trap, but she would do anything to get Passatine back. Julia was now a mother and intended to keep her child safely in her and Nathan's arms at any cost to become a beautiful family. She pursued with determination.

However, the carriage then came to a halt. She looked out the window, as she saw an arrow rip through the air and puncture a Royal Guard's heart. Disoriented, the men drew their swords. Suddenly, an ambush of Remora warriors came out of hiding and attacked.

In all of the chaos of the soldiers battling, one member of the Remora stole the carriage with Julia inside of it. Trying to keep her balance, she stood opening the door planning to jump. Out of the corner of her eye, another associate sped fast on his horse following and leaped onto the fast moving carriage. The door then hit a tree, shattering into millions of splinters.

An axe smashed through the roof. He then made his way in the interior, searching for her. When he came to the opening from the missing door, she clung to the side of the carriage, and then pulled him out of it. He hit a tree and landed on his back.

Still clinging to the side, she finally decided to jump. She prayed that her baby boy would not be harmed in the process. Catching her just in time, Carson was on the ground.

Getting up, he hushed her, "Get down."

As she hid, he fought with the soldiers that had followed. Winning, he grinned. One came behind him with a dagger, so he plunged it into his stomach.

With none remaining, he did a quick search. When done, he helped her get back on her feet. Julia closed her eyes, remembering him saving her in the very same forest over a year ago. Emotions of admiration, gratitude, and love for Carson flowed back into her all over again. Tears of guilt from these feelings came to her eyes as she stood unmoved.

Carson held her hand as he led her to the waiting horse, "Come on. Let's go." and helped her onto the stallion.

Waiting for the Remora on the battlegrounds, Nathan grew impatient. He also wanted to save his daughter. Out of the blue, he remembered what the Oracle had said- Alek was immortal.

The King turned his steed to face the Songbird, "Alek, I want you and Cassidy to save my daughter," he looked to Cassidy, "I let you read the note. You know what to do."

Both bowed their heads, "Yes your majesty." and steered their horses to the yearning forest beside them.

"Why did you risk your life for me?" Julia asked to Carson, holding his torso behind him for balance.

"I didn't."

"They could've killed you. And after everything…you still saved me?"

"I'm not that easy to kill."

She recalled some of his first words he spoke to her when they had met, 'a large thank you would suffice'. She smiled and put her head on his shoulder. He looked back mystified, but she replied, "Thank you." her emotions were uncontrollable after so long of her stubbornness and being head strong.

"You're welcome."

"Where are you taking me?"

"Back home."

She became a little angered then, "No! I have to finish what I started. I have to save Passatine."

Then, she saw the creek. The creek she'd come out of, how she came to Renata. What made her frightened and found Carson. What made her the woman she grew up to be.

He helped her down from the horse, "I know that. I just wanted to show you whom home you will go to."

"What?"

"Your diary wasn't the only way to get back. After we rescue Passatine, I want you to go back home-your home- to protect yourself. I will cast the communication spell on silver bands for you as I did with Peter…This is the only way you can be safe. I just wish…" he stopped.

Julia stepped up to his stance once more, fixing his armor, "Come with me."

Carson stared blankly, "What?"

"You need to live instead of exist," her eyes were red, "I can't fight these feelings for you anymore…please," she paused with heavy eyes, breathing deeply, "I'm asking you…"

He studied her for a moment and felt weak as he gasped and unleashed his long-drawn-out, unvarying lust for her after so long. Their lips met with a heated passion. Her back went up against a tree as he lifted her. Each touch of his burned and his lips smoldered like fire. Tears streamed down her cheeks as he kissed them away and moved to her neck. Neither of them could contain their emotions of their prolonged love. Neither could or wanted to part from each other. Their fingers intertwined with each other. His perfect lips, the pungent smell coming off of his lightly tanned skin, his voice, and his eyes all contributed to the spinning of her world around her. Everything seemed to fit into place as they kissed and fought their common sense to be with the missing piece of their souls.

Hearing a twig break was only then when they finally parted, "Hold onto me." he said with fear.

He started to cast a barrier around them using his light. As it almost completely surrounded them, an arrow was shot through the narrow gap in a split second. Julia let out an ear piercing screech into the forest wind.

Cassidy and Alek came up to the cottage that the Remora had indicated and described in the letter. Alek drew his sword and kicked the door open. The entire chalet was filled with Remora soldiers.

Aldrich then walked insight of the opening, "Well, you're not the human." he smirked.

All of a sudden, a shriek of terror shook and echoed through the trees. Everyone looked up to try to guess where it came from. The sound was blood curdling.

"What was that?"

Aldrich laughed, "I believe that's our cue." he then snapped his fingers to disappear with all the warriors.

Cassidy ran to the crib in the center of the cottage. Passatine was perfectly fine. She sighed in relief.

"Something doesn't feel right…Julia was supposed to be here."

She turned slowly to him, with her heart almost stopping from his words, "What did you say?"

"She said she was going to-"

Cassidy interrupted, "I heard what you said you damn fool. What did you do?"

"She was begging me to let her out."

"Nathan locked her in there for a reason! She's pregnant!"

"Oh…my…"

"And you fed her to the wolves…"

"Cassidy…I didn't know."

She shook her head, "Go back to the King. I'll protect the baby." she said casting the teleportation spell.

"Julia! Julia!" Carson cried desperately, trying to give her healing potions as she lay in his arms.

Nothing was working. He turned her around and ripped the back of her dress to get a better look at the wound. He blew onto Ceylon and placed it onto the bloody mess, but it did not heal. She cried from the immense pain it had caused her.

Laughter was then heard. A man in all black armor and a black helmet came from the shadows. Carson rested Julia beside a tree about to fight him, but he was stopped by an invisible force, "Nothing is going to heal her, my friend."

"What did you do to her?"

"She is a human. I'm just doing my job," he pointed to the sobbing Julia, "Careful, it looks like she doesn't have much time left."

Carson knelt down to tend to her, but then felt a sharp, throbbing stab in his back, "What are you doing?" he gasped through the pain.

"I'm only transferring some of her pain to you. The closer you are, she has less pain, but you gain it in return. I want her death to be slow and excruciatingly painful."

Carson cried out, "Who…who are you?"

He took off the helmet. Both Julia and Cason struggled for air in their pain, looking upon the face threatening their lives. Dark hair, twinkling black eyes, and a thin scar on his right cheek, "Don't you recognize an old friend?"

"Christopher…how…how could you?" Julia asked gasping for air.

"I was the one who told the Remora of a human being among us. I'm their leader," Aldrich came from the midst of the tress, "Perfect timing. Tie them up. They won't be able to escape with the amount of pain they're in."

"You bastard!" Carson tried to yell to him.

Aldrich shackled the bleeding King on his knees to a wooden plank with wheels at the bottom. He also handcuffed his hands behind his injured back, making his wrists begin to hemorrhage. Julia was set in front of him, with a steal dome placed above them to conceal them as a barrier.

They then began to move, feeling every fissure and crevice as Carson's pain grew more and more from being so close to her. His blood dripped from his back and hands. Julia wept even more in the darkness, seeing her love in such pain.

"I'm so sorry Carson."

"It's not your fault."

"It's entirely my fault! You shouldn't have to go through so much pain."

"If I had cast the barrier a little faster…"

"Don't say that," she held him in her arms kissing him, "I'm so sorry my love," the pain still hurt her, causing her to shudder from the sudden cold seeping slowly into her body, "What do you think happens if I die in this world?"

"For as long as I live, I promise you will not die."

On the battlegrounds, the Remora thundered as they came down the hill to convene the King's army. Both had a total of two thousand soldiers. To hide his identity, Christopher kept his helmet on and called down to Nathan, "My King…before we begin war, I have something to show you," he brought out the steal dome King Carson and Queen Julia were in, "Meet with me."

Nathan brought Bade, Jarvis, Lori Linda, Veronica, Alek, and five Royal Guards with him. Christopher brought Aldrich and nine other soldiers into the center of both armies. The King studied him and the dome.

"Reveal yourself first."

Christopher removed his helmet and threw it to the ground. Everyone gasped. Alek growled and cursed under his breath.

"I'm surprised none of you knew I was the leader."

"You traitor." Nathan snarled.

Christopher chuckled sadistically, "That I may be, but I had no intention of letting a human reside in Renata. What my intentions were, however, were to gain the trust and eventually be in Parliament to overthrow you, my King. Yet, now I found a more interesting place to rule my new people."

"Renata will never be yours. No one's for that matter."

"You fool. It's not Renata that I want."

Nathan's eyes grew large, "You don't mean-"

"Yes," he pat the dome with the palm of his hand, "With a little help, I found the gateway to Julia's world. I plan on taking it for myself." his black eyes twinkled.

He then let Aldrich open the dome to expose Carson and Julia chained. Nathan started to move, but Aldrich unlocked them both to have a guard hold each of them. Being farther apart, Julia felt the pain submerge in her back again. She made a great effort to resist with the blood staining her white gown.

"Carson," Christopher started, "When we first met, you found me in the cottage your King's precious baby girl was saved from. Am I wrong?"

"No." he panted.

"Do you know what I was looking for? I was in search of the diary that evidently, Julia and her family had the entire time. Luckily, I don't need it anymore to travel to her world. I shall enter through the creek and burn that repulsive human world to the ground, with a new King raising from its ashes- me."

"You will never touch my home! Why do you even hate humans? What did we do to you?"

"They took my family. A long, long time ago. I'm the direct bloodline to the first Remora leader. She was once a great Queen. Then when that human came, her honor and title were stripped from her. Everything she'd worked for crushed. Banished to never be found again…until she formed the Remora. By killing each human, our honor slowly regains."

Julia shouted behind tears, "But not all humans are like that!"

"Humans are disgusting. Slippery as snakes. Always spinning webs of lies around each other like spiders. Thieves scurrying like rats with no repentance. They *all* have cold hearts. All they care about is hurting each other and others who aren't like them. Some never see the true meanings and reasons for things that happen. They're horrible, greedy, and inhospitable creatures." yelled Christopher.

"That's not true! Julia is *not*!" Nathan yelled.

"Oh, really? Did she ever mention that she doesn't even love you King Nathan?" he looked to her scared eyes, "I thought not."

"Christopher," Carson said trying to reason, "this won't bring your family back, you know. It'll only make things worse for you."

"No. No, it won't bring my family back, but it'll bring their honor back for the Remora!" he shouted Remora with his followers cheering and then continued in a raspy, low voice, "And that makes me feel a hell of a lot better!"

"You let them go now." Nathan said as sternly and as coldly as he could.

"Or what?"

With Carson's strength regaining, a highlight of his eye turned and grew into a massive gold dragon made entirely out of light into the sky. It circled both armies, with soldiers cowering at the sight of it. On its way back around, Christopher gradually made it smaller, fading away and vanish when he closed his hand, "Pathetic…I didn't want to have to kill you, my old friend." he signaled and the soldier holding him, suddenly plunged his sword into Carson's chest, near his rapidly beating heart once more, spraying blood and making him fall to the ground as he tried to breathe.

"No!!!" Julia screamed, kicked, and thrashed as tears became rain from the storm of fury in her eyes.

In a quick second, people started to fight from every angle. Christopher held Julia's chin as he bit her lips with his demon fangs, releasing a deathly venom into her body. Darkness caved all around her as she made her way to Carson. Nathan swung his sword at Christopher, but was too late. He quavered and changed the ground as he made pillars for him and Aldrich to watch the chaos below them.

Julia found Carson in her blurry vision and throbbing pain as she created a barrier around them. She put her hands on the sides of his face, wiping his tears. Her own tears drenched her neck and soaked her sleeves as she tried to wipe them away with.

"Carson." she called trembling, trying to use Ceylon to heal him.

"Nothing will work...my love. When I gave up my immortality, they told me I couldn't be healed by anything...ever again. That's why I had to always protect myself, and try to be a great fighter...but I never expected this."

"Immortality?"

He nodded, "I'm sorry Julia."

"Carson please don't die," she noticed the grass he lay upon stained with his and her own blood, "If you do, I won't be able to survive."

"You will survive Julia. I love you too much to let that happen to you," he kissed her, "I will protect you my Queen. You are so brave."

She shook her head violently, "If I was, I'd be able to save you."

"Nothing can save me. But you can save yourself."

Julia kissed him more and more now that he was finally back with her, "Carson I love you. Please. I need you. I've always needed you. Don't leave me now."

"I can't let you die," his pacific blue eyes were starting to turn gray, "Kiss me one last time," she did, as long as she could with tears in a never ending flow, "Close your eyes and cover your ears. I love you," he longingly kissed her forehead and howled like a beast as he screamed, "I Will Not Let You Die!"

Light shot out from his roar, crossing the barrier towards the sun and turned into a three-story tall spirit of a lion made exclusively out of light. He roared as well and knocked the crumbling pillars Christopher and Alek Aldrich stood on. Soldiers cringed, terrified of the beast. The lion charged at the Remora army and defeated many of them.

Julia opened her eyes to Carson's cold, comatose, beautiful, and lifeless body, "Carson..." she wept, "Open your eyes. Please." but he did not move, with one tear resting on his cheek.

A new sensation rose in Julia. She took the barrier away and stood. A bow and arrow set was created out of light and placed on her back. She reached behind her, took an arrow, said a spell, and aimed it at Christopher, "You...you killed him!"

The arrow tore through the air, aimed right at Christopher's heart.

In the blink of an eye, Soren shoved him out of the way and blocked the arrow, slicing his mouth. Aldrich set up a barrier rapidly. While Soren screamed, Julia cursed, and Christopher smirked. He snapped his fingers, making him and the rest of the Remora warriors disappear, along with the venom in Julia's bloodstream to take its course.

Her veins pumped wildly, spreading dark blood all around her body. She fell to the ground in an instant. Nathan caught her in his arms, trying to heal her with potions and Ceylon.

She gasped for air as the venom moved more. Her ribs were throbbing in her chest and her heart...broken to never be mended again...The baby boy added more pain to her. Her will to survive was fading, along with her son's. The sharp agonizing toxin was crushing her worse than the rocks from the landslide in the previous war did. The pain was unbearable. Her heart beat accelerated too fast in such little time.

Everything became numb. She was blinded, almost deaf. Julia screamed and thrashed against her husband's arms. The pain was poking at her scalp like a fire. The last of the ache was her blood curdling scream once more.

"Julia! Julia please...you can't go. You have to fight!"

"Nathan," she reached up weeping, "Don't think I never loved you. I did. Take care of Passatine and the Kingdom."

He tried to stay strong, "What about the baby?"

"I don't think I can pull through. You'll have to live on without me. They call it the Kiss of Death for a reason."

"You can't leave me now. I love you my wife, my Queen, my everything." he kissed her.

She felt her own life fading away, "I..." she saw her parents crying, "I'm..." she saw Carson crying himself, "I'm so sorry Nathan..." she saw her unborn baby in her mother's arms, "my love."

Darkness concealed her. Julia saw a glimpse of light and reached out to it. White overpowered the darkness around her. Peace, harmony, and tranquility. She couldn't move a muscle. She was like stone with no more pain. She closed her eyes for the last time. She was gone.

"No...no! Julia!" he shouted to the heavens and skies above, "Julia," he felt her lips once more, "Come back. Come back."

For a moment, only his weeping could be heard. Then, absolutely nothing even though he was shouting his tears away. Not even the wind made a sound. He got up, trying to make his way to the forest.

Bade stopped him, "My King."

Nathan had to hold onto his forearms for support, "Julia…She was carrying my son…she's gone. She's gone!" he yelled desperately, trying to breathe and Bade let him walk off a little, looking down.

King Nathan fell to his knees and cried his heart out. Lori Linda sobbed onto Jarvis's shoulder. Veronica was being held by Bade in his arms. Alek shed tears mutely to himself. All of the army was silent. No one dared to speak a word as their King was on his hands and knees, weeping over his whole life swept away and taken from him.

Chapter 40

RENATA: THE BEGINNING

May 27th, 2001: Julia Myers and Carson Tabor's funeral. People from each Kingdom mourned for their loss King and Queen, standing on the sides of the yellow stone road all the way up to the entrance of the Tabor's Castle. White flowers and petals surrounded the dark area.

Carson was dressed in the Pierre Kingdom's colors with a golden crown and holding a jewel encrusted sword. Julia was clothed in elegant fabrics of the Felpierre Kingdom's colors with a gold crown and beautiful jewel encrusted sword as well. A necklace with a piece of Ceylon was placed around both of their necks. They were buried in the cave of Ceylon in impenetrable, golden caskets, and blocked off with a new entrance. Only those with the Tabor's blood flowing in their veins could open the doorway to Ceylon from then on.

Theodora and Nathan waited in the courtyard of the Tabor's Castle until the gateway was completely shut. So many memories, such little time. Tears were shed nonstop by all close friends of both Julia and Carson.

Prince Philip stood on a ledge to get everyone's attention and gave a speech, "Let us not take this great bearing alone only in our hearts, but in our minds as well. We are in a dark place, but let us not put the blame on Julia or Carson. It was not their fault- and should not be to blame. In fact, they showed us what we were lacking in our knowledge and opened our eyes. This time...this time of need, of darkness is not because of them but because of us. We were blind and did not see it. We were human in a way. This isn't just about humans or even Renata now. It's about power. If this is what the Remora is willing to do, we shall strike back. No looking back. It will be the final threshold. Guide ourselves into the light. One strong, final battle."

Both Kingdoms clapped for the young, but also wise Prince. Indeed those were dark times. Any changes would have to be made to protect and help the people of both Renata, and Julia's world.

Back at King Nathan's castle, Prince Philip was talking with his brother. Most of the changes discussed were the security of Passatine and Julia's own world. Nathan intended to do everything he possibly could while trying to contain his rage. He wanted **_revenge_**.

Earlier, he had found the speech Julia had wrote many months ago. It was titled We Are One. Through talking with his brother, he read it.

*If I have learned anything in my few years of my tiny life that I can remember, it is the life is the most precious thing we people hold dear, for it is so very fragile. It can be taken from us, and we'll be tested. Our very own souls, minds, and hearts will be tested. To see what we can do, will do, and have done. It is a person's time that's held dear to them, to us, and to others. Time can be lost. Time can be taken. Time can be fast. Time can be slow. Time is the measurement of us beings. Time can also never be given back. Once it's lost, it's gone. A nonrenewable resource. Extinct. A gift that cannot be returned. A treasure that cannot be found. Most of us take it for granted, but if you measure the moments you've wasted, you've not only wasted time to do something great, but also someone else's time. Someone on the verge of death, waiting for an angel to sing to their newfound sleep. Tears are shed, hearts are broken. But the life is exactly like time- can never be found again- gone forever and never to return. You may think "Well, **I** didn't know them," but from the forgotten laws of common courtesy, we are all brothers and sisters. A family; and we must learn to love and to care for our family. We all need the strength and support we can receive from each other. I have also learned that we will all...fall. We will eventually fall and lose. No matter how great the battle. No matter how great the adversity. Crying and begging, we will be down on our knees wanting mercy, joy,* *forgiveness, or comfort. Maybe even something else entirely. But it is the journey that counts. On Earth, we are gathered as one. Let our hearts beat as one. Let our minds think as one. Let us become one with each other and ourselves. Let's all stop, take a look around, and become one. We are one.*

"Do you think this will be the end of Renata?" Prince Philip asked remorsefully, looking out the window then to King Nathan.

"No brother. It's only just the ***beginning***."